The Boy I Once Hated

Love & Hate Duet

C.R. Jane

Ivy Fox

The Boy I Once Hated by C. R. Jane and Ivy Fox

For permissions contact:

crjaneauthor@gmail.com

ivyfoxauthor@gmail.com

Cover Design: XF Des (X-Factory Designs)

Photogapher: Michelle Lancaster

Editing: Jasmine J., Rumi Khan

Join C.R. Jane's Readers' Group

Stay up to date with C.R. Jane by joining her Facebook readers' group, C.R.'s Fated Realm. Ask questions, get first looks at new books/series, and have fun with other book lovers!

Join C.R.'s Fated Realm

Join Ivy Fox's Readers' Group

Join Ivy's Sassy Foxes to chat directly with Ivy and other readers about her books, enter giveaways, and generally just have loads of fun!

Join Ivy's Sassy Foxes

To the girls who hide in the shadows, just waiting for a chance to shine.

The Boy I Once Hated

I've always heard there's a fine line between love and hate.

No one told me that line could destroy me.

Noah Fontaine.

King of the school.

My living nightmare.

The object of my fantasies.

My new stepbrother.

I did whatever it took to survive him.

Every day he took more of me.

I just didn't expect him to take my heart.

Because of the boy I once hated, I'd never be the same girl again.

TBIOH Soundtrack

Lavender Haze
Taylor Swift

Opera House
Cigarettes After Sex

Still Don't Know My Name
Labyrinth

Watercolor Eyes
Lana Del Rey

Are You Bored Yet
Wallows ft. Claire

Happiness is a Butterfly
Lana Del Rey

Keep Breathing
Ingrid Michaelson

Chasing Cars
Snow Patrol

The Infidel
The Republic Tigers

Something About You
Cary Brothers

Tainted Love
Claire Guerreso

Feels Like The End
Milky Ekko

What The Heart Wants
Selena Gomez

Sweet Nothing
Taylor Swift

Listen to the full playlist here.

"The only thing worse than a boy who hates you, is a boy that loves you."

— Markus Zusak, The Book Thief

Part One

Prologue

Skylar

I once knew a boy whose stormy eyes stole my very breath away just by looking directly into mine. Either in fear or morbid fascination, he always managed to captivate me. Too young and dumb to know any better, his stare was enough to leave me an emotional wreck. I was either intoxicatingly enamored by his tumultuous sea of blue or overwhelmed by the notion that diving into such deep waters would be my ultimate ruin, drowning me once and for all.

From the tender age of fifteen, his eyes promised me so much.

Promised me pain, suffering, and almighty misery.

And for years, he made good on all his promises.

He became the bane of my very existence. The boy that sought me out, only to torment me, purposely casting a shadow on every joyous moment I had in my pathetic life.

I'm not going to lie to you, my life was definitely an endless ocean of dullness.

Especially considering the only rush that excited me—the only thing that made me feel alive—was taking him on and provoking his wrath at every turn. I never shied away from his bullying. I didn't curl up into the fetal position and take his abuse. Oh no, I always fought back. I made it a point of showing him he could never break me, no matter how ingenious his attempts were. My world could have been falling on top of me and I still would've mustered the strength to give him the same hell he showered me with.

And what glorious battles we had.

I thrived and yearned for them.

But not once did I think I'd lose the war.

It never occurred to me what his true end goal was—that somehow, against all odds, he'd be capable of stealing something as precious as my heart.

Like a fool, I gift wrapped it for him, naively believing that somehow it would be safe in his malicious hands.

He played the long game, I'll give him that.

So much so, that right up until the very end, I never saw it coming—how deviously cruel his black heart really was or how calculating he'd been from the start to make me fall the way I did.

He played his part beautifully, and like a sucker, I fell for it.

Kudos to him.

He really did a number on me.

Because of the boy I once hated, I'd never be the same girl again.

Chapter One

Noah

Fifteen years old

"You're going to have to do something about this hair, kiddo. If you let it get any longer, you won't be able to see a thing in front of you," my mom teases, running her fragile fingers through my blond locks and giving one strand a meager pull in playful reprimand.

"Guess you better get well soon then, because no scissor is coming within an inch of my head if the person who's wielding it isn't you," I reply with a mischievous wink, gaining a small smile out of my frail mother.

Still rooted to my chair at her bedside, I slouch as much as I can toward her, just so my mom can get her fill. When she starts humming in delight while carefully combing my hair with her fingertips, I close my eyes and pretend I'm five years old again. In my mind, I'm the one who's bedridden while my mother sings me to sleep, toying with the strands of my hair exactly like she used to do anytime I got sick. Her tune isn't as strong as it once was, but the raindrops on the windowpane camouflage it enough that I almost believe we're in my room back home and not in the sterile environment of Falmouth Hospital.

But this small reprieve is quickly stolen from me when one of the nurses comes in to do her daily routine of checking my mother's stats. Resentment for the woman who just entered the small room consumes me when my mom quickly pulls her hand away from my hair and straightens up on the bed, trying to appear stronger.

"Is your father coming today?" she asks after a long pause, her eyes never straying from the nurse going about her business.

"He's on a fishing expedition. He'll be back in a couple of days. We told you that last week when we were both here. Remember, Mom?"

Her face drops at the reminder, making her look even more fragile than she did when I first arrived. The sick feeling in the pit of my stomach always increases every time I see my mother deteriorating like this right before my very eyes.

Her memory not being as sharp as it once was, isn't the only noticeable side effect of her illness. My mother's sunken cheeks and ghostly pale skin are a testament to the ways her cancer has taken most of her natural beauty and jubilant nature away from her. The fact that she still has the frame of mind to wrap a scarf over her naked head and cover most of her skin-and-bones body under her hospital blanket before visiting hours is astounding to me.

But that's my mom for you.

She hates to show us how truly weak she is and cause me and my dad any more concern than the ones we already have. Even before my mom got sick, she was always the type of person who hated to cause a fuss, so I get her need to try and downplay her sickness for us.

But sometimes I wish she didn't.

Especially when she's in so much pain.

A few months back, her doctor warned us about her blatant refusal to take any morphine whenever dad and I came into the mainland to visit her. Her stubbornness in not taking the drug has gotten so bad that I have to call the hospital first to see if she's having a good day or a bad one, before I even think of coming to visit her. If the nurse on call tells me she's having a rough day of it then I don't come and make up an excuse as to why I have to stay back in Thatcher's Bay. I won't have her choosing to be in excruciating pain just so she can put on a brave face for me. It's bad enough that I have to put one on for her.

I do understand the sentiment behind her not wanting to be all doped up around us though. The drugs make her loopy and it's hard to have a coherent conversation with her when her veins are polluted with that vile stuff. And although I would prefer to know she isn't suffering, anytime I come by and see that she's lucid, I can't help but hold on to that feeling of hope that somehow a miracle will happen and my mom will eventually beat this beast of an illness that has consumed her from within. When she's all drugged up and zombie-like, it's harder to keep that hope alive.

Just like me, my mom knows that all the days we spend together are precious. We might hope for the best, but deep down, all of us expect the worst. Her need to make each day count and be fully present for me, as selfish as it sounds, is what has gotten me through these past few years.

I really wish my father was here though.

I get that he has to work. With mom being so sick, we only have his paycheck to survive, and my mom's health insurance only covers so much. If my father isn't working, or here at the hospital, he's home with the phone glued to his ear, negotiating with the bank and insurance company. Unbeknownst to him, I know fully well just how deep a hole my mom's cancer has gotten us into. I hear his frustrated whispers on the phone, trying to come up with ways to pay for mom's treatment. He's taken out so many loans, it'll take his and my lifetime to pay them all.

So, he works.

He goes out on his trawler, praying that the sea will be his friend and offers up a haul that will get us out of this ditch we find ourselves in. Even though I know this, anytime I come to visit mom and he's not with me, I still can't help but resent his absence.

But lately, it doesn't even measure up to the resentment I feel when he does come.

When he is here, a part of me wishes he would go back out to sea and never come back.

My father has lost hope.

It's clear as day in his eyes.

Mom sees it too, and it kills me that he can no longer pretend around her.

"Noah, sweetheart, tell me about school," Mom probes, finally averting her eyes from the blonde nurse.

I offer her a smile and talk about my lame ass shit so she can feel like she's a part of it. She patiently listens to me moan about teachers and friends alike. I wish I was the type of kid who got straight A's and could make her proud. But I'm not. C's are a win for me.

But even those have been hard to get these last three years.

My head isn't on school—it's on her.

The woman I love most in the world.

The woman who cared for me every day of her life.

God is cruel to have given her this fucking illness.

Fuck that.

God doesn't exist in my book.

How could he when my good-hearted mother is literally lying on her deathbed, while bad people live long and prosperous lives?

Mom hates it when I say shit like this, so I keep these thoughts to myself while I tell her about the latest news and gossip from our little island. Not that anything noteworthy really happens in Thatcher's Bay, but I still fill in the gaps, hoping it's enough to keep her entertained.

We continue with our visit, and when one of the other nurses on call pops his head into my mom's room saying that visiting hours are over, I promise my mom that I'll come back the next day.

"I love you, kiddo," she whispers as I place a kiss on her cheek.

"I love you, too, Mom," I reply, hating how my voice sounds strangled and hoarse.

She doesn't need that shit from me.

If she can be strong, then so can I.

I plant a wide smile and stand up straight so she can see that I'm okay, even if inside, my heart is shattering, piece by piece.

"I'll see you tomorrow, okay?" I say, squeezing her dainty small hand in mine.

"And I'll see you in a bit. In my dreams," she retorts with a tired smile.

I kiss her knuckles and her forehead before turning around and finding the male nurse standing at the door looking guilty as fuck at the pair of us.

"Sorry, son. I tried to leave you in there as long as I could."

"I know," I mumble, taking one more quick glance at my mom over my shoulder and seeing that she's already nestled in her bed, eyes closed.

Lately, any time I come over, it takes more than its toll on her. She's out like a light even before I've left the room. I wonder how hard it must be for her to keep herself awake when I'm here. Maybe I shouldn't come over tomorrow and let her rest, but since I already promised I'd come, I can't back out now. She always sees right through any excuses I make up anyway.

"You good, son?" the nurse asks as we step out of the room.

"What do you think?" I snap, shoving my hands in my jean's pockets and walking as fast as I can out of there.

Even though this is technically a hospital, my mom is in a separate wing of care.

She's stashed away on the hospice side of the building.

In other words, the only thing the doctors and nurses are doing now is keeping her as comfortable as possible and waiting for the day her body gives up on her.

Like my dad, they've lost hope, too.

At least he was able to do one thing right.

Back at the island, the care facility she had been in was goddamn awful. She was there for less than a month before she started fading away from us at rapid speed. The straw that broke the camel's back was when dad found bed sores on her back. Dad did the only thing he could do in those circumstances. He punched the orderly that had the gall to say *these things happen* and took her out of there that same day.

Unfortunately for us, the only proper facility we could take her to was on the mainland.

We knew this meant the price tag would be steep as fuck, but it also meant that seeing her every day would be challenging for us. Still, it was the only solution we could find. The hospice wing of Falmouth Hospital is reputable, clean, and the staff treats her well.

Well, maybe not all of them.

I'm hit with the memory of how my mom gave the side eye to that blonde nurse earlier today.

There was definitely hatred in my mom's eyes.

Could that nurse be treating her badly?

Did she say something to offend her?

Mom has never been one to hate anyone.

She used to be a kindergarten teacher, for crying out loud. Mom doesn't have a mean bone in her body, so if she was scowling at the woman, then she must have done something to piss her off.

I vow to keep my eye on the nurse and have a word with her in the morning. I have half a mind to turn around and have a talk with her now, but that would mean I'd miss the last ferry back to Thatcher's Bay. If I did that, I would either need to sleep in the waiting room of the hospital or find a bench in some park to sleep on for the night. It's not like I haven't done it before, but with the rain coming down so violently as it is now, I would rather sleep in my own bed tonight and confront the nurse tomorrow.

When I step onto the ferry that will take me home, I don't waste time and walk towards the empty upper deck, needing a few minutes to myself. Although the rain is heavier now, I prefer to stay up here and allow the rain to drench my face.

The dark gray sky resembles how I feel—angry at the world while filled with a deep melancholy.

But unlike the saddened sky and its tears streaming down my face, I don't let myself cry. Although no one can tell the tears from the rain, I refuse to show weakness when my mother has been so fucking brave.

Between the three of us, she's the one who has kept her shit together.

In the beginning, I used to hear dad cry every night in his room.

And hated him for it.

It was so selfish of him to simply cry like that.

Didn't he know I could hear his wails of misery?

Didn't he realize his pain would only increase my own?

Every night for two years, he broke down, and I swore to myself that I would never be as selfish as he was and let everyone witness my suffering. I resented him for being so weak when my mom has been nothing but courageous.

But my dad doesn't cry anymore.

He hasn't cried in months.

And that has widened the rift between us.

I resented his suffering.

But I resent him for giving up on her even more.

These are the thoughts that filter through my mind as the ferry pulls up to the island I call home. Fifteen minutes later, I walk through the front door of our two-story house and let out an exhausted exhale.

Everything is a mess.

Not that it surprises me anymore.

What can you expect from two guys with no woman around telling them to clean up behind themselves? I let out another groan and walk over to the kitchen so I can clean up before I nuke some leftover takeout in the microwave.

Mom would give us hell if she saw her house this way.

And the smell.

God, the smell.

Fish.

Dad says after all these years that I should be used to the stench already.

I'm not. Nor will I ever be.

When Mom was still living with us, our home always smelled lemony-fresh. I don't know how she pulled it off or what her secret was, but not once did our place smell this bad. You would never have guessed this was a fisherman's home when you stepped foot inside of it.

Now it reeks of fish guts.

Fucking nauseating.

Disgruntled that this is the new norm, I start to straighten everything up, knowing it won't be enough to erase the stink. After the kitchen and living room are somewhat livable again, I bring my dinner upstairs to my room. I crack a book open in an attempt to get some homework done, only to quit ten minutes later.

Fuck this.

It's not like I'll need any of this shit anyway. My future has been set in stone since birth. I'm to be a fisherman like my dad and his dad before him. No one gets out of Thatcher's Bay. We all lead the same lives our parents did and their parents before them.

It's a waste of a life but it's all I have.

That shit never bothered me so much when mom was here. She made even the crappiest of moments bearable. I didn't care that I was poor or about the impending future that awaited me. I didn't care about any of it since mom gave me room to simply be a kid and enjoy my childhood, free of all obligations and concerns. Even though I'm only fifteen years old, I feel like I'm fucking fifty, having lived more heartache and suffering than any of the kids my age could even manage to comprehend.

And soon I won't even have these small moments of reprieve that my mom offers.

It will only be me and my dad.

In this lonely house, going through the motions of our pathetic existence, until we meet her on the other side.

Not wanting to let that forlorn thought grow roots in my brain, I put on my headphones and start my playlist, praying that the loud, angry music will do its job of eviscerating every thought in my head. After kicking off my secondhand Jordans, I lie down on my bed. It still has the blue comforter with white sailboats that my mom bought for my tenth birthday.

"It's to help you dream. Never give up on your dreams, kiddo," she said when she placed it over my bed. "They might just surprise you and come true."

There was a time where I actually believed her. I may not like the idea that I'm predestined to become a fisherman like my father, but I've always been enamored with the ocean. Sometimes I let myself daydream of a life where my mom waves to me from a pier, as she watches me sail off in a thirty-foot-long boat, as I go on an adventure and cross the Atlantic Ocean just to see what's on the other side.

But that's all it is.

A daydream.

A wish for a tomorrow that will never come.

But it's with this elusive vision playing in my mind, that sleep comes to me and takes me under, dreaming about open skies and a tame vast ocean on the horizon. I let the dream take hold, as I live a life that is not in the cards for me. But my blissful dream is all too soon stolen away from me when I hear a distant voice call out my name.

"Noah..."

"Noah..."

"Son..."

I stir in my bed as the strangled voice successfully pulls me from my happy place and back to the darkness of my bedroom and my bleak reality. I rub the sleep from my eyes as they get accustomed to the dim-lit room, a dark shadow sitting right at the edge of my bed. It takes me a minute to focus on my father's frame, and another minute to realize how distraught his facial features are. His eyes are swollen and red, and when he uses his forearm to clean them, I realize he's silently crying as he stares at me.

I don't ask him why he's back early from his fishing expedition.

I don't ask him why he's in my room crying.

I don't ask him anything.

Because I know.

I know the next words that will come out of his mouth before he's even uttered them.

I know.

I know.

My mom is dead.

While I was dreaming of the sun on my face and the vast blue ocean all around me, she died.

It's just as I thought.

There is no God.

She's gone.

And all I have left now is him.

I will never dream again.

Chapter 2

Skylar

Sixteen years old

ten months later

"Whatcha doing?" my sister Daisy singsongs as she walks into my room and jumps on top of my bed, making the whole thing shake beneath me.

I continue to write in my notebook, ignoring her presence as she drops flat on her back beside me. Unfortunately, my big sister has never been the type of girl who takes being ignored lightly. A fact that is all too evident when she starts tugging at my ponytail to grab my attention away from writing and onto her.

"Do you mind?" I mumble, annoyed, slapping her hand away from my hair.

"Not at all," she taunts with a sly grin, using the distraction of me fixing my ponytail to snatch my book away from me, to flick through its pages.

Argh!

It's official.

My sister has no sense of boundaries.

"I thought I told you to knock?" I exhale, frustrated as she continues to read passage after passage of what I've written so far. "You know I don't like it when people barge into my room whenever they feel like it. This is my personal space, Daisy. Not yours."

"Relax, Sky. Jesus." She laughs, amused. "Someone seriously needs to take that stick out of your ass. You're too easily wound up. I'd offer to do it myself, but this bitch got her nails done this morning. I love you, Sis, but no way will I chip a nail on your account. That stick is so far jammed up there, it's sure to ruin any manicure." She continues to giggle.

"Ha. Ha. Hilarious," I scold with an eye roll. "Now that you're done with your one-woman comedy act, how about you give me back my notebook and leave?"

"Nope. Not yet. Do you finally have your sexy-ass Pirate Barbosa getting it on with Lady Jane?" she asks while flipping through the pages of my book.

"Hate to disappoint you but they haven't even kissed yet."

"For real?" My sister gawks in astonishment, her eyebrows going so far up her forehead they almost touch the roots of her blonde hair. "But he's held her prisoner on his ship for over a month now. A whole ass month! How have they not kissed?"

"What can I tell you? The opportunity hasn't presented itself yet." I shrug, not seeing the problem that my sister obviously does.

"Poor guy. Barbosa must be suffering from a bad case of blue balls. By the time you pull the trigger and get to the sexy times, he won't even remember how to use his dick."

"Can you be any more vulgar?!" I snap.

"Can you be any more prudish?" she rebukes with a chuckle.

"I'm not a prude. They will have sex. Eventually."

"But you said that they haven't even kissed. How the hell are they going to jump each other's bones if they haven't even gotten to first base yet?"

"It *will* happen. Organically. Naturally. You do know that not everyone jumps into bed with the first guy they meet, right?"

"Is that a jab at me, squirt?" She laughs joyously, not one bit bothered by my remark.

"If the shoe fits," I taunt, stealing away my journal.

Anyone else would be offended by the insinuation.

But not Daisy.

Not my sister.

Daisy has never cared what people think of her. She's one of those rare individuals that lives free of all judgment. I would never tell her to her face, but my big sister is kind of my idol.

My aspiration—the type of person I dream to become one day.

So when she starts laughing at my sass, I'm not even surprised. In fact, it warms my insides to witness her 'fuck it' attitude up close.

"I know why you're having such a hard time getting to the sex scene," she muses, turning to face me.

"Okay, I'll bite. Why?" I reply, turning to look at her with my elbow on the pillow and my hand on my cheek.

"Isn't it obvious?" she retorts, her blue eyes softening. "It's because you're still a virgin. How can you write a sex scene when you haven't even done the deed yet?"

I don't remind my sister that I just turned sixteen a few weeks ago and haven't mustered the courage to let a boy kiss me, much less do the dirty with. Using that as an excuse on my sister would be pointless since I'm pretty sure Daisy had her sexual awakening around the time she was in junior high and has never looked back. She sees sex as simply having a bit of harmless fun, while I've built it up so high in my mind that it kind of scares the living shit out of me.

When her spirited expression turns into concern that she's hurt my feelings, I plant a playful smile on my lips.

"That's what the imagination is for." I flick the center of her forehead to drive the point home. "And besides, I know the mechanics of it, thank you very much."

"Knowing where a cock fits into a vagina isn't enough. You'll never be able to do it justice if you don't let yourself experience it first. How else will you be able to describe the intensity in your lover's eyes? The smell in the room? Or how his warm skin slides up against yours, making your heart skip? Or how the sweat drips down your brow as you beg him to give it to you harder. Shouting more, more, more!" she yells, slapping her hand on the mattress in the space between us.

"You're a freak, you know that, right?" I laugh.

"And you're my favorite little weirdo." She giggles, ruffling my dark brown hair. "But I guess you still have plenty of time for all of that good stuff. All I ask is that you at least write one good kiss scene. Please don't make me wait ten fucking chapters to get it."

"Fine. I'll have them kiss in the next chapter," I concede.

"Barbosa's blue balls thank you. And remember, if you need any help with the sexy times, you know who to come to for advice." She wiggles her eyebrows at me as she pretends to hump the air.

"God, you're gross."

She cackles.

"Speaking of gross," she starts to say when she's calmed down, "I think Mom is getting nailed on the daily now. Good and proper by the way she's always smiling."

"Oh my God, Daisy! Can you not?! I don't want to have the picture of our mom doing it in my mind."

Another cackle.

"Doesn't make it any less true. She didn't come home again last night. It's the fourth time this month."

"Yeah, I noticed." I chew on the corner of my bottom lip.

"So, you know what that means?" Daisy smiles mischievously while jumping up on top of my bed again. "Mom has ditched all those fuck boys that never call her back after getting some and she's got herself a real man. Bow chicka wow wow!" she hollers, spanking the air in front of her as she jumps up and down.

"You're going to break the bed!" I shout, laughing while trying to pull her back down.

She just laughs away, dropping down beside me.

This, ladies and gentlemen, is my big sister. Always happy. Always a perv, and always the life of the party.

I'm the total opposite.

I'm the serious one.

My nose is either stuck in a book, or on my laptop writing up a storm. To say I'm socially awkward is an understatement. Give me fictional heroes any day of the week compared to the idiots I go to school with. Daisy, however, is the *it* girl at our school. I think that's why I'm not bullied even if the kids there think I'm a freak. I'm Daisy Ames' little sister, after all. If you mess with me, you mess with her. And no one wants to be on my sister's shit list.

I should be thankful, I guess.

But if I'm completely honest with myself, at times I resent her a little. The things I love about my sister are also the things that make my existence extra hard. If she would only tone it down a notch, no one would think I'm such a letdown all the time in comparison.

"So?" she asks, pulling me out of my shameful thoughts.

"So?" I retort, confused.

"So what do you think about Mom and this new beau of hers?"

"Do people still say beau?"

"I'm trying to use words you will understand. Give me a break, squirt. Just stop acting all Skylaresque for a bit and tell me everything. I know you're always eavesdropping on us—"

"Hey!" I blurt out defensively.

"I'm not accusing you or saying it's a bad thing," she's quick to add. "I know that's how you get your creative juices flowing and come up with story ideas. It's your process and I respect the hell out of your commitment to your craft. All I'm asking is if you know the scoop about this guy or not? Spill it."

Shit. She has me there.

I have been eavesdropping.

I always do.

At school. At the supermarket. At the coffee house. Even at the bus stop. I can't help it.

The human spirit and people's interactions with one another fascinate me.

Since I'm unable to tap into my own experiences—since, let's face it, I've had none worth mentioning—eavesdropping and spying on strangers has become my favorite pastime. Sometimes all it takes is listening in on an innocent phone call to have my imagination working double time. I don't question the morality aspect of it anymore. The hit of dopamine I get when inspiration hits is far more alluring than worrying about the implications of my less than above water actions.

When I grow quiet for longer than acceptable, Daisy snaps her fingers in my face.

"Sky! Get out of Lalaland and tell me what you know," she insists, frustrated.

"Fine," I relent. No use in pretending I'm in the dark when it comes to my mom's new boyfriend. "His name is Curt, and he lives in Thatcher's Bay."

"Okay," my sister mumbles, taking in that piece of information.

"That means they can't see each other as much as they would like. He's also a fisherman, which means he goes out to sea for long periods of time sometimes."

"What else?"

"I don't think their relationship is something new. I think they've been seeing each other for a while now. And I'm not completely sure about this next thing, but I think he might have a son. I heard Mom saying something about Curt needing to give someone named Noah time to heal and grieve or something. I'm guessing someone close to them must have died a few months back. A woman by the sound of it. Maybe a grandmother."

"Or maybe his wife," Daisy interjects, making my eyes snap in alarm at her.

"You think? No, that can't be. By my count, they've been dating for over six months and whoever passed away sounded like it happened pretty recently."

"Keeping track, huh? I knew I could count on you for dirt," she praises, fake punching my chin.

I slap her hand away.

"Whatever. All I know is that it's getting super serious between them."

"How come?"

I maul my lip, since what I'm about to confess is far worse than eavesdropping on my mother's private conversations.

"I might have gone on Mom's computer last week," I admit with a cringe.

Instead of the reprimand I expect to hear from my sister, all she does is wait for me to continue.

"And?" she insists, with wide eyes anxious for me to get on with it.

"And she's been sending resumes to hospices, clinics, and the hospital on the island," I finally say.

"Shit. For real?"

"Yeah." My shoulders slump.

"Do you think that means she is thinking of moving us to Thatcher's Bay to be closer to him?"

"She isn't applying to jobs on the island just for kicks, Daisy. Yes, I definitely think that's where her head is at."

"Ah, man. That's a bummer."

"Is that all you have to say? Mom is probably going to uproot us from our childhood home and all you have to say is that it's a bummer?" I ask incredulously.

She shrugs.

"That's life. What's true today, might not be tomorrow. You just have to roll with the punches. So, we'll move. Big whoop. Think of it like a new adventure. New school. New friends. You can even create a whole new you if you wanted."

"But I like who I am." My brow furrows at that remark.

"I know you do. But I think you'd like yourself a whole lot more if others did, too."

I turn my face away from her, since I don't want my sister to see how her words cut into me. I always pretend that I'm like Daisy and don't care what people think about me either, but it's a big fat lie. In truth, I'm getting pretty sick of everyone treating me like a basket case just because I prefer to spend my precious time with the fictional characters in my head than with flesh and blood people.

Real life has a knack of disappointing you.

Fiction never does.

The air in the room grows tense and I can feel that Daisy wants to say something or maybe even apologize for the callous remark, but thankfully, a rap on my bedroom door prevents her from saying anything else.

"Hey, girls." My mother smiles that big-ass grin she's been sporting lately. "Do you mind if we talk for a minute?"

"If it's to apologize for doing the walk of shame when you got home this morning, then no need. We're good. Although, I do want you to remember how empathetic I'm being right now when it's my turn to come home at all hours of the morning," Daisy states, hiking up a mischievous brow.

"Noted." My mother laughs softly as she takes a seat on the edge of my bed, unable to hide the blush that blooms on her cheeks. "In fact, that's what I wanted to talk to you girls about."

"Ew, Mom. No," Daisy starts, scrunching her face like she just sucked on a lemon wedge. "I know you like us to share what's up with our lives and all, but knowing the details of you getting it on with your new man is where I draw the line. I'm more than happy to tease you about it, but I really don't need to know how many times you and your new boyfriend have been bumping uglies."

"Daisy!" My mother lets out an exaggerated exhale. "Can you please act like the well-behaved young lady I raised long enough for us to have a serious conversation? Please?"

Daisy takes her phone out of her back pocket, fiddles with it for a bit, and then turns the screen over to our mother.

"You got five minutes. I'm timing you."

"Fine," my mother retorts, grabbing my hand in hers so I can feel included in their banter. "As you girls know by now, I've been seeing someone."

"You mean you've been fu—"

"Daisy, please. Five minutes. You promised," our mom warns, her cheeks turning redder by the minute.

"Please proceed," Daisy snickers, wrapping her arms around my waist and plopping her chin on my shoulder.

"As I was saying, I've been dating Curt for a while now. Six months, to be exact, and, well...things are serious."

"Seriously dirty, she means," Daisy whispers in my ear, but thankfully my mother doesn't hear the hushed innuendo.

"How serious?" I ask, ignoring my sister's need to add her own commentary to the situation.

"Serious enough that he would like to meet you girls." My mom smiles widely, while wringing her hands together.

She's nervous.

Really nervous.

But she's also extremely happy.

I don't know which is cause for more concern.

"Is that it? All this for only a meet and greet? I was sure you were going to tell us that he popped the question or something." Daisy squints her eyes, unimpressed with the anticlimactic conversation.

"Actually, I think he might." Mom beams, her shy smile growing ever wider.

"Holy shit," my sister blurts out.

"Daisy!" Mom reprimands my sister on her outburst. "Please try to be on your best behavior tomorrow and refrain from cursing like a sailor. I know it's a big ask, but please try and behave."

"Tomorrow?!" I croak, finally adding my two cents to the conversation.

"Yes," my mother answers, her features going soft. "Is that okay?"

Is that okay?

Do I have a choice in the matter?

But instead of saying what I'm really thinking, I fake a smile for her and nod.

"Good. I'm glad. We'll have to leave early, though, to catch the ferry. Curt still hasn't talked to Noah yet about this lunch, but we both feel it would be better if we met for the first time in Thatcher's Bay instead of here on the mainland."

"Noah?" I repeat, wanting to know who this mysterious person is.

"Curt's son. He's only a few months older than you, Skylar. I'm positive you two will hit it off with a bang and become the best of friends."

But even as she says those optimistic, hopeful words with a broad grin, it never reaches her eyes.

As I connect the dots, it becomes blatantly obvious to me now that it's Curt's son, Noah, who they have spent endless hours talking about over the phone.

He's not even a part of my life yet, and already my mother is more concerned how he'll react to her relationship with his father than she is about how I feel about it. It stings, how even to my own mother, I'm always an afterthought. That I'm expected to smile and accept whatever hurdle she throws at me like the good girl she perceives me to be. I guess it all comes down to the fact that, unlike Daisy, I never cause any waves regarding anything. Not that at times I haven't wanted to tear the whole roof off. It's just easier to suck it up and pretend nothing affects me. I know it's definitely easier on my mother.

"How do you girls feel about all this?" she asks, trying to gauge where we're at, but inwardly praying that we won't object.

Again, I stretch out my smile and grab her hand in mine.

"We're fine with it. Aren't we, Daisy?"

My sister takes longer to reply, because she knows it will drive our mother up the wall. It wouldn't be Daisy if she didn't make things more difficult than they need to be.

"Daisy?"

It's only when her phone starts blowing up that Daisy finally reacts, jumping out of the bed with her phone already to her ear.

"Daisy! Aren't you going to say something?" my mom calls out before my sister is able to leave the room.

"Hold on," Daisy says to whoever is on the other line. "Yeah, Mom. We're good. Set up the lunch or whatever. Can't wait to meet the new guy," she says with a wave before she struts out of the room.

My mother's shoulders slump in defeat.

"That girl never takes anything seriously, does she?"

"It's just Daisy being Daisy, Mom. But she's happy for you, even if she didn't say it," I try to console.

"Do you really think so?" she asks, insecurity hugging her every word.

"I do." I smile.

"What about you?"

My front teeth immediately go to chew on my lip, but I stop myself before she sees the nervous tic.

"If you're happy, I'm happy."

"How did I ever get so lucky at having such a sweet daughter like you?" my mother coos, cupping my cheeks in her hands and placing a tender kiss on my forehead.

I just smile, because telling her the truth would break her heart.

I'm not sweet.

Sometimes, I don't think I'm even nice.

But I work damn hard at pretending that I am.

Fake it until you make it, I guess.

If my mother knew how angry I was all the time, it would scare her. And thanks to me, she's had a rough life as it is. She doesn't need me to pile my baggage to her already heavy plate of misfortunes. So I smile and I nod, hoping she doesn't see how broken and flawed I truly am on the inside.

It's a twenty-four-seven job.

One that will become more difficult to pull off if we move to Thatcher's Bay.

As the saying goes, you can fool some people some of the time, but you can't fool them all, all of the time.

Maybe it won't be that bad.

Maybe this Noah guy will put up enough of a fight that will make my mom reconsider moving us altogether.

A girl can only hope.

Chapter 3

Skylar

Sixteen years old

The wind whips at my hair, throwing it across my face like it's trying to punish me for the negative thoughts battering at my skull. Daisy's beside me, typing away on her phone like this is just another day, another normal moment, and not the probable start of a whole new life.

My mother is...a mess. Vibrating between huge, awkward smiles and nervous looks, she spends her time staring wistfully between the strip of land in the distance and us. I don't know what she's so nervous about. I love my mother. But she's already started down this path. She's already taken our choice away from us. Even if I go to this lunch and hate Curt, even if I scream and curse and tell her she's ruining my life, it won't make a difference. She's already made up her mind, and nothing I say will change that.

It's helpful knowing that going into this so I can manage my expectations accordingly.

Fuck. I sound like I'm an eighty year old woman—even in my own head.

Daisy snorts and then throws her head back, practically howling. People glance over at us, soft smiles on their faces. It's the reaction she always gets.

The boat rocks as we hit a wave and my stomach twists and rolls, a wave of nausea hitting me hard.

Have I mentioned that I hate boats?

I'll add that into the win column for how my mother's relationship, with a fisherman no less, is going to be perfect for me.

It's also one more thing that proves just how unseen I really am.

Right now she's not worrying about my fear of the sea and drowning. All she's worried about is whether we'll make this easy or not for her.

I grit my teeth and squeeze the railing as we hit another wave. Daisy drops her phone on the deck with a curse and a cute boy with auburn hair and a brilliant smile swoops in from nearby and grabs it for her. I roll my eyes as she giggles and plays with her hair. He's staring at her like she's the best thing he's ever seen.

Jealousy pulses through my insides.

What would it feel like to have someone look at me like that?

Water hits the side of the boat and sprays all over my face. And I've honestly had enough. "I'm going to wait inside," I tell them, not waiting for an answer as I hustle to the doorway that leads to the near empty inside. Every normal person is out there on the railing, enjoying the view and the fresh air.

I slide into a hard, plastic bench seat, the coolness of the plastic seeping into my damp shorts. I wrap my arms around myself, muttering affirmations inanely like that'll help me overcome my fears.

For about the millionth time, I curse my father, Grant Ames, for setting me up so well for life in a seaside town.

"It's a beautiful fucking day today, little bird," my father hollers as he starts our old rusted boat and sets off for the open water.

I cling to the edges of the boat, terror gripping my insides as the waves dash against the sides. It is not a beautiful "fucking" day. The high winds alone are alarming, and if Mom knew that I was in this sketchy boat alone with my irresponsible father, she would definitely be freaking out.

But that's my dad for you. A force of nature that relishes in skirting the edges of disaster. And I have never said anything to discourage his behavior because I want to be around him.

My hair smacks my face, while salt water sprays my skin as we keep smacking into wave after wave. Each time the boat hits one, I'm bounced off my seat.

"Hold on!" he yells, his face lifting to the wind as he lets out a loud "whoop" that I can hear even with the cacophony of noises assaulting my ear drums.

And that's when it happens, right after he says it, a particularly violent wave blasts the front of the boat and I lose my grip on the sides and tumble...overboard.

I lose my breath as I hit the icy water, inhaling a barrel of it down my throat as I crash under the surface into its dark depths. I kick my legs furiously and, miraculously, a second later get my head above water. The boat isn't turning around; he hasn't even noticed I'm gone yet.

"Dad!" I try to scream, but unlike my father's voice, mine gets caught in the elements and I doubt someone next to me could have heard my cry.

I'm not a strong swimmer, never have been. Swimming for me consists of doggy paddling, and I'm even crap at that. Add the fact that I'm also not wearing a life jacket, and my clothes are so heavy, they feel like an anchor pulling me down. I'm having what can only be described as a panic attack. I'm treading water the best I can, but I'm so cold that with each wave, I end up sinking under the surface once again.

The boat finally starts to turn around, but it is so far away...and I'm so tired.

Just then, a huge wave crashes over me, pushing me much farther under the surface than the previous ones have. I struggle to kick my feet but in my panic, I breathe in another huge gulp of water and...

I begin to sink, the dim light of the surface above me fading as I fall through the water.

And I wonder as I drown...if anyone will even miss me.

"Sky!" Daisy's voice cuts through the noise in my head, coaxing me to come back to the present. Suddenly, I realize we've somehow managed to dock in the time I'd been lost in my tumultuous thoughts. "Ready to go?" she asks, examining me closely when I refuse to move.

I shake my head, trying to clear away the bad memories as I give her an awkward smile.

"Ready," I try to say cheerfully, but I know my sister can see right through me. She links her arm through mine and we walk back on deck where we follow our eager mother off the boat and down the ramp to the dock.

"Clara!" a deep voice rumbles from a few feet away. I turn in the direction of the voice, only to see a tall, rugged-looking man with a thick, maroon cable-knit sweater and wavy dirty blond hair come rushing towards us with long strides.

He comes to a stop awkwardly a few steps away, obviously unsure of what he is supposed to do since my sister and I are here. My mother has no such worries, flinging herself at him, her arms wrapping around his neck as she lets out a tinkling laugh. He wraps her up in his arms and lifts her so her toes are dangling above the ground. They stare at each other for an absurdly long stretch, obviously in love, and Daisy and I exchange incredulous glances.

When they both finally remember that we are also standing here, Curt sets my mother down. She grabs his hand and turns towards us proudly.

"This is Curt," she gushes. "Curt, these are my babies!"

My mother instantly seems ten years younger at this very moment, a soft light wrapped around her.

Is this what everyone looks like when they're in love? I can't remember mom ever acting this way when she was with our dad.

"Nice to meet you," greets Daisy, in a posh, British accent, holding out her hand for him to take like she's the Queen of England.

My mother sighs, feigning annoyance, but Curt lets out a deep, amused belly laugh as he takes my sister's hand and shakes it.

"Your mother has told me so much about you two girls, I feel as if I already know you, Daisy," he says with amusement in his tone.

I examine his face closely, noting how blue his eyes are, standing out from his tan skin and his dark blond hair streaked with gray around the temples. He is good-looking, I'll give him that, but it's his earnest features, like he's actually happy to meet the two of us, that catches me off guard. So when Curt turns his attention on me, holding out his hand for me to shake, it takes me a minute to register it.

"Hi, Skylar," he murmurs, a small smile playing on his lips. Words are stuck in my throat as I shake his hand on autopilot, the size of it enveloping mine completely.

"Hello," I finally squeak out, eliciting a snort from Daisy who has never been awkward a day in her life, of course. My mother stares at the three of us with a goofy smile on her face, like we have just succeeded in making all of her dreams come true.

"I hope you ladies like seafood," Curt announces once he's let go of my hand.

I hold in an eye roll, mostly because I'm not sure that you are allowed to hate seafood in a fishermen's town like this. And Mom has already told us he's a fisherman, so it definitely wouldn't be a great start for me to admit I'd like to eat literally anything other than seafood.

"Sounds wonderful," Mom coos, giggling when he pushes a piece of hair away from her face.

They walk off down the cobblestone road that leads into the quaint island village, lost in their own rainbow-color world, while my sister and I trail behind them.

Daisy slings her arm across my shoulder, leaning in to whisper in my ear.

"Well, at least he's hot for an old guy."

"Daisy!" I reprimand, thankful she didn't just say that loud enough for them to hear.

"What?" she retorts, unabashedly.

"You can't say stuff like that!"

"Can't say Mom's boyfriend is a DILF? What about Zaddy? Can I say that?"

I blush at my sister's creative vulgar vocabulary.

"Daisy, that could be our new...stepdad."

"Well aware, squirt. Still hot though. Way to go, Mom. I knew I got a good eye from someplace." She smirks, then starts ogling our surroundings. "Hmm. I wonder if this place has anything fun to do," she thinks out loud, glancing around the storefront windows we pass by.

"Um, I don't think Mom is going to be happy if you sneak off during lunch," I answer, reading her thoughts.

"Obviously. But if we're going to be living here..."

"Living here?" I ask, my insides growing cold.

I'm not sure why the idea of living here chills me to the bone, but it does. I mean, it shouldn't come as a surprise to me. Mom has told us repeatedly what Curt does for a living, making sure we understood her underlying meaning. Mom can do her nursing job anywhere. Curt's job, however, isn't as flexible.

"You think they're that serious?" I ask quietly, even though I'd been so positive about that yesterday. It's just a different thing for the reality of it to be in my face.

Daisy nods her head at Mom and Curt. Their arms are locked so tightly around each other, I'm not sure how they're even capable of walking...or breathing, for that matter, without one another. Daisy and I have ceased to exist at the moment, and the only people alive in their bubble are the pair of them.

My shoulders slump and I stare at the town around me, trying to imagine living here.

It...doesn't look that different from our town. Just older. A little more rundown. Passersby call out to Curt as they walk by, staring at us curiously. That's different. Would I like that about living on a small island, everyone knowing everyone and everything about their lives?

Definitely not.

Daisy chatters while I watch our surroundings carefully. Five minutes later, we're at a small diner called The Scarlet Letter Cafe. I frown, thinking it's a strange name for a restaurant, but when we walk in, I immediately see that the owner of the place is obsessed with Nathanial Hawthorne. There's scarlet letter wallpaper, and pearls, and scaffolds here and there, decorating most of the walls and tables.

Really, really odd, actually.

"Mmh. Always did hate that book," Daisy mutters, glancing around in amusement.

Meanwhile, our mother is gushing about what a quaint place it is.

I'm a little worried that an alien has taken over her body. She's just referred to it as "quite lovely." Definitely not her typical language.

Curt glances at his watch with a frown. "Noah should have been here by now," he grumbles...right as the door flies open and in walks...

A god.

That's who walks in.

A living, breathing god amongst men.

Hair touched with a thousand shades of gold. Soulful blue eyes, like a glacier reflecting the sky above it. Warm, tan skin without a single blemish or freckle. Built more like a man than what he should have been.

A teenage dream.

My insides shift uncomfortably, something unrecognizable stirring as I gaze at him.

And I just want to keep gazing at him. I don't think I'll ever get tired of it.

He doesn't seem to be having the soul crushing awakening that I am at the moment though. He's staring at his surroundings, bored, as he strides towards us, finally deigning to give us a glance once he's a few feet away.

"I do love some eye candy," Daisy murmurs, unabashedly staring him up and down.

Normally, I would have said something to chastise her, but I have nothing. He is eye candy. The best and the worst kind. The kind that gives you type 2 diabetes.

"Well, I'm here," he snaps just as he glances at my mother, his mouth dropping. He looks momentarily shocked for a second before he puts on his perfect arctic mask again.

I shiver just watching him. I've never seen someone able to do that. Go from warm and hot, to ice cold...simply with their gaze.

Curt clears his throat, a brief flicker of annoyance in his features before he schools them for a placid smile.

"Glad you could make it, Noah." He pulls my mother closer with the arm he has wrapped around her waist, his fake smile blossoming into a real one as he glances at her.

A sick feeling spreads through my veins. This is his son. Which means if this is as serious as it seems to be...he's going to be my...

"This is Clara," Curt announces proudly, his eyes shining with adoration as he gazes lovingly at my mother.

Again, I can't help but wonder, had my father ever looked at my mom like that? Like he couldn't exist without her? For the life of me, I can't picture it.

Noah's completely silent, not even giving her a head nod. But his stare has gone from blank to glaring, as he looks my mother over with his nose scrunched like he just took a whiff of sour milk.

Not a big fan of the union then, I take it...

Curt's smile dims at his son's reaction. He clears his throat and turns towards us.

"These are Clara's lovely daughters, Daisy and Skylar."

"Sky," I blurt out, drawing everyone's attention to me. As soon as it slips from my mouth for whatever inane reason, I want to run and hide under a table.

Daisy is silently laughing next to me, her whole body shaking, but Noah doesn't seem fazed by my awkwardness. He gives us a brief, bored stare before heading to an empty table and sliding smoothly into a seat, pulling out his phone and typing something.

"Charming." Daisy laughs, grabbing my arm and pulling me towards the seats at the end of the table and as far as we can get from Noah.

I watch as Curt whispers something in my mother's ear, as she stares at Noah with alarm. Whatever Curt just told her works like magic, because her shoulders drop and her face relaxes.

"So, Noah," Daisy begins teasingly. He doesn't put his phone down or turn towards us like he's heard her at all. Daisy, of course, isn't about to give up. She puts both hands to her mouth and calls loudly, "Hey! Earth to asshole! Anybody home?"

"Daisy!" my mother calls out, shocked, right as Noah's burning stare focuses our way.

It's hard to think with him glaring at us like this. Like he's seen below our skin and found us wanting.

"You rang," he drawls.

Mom stares between Noah and an amused Daisy in a panic. Curt shepherds her to a chair and pulls it out for her to sit down, seemingly unbothered by Noah's sarcastic response, although the slight frown on his face belies that.

Maybe he's used to this attitude from his son.

A beaming young woman who appears to be around my age comes bustling over to the table, her gaze like a laser beam on Noah's face.

Noah turns away from Daisy before she has time to say anything else, and I watch as the asshole fades away, and in its place is a sexy beast.

Sexy beast. Had I really just thought that?

Kill me now.

"Hi Noah," the girl purrs, bouncing her pen on her tiny notebook, completely ignoring the rest of us seated at the table.

Curt sighs loudly, but she doesn't seem to hear it. She's a pretty girl, with dark red hair and vibrant blue eyes. Someone who could hold a boy's attention for sure. My hand drifts up to touch the ends of my plain brown hair that's badly in need of a trim.

"How have you been?" She giggles, like he's said something funny...even though he hasn't said anything at all yet.

But maybe he doesn't have to say anything. The way he's lazily eyeing her, it would most likely cause hysterical laughter out of most people.

"Better now that I'm seeing you," he finally answers in a silky voice. Daisy snorts and pretends to gag, drawing a furious glare from Noah.

My mother pales, her eyes a little too wide and desperate like she's in danger of passing out.

I pick up my menu, fiddling with the page anxiously as Noah turns his attention back to the waitress.

"Looking forward to summer vacation? I'm so ready to be done with school," she says in a choked voice, a blush darkening her cheeks. I can't help but sneak glances at their conversation even as I try to distract myself with deciding what I want for lunch.

Daisy is now fluttering her eyelashes, pretending like she's fainting, while Noah ignores her and continues to give the waitress his full attention.

School. I can only imagine how a boy like him is received at school. Do the girls faint as he walks by? Do the other guys bow in utter awe? One thing's for sure. No way does Noah fade into the shadows like I do. Of that, I'm certain.

I wonder what that must be like...to be seen.

"I think we're ready to get our order taken," Curt interjects gently, before Noah can answer her question about school.

The redhead has been so consumed in leaning towards Noah, thoroughly enthralled in the planes of his face, that she practically jumps at the sound of Curt's voice and at being reminded that she's on the clock. She hastily wipes her sweaty hands on her apron and straightens up.

"Right, of course." The girl pretends to give her attention back to Curt and my mom as they think about their order, but she can't help herself from sneaking glances towards Noah from time to time.

Noah, for his part, has a smug grin on his face and a cocky air about him. He seems secure in the knowledge that he controls this girl.

"The chowder is really good here," comments Curt to us. My mom nods, apparently recovered from her embarrassment over Daisy's behavior and back to swooning over her man.

Jesus. She's as bad as the waitress is.

I'm now a little mortified.

"Chicken tenders, french fries, and a side of hushpuppies," Daisy throws out before my mom can order.

Noah snorts.

"Oh, did I copy your order?" asks Daisy innocently.

For as worldly as my big sister is, her comfort foods are definitely more akin to what a toddler would eat. Her order might have signaled to me...and maybe my mother too, that she's actually more uncomfortable than she would allow us to believe...but she was also trying to insult Noah with her comment.

I wish I had half of her bravery...or foolishness. Sometimes her actions could go either way.

"The chicken tenders are really good," the waitress adds eagerly, obviously missing the joke.

My mother hasn't though. Not by the way she's glaring at Daisy once again.

Up until this point, I'd been doing such a good job of staying quiet. But to my dismay, I release a snort, provoked by her naive comment.

Big mistake.

Because now Noah's sharp glare is on me...and I'm frantically trying to throw water on the inner fire I'm suddenly feeling.

"Something funny?" he asks casually, his stare intense on my features.

Gulp.

I'd never had anyone look at me like this.

It's...too much.

For as much as a part of me craves attention, the far bigger part of me prefers to stay blended into the scenery. Noah's stare seems to see all of that, and then some. Somehow, in that moment, I know I'll never be able to hide from him again, for as long as he's in my life.

That's...unsettling.

"You'll have to forgive Sky. She's frequently embarrassed of me," inserts Daisy, saving me from having to reply to...*him*.

"Do you not talk?" Noah presses, cutting me off from the fantasy world where I did indeed not have to talk.

I open my mouth to answer, but nothing comes out.

"I'll have the clam chowder," my mother says quickly trying to fill the awkward silence. "And some of those cheddar biscuits for the table."

Everyone else's attention moves back to ordering, but not Noah's. He's still studying me, a knowing smirk on his pretty lips.

I quickly stare down at the menu, feeling the tips of my ears growing red. At least I was able to hold in my blush for a minute.

Stupid. Stupid. Stupid, I think to myself.

Daisy kicks me under the table and when I glance up at her, she's shooting me a sympathetic frown. "Fuck him," she mouths, and I grimace at her...still feeling his stare on the side of my head.

"And for you?" the waitress asks me, her lips now laced in displeasure as she examines Daisy and me...almost like she's sizing up potential competition for Noah's attention.

Down girl. There isn't a world where I'd be a threat to you...and Daisy's just added him to her shit list for making me squirm like I did.

"The shrimp salad," I answer quietly, proud that my voice actually comes out steady. The whole situation is overwhelming me. It was hard enough meeting Curt...but adding Noah to the mix? I'm ready to either throw up...or faint.

She nods and sniffs, like she finds my order underwhelming before turning back to Noah, her frown changing to a wide, simpering grin.

"Thirsty much?" Daisy mumbles under her breath, but Noah catches it all the same.

He pulls his eyes away from me and my sister and directs them back to the waitress.

"I'll have you when you're off," Noah answers at last, and I choke on my water. Literally choke.

"Noah!" his dad barks, obviously having enough with his antics. Meanwhile, the poor waitress seems to be melting in place, a puddle of lust at her metaphorical feet.

"A burger and some fries," Noah says with a wink, not seeming put off at all by his dad's obvious fury across the table. Even his order seems to be mocking his dad. Like it had been intentional that he hadn't ordered seafood.

But maybe I'm just reading into things too much.

"Of course," she squeaks before scurrying off as fast as she can, only throwing a few glances over her shoulder at Noah as she moves.

"Noah, could you try and at least act like your mother and I raised you right for the duration of this lunch?" Curt sighs, his voice sounding like he's been carrying the weight of the world on his shoulders–Noah comprising most of that weight.

Noah's face flickers in displeasure before he schools it into the carefully crafted air of nonchalance that I'm learning is his go to.

"Not sure what you mean, Pops."

Curt shakes his head and turns his attention to us, throwing an arm around the back of my mother's chair.

"Girls. Tell me about yourselves. What do you like to do? What's your favorite subject in school? What do you want to do after you graduate?" he asks eagerly, leaning towards us now, a soft smile on his lips.

And of course, my mother is practically purring in adoration next to him. She's staring at him like he...completes her.

Like she has always been the other half of his soul.

Daisy jumps in...as she always does. Good thing too, since her life is a hell of a lot more interesting than mine. If I'm lucky, she'll talk long enough for the food to arrive and then I won't need to talk at all.

As hoped, she chatters away. My sister is insanely talented...if a little flighty. Which means that she's always doing tons of activities and skipping from one hobby to another...wherever the wind blows her.

There were occasional guitar lessons...which ended with her having a brief foray with a band that practiced in our garage after class—although, not to be biased, Daisy really had been the only highlight in that experience. There were photography classes and the brief idea that Daisy would be a nature photographer. That is until she discovered how badly she hated bugs after a hike to a nearby waterfall for pictures. She's also a naturally talented athlete but thus far had decided "team sports" weren't her thing. I think she's been taking cooking classes lately, but judging by the eggs she burned for breakfast the last five days in a row, I'm pretty sure that, unlike the many other things she was good at and could possibly turn into a career, a chef was not one of them.

Daisy is still talking about the Arabic class she's been taking when the waitress comes back with another waiter, their trays loaded with food.

The waiter gives a chin lift to Noah before moving the plates onto the table.

It all smelled...really good.

"Well, hello there," he murmurs to me flirtily, as he sets my salad in front of me. He's cute. Dark brown hair and vibrant green eyes. Cute, but not heart-stopping.

Before I can say anything in return–not that it was a sure thing I could get the words out if I tried anyway–Noah cuts in.

"How's baseball training going?"

The guy moves his attention eagerly to Noah, seeming a bit in awe that he's actually speaking to him. It doesn't take him more than two seconds to start a conversation with Noah, forgetting that I exist entirely.

I find myself frowning...although I'm used to being forgotten, it always stings when it happens. Daisy knocks me gently with her shoulder, and throws me a lopsided smile.

She knows I tend to go to the worst case scenarios in my head when it comes to my self esteem. She's probably the one person who always makes an effort to ensure I feel like my presence is needed. Wanted, even.

The waiters walk away after delivering the food, helped along their way by an annoyed glare from Curt, and we begin to eat.

I pick at my meal, my stomach churning with anxiety as I sneak glances at my mom and her boyfriend...and sometimes Noah.

"I haven't heard from you yet, Sky," Curt says suddenly, and my gut churns even more as my fork clatters to my plate.

"Not much to say," I finally retort with a false grin, while my mother frowns at my answer.

"Sky's always too modest," my mom begins, but Daisy cuts her off before our mom says anything overtly embarrassing.

"What Sky is trying to say is that she's an amazing writer. Like the best I've ever read," Daisy gushes. My cheeks flush hot under her praise, quiet pride building in my chest.

I wouldn't say I'm an amazing writer like my sister is currently boasting, but it is something I'm good at and enjoy. I've loved doing it for as long as I can remember. I lie in bed, coming up with a million different worlds and then race to get them down on paper or on my computer as soon as I wake up. Telling stories has somehow always been ingrained in me. Like my brain is wired to make fantastic tales and put them onto paper. Sure beats real life.

"Really? I'd love to read something you've written," Curt comments politely, and I give him a weak smile.

I don't let many people read my writing. And by many...I mean the only person I allow to read any of it is Daisy...and sometimes my mother if she begs...and my teachers when I'm forced to turn in my assignments. However, I make it a point to always turn my teachers down every time they ask if I can read one of my short stories in front of the class.

Yeah. That isn't happening.

Of course, sometimes I let myself dream of a million people reading the words I write but that's something I keep to myself. I don't know if I'll ever be brave enough to actually publish anything I write. The whole idea that someone can scrutinize my words is too daunting for me to wrap my head around. Right now, I write for my own pleasure. It's my own lifeline to sanity. To add any pressure to it would only steal the joy it brings me. And in my pathetic excuse of a life, I can't afford to lose the one thing that actually still makes me happy.

"Maybe," I finally answer lamely.

Noah coughs and I glance at him, only to see that his face is curled up in laughter.

And that is why I don't talk about my writing with anyone. No one expects something incredible to come from someone who appears to be so completely average.

The table descends into silence as we all continue eating. The shrimp salad is probably wonderful, but it might as well be leather with how uncomfortable I'm feeling. Still, I can't keep my eyes off my mother. Curt's been fawning over her ever since we got here, even going as far as buttering her freaking biscuit for her and feeding her little bites of his meal. My mother's still glowing from the attention, confirming that she seems to be at least a decade younger under his care and attention.

"So...you look familiar to me, Clara," Noah comments after a few minutes. "I wonder where from. Any guesses?"

For some reason, Curt and my mother freeze at his comment.

Curt clears his throat and shifts in his chair.

My mother almost appears ...shamed. That's odd.

"You might have seen her here and there," he finally answers his son, not glancing up at him and instead shoveling some of his soup into his mouth.

"Where would I have seen her?" Noah presses. And the question comes out innocently enough...but still, there's something mocking about it, something I can feel slithering along my skin.

"Well—" Curt's voice fades away as if trying to grasp the right words to say and failing.

"I was one of the nurses that took care of your mom in Falmouth Hospital," Mom finishes for him gently, sliding her hand into Curt's on top of the table. "Before her passing."

It takes me a second to connect the dots—Daisy flinching long before I do—but then I realize why they're acting so weird.

Noah's mother died. And it was highly unlikely that my mom and Curt had happened to *fall* for each other conveniently after she passed.

Fuck, Mom.

I side-eye Daisy, who's unusually quiet. Her brow is furrowed and there's a tightness to her jaw, as though she's trying to keep from saying something she might regret.

I mean, they could have fallen for each other after. It's not unlikely.

Right?

I'm imagining my mom pushing her cart in a grocery store and Curt reaching for a can of beans at the same time she did. A reunion of sorts outside of the professional way they'd acted when she was caring for his wife.

I wish that was how it had happened....but judging by how... guilty...my mother seems, I somehow doubt that's the case.

"Yeah, I remember you. I remember you well. So tell me. Did you enjoy fucking my dad while my mother was literally dying in her hospital bed?" Noah asks, eerily calm.

Holy fuck.

You could have heard a pin drop as Noah sucked all of the happiness from the air.

Curt stands abruptly, his chair slamming to the ground behind him. My mom's face is scrunched up and pale, like she's about to throw up at any moment.

He marches over to Noah, who's glaring at him furiously, and grabs him by the collar of his shirt, yanking him back towards the bathrooms while the rest of us watch in shock.

I've always had a relatively easy relationship with my mother. She doesn't understand me, not like Daisy does...but I've always known that she cares, and she works hard to provide the best life she can for us.

She feels like a stranger to me at the moment, though.

Although she'd never confirmed it, it had been pretty much a given in my head that Dad had stepped out on her. She always told us that he needed his freedom—he told me the same thing himself. I always assumed that other women had been a part of that freedom.

So for my mom to do it to another woman...I'm at a loss for words, quite honestly.

Which is unusual for me since words are the closest allies I have...but still they fail me now.

"Mom?" Daisy asks uncomfortably, the expression on her face hard to read.

My mom stares at the table in front of her, her hands clenched on top of her lap, the glow she'd had a moment ago nowhere in sight.

"This isn't something we should talk about. It's something we *need* to talk about," she corrects herself. I watch, gobsmacked, as her chest rises and falls sharply as she takes a deep breath and finally lifts her head to stare at us. "It wasn't how I imagined finding my soulmate. And it's not something I'm proud of. But sometimes—sometimes love hits you when you least expect it. I can't regret meeting him. Besides you girls...he's the best thing that's ever happened to me." Her lips tremble as she stops speaking, and a swell of emotion pummels at my chest.

I try not to judge people. I really do. When everyone sees you and immediately puts a label on you...your whole life...you try not to do the same to others.

But this?

"Did she know?" Daisy asks quietly, making our mother immediately turn away, a slight tremor to her body.

"I—I don't think so. But sometimes she would look at me and..." She drags her gaze back to ours. "No matter what you're thinking, Curt really is an incredible person. Her death was so hard on him... watching her sick for all those years." Her voice trails off. "It wasn't something that anyone planned. It wasn't physical... before...but our hearts...they just fell..."

Wasn't physical. Well...I guess there was that. I'm sure my father's affairs were definitely physical.

Before we can answer her, I see Curt and Noah, who seems more subdued if his lowered head and hunched shoulders are anything to go by, beyond my mother's gaunt features, walking towards us from the bathrooms. Curt's face is tight. There are lines around his eyes that I swear are deeper than before Noah decided to drop that little bomb on the table. Daisy and I don't say anything else as we watch them approach.

Noah slides in his seat once he reaches the table, but before he does...

He shoots me a glare of loathing that has me quaking in my seat, leaving me utterly confused.

What did *I* do?

I quickly look away, determined to table that little conundrum for the moment. I've got enough on my plate as it is. What I thought was going to be a meet and greet of my mother's new boyfriend has turned infinitely more complicated.

I study Curt as he brushes a soft kiss across my mom's forehead and squeezes her shoulder reassuringly. Had he cheated on his wife before? There's that old adage about once a cheater, always a cheater...could she trust him? Could he trust her?

Was my life going to be completely uprooted for something that's doomed from the start?

You're getting ahead of yourself, I chide my overactive brain.

"How do you girls like your food?" Curt asks, his voice holding no sign of what's occurred.

"Great!" Daisy says cheerfully, or at least to a stranger like Curt it would seem cheerful. I can hear the sarcastic intent behind Daisy's answer the same way I could read between the lines of Noah's earlier benign comments.

Curt totally misses it and his shoulders relax as if he thinks we don't know anything... or we've decided not to make it a thing. He presses another kiss against my mom's hair and she relaxes into him, her whole body curling towards his, like he's her safe place.

I'm sure his wife had thought he was her safe place, too.

We all descend into another long silence...this one painful, before the waitress is back, standing as close to Noah as she can get. She offers us dessert even though our plates have barely been touched. Except for Noah's, that is. Evidently, the situation didn't quell his appetite because he's the only one with a clean plate.

"Would anyone like dessert?" she practically coos, curling a piece of her pretty hair around her finger and smacking her gum like she thinks it's the key to Noah's heart. Or as Daisy would bluntly put it—his cock.

"Let's have a slice of key lime pie for everyone," Curt says enthusiastically, before remembering he doesn't know us. "Does everyone like key lime pie? It's one of their specialties. They also have chocolate cake and cheesecake made fresh daily." His words are rushed. A bit desperate, actually.

I feel like he's trying to sell himself. Like he's also made fresh daily and we'll like him if we give him a chance. An unbidden laugh shoots from my mouth at the thought, bringing, of course, everyone's attention to me. The waitress is staring at me with a cocky smile like she's no longer worried that I'll pose a threat to her and lover boy. But as I continue to gasp for breath, her smile drops and her brows pinch together, and I know she's wondering if I'm actually insane.

Jury is still out on that one.

"Key lime pie sounds great," I squeak, once I've gathered my composure.

My awkwardness brings a smile to my mother's face, the first one since the origins of their "love story" was revealed.

"How about you, Noah?" she asks breathily.

He doesn't seem as keen on playing with her as he did earlier. In fact, he ends up shooing her away. I blink twice to make sure I'm not seeing things.

Did this really just happen?

I mean, Noah must be around my age and yet he shoos this girl away, like a parent would an insolent child. And worst of all, she listens to him. She practically runs away, and it's obvious by the tremor in her shoulders that, after she places the order for key lime pie, she'll spend the rest of her shift sobbing in the bathroom.

And just like that, Noah becomes infinitely more terrifying to me.

Unlike me, Daisy seems amused, like she's found her kindred spirit for trouble making at the table.

Curt...Curt seems conflicted...like he wants to chastise Noah, not that it'll get him anywhere. He's done plenty of reprimanding so far during this one meal and we've only been here an hour.

The longest hour of my life, by the way.

He sighs and turns his attention back towards Daisy and me, covering my mom's hand on the table.

My insides clench, my intuition already two steps ahead, knowing exactly what's about to happen.

"I'm so glad that I could meet you girls today, and I hope that we'll get to know each other very well in the future. But the real reason why I asked your mother to bring you girls to this lunch is because I wanted to ask for your blessing as well as your permission today."

Daisy side-eyes me again, and I can see the inner eye roll she is somehow reining in.

This isn't Daisy's thing. Marriage, I mean. Not that I could picture Daisy ever settling down even if it was, but if she somehow wanted to, the last thing she would want was for her guy asking for *permission* to marry her.

Fuck. Marry her. How did we get here?

Everything is about to change.

And I'm not sure if it's for the better either.

"I never thought I'd find love again after Noah's mother, Annabelle." He glances over at Noah's completely blank face; the only sign of tension is the way his hand is clenched at his side, something I'm the only one privy to because of my spot at the table.

Curt takes a deep, almost conflicted breath, tears his gaze away from Noah, and turns it back to us. "Your mom...she's a miracle. My miracle. A second chance at happiness for me when I thought I'd never smile again. I'd like to spend the rest of my life with her." There are tears threaded through his voice, and maybe normally I'd be swooning with how sweet he was being to my mom...

But who has time for that when I'm freaking out on the inside.

"I'd like to marry her. I'd like us all to become a family. I'll do my best to make us all happy. To make sure your mom knows how loved she is every day of her life."

There's an uneasy silence after his announcement.

My words are caught in my chest...as usual.

But also as usual...Daisy knows exactly what to say.

"Do you promise not to break her heart?" she asks, her gaze boring holes into his skull.

He nods solemnly before she even finishes the question, and when he glances at my mom, I wonder how it was possible that he could have loved his first wife at all considering the depths of emotion I can see in his eyes now.

"I promise," he finally answers.

I peer over at Noah, who's staring away from the table, out the window where you can see the waves crashing on the dock in the distance. But even though he tries to hide his face, I recognize the expression on it all the same—he's in agony.

Daisy pauses for dramatic effect before she gives him her answer. It's long enough to leave Curt on the edge of his seat in anticipation, as is Daisy's style.

"Okay then!" she finally answers, lifting her glass of water in the air. "To the engaged couple!"

I lift my glass in the air too, hoping Curt takes it as consent to marry my mother without me having to verbalize it. Ecstatic, both Curt and my mom lift their glasses to join our toast, but Noah doesn't so much as budge from his perusal out the window.

And the sad thing is...I'm the only one who seems to notice.

Chapter 4

Skylar

sixteen years old

Evidently things move fast when you're head over heels in love. Not two months have passed since that memorable lunch and here we are, walking up the steps to City Hall, about to watch my mom and Curt get married.

It's unusually chilly for a summer's day at Thatcher's Bay, or at least that's what Curt has commented. And like the unpredictable weather, everything on the island is still so unfamiliar to me, and I'm not looking forward to getting lost all the time here.

We'd gotten ready for the wedding at his house—I guess our house now. Or it's about to be. After the ceremony and small lunch they have planned, my mom and Curt will leave for a short honeymoon at a bed and breakfast a few hours away. As they do that, movers will pack our house on the mainland and bring it to Curt's house here on the small island.

I shiver as I walk through the hallways of Curt's place, wondering how my mother can even stand to step foot inside it. There are traces of his first wife everywhere. In the candles scattered around as decorations, and the cozy throw blankets placed on the couch. The warm woven rugs in front of all the places a person would stand and yearn for comfort. There are even some pictures of her on the wall. The first time Curt walked us down the upstairs hallway to show us the rooms we'll be sleeping in, I caught a glimpse of one of their wedding pictures still hanging on the wall. When Curt saw me staring at it, he flushed a thousand shades of red and grabbed it from the wall, dropping it off in his room before we resumed the tour of his house. Not that the tour took very long. I'm sure as a commercial fisherman he did alright, and with my mom's contribution, everything will be comfortable, but the house definitely doesn't resemble a manor.

Thankfully, I've been given my own room. The only drawback is that Noah's room is right across from mine. The previous guest room will be Daisy's. Not that she's too happy about it since mom and Curt's room is right across from hers. But instead of complaining, like I know she's dying to, she agrees to occupy the room, saying she won't bitch about it on Mom's wedding day.

I, on the other hand, am itching to complain about mine and would trade with hers in a heartbeat if I thought it wouldn't seem suspicious.

I don't know what my life will be like with Noah living in such close proximity to me at all times. I haven't seen him once since that awkward lunch, even though Curt has been to our place a few times and we've come to the island for two more dinners. He always makes excuses for Noah's absence, but it's not like we can't read between the lines—his son is doing everything he can to avoid us.

Now, any time I want, I can stare at his closed bedroom door, wondering if he's in there, hiding away. I know I won't forget the look on his face when his dad announced his intention to marry my mom. Clumsily, I trip on the stairs leading up to City Hall, jarring me out of my deep thoughts. Daisy snorts next to me, lifting an eyebrow teasingly, knowing my clumsiness must have been provoked by me being lost in my head, as usual.

She's dressed in a light pink sheath dress accented with a thin, dark brown belt, holding mom's bouquet in her hands, a collection of white roses, forget-me-nots, and pink Gerbera daisies. She looks much more demure than usual with her hair pulled back in an elegant chignon and pearl studs in her ears. Usually Daisy's free spirit is reflected in her clothing, her hair loose and wild, and her clothes a million different styles depending on how she's feeling on that day. Today she's dressed so proper that if you ignore the hint of crazy in her gaze, you'd believe she was the epitome of calm and tranquility.

I'm dressed in a matching outfit, but my hair is half up half down. Unlike Daisy, this outfit is pretty normal to how I dress on a daily basis, prim and proper...nothing that stands out. Of course, if given the choice, I always feel more comfortable in a hoodie or a simple t-shirt and shorts. However, I doubt my mom would appreciate such attire on her big day.

As I think of her, my eyes land on my mother reaching the top step, and I admire her for a moment. She's forgone the traditional white wedding dress and instead is wearing a lacy cream-colored cocktail dress that ends at her knees. It shows off her athletic form and perfectly accents her smooth skin. She has an almost fifties style short veil on her head and her hair is pulled back in a loose bun with tendrils framing her face.

She's gorgeous, her eyes sparkling, and the same rosy hue to her cheeks that has been there from the moment we suspected she met someone.

I haven't seen any evidence that my mom's nervous about today. In fact, all I've seen is the exact opposite of bride jitters. She keeps glancing at Curt like she can't believe her good fortune, mimicking the same sappy expression on his face. My new stepfather looks dashing in his navy suit paired with a light pink tie that matches our dresses. Noah hasn't arrived yet, but if he ever shows up, I assume he'll be wearing something similar to his father. It'll only be the five of us at the wedding, but my mother insists that today feels like a celebration.

Once we start walking inside the building, I almost trip again, only this time, a strong pair of arms catch me around my waist before I can fall on my face. I flinch when I'm pulled against a hard chest, and it only takes me half a second to know exactly who's helped me into his arms.

Noah.

I can't help but inhale the tangy scent of oranges and cinnamon washing over my senses. He quickly lets me go, but I could swear there was a moment where his hands almost seemed to tighten around my waist. I flush as I glance backwards and see him standing behind me, staring forward in annoyance, dressed in an identical suit to Curt's. His blond hair is falling in his face, and the suit's a bit wrinkled, like he rolled out of bed and picked it up off the floor, not daring to appear put together for the wedding he didn't want to attend in the first place.

"Try to be more careful, princess," he drawls as he brushes past me, walking over to where my mom and Curt are talking to someone at the front desk.

Errant goosebumps crawl along my arms from his touch, and I can't help but greedily watch his form as he smoothly prowls away.

"Aw, does my little sister have a crush on the asshole?" Daisy teases, pinching my side.

My blush only grows and I smack her hand away, leveling her with a disgusted glare I hope throws her off the scent. I don't have a crush. The guy's about to be my stepbrother, not that that fact alone is a big deal—it's not like we'll be blood related—but there is no way I'll let myself pine over someone I have to live with. Someone who hates me on mere principle alone.

"Shut up," I whisper-yell at her.

Her answering giggle seems to reverberate around the room, making me shift my weight nervously from one foot to the other.

"It would probably give you lots of great writing material to work with. Can you imagine if you guys ended up fucking? Oh, the juicy chapters I'd get to read if that shit happened!"

"I can't believe you," I murmur in shock, even though I shouldn't be so surprised.

This *is* Daisy we're talking about, after all. She always has her head in the gutter ninety-nine percent of the time.

Not wanting to feed into her pervy imagination, I move away from her as quickly as I can, practically dashing after Noah still walking towards our parents. I might have been running away from her but I was also running away from the brief flash of lust that pooled in my gut at her words...just imagining them becoming a reality.

My mom gives me a warm smile once I reach them. My cheeks are still flushed, but she doesn't seem to notice, turning her attention towards Curt and Noah.

"Glad you could make it, Son," Curt says quietly in a tired voice that hints to the fights at home I'm sure they've been having since the wedding news.

"No problem," Noah replies flippantly. Curt's eyes practically roll to the back of his head as he stares at the ceiling in a "God help me" kind of way.

"Noah, I really am so thankful that you're here," my mom says in earnest, but I know her heartfelt words are lost on him.

Her attempt is met with nothing but silence. Noah must realize that it's the most effective weapon he holds, making Mom fidget with the lace on her dress nervously as it deepens.

"Here you go, sir," the receptionist interrupts, cutting through the tension of the moment.

"Thank you," Curt tells her, reaching to take the wedding license she's holding out for him.

"If you go sit in those chairs over in the corner, someone will be with you shortly to take you before the judge," she continues, looking frazzled with her curly brown hair sticking up everywhere and the glasses on her face in desperate need of a good cleaning. Daisy makes it to us finally, evidently deciding to amble around the room before coming over. I decidedly keep my gaze away from hers, knowing she isn't done with her teasing. Not yet, anyway.

We make our way over to the chairs, and Curt pulls my mom onto his lap, eliciting a scoff from Noah. His cheek is pulsing and I wonder how everyone is missing the rage in his blue gaze. He's clearly not even close to being ready to forgive their indiscretion. Not that I really blame him. I've tried to put myself in his position, thinking about how I would feel if the roles were reversed, and I've come to the conclusion that his rage is warranted.

Which doesn't bode well for the happy couple.

It doesn't bode well for me either if he makes their marriage hell and things end up falling apart because of it.

Daisy fidgets about on her phone, I'm sure passing the time by talking to the forty million people that follow her every move on social media. She takes a selfie and I know she'll add some witty phrase to the post alongside her pic. Probably something about being a "lady in the streets and a freak in the sheets." I laugh softly to myself and Noah stares at me, shooting me a glare that tells me he thinks I'm an idiot.

My quiet grin fades and I find myself wishing that I hadn't left my phone at home. I don't know why I thought it would be a good idea. I was probably trying to be the dutiful daughter once again, and making sure that I was giving my mom the attention she would want.

I'm an idiot.

Glancing at her, I'm not sure she can even remember she has daughters right now. Not when her eyes are set on her groom to be.

Time stands still as we wait. It seems to take forever before a woman in hot pink sky high heels and a tight black dress opens the door a few feet away from us.

"Are you the Fontaine family?" she asks in a bored voice. My chest flips at the name. Not that it has been discussed, but I have no intention of ever being adopted by Curt. Which means that in a few short hours, I'll be an Ames and my mother will be a Fontaine. I'm not sure how I feel about that.

My mother doesn't seem to be struggling with her name change judging by the way she eagerly hops off Curt's lap. For a second, I worry that they'll break out in a sprint in their eagerness to form their union.

"Yes, we are," my mother comments excitedly, confirming my suspicions from a moment ago. Curt wraps his arms around her and presses a kiss to the side of her neck.

"Blah, their cuteness is going to make me sick," huffs Daisy next to me, shaking her head. I know she's not actually disgusted though. Even if the idea of marriage absolutely terrifies her, she's happy for our mother. She told me as much the other night.

"I think Mom gets happier every day," Daisy muses, lying on her back beside me on my bed.

"Yeah, I know. It's pretty crazy, isn't it? Just the other day, I caught her dancing in the kitchen. Literally dancing. Like she's turned into a Disney princess overnight. I half expected birds to come swooping in the open window and start talking to her."

"I wouldn't have been surprised if they had." She chuckles. "I always dreamed about her meeting someone, but I never could quite picture what it would be like. I have to admit that it makes me happy to see her so happy. You know?"

"Yeah," I whisper, but my insides are churning. In a few days, we'll be moving out of our family home and starting a whole new life with strangers.

"Don't be scared, Sky," she murmurs like she can read my mind as I stare at the ceiling in the darkness, my mind racing with all the changes yet to come.

"I'm not," I huff, before sighing deeply.

She laughs softly, and even though I can't see her, I know she's shaking her head, a fond smile on her lips.

"Think of it as an adventure, or like you're the heroine in one of your stories, setting off to become the new queen of the high school."

I think I'd written a story about that once, but the idea that it could actually come true in real life is beyond laughable.

"Do you think the school there will be similar to the school here?" I ask, keeping my voice quiet even though my mom's on night shift and there's no one in the house but us. It's a strange thing, really, the tendency of humans to whisper in the dark, like we're afraid there's something out there we can't see that's going to take our confessions for themselves.

"No," she responds. "It'll be small. Everyone on the island goes to the same high school, but even then I'm sure it will feel small compared to our school."

That was probably a safe assumption. There were seven thousand people at our high school, and it felt like that. But I'd always liked it because it made it easier to disappear. When there were that many people crammed in the hallways, you couldn't focus on anyone other than the "bright lights" of the school. And I had never been one of those bright lights. But Daisy had. For her, the whole world was a stage. I wondered if the intangible quality that she always seemed to hold–to grab life around the neck and make it her own–would stretch to this new school as well.

"You'll probably have to talk in class there. There won't be fifty people crammed into one classroom. Half of that at best. And you just know they'll make you introduce yourself on the first day. So be ready for it. I will." She laughs to herself, probably imagining her grand entrance, an invisible crown already on her head as she deems herself queen of this new school.

My thoughts instantly turn to Noah, wondering what he's like walking those same halls.

"God, I hope there's lots of hot island guys to play with. I mean, if push comes to shove, I can still go for the teachers, but it would be nice to have a few hot guys my age to corrupt."

"Daisy," I chastise, my mind instantly flipping to the rumor I heard about my sister and one of the football assistant coaches at our current high school.

She'd been dating the quarterback of the team at the time those rumors had spread around, but she hadn't seemed the least bit ruffled about them. I'm not sure why I never asked her if they were true or not. I guess it's because I was afraid of what her answer would be.

"It'll be good to have a fresh start," she whispers more seriously.

I want to agree with her. I want to think that things could and will be different. But I've always hated lying to myself.

"I wonder what Dad's going to think about all this."

"Who the fuck cares," Daisy scoffs.

While I've always made sure I was available when our dad deigned to give us the smallest hint of attention, Daisy isn't quite so agreeable. Which is kind of strange because I feel like they are both cut from the same cloth. Of course, unlike our dad, Daisy is infinitely more loyal to the people she truly cares about. No one can deny there's the same wildness about them, a devil-may-care attitude that Daisy certainly didn't get from our mom. Still, my sister has never been a fan of our father. Maybe when two people are too much alike they end up repelling each other, unable to stomach seeing their flaws staring back at them.

"Get some sleep, Sky," she orders, no longer in the mood to talk now that I brought up our dad.

Instead of going back to her room, she makes herself comfortable in my bed. I don't ask her to leave, since I kind of like her being here when Mom is on a night shift. It doesn't take long for her soft breaths to echo around the room. Meanwhile, I continue to lie here, staring at the ceiling for answers I'll never get tonight.

"Sky," Daisy hisses, and I blink as I stare at her, realizing that I've walked into the courtroom with everyone without even realizing I was doing it. However, I must have stopped halfway across the aisle, while everyone else had made their way to the front to stand in front of the judge.

My mom didn't seem to notice though, since she's too preoccupied holding hands with Curt and staring lovingly into his eyes. I wonder how long it'll take before she sees *us* again. How long will the haze of lust and love cloud her vision to anyone but him? Is that what love does? Makes you forget everyone in existence after you've met the *one*? Lose yourself in him so completely that you can't focus on all the other things that matter to you? If that's love, then maybe we're all better off without it.

Begrudgingly, I hustle over and take my spot next to Daisy, staring at the thread-worn carpet that needs to be updated. As a throat clears, I glance up to find Curt now staring over his shoulder at Noah, who, of course, is on his phone.

"Son," he states exasperatedly.

Noah lifts his phone, clicking the camera, and signaling he's taking a picture.

"Just trying to capture the moment. Who knows how many of these you'll get." Curt turns back to the judge, shaking his head, right as Noah whispers under his breath, "Mom is probably rolling in her grave. Hope you're fucking happy."

I was apparently the only one paying close enough attention to him to hear his whispered comment, because there's no shocked inhales. Curt never even flinches at the remark.

When the judge starts speaking, I try to concentrate on his words, instead of appearing dumbfounded that everyone is so wrapped up in this wedding that they don't pick up on the somber vibe Noah is giving off. While Curt and Mom hold each other's hands tightly, gazing dreamily into one another's faces, Noah hangs his head, returning to his phone. As the judge talks about true love, my attention keeps straying to Noah, who's typing feverishly on his phone. It's only when his hand tilts that I realize he's playing Candy Crush.

Well, okay then.

"Clara, will you please repeat this vow after me," the judge announces.

"I, Clara, take you, Curt, to be my husband. To have and to hold from this day forward, for better or for worse, for richer or for poorer, in sickness and in health. I promise to love and cherish you for all of my days," my mom repeats.

A tear trails down her face and I feel the same moisture building in my eyes. I'm not sure that I'm experiencing quite the same mix of emotions as she is at the moment...but there's definitely some happiness built in for her along with everything else.

"I, Curt, take you, Clara, to be my wife. To have and to hold from this day forward, for better or for worse, for richer or for poorer, in sickness and in health. I promise to love and cherish you for all of my days," repeats Curt, his voice trembling with his own emotion.

Unable to stop myself, I glance at Noah again, wondering if he's turned his attention to his dad at all in this defining moment. But nope, he's still intent on finishing his game.

I guess we can all be glad he deigned to put his phone on silent so we don't have to hear the irritating music of his game.

It's time to exchange rings when I turn my attention back to the happy couple. Daisy is handing Mom Curt's wedding band. Curt clears his throat in annoyance as he holds out his hand to Noah, presumably waiting for him to hand over Mom's ring.

"Here you go," Noah drawls, his gaze filled with displeasure as he drops the blue velvet box in his father's hand.

Curt's eyes flash at Noah's insolent tone, but he says nothing as he takes the ring from Noah's hand and gives him a tap on his shoulder. I can tell it's a little heavier than a friendly clap would be, but from the little I know of Noah, he's probably done or said something that deserves a smack upside the head by his father, so I'm impressed with Curt's restraint.

Noah turns back around towards my mom, and I watch as his hands clench into fists, so hard that his knuckles turn white. His face is an almost green color, and the disinterest in his gaze has faded to one of...abject sorrow.

And still...I'm the only one who seems to notice.

I wonder if that happens a lot to Noah, that the world sees one face and completely misses the other.

Maybe we're both actually not seen...only in different ways.

He brushes a tendril of perfect golden hair out of his face, and I almost take back my thought.

Who could ever not notice him?

"You may now kiss the bride," the judge proclaims, his words bringing my attention back to where it should be. For being practically a stranger, Noah seems to occupy my thoughts much more than I would like.

I need to get a handle on that.

My new stepbrother doesn't deserve my attention unless he earns it.

And thus far, it doesn't seem like he does.

Curt dips my mom in a dramatic, Hollywood style kiss, and when their lips finally detach, she has a dark, attractive flush to her cheeks. She looks happier than I've ever seen her. Truly, blissfully happy.

I smile when my mom peers over at Daisy and me, gratitude that we're here to celebrate her big day plastered all over her face. But the instant she turns away and is once again distracted by her new husband, I slip outside the courthouse and don't stop walking until I'm breathing in the sea-tinged air.

Change.

It's here.

I've spent so much of my time avoiding it, and yet it's come for me anyway. I'll be starting a new school in just a few days, living on an island that is completely foreign to me, and spending my time in a house that doesn't feel like mine.

Will this new life, with all these chances, be exactly like my old one?

Will I be a perpetual wallflower once again?

Or maybe the better question is do I want to be anything other than that?

For a second, I have the alien urge to scream out my frustration and anxiety to the whole world. I want everyone to hear how conflicted and angry I am that I feel so powerless to all these new unexpected changes. The urge passes though, and I allow my despair to slip back into the cracks of my heart where I usually keep it locked up tight.

I hear the heavy double doors open behind me, and a second later, Daisy's standing next to me.

"What are you doing out here? Brooding?" she asks lightly, playfully nudging her shoulder with mine, even though I can hear the concern in her voice.

I immediately feel the urge to deny I'm brooding, but I let it pass and actually tell the truth for once.

"Sometimes my head...it's too much," I whisper softly.

"I feel that, babe," she responds, and my fierce, take the world by the balls sister actually sounds...sad.

I quickly glance at her but there's no sign on her pretty features of the pain I just heard. She pretends not to see my bewildering stare, and lightly socks me in the arm instead.

"Let's go back in there and meet up with the fam. Everything will be okay. You'll see."

I follow her inside, but all the while I can't help but think that Daisy lied to me.

* * *

The newlyweds have planned a lunch after the ceremony, ironically at the same restaurant where our lives changed forever. I'm not sure I would have ever picked such a themed place for my wedding reception, but here we are.

The restaurant reserved the giant room in the back for the occasion, even though it's only the five of us again. We settle in and take our respective seats around the table. The whole ambience is a little awkward since the only people talking are Mom and Curt...and that's to each other.

Noah's tie is hanging loosely around his neck, and the bored expression has returned as he continues to play Candy Crush on his phone. Daisy's also tapping away on her phone, leaving me to stare at the ceiling, idly wondering who painted all the "As" up there, tangled amidst the fishing net decor.

"Why did you pick this place to have your reception, Mom?" I ask curiously, thinking that my shrimp salad hadn't been anything to write home about the last time we were here.

"This was where Curt and I went for our first date on the island," my mother coos dreamily, as if it was the most romantic thing ever.

Daisy and I shoot each other a look, and there's mirth sparkling from her gaze.

"Hmm, that's interesting, isn't it? Since this was where I believe he took my mother for her first date as well," Noah remarks casually, freezing the air in the room. "How unoriginal."

Curt shifts awkwardly in his seat while my mother's cheeks flush; this time it's not with happiness but with utter embarrassment.

"I'm sure we'll make a lot more good memories here then if it has such a rich history," Daisy gently inserts, coaxing thankful smiles from Curt and Mom. "Makes sense why you would want to celebrate here. It has meaning. I think that's pretty damn original to me."

Noah huffs in annoyance, but whatever vitriol he had built up in the tank is cut off by the entrance of our server—the same one he flirted with last time we were here together.

All glimmers of resentment and pouting fade from Noah's features as her gaze immediately flits to his. She stutter steps for a moment before glancing over at Mom and Curt, who I'm sure she'd been apprised were celebrating their wedding.

"Hello again," she squeaks, and I'm getting déjà vu.

This place really is the gift that keeps on giving.

"A bottle of champagne for the table," announces Curt before Noah can begin flirting—which I can tell by his upturned lips and heavy lidded gaze is definitely going to happen.

"Alright! Now that's what I'm talking about!" cheers Daisy. "I knew I liked you, Curt."

Mom rolls her eyes since we definitely have a *no alcohol for minors* policy at our house...or at least we had a strict 'don't let me ever find out' policy. Daisy has been partying for at least a few years, and I know she's snuck in drunk quite a few of those nights.

"Only a sip." Mom smiles, but it's obvious she's too happy to really care if we do more than sip.

"Of course," the waitress responds, appearing eager all of a sudden. The way she rushes from the room gives me the feeling they don't have very many of those requests here, even though champagne is the first thing listed on the drink menu.

There's a long, uncomfortable silence after she leaves, until Curt clears his throat.

"Anything you girls need for moving in to make things more comfortable?" he asks sincerely.

It's almost weird to see him being genuinely nice. My father's kindness comes with strings. Usually, he's only nice when he wants something or is making up for all the times he's disappointed my sister and me.

It never works because we can obviously see right through it, even if we don't call him out on it. Scratch that. Even if *I* don't call him out on it. Daisy isn't shy about throwing it in his face. The many visits he's missed over the years have resulted in quite a few random gifts. Daisy doesn't even so much as open the wrapped presents, throwing them in the trash immediately. But I keep everything. Because a gift from him is better than nothing when you're desperate for a father to love you.

"I mean, if you're offering, I'd love a car," Daisy teases, wondering just how far Curt will go to win our affection.

"Daisy!" my mother admonishes, eyes wide in mortification.

Daisy and I burst out in a fit of giggles since one of our favorite games is seeing how exasperated we can make our mother in public.

"I'll see what I can do," Curt promises, putting an end to our laughter when he actually appears serious.

My sister's eyes almost glaze over at the thought she can actually win a car out of this marriage, but before she has time to say something, one of Noah's trademark scoffs sounds in the room.

"I'm going to take a piss," he announces angrily before jumping from his chair, almost sending it toppling to the floor, and striding out of the room.

Silence descends once again with his retreat. Curt stares after his son, frustration and annoyance written all over his face with each step he takes. It's only when Noah disappears that Curt finally sighs.

"I'm sorry about that, girls. Noah...is having a rough time."

"As anyone would if they lost their mom," I respond coldly, surprising everyone with my slip of the tongue, including myself.

I have no idea why I'm defending him, but it seems like Curt expects Noah to be over it already...like he seems to be. And that's not fair at all. If you truly love someone, and you lost them, the pain never goes away. Grief isn't something you can simply switch off, and asking someone to get over such loss when it's no longer convenient for you is not only selfish...but purely shitty.

Which makes me wonder how much Curt loved his first wife in the first place.

"I'm going to use the restroom too," I say quietly, not liking the edge of disappointment in my mom's gaze, like I've done something wrong.

I hurry out of the room and head towards the bathrooms, not really having to pee, but needing a break.

I push open the door to the ladies room, coming to a screeching, surprised halt when I see Noah in there, leaning against the wall across from the mirrors, his gaze half-lidded in pleasure as our waitress kneels on the floor in front of him...

Sucking his dick.

I can't take my eyes off the scene. The girl either didn't hear me come in or doesn't care, because her pace never falters. Maybe she's simply happy to get the chance with a god like Noah and doesn't want to lose it...even if she has an audience.

The girl might not be paying me any attention...but Noah is.

His head tilts towards me, his gaze focused on my face, a smug grin tugging on his beautiful lips. I stand there paralyzed as he threads his fingers into the waitress' hair, pulling her to meet his punishing tempo. His eyes never falter away from me as the girl slurps and gags on his cock. But her skill in giving him a blowjob isn't what has me at a loss for words. It isn't what has me frozen to my spot, unable to move. It's his smile.

He's enjoying this.

He's enjoying putting on a show for me.

He's enjoying putting on a show for his new *stepsister*.

And worse...I'm enjoying it too.

My heart feels like it's about to break through my chest with how hard it's beating. My skin is flushed and I feel...achy. Something I've never felt before.

"That's it, little slut, suck my big fucking dick."

My gaze widens at the fact he calls her a slut but her tempo doesn't change. In fact, by the way she moans out it's as if it's her favorite thing to be called.

I should run away. I really should. I have no idea why my feet refuse to move, or why my eyes remain locked with his, but here we are, connected in the most sordid of ways.

"Such a good little slut."

The way he grunts out those words, it's almost like they are meant for me.

Daisy had talked to me about blowjobs before, how there was no end to what you could get from a man once you mastered them. I'd listened avidly, a blush to my cheeks that she teased me mercilessly about. Evidently, Daisy was one such master.

But she had mentioned one thing that stuck with me now as Noah yanks on the girl's hair so hard I'm surprised she's not crying out in pain. Daisy preferred to be warned before a man came in her mouth.

Noah gives no such warning. His face scrunches up in euphoric bliss as he cums. His moan echoes around the room so loudly I'm sure the whole restaurant heard him.

And through it all...he stares at me. His gaze burns into me like he's trying to reach inside me and yank my heart out.

The girl gulps on his dick. Literally gulps, like she's just finished working out and she's desperate for water. Except the water in this case is, of course, his cum.

She finally slides off his dick and stares up at him desperately, like it's been a privilege for her to offer him that service. As if her grateful submission is my cue to leave, my feet finally regain the ability to move. Not wanting to stay for the second act of the show, I yank my gaze away from his and haul ass out of the bathroom.

I'm a different person when I enter the room where my mother is beaming with love. I collapse in my seat, shaking slightly. Daisy shoots me a confused look, and knowing her, this is the exact little bit of gossip she would love to hear about. And before this very moment, I would have told her. Immediately.

Because I tell her everything.

But for some reason, all I do is give her a reassuring smile, smooth my hair down, and pretend to study my dinner eagerly.

And when Noah walks in, I don't dare glance at him once.

But I can feel his gaze on me for the rest of the fucking night.

Chapter 5

Skylar

Sixteen years old

"You can do this," I whisper as I fidget with the dark blue blouse Daisy picked out for me last night. I'm not usually one for pep talks, but the situation seems to call for it as I get ready to start my first day at our new high school.

Today had arrived before I even had time to blink. A moment I'd been both dreading and anticipating when it had finally sunk in that the marriage was happening and that mom would be moving us from the mainland to Thatcher's Bay.

"I knew you'd look good in that," Daisy comments from the doorway, and I jump. She laughs and slides all the way in, shutting the door behind her. "You're freaking out."

"I'm not freaking out," I snap back, a little more bite to my voice than usual because, let's face it, I *am* freaking out.

Daisy looks like a supermodel with her tight white jeans, so tight that I can see the outline of her black thong. Her red shirt is designed to catch everyone's attention, showing off a sliver of her toned stomach. Her hair is pulled up into a haphazard ponytail and her make up is expertly applied. Staring at my gorgeous sister in her get-up only manages to do one thing—make me second guess what I've got on.

I suddenly hate my outfit.

I pull on the shirt and then pick up a brush, sighing as I tug at my hair.

"Stop," Daisy orders, yanking the brush from my hands and throwing it on the dresser with a loud clatter. "You can't be trusted with this brush. This is not a weapon, Sky. It's supposed to make you look beautiful, not bald." She smirks teasingly while gathering some bobby pins before working her magic on my hair. A few minutes later, she's done more with my hair than I've been able to do for the last thirty minutes.

"My pretty little sister," she coos as she stares lovingly at me through the mirror.

Just one of the reasons I love Daisy and would do anything for her—she actually means it when she says things like this. Somehow, she really believes it. She looks in the mirror and sees me standing next to her like a star standing next to the sun. She sees something I don't.

And I never will.

Not wanting Daisy to be aware of the pitiful thoughts rummaging around my head, I shoot her a wan smile and she plants a smacking kiss on my cheek before sauntering back towards the door. "We need to leave in five. I'm fine with being late, but I don't want you to have a heart attack on your first day."

I stick my tongue out at her, even though a glance at my phone tells me I did lose track of time trying to get ready.

And that does in fact make me panic.

After one last peek in the mirror, I rush to grab my backpack and race out of the room...smacking right into Noah. I almost fall backwards, but he quickly reaches out and grips my arms, saving me from falling on my ass.

"Aren't we in a hurry?" he drawls in that lazy, mocking way of his. I try to step away, but his hold remains tight.

"Sorry," I murmur, biting down on my lip as we lock eyes.

You would assume that I would be used to having a stepbrother by now, but you'd be wrong. Noah has made himself scarce since the wedding, a fact that, up until this very moment, I didn't realize how much I appreciated. Because all I can think about as I stare at him is that I know what his face looks like when he has an orgasm.

Awkward.

I clear my throat, a countdown starting in my brain of how much time I have until I'm late. His eyes are glittering with amusement, like he can see the numbers in my head. But that isn't the reason why his stare is so unnerving to me. It's the way Noah slowly traces my skin with his gaze, all the way from my face to my toes.

"Trying a bit too hard to impress on your first day, aren't you?"

His stare feels like a physical caress across my skin and it's all I can do not to shiver.

I roll my eyes at him, proud of how steady I'm acting even if my insides are shaking.

His lazy grin widens and he leans forward.

"Well, color me impressed," he whispers before he brushes past me and disappears down the hallway to the bathroom.

My nerves are even more messed up as I go the opposite direction, out into the living room where Daisy is sprawled on the couch, scrolling through her phone.

"Ready to go?" she asks expectantly. I nod, unable to form words after whatever the hell that had been back there. My sister is used to my awkwardness though, so she doesn't think to question it.

I follow her out to the beat up Honda that she's taken to driving so proudly, like it's actually a Rolls Royce. When Daisy asked Curt for a car on that harrowing wedding day, none of us thought he'd actually give her one. So imagine our surprise when he drove the old thing up the driveway a week later, handing her the keys to it. I doubt Daisy heard a word about how the car was so that we both had some kind of dependable transportation to use to and from school. All she heard was the sweet sound of freedom. Sure the car is older than me and her combined, but Curt won her heart that day. I wish I could say the same. The Fontaine men are something I'm still trying to decipher.

Daisy chatters the entire drive to school, but I wouldn't be able to pass a quiz on what she says even if I tried. All my thoughts are centered on what lies ahead.

And to my chagrin, my mind also comes back to that peculiar interaction with Noah in the hallway.

It's like he's been put on earth to destroy me. At least that's what it feels like, thanks to the cornucopia of awkward encounters that are stacking up.

Stop it, Sky. You've got bigger problems on your plate than your stepbrother.

I shake all thoughts of Noah away from my mind and force myself to think about school instead. Is everyone going to stare at me constantly because I'm the new girl? Will it be worse if they don't? If I somehow slide past their scrutiny because I truly am the afterthought, the shadow that no one sees, will that be better?

God, I hate my brain.

Before I can get my anxiety in check, we pull into the school parking lot that's already teeming with students.

"Chin up," Daisy commands softly as I stare at the red brick building that looks like something out of a storybook. Our last high school was a gray concrete monstrosity that resembled more of a prison than an institute of learning.

This place...it's quaint. With ivy carving its way up the brick and large white windows. The windows in our other school were tiny slits, a style of architecture that was popular in the seventies. You couldn't see anything clearly from inside, and maybe that was the goal. So you felt trapped.

This school, though, doesn't look as scary as I had made it up in my mind. At least not at first glance.

I take a deep breath, inhaling the scent of the sea that permeates everything here, and smile.

Maybe it's the one thing I don't actually hate about Thatcher's Bay. In fact, the sea breeze is starting to grow on me. And if I can get accustomed to that, maybe I can feel at home with other things too. But with each step that Daisy and I take toward the building, no matter how hard I try to hold onto that sliver of hope that things will be different for me here, it quickly begins to fade. And in its place, panic sets in, my anxiety reminding me that it's never far away. I can almost hear it laugh the second we pass through the school's doors, and all eyes fall on us.

Fuck my life.

"I bet we're the first *new* people they've had in years," Daisy muses, shooting a group of letterman-clad jocks a flirty smile as we pass. I feel the tip of my ears redden, and I find myself trying to shrink and hide beside her as their gazes bore into my skin. "Mmmh. So far, so good. I'm starting to think that the ocean air does something for the boys here, cause they sure grow up nice around these parts. I've already seen some delicious ones I'd like to nibble on."

I squeak when one of the so-called 'delicious ones' pops up next to me and shoots me a winning smile.

"Well, aren't you a sight for sore eyes," he teases, as if he knows exactly who we are.

He's the epitome of tall, dark, and handsome...with dark blue eyes that remind me of a midnight sky. Unlike Noah's, whose eyes look like the vast ocean on a summer's day. Either it's the thought of my stepbrother's eyes sneaking its way into my head without permission, or the fact that this Adonis is still walking in step with us, staring at me like I'm some candy he wants to put in his mouth, I lose the ability to speak.

"Yes, we are," sasses Daisy next to me, saving me from actually having to form words. The guy flicks his attention her way briefly and grins before bringing it back to me.

I almost faint.

I hate the attention. Especially from strangers. Even cute strangers like him.

"Kyle," he says, holding out his hand for me to take.

My mouth opens and closes, and I swear I'm trying to force words out. But nothing fucking comes from between my lips.

"Skylar. Her name's Skylar." Daisy saves me yet again, but I know my sister well enough that she's doing her best to stop herself from laughing at how ridiculous I'm being right now.

"Skylar," he repeats, like he's savoring the taste of my name on his lips. "Welcome to Bayshore High. Hope to see more of you."

Before I can get a "me too," or anything out, someone calls his name ahead of us. He shoots me one more smile and then strides off, leaving me in a puddle of regret.

"I really didn't think you could level up any further from how awkward you are, but it seems I was wrong," she groans with an exaggerated exhale, after she's made sure no one is close enough to hear her. I shoot my sister a glare, wanting to find a hole to bury myself in. But of course she's not done with me yet. She places both her hands on my shoulders and gives me a supportive smile. "Repeat after me. 'Hello. My name's Skylar. Do you want to be my friend?'"

I giggle, remembering myself on the playground with pigtails repeating those exact words in kindergarten. Who knew I'd still be needing that same script years later?

"You think you can handle that?" she asks with her manicured brow arched up high.

"Yeah, I can handle that." I laugh half-heartedly, praying that I'm not lying to my sister.

"Good." She grins, throwing me a wink before releasing her grip on my shoulders so we can continue on our merry way.

We endure more curious stares as we walk to the Admissions office, but thankfully no one else tries to talk to us.

When we walk inside, we come face to face with a lady sitting at a computer behind a long white counter with black granite on the top. She must be pushing sixty at least, but by the loud red dress she's wearing, I don't think age is something she's too concerned about. She's the very definition of a cougar if I've ever seen one. Not only is the dress she's wearing a vibrant red that you almost need sunglasses to stare at it, but it's also tight. And I mean tight. I can literally see her nipples from what I can only assume is a very expensive boob job, poking through the fabric. But I'm thankful that there's fabric at all. Because the dress is so low cut that her nips are in danger of popping out if she takes too deep a breath. Her hair is dyed an almost fluorescent yellow, and she's got so much makeup on, I bet if someone pressed on her face, their finger would push in at least an inch.

"Well, hello girls," she coos in a very thick, very fake, southern accent. Daisy and I trade wide-eyed glances. This woman is a character and I can already envision writing her into one of my stories. "You must be the Fontaine girls."

"Ames," I rectify quickly, surprising even myself with the vehemence in my voice. But I have to make it clear, my mother may be a 'Fontaine girl' now, but we are still Ames girls.

Daisy shoots me an approving smile, but the woman frowns.

"Alright," she drawls, "the Ames girls."

"Daisy and Skylar," Daisy presses as a bell rings in the hallway behind us.

I begin to panic. That's the start of school bell. Which means I'll be walking into my first class late. Which means everyone will stare. Which means there is no way I'll go unnoticed today even if I tried. The buzzing sound in my ears increases until it's the only sound I hear.

Daisy cuts off my impending panic attack by grabbing my hand and squeezing it tightly. She knows all the signs for when I'm about to lose my shit. I take as many non-descript breaths as I can, trying to avoid the woman's attention as she types on her computer.

I'm almost all the way back to normal by the time she glances back at us. "All honors classes?" she asks me with a raised eyebrow. "Are you sure you can handle that?"

"My sister is basically a genius," pipes in Daisy.

I flush under both of their stares. The woman is frowning again, her red lips showing off a myriad of wrinkles. Mercifully, she doesn't push anymore. She simply hands us both a packet. "Class started ten minutes ago, so head right there," she chides as if we were the ones moving at a snail's pace. I didn't even know people could type that slow. Especially school admin personnel whose main job is to type.

The panic threatens to burst forward again at the thought of walking in so late, but I do my best to hold it at bay.

Daisy shoots the woman one of her trademark mocking smiles that always seems to make people fall all over themselves, and then we're blissfully free. We walk out into the perfectly still hallway.

"You're going to write about her, aren't you?" Daisy teases.

I shoot her a sly grin. "How could I not?"

We both erupt into giggles, and it's all I can do to pull myself together as I open my folder to look at my class schedule.

I've got Honors Algebra II first. Math is the bane of my existence. It's the subject I have to work ten times as hard in as everything else, but the guidance counselor in our last school had told me it wouldn't reflect well to colleges if math was a regular class, so I'd been forcing myself into torture every year since then.

There's not a single honors class on Daisy's schedule, and that's how she likes it. Daisy has no plans for college; she has no idea what she'll do. She just knows she'll do something, be something. My stomach clenches because I know the second she graduates, Daisy will be gone, and I worry I'll never see her again.

But that's my little secret too. I know that Daisy is going to leave the second school is over...but then again, so am I.

"Ready?" Daisy asks, finally recovered from our bout of laughter.

I nod and square my shoulders, ridiculously wishing Daisy and I were actually twins so I could be in all of her classes with her and not one year behind. She waves at me and heads off in the opposite direction of where I have to go.

And then I'm all alone. I trudge to class, every step feeling like a death march. I know I'm being dramatic. Starting at a new school is the least of most people's problems, but with my anxiety, it feels like I've been asked to climb Mount Everest...butt naked.

I'm finally standing outside the door. I can see the teacher behind his desk, standing up and talking to everyone. For a brief second, I think about dropping everything and running out of the school, disappearing forever. But since that wouldn't go over too well with my mother, I find myself pulling down on the lever to open the door.

It's exactly as I envision it, except maybe a million times worse. The teacher's voice trails off, and I can immediately feel the room full of people staring at me. I make sure to keep my eyes locked on the teacher's and not on the rest of the class.

"You must be Skylar," he says, except he pronounces the "ar" part of my name all wrong.

"Skylar," I gently correct, impressed with myself that I was able to even do that. It's not a hard name to pronounce, at least I don't think so, but people do it all the time. My first grade teacher actually called me the wrong name for half the year and I never had the courage to correct her. Look at me now, growing a set of balls, if balls were what it took to have someone actually say your name right.

Daisy would be proud.

But just as that fleeting thought crosses my mind, I start to panic again when I realize the teacher asked me something, and I completely missed what he said.

Some of the class titters at my awkwardness.

"Why don't you head to that desk in the back and I'll get back to it," he says gently, and I already like him. He has kind eyes, dark brown, sort of like a puppy's.

With flushed cheeks, I nod, turning towards the class, right as a familiar voice cuts through the room.

"I think she should introduce herself, don't you think, Mr. Evans?" the cold voice drawls. I say cold, but the sound of Noah's voice is enough to set my blood boiling.

As if his gaze has a tractor beam on it that's forcing me to stare at him, I find him immediately. His seat is of course next to the only empty one. There's another jockish dude to the right of him, and three pretty girls in cheerleader uniforms in the other seats surrounding him. He's sprawled back, his hair a mess, looking unbelievably gorgeous—no, I didn't just think that.

Argh, Sky!

Get a grip girl.

There's a challenge in his gaze, like he expects the idea of speaking in front of the room to send me running for the hills, which it very well could.

I glance back to Mr. Evans, I'm sure a plea written all over my face. He glances down, a small frown on his face, and he fidgets with the buttons on his long sleeve dress shirt, like he has issues not doing whatever Noah says.

"Well—" Mr. Evans begins.

"It's been years since there's been a new face in the school. We should make it the big deal it is," Noah continues. Unlike with Daisy, there's no missing the mocking air in his tone. I highly doubt Noah thinks my starting school here is a big deal.

"Well then, go ahead," Mr. Evans says sheepishly, a note of apology in his gaze as he flicks his head at me.

I immediately feel lightheaded. There's only around fifteen people in the class, but it might as well be a thousand.

"My name is... Skylar," I begin in a choked voice. My hands are shaking, and I wonder if I really might pass out. My gaze locks with Noah's though, and somehow it gives me the strength I need to muster through. Because he's such a freaking asshole, it makes me want to run over to him and punch him in his too perfect face. "I just moved here from Falmouth...and if I'm honest, I really, really hate math." I finish lamely, causing a few people to laugh.

And for once, it doesn't feel like they're laughing at me...it kind of feels like they're laughing with me.

Noah's face scrunches in annoyance as I head to my seat. I don't meet anyone's eyes on the way there, and it feels like I've accomplished something when I finally slide into my seat.

"Hopefully, I can change your mind about math," Mr. Evans says with a smile, looking as relieved as I feel that it's over. He flips the page of the math textbook on his desk and then asks us all to turn to page thirty.

My hands are still trembling as I reach into my backpack and pull out a notebook, praying that I can follow the lesson without the textbook that I failed to bring.

"You looked like you were about to pass out up there, little stalker," he murmurs, casually twirling a pencil in between his fingers while Mr. Evans talks about complex numbers.

It takes me a moment to realize the nickname he's called me.

"What did you just call me?" I snap, my voice a little too loud.

I wince and sit back in my seat, determined to ignore him as I try and listen to what Mr. Evans is saying.

But it's freaking hard to concentrate when Noah's sitting there... clearly not paying attention at all. And then there's a girl seated in front of me, who keeps turning to stare at him and give him flirty smiles. In fact, it's not only her...it seems like the whole class is taking turns trying to stare at him. Like he's some Hollywood star they're desperate to get the attention of.

It's really...weird.

And really bad for Noah's ego. I've never seen someone occupy so much space in a room. I mean, he's tall, already over six feet. But it's like his aura is a living, breathing thing. Or maybe that's my writer brain imagining things again.

I guess I'd been hoping that the waitress's worship was a one-off. But it's obvious it's not, because everyone else in the room is doing the same thing she was. Bleeding all over themselves for his attention.

The jock next to him, who is handsome in his own right, glances over at Noah every few seconds, like he's checking to make sure Noah approves of the way he's breathing.

It's all very...gross.

And fascinating.

And what did he mean when he called me "little stalker?"

The boy strode through the hallway, a devilish gleam in his gaze...

"Ms. Ames, can you please tell us the answer to question number four?" Mr. Evans' voice cuts through the story I'm writing in my head.

My cheeks flush and I eye my empty notebook page in a panic, searching for question number four that of course isn't there. Agitated, my gaze falls to Noah's open textbook on top of his desk, slanted in a way that I'm able to perfectly read the problem I've been called to solve.

$4x+(3y+4)i=21+7i$

Evaluate y.

Okay, complex numbers, what do I remember about complex numbers?

Y=, y=....what does y=?

"Y=1," Noah drawls, sounding bored, but ultimately saving me from further embarrassment.

"I don't think your name is Ms. Ames, Mr. Fontaine," Mr. Evans chides. "Please give your new colleague time to get the answer herself."

"Then we'll be here all day waiting for her to get the answer right," Noah quips back.

The class laughs, and tears threaten in my eyes.

Get your shit together, I curse myself. The last thing I need is to burst into tears right now. I'm sure Noah would have a field day with that.

I really would have to run out of the school in that case.

With a slanted frown, Mr. Evans moves on, and thankfully doesn't call on me for the rest of class.

But the lesson has been learned. Noah won't be my friend here.

It feels like hours later that the bell rings, signaling class is over. I'm exhausted, like one period has been the equivalent of half my life span.

Noah strolls out of the room without a glance back, a gaggle of people following him desperately.

Mr. Evans shoots me a sympathetic smile as I drag myself from my desk.

"Just try and stay out of his way. School will run much smoother if you do," he says softly, and of course I know he's talking about Noah.

Hysterical laughter bubbles up inside me...because how do you stay away from someone you live with?

"And if you need extra help, I have tutoring available," he adds helpfully.

"Thank you," I squeak, before rushing out of the room. I've done such a good job of setting myself up with a stellar first impression. The man probably thinks I'm a moron.

I spot Daisy as soon as I walk out into the hallway, and my jaw drops. Not with shock, but in utter awe. The girl is basically holding court. Similar to the way Noah is across the way. She has at least twenty people gathered around her, all of them listening avidly to whatever story she's telling.

I love my sister. But I can't help the hot envy that catches in my throat. I've just embarrassed myself for an hour and a half, and in that same time she's managed to cement herself into school lore.

The envy is laced with self-loathing, and I put my head down and tuck my backpack close to my chest as I rush down the hall to the class I'm hoping will offer me some sort of solace.

English.

I'm early as I step into the room; the bell won't go off for another few minutes, but as the door closes behind me, it immediately feels like a safe place.

There's a woman in a navy cardigan typing at a laptop, her hair in a haphazard bun, and a pair of librarian glasses perched on her nose. Exactly what I like to see in an English teacher. As the door closes behind me, her eyes meet mine and she offers a stiff smile that's not unkind. It's like she's awkward too, and that's the best she can do under the circumstances. My schedule said the teacher's name is Ms. Julian, so I assume that's her.

"You're Skylar, aren't you?" she asks quietly, pushing her glasses up the bridge of her nose. When she pronounces my name correctly right off the bat, I like her even more.

"Yes," I answer...just as quietly.

"One of your teachers actually reached out to me from your old school." She shuffles through some papers on her desk before grabbing one. "Mrs. Higgins?"

I perk up. Mrs. Higgins was my favorite person at that school. I'd had her as my English teacher for the past two years and like Daisy, she had this thing about her. Like she'd seemed to believe in me and my capabilities. I'd shown her my stories, something I didn't show anyone. And she'd always acted like she liked them, giving me constructive feedback whenever she'd felt I could learn from it.

"Oh?" I respond.

"She was raving about you. Making sure I knew I had a real writer on my hands." She giggles nervously, like the thought of that actually scares her.

"I don't know about that. But she was a great teacher."

Ms. Julian nods. "Well, better get to your seat," she says, even though the classroom is still empty. I nod gratefully, sensing she needs the out from our conversation as much as I do. Introverts unite and all that.

People start trickling in, and I check each time the door opens, my stomach clenching at the thought of Noah being in this class as well. The thought of having to be on guard in my favorite class sends terror running through my veins.

The door opens and a familiar face appears. Kyle. He makes a beeline for the desk next to me when he sees where I'm sitting, offering me a boyish grin. There's someone at the desk already, but that doesn't stop him.

"Get up," he says casually to the girl sitting there who had just pulled out her notebook.

I wait for her to say no, or just say anything really, but she only shoots him a nervous smile and immediately gets up. I watch in wide-eyed amazement as she finds another desk without a word.

Kyle settles into the seat nonchalantly, like that's a normal, everyday occurrence. I'm starting to wonder if there really is something in the water here that they're feeding certain people to give them this exaggerated sense of self importance and outright entitled douchery.

"How was first period?" he asks, and butterflies take flight in my stomach as I realize I'll actually need to talk this time.

I'm not used to this, people...seeing me.

He catches me off guard with his question. Why is he bothering to talk to me when he's shown himself to be an asshole by making that girl move?

"It was fine," I finally say, watching as his grin transforms into something even more spell-binding.

"She does talk," he teases, and I curse myself as I blush for the umpteenth time that day.

"She does," I answer.

He's about to say more, but Ms. Julian stands up and hesitantly clears her throat. I like that Kyle settles back in his seat and doesn't try to talk over her. I doubt she would say anything if he did. She seems too nervous for that, so it's nice that she doesn't have to and that she can give her class in peace and without fear of being interrupted.

My thoughts drift from Kyle to Noah, envisioning what he'd do in the same situation.

It wouldn't be pretty.

He'd eat Ms. Julian alive.

Which is unsurprising since wallflowers like us could never survive the beat down of a merciless tidal wave.

And make no mistake. Noah is a tsunami in the making.

* * *

"Can I walk you to the cafeteria?" Kyle asks after he's helped me find my locker.

I nervously chew on my lip, not accustomed to so much friendly attention from someone I've just met.

"Actually, I brought my lunch with me," I tell him, taking out the tuna sandwich I made this morning from my backpack.

"Ah, come on? You can't eat that on your first day at Bayshore High," Kyle retorts playfully, shoving my sandwich back in my bag and closing my locker for me.

I'm uncomfortable with his assertiveness, but he's been nothing but nice to me all day so I don't have the heart to tell him no.

"Sure. Okay," I concede with a thin smile.

"Awesome!" he cheers, like I just made his day.

Kyle leads me through the school hall towards the cafeteria, chatting away like he's known me all his life. In return, I nod and offer him a few hmms and aahs to show him I'm listening.

I'm not.

How could I be when my anxiety is playing its games with me?

All I can concentrate on is the curious stares from the other students flicking our way as we walk down the hall.

Daisy was right.

These kids haven't had fresh blood in this school in a long ass time, which means there was no way I would have ever passed under their radar. It only gets worse when Kyle and I enter the busy cafeteria. Kids pry their gazes from their lunch trays to gawk and stare at me. It's almost like I'm some beacon, attracting all this unwanted attention.

It's unnerving.

Kyle, however, seems to be utterly oblivious to it all.

Or maybe, he's just pretending to be.

"See? Isn't pizza better than a tuna sandwich?" he teases, placing two slices of pepperoni pizza on my plate.

I'm a little miffed that he just assumed I wanted pizza instead of anything else on display. Honestly, my anxious stomach won't be able to handle it, and I would rather have had a simple salad than greasy cafeteria junk food.

Still, instead of getting what I want, I let him pay for my lunch, making a note of only having a few bites so I don't get sick later on.

"Hey, you're in luck. There's an empty seat at your brother's table," he proclaims excitedly, heading to a large round table at the corner of the room.

"I don't have a brother—" I start confused, then slam my mouth shut when it hits me.

He means Noah.

Fuck.

Word sure gets around here. I bet Kyle knew who I was before he even laid eyes on me this morning.

My gaze scans the table in question, and just as I suspected, Noah is surrounded by what I can only assume are his friends. Yeah, no way am I sitting there.

"Kyle!" I call out, but he's too far away to hear me.

Goddamn it!

I take a deep breath and plant the fakest smile I can muster as I follow him.

One lunch.

I can survive one lunch with Noah.

If I can survive family dinners with him, I can survive this.

I think.

"Hey, look who I found?" Kyle says when he reaches the table, me now at his heel. Everyone stops what they are doing to see what Kyle is going on about, but it's not their prying eyes that churn my stomach —it's *his*.

After Kyle places his tray on the table, he grabs an empty chair for me, which to my chagrin, I have no choice but to sit in.

"Thought it would be nice if your sister could have lunch with a familiar face, being it her first day and all," Kyle adds cheerfully after he's taken the empty seat next to me.

"Haven't you heard?" Noah says, not taking his eyes off his phone. "The road to hell is paved with good intentions." He then breaks his gaze away from his screen just long enough to stare me in the eye. "And that...is not my sister."

My cheeks flush crimson with the few chuckles that erupt from the table.

"Fine. *Stepsister*. Don't be a dick." Kyle waves him off like he's used to this type of bad behavior from Noah.

But then again, maybe he is. Perhaps they all are.

And I'm the one who needs to get with the program.

With my head hung low, I fiddle with my food while Kyle tries to entertain me. When he sees that I'm not the talkative type, he starts a conversation about basketball with the two guys across from us wearing the same letterman jacket he is.

God, I wish Daisy had the same lunch hour I have.

I could use her as an excuse to get up and walk away from this wretched table.

Twenty minutes.

That's all the time I'm going to give this awkward lunch. Twenty minutes should suffice to appease Kyle and not have him be offended by my bailing.

Satisfied with that plan, I inwardly start counting down the minutes while playing with the food I have no intention of eating.

But then it happens.

A nagging feeling that this awkward lunch is about to get a whole lot worse.

I lift my head and discreetly look over to where Noah is seated, knowing he's the only person here who could make my life difficult. His eyes are no longer on me but on a familiar redhead that is sashaying past our table. His smug smile is all the coaxing she needs to come and talk to him.

It doesn't take long to realize where I know her from. She's the waitress from The Scarlet Letter Café. The same waitress I saw on her knees for Noah.

It's only when she gets close enough that I see her staring at the raven-haired girl sitting beside Noah with apprehension. When said girl rolls her eyes at her and dismisses her presence by continuing to talk with her friends, does the redhead eat the distance between her and Noah.

"Ah shit. Things are about to get heated." Kyle laughs beside me.

"Why?" I ask curiously, not bothering to look at him since I'm too focused on Noah and his hookup talking to one another.

"See the girl sitting right next to your brother? The one with the high ponytail to show off her Tiffany diamond studs? That's Noah's girlfriend, Stacy. Or maybe she's his ex now. You never know with those two."

My jaw goes agape at this piece of gossip. So much so that instead of me staring at the redhead blatantly flirting with Noah, I'm far more interested in Stacy, who doesn't seem to mind that another girl is talking to her boyfriend in such an intimate way.

It's only when Noah crooks his finger to the waitress, ordering her to bend down so she can get close enough for him to whisper in her ear, that Stacy ends whatever talk she was having with her friends to listen in on what he's saying. Whatever he says can't be good because both girls start to stare at me for some reason. While the waitress looks embarrassed by what he just told her, with the way her cheeks flush all sorts of red, Stacy seems disgusted.

Noah, though... looks like the cat who got the cream.

The waitress quickly retreats from the table, rushing away like she can't get far fast enough. Stacy, however, stays seated precisely where she is, throwing me an ugly smirk and whispering in her friend's ear. Her friend's eyes widen as she stares at me, and before I know it, she's whispering to the girl sitting beside her, too.

It all feels surreal, this juvenile game of telephone.

And it was all provoked by something Noah said to the redhead, loud enough that he knew Stacy would pick up on it.

What did he say?

What the fuck did he say?

But just as the question pops into my head, Stacy's quick to clarify for me.

"Stalker!" she shouts while pretending to cough out the word.

The tip of my ears begins to heat when everyone around the table takes Stacy's cue and begins to cough out the word 'stalker.' They don't even have the decency to pretend they aren't talking about me, staring directly at me as they laugh away at my ridicule.

Stalker.

That's Noah's favorite word for me.

All because I caught him with his pants down, literally.

He was the one in the ladies' bathroom getting off, but I'm the one being judged for it.

You did watch.

You stayed and watched.

That's why they're laughing at you.

Because you stayed. Because you enjoyed watching him.

And now everyone knows it.

Not waiting for the twenty minutes to pass, I get up from my seat and walk away. I don't even care to look back when Kyle worriedly calls out my name.

I can't look back.

Because *he's* watching me. Taking pleasure in my embarrassment and humiliation.

If I thought Bayshore High would be different from the school back home, then I was right.

Going to school here is going to be so much worse.

All because of my asshole of a stepbrother.

Isn't that a kick in the head...

Chapter 6

Noah

Sixteen years old

I've never been a fan of Bayshore High.

Scratch that.

I've never been a fan of school, period.

Classes, teachers, grades...

Their demands of academic perfection do my head in.

I have no interest in learning a second language or the politics of this nation. I have no interest in discussing prose or poetry. If I can't see its use for the future I'm about to lead, I don't see the point in it. It's all a fucking waste of time to me.

There are some precious few subjects that do spark my interest though.

Give me physics, geography, geometry, algebra, or trigonometry, and then you are guaranteed to have my full attention. Sure, they're hard as fuck to learn, but they're also the building blocks you need to be a good sailor. If you mess up on even one while you're out in the vast, unforgiving ocean, you're fucked. And if, by some miracle, I can afford to have my own sailboat one day, I'll need that shit to survive on my own. There's no time out there. No one you can call for help. No second chances to get it right. You either know your shit, or you have no business being out there in the first place.

And my place has always been out in the deep.

But as I said, these subjects aren't for the faint of heart.

They're grueling.

Especially for a guy like me, where nothing comes easy. Not even learning.

So is it any wonder why I'm fuming right now?

I'm supposed to be attentively listening to Mr. Evans solve the algebra problem he has on the whiteboard, but instead my head is on *her*.

Skylar.

Fuck.

Out of all the classes she had to be in, she just had to be in this one. *My one*. The one I've been working so damn hard since freshman year to master.

I fucking can't catch a break.

Not only do I have to suffer walking around *my* house smelling her cherry blossom perfume everywhere, I now have to smell it here too. Since the big guy upstairs loves to fuck with me, he made sure that the only available seat in this whole classroom was right beside me.

So here I am.

Pissed beyond measure because for the remaining thirty minutes of this class, her very presence will be enough to distract me from what really matters.

The only thing that gives me some sadistic satisfaction is the way she's cowering in her seat, that dark chestnut long hair of hers covering her entire face as if it is enough to protect her.

She's hiding.

From me.

You can hide all you want, little stalker, but I see you.

The corner of my lip pulls upwards at the thought.

"Ms. Ames," Mr. Evan calls out. "Can you tell me what I must do to solve this equation?"

Sky lifts her head and tugs her hair behind her ear, showcasing her long neck, to stare at the problem in question. She bites her fat bottom lip, taking a minute to consider all her options. I don't even register her answer, but it must be right by the big bright smile that ends up cresting her lips.

And suddenly, my chest feels like someone just poured cement all over it. Because for that one split second—she's happy.

Fuck her happiness.

Not wanting that smile to prolong, I extend my leg and kick her chair, startling her.

Silver eyes that remind me of pale moonlight stare at me in astonishment.

I offer her my cruelest smirk, and she throws me an aggravated glare in response. But her bravery is short-lived when a faint 'stalker' is mumbled from somewhere in the room. Sky immediately shrinks in her seat, head hung low, her hair once again, the curtain she pulls to keep prying eyes away from her face.

A better person would feel guilty for making her a pariah at school on her first day.

Me?

Not so much.

Misery loves company, after all.

And if I have to live in utter torment with this goddamn union my father forced on me, why shouldn't she?

Only fair.

At least, that's how I see it.

And who knows? Maybe I can make her life bad enough that she cries off to her mommy. Tells her how she hates it here. How she wants to move back to whatever hole they came from. Maybe it will be the wedge that comes between my asshole of a father and his wife —no harm in trying.

Shit can't get worse than it already is.

When the sound of the bell rings, I curse under my breath, hating that instead of spending the time in class learning, I spent all of it thinking about Skylar.

The girl has been in my life for less than a couple of months, and already, she's a pain in my ass.

Not wanting to be in the same place she is, I bolt out of my seat and make my way to my locker. On the way, my phone vibrates in my pocket, Stacy's number flashing on the screen. I decline the call, not caring what she has to say.

I already know what's on her mind.

Leave it to my ex to not care about the little blow job I got at my father's wedding reception. Instead, she's worried about the new stepsisters I just begrudgingly inherited. I could probably fuck the whole goddamn school, and Stacy wouldn't bat an eye. But tell her that I'm living with two hot as fuck sisters, and she goes bonkers.

Not my problem.

"Yo! Noah!" someone calls out my name.

I bite my inner cheek when I realize it's none other than Kyle and his steroid-aficionado besties.

He waves me over to his locker as if I'm some dog he can summon with a whistle. I have half a mind to ignore the prick, but my curiosity wins out.

"What?" I grunt the minute I reach him.

"Is that any way to greet a friend?" He laughs off.

"We're not friends. We just grew up together because this island is too goddamn small for us not to. Don't get it twisted."

I smirk when his All-American good ol' boy mask falls a smidge.

"You really have to get back with Stacy asap. You're turning into an asshole," he teases, his way of trying to do damage control.

When I stand there, stone-faced, he quickly takes the hint that he needs to explain why he called me over here.

"Look, Noah. I know we all live by the bro code and all, but would you be okay if you made an exception in my case?" he asks.

"A second ago, you told me to get back with my ex, and now you're asking for permission to date her?" I laugh.

Have it.

Stacy would fucking eat you alive and spit out your bones before you could even blink.

"Nah, man. I'm not talking about Stacy. I mean...Skylar."

His friends begin to howl at his request while my blood starts to boil in my veins.

"Dude, why the fuck are you interested in her? Have you seen her older sister yet? Daisy? I'd give my left nut for the girl's digits," one of Kyle's friends says, biting his knuckles to drive the point home.

All the guys start talking about how hot Daisy is, but it doesn't go unnoticed to me how Kyle doesn't join in, staring me down until I give him an answer.

Fucker.

He's got his sights on the easy prey.

While every last guy at this school with a working pair of balls will be jonesing for Daisy's attention, Kyle knows that Sky is easy pickings. The fucker sure didn't waste any time moving in on her.

Not that I wasn't expecting some asshole to try.

The whole school knew that both Ames sisters would attend Bayshore High. It had been the talk of the summer. Not only was the island reeling with the fact that my father remarried so soon after my mom passed away, but also that his new wife brought two teenage daughters to live with us.

Kyle probably got to school bright and early yesterday and waited to see the both of them arrive in the parking lot to make his pick. And then, to put his plan into action, he pretended to bump into them innocently, ensuring he'd be the first to creep his way into Sky's life.

Of course, I don't have any proof.

But I've known the fucker his entire life.

He might act like the boy next door, but he's just like the rest of them—another rich asshole who needs the clout of having what others don't.

His friends are now on their phones, drooling over Daisy's IG account, asking if they, too, can break bro code. Like any of these motherfuckers live by any code.

"So?" Kyle insists. "Can I ask her out or what?"

I run the pad of my thumb over my lower lip, using his friends being distracted to my advantage. I lean into him, my head right next to his, and whisper, "I'd think twice before you ask me that question again."

"Yeah? Why?" the arrogant fuck has the nerve to counter.

"You heard the rumors," I explain, grinning when his body stiffens. "About how she likes to watch. Watch me, her stepbrother, get his dick wet. Hate to say it, Kyle. But I doubt after she's seen what a real man can do, she'll be interested in your two-inch cock."

His nostrils flare, but he's got the good sense not to say anything in return.

Good.

Smart.

I pull away and gift him my winning smile.

"Need anything else?"

"Nah, I'm good," he retorts coldly.

"Glad to be of help then." I smile and walk away, feeling like a weight has been lifted off my shoulders.

Not that I care if Kyle tries anything with Sky.

I don't care.

But knowing that I'm the only one that gets to play with Thatcher's Bay's new toy puts that added spring in my step. Maybe it wouldn't be all that bad to keep her around a little longer after all.

It looks like it may have its advantages.

Chapter 7

Skylar

Sixteen years old

If I had harbored a smidge of hope that life would be easier for me when I moved to Thatcher's Bay last month, I was sorely mistaken. In reality, it's only gotten worse.

Back at my old school, I could at least take comfort in the knowledge that I was just a blip on everyone's radar, and that most of my days were completely uneventful, with nothing noteworthy to look forward to. As boring as that may sound, I relished in the mundaneness of it all. Most of the kids at school would leave me alone out of fear of Daisy's retribution if they ever even thought of messing with me, and I, for one, was happy to reap the spoils of that fear and live my life without the added worry that I would be put on some sort of spotlight.

But the minute I stepped foot on this island, all those perks went away.

Where before I was just Daisy's younger sister and no one of real importance, now I'm Noah's stepsister, and by the looks of it, that makes me public enemy number one. I wouldn't be surprised if Noah sent out a newsletter or a tweet to all his minions, telling them that whoever made my life extra miserable would be in his good graces for life.

I'm not sure how I ended up being on his shit list, but not only did I get on it, I'm pretty sure my name is listed right at the top of the damn thing. That's not true. I know exactly what got me there. It was that stupid blowjob. Walking in on him while some girl got him off was Noah's special brand of welcoming me into the family. It told me that he didn't give a shit what I thought of him, and that he would make it so that the world wouldn't give a shit about me either.

To say that school has become my least favorite place in the entire world is the understatement of the decade.

There hasn't been a day where I could walk through Bayshore High's halls without someone accidentally bumping into me hard enough that I end up falling to the floor on my hands and knees. It's happened so many times now that it's no wonder the first person I'm on a first-name basis with is the school nurse. The amount of scrapes and bruises I've gotten in the past few weeks is ridiculous, and frankly, they're starting to be a little hard to hide from my mother and sister. Not that they've had much time to notice them. With Mom starting a new job and still being in her honeymoon phase, she's been too preoccupied to see that I hate it here.

And as for Daisy...well...Daisy is just being Daisy.

Coming to Bayshore High has become sort of a challenge for her.

She won't be satisfied until she's left her mark on the school.

And in true Daisy fashion, I'd say that before the year is through, she'll get her wish. If Noah told his followers that, like me, my sister was persona non grata at Bayshore High, then they didn't get the memo. It took less than a day for Daisy to have everyone eating out of the palm of her hand and have them all hanging on her every word. Where I've hated every minute of living on this godforsaken island, Daisy took to it like a fish to water. It's like she has lived here all her life and grown up with these assholes.

The ugly and resentful side of me sometimes wishes she wasn't having such a good time and was just as miserable as I am. If she was having a hard time settling here, then I at least would have someone to bitch with.

But just like back home, I have no one.

All I have are the fictional characters in my head to keep me company.

Say what you will about being an outcast, but it does have its strong points.

Never has my muse been more pronounced and active as it is now. It's like it thrives on every moment of hardship, helping me create the most interesting situations and complex villains I have to date. And boy, is one particular person the muse for my overactive imagination.

Noah.

The blue-eyed boy that hides his stellar eyes behind long dirty blond hair.

The bane of my existence is also the source of the best writing I've ever done. Sometimes when I come home after a grueling day at school, my hands can't write all the ideas that pop into my head fast enough. Sure, my scribblings are mostly ways of inflicting pain on my nemesis, but hey, when inspiration strikes, you roll with it.

I hate to admit it, but his hatred of me has inspired some of my best work.

Tales of revenge.

Scenes of utter carnage and destruction.

And...this is a big one...my first sex scene.

I don't want to dissect why it was so easy for me to finally write such a scene with Noah in mind, but I can't deny that it was. It felt natural. Almost inevitable. The ripping of shirts and buttons flying left and right across a room. The hungry stares and shallow breaths. The loud drumming of two heartbeats. I could see it so clearly in my mind's eye. I could even taste it. Taste him.

Again, I don't want to think too hard on why that is. It would only block my words from pouring out so fluidly and effortlessly like they have done if I were to question the reason behind this spurt of creativity. And if this is my only silver lining of living at Thatcher's Bay, then so be it.

I once read an article somewhere that an artist needed to suffer for their art for it to be truly great.

If that really is the case, then I willingly volunteer to become the puppet on a string of my stepbrother's cruelty. His white-hot anger fuels my own. Every snide remark and dirty look taps into a part of me that I've kept bottled up for far too long, and it's oddly liberating to just let it all out without fear of being scrutinized or judged for it.

If I had to put into words how I feel when Noah is showing me his worst, coaxing me to rise to his level, I would have to say that it feels a lot like freedom. The air tastes different on the tip of my tongue when I'm cursing him out. My skin feels hot to the touch while my heart threatens to explode in my chest with how hard it starts beating. All of me feels like a flickering flame, heating up to brand-new heights anytime he forces me to confront him.

It's terribly addicting.

Although I'm pretty sure none of this is healthy.

How could it be?

Even though this little game of ours is far from normal behavior, I can't find the will to stop. Not when it feels like I'm finally living.

Huh.

Who would have thought that hate could taste this sweet?

Be the inspiration I needed to push my writing to the next level?

Chaucer and Nietzsche sacrificed their mental well-being for their art, right? So why can't I?

Because let's face it, kindling this rivalry between Noah and I just for the sake of writing a good chapter, is not what a sane person would do. A mentally stable person would try to go out of their way to make peace, whereas I am doing everything in my power just to piss my rival off further.

Hence why I decided that today I would step it up a notch and see if I could push his buttons in some other way besides merely existing. But to do that, I need to gather some intel and do a little reconnaissance mission. A sneak peek into the mind of my bully, if you will. What better way to learn your enemy's secrets than to sneak into his room and see if he has any of them lying around.

With our parents at work, and Daisy off to God knows where, the house is completely empty of anyone who could spoil my fun. As per usual, Noah is outside in the garage fiddling with his bike. I've lived here long enough to know that's how he likes to spend his afternoons, listening to loud rap music while he messes around with his precious Yamaha. He's an animal of habit, so I know I've got a few hours before he comes upstairs to take a shower before dinner, giving me ample time to get the job done without him being none the wiser about it.

Fueled with palpitating adrenaline, I leave my room and walk across the hall over to his. Ever so slowly, I turn the doorknob to his bedroom and smile when I open it with ease. On bare feet, I walk inside, my gaze soaking up every dust particle in the room. The first thing I notice is that for a teenage boy, Noah sure keeps his devil's lair spick and span. His bed is neatly made. His textbooks on top of his desk are carefully stacked into one arranged pile, and there isn't a piece of dirty laundry on the floor like I expected to find. In fact, Daisy could take pointers from Noah on how to keep a room so clean. It's immaculately spotless.

Hmm.

That doesn't bode well for my investigation.

No matter.

It just means I have to dig a little deeper.

Without a minute to lose, I go to his desk and open his laptop, hopeful that maybe I can find some dirt, or at the very least, some embarrassing porn that I can use against him.

"Damn it," I exhale, frustrated when I see that his computer is password-protected.

My shoulders slump as I look around his desk, trying to see if there is any piece of information lying around that can help me crack into it. Unfortunately, after a quick glance, there doesn't seem to be much here that looks to be of use to me. Not one to be defeated so easily, I start opening his desk drawers, one after another, and again I'm disappointed to find there isn't anything in them that shouts out password. Just some old motorbike magazines and some discarded change.

I spin around the room, hopelessness starting to set into my bones that this clandestine endeavor of mine will end up bearing no fruit. It's only when my gaze falls on Noah's bedside table on the other side of the room that I pause. Even though it's a bit far from where I'm standing, I can still clearly see the photograph of a woman pushing a young boy on a swing set. My feet move before I even tell them to and walk over to it, picking up the frame in my hands to inspect the image closer.

There is no question in my mind that the boy in the picture is Noah, even if it doesn't remotely look like him anymore. It isn't the fact that the boy in the picture is so much younger than Noah is now —maybe only seven or eight, if I had to venture a guess—it's the significant change in him. It's the fact that he's smiling that is so alarming. A real, genuine smile. One that I've never seen on his face before. I didn't even think he'd be capable of such a thing.

And God, it's beautiful.

Blindingly so.

My chest tightens seeing how happy he had been once. Such a contrast to the bitter, angry boy who has put my life in such a tailspin lately. If this version of Noah still existed, maybe we could have actually been friends instead of sworn enemies.

My gaze trails from his cheerful face and chubby cheeks to the cause of such happiness. The woman who stands behind him with a beaming, wide smile, laughing at her son's joy. She has the same blonde hair and playful twinkle of mischief that her son's eyes carry.

She is beautiful. Happy. Loved.

"Annabelle," I whisper softly, the fist around my heart squeezing it to a pulp.

When I decided to invade Noah's personal space, it was with the sole mission of finding something embarrassing that would put us on an even keel. I never thought I would find such raw vulnerability that this memento of Noah's mom represents. I swallow dryly, looking back down on his bedside table and see that this photograph isn't the only thing he has of her. On closer inspection, I can see that there is a small shrine of sorts just for her.

A handkerchief with her initials embroidered in blue on it.

A butterfly hairpin, the same one she's using to pull the hair away from her face in the photograph in my now trembling hands.

A book of poems.

And a velvet ring box that I don't dare open.

Feeling overwhelmed with the display of such sad devotion, I carefully place the frame back on the table. I then take three huge steps back, not wanting to tarnish Noah's need to keep his mom's memory alive with my uninvited presence. Suddenly, my plan to sneak into his room for dirt feels like I've stepped over an invisible line that I should have never crossed.

I know what it feels like to lose a parent.

To not have them around anymore.

But my pain is so different from Noah's.

My father chose to leave me.

His mom had no say in the matter.

She was ripped from his life in the cruelest of ways, and those types of wounds never heal fully.

It's easier to pretend that you're better off without a parent when they don't want anything to do with you. But to accept a loss like Noah had to suffer feels excruciating to me. I'm not sure I could ever recover from it. If I lost my mom like that... God...just thinking about it makes me want to curl into a ball and cry.

This is not what I expected to find when I came in here.

Not by a long shot.

And it sure as shit wasn't meant for me to actually feel for Noah.

To care for him.

I shake my head, needing to expunge those thoughts from my mind and quickly turn around to leave. But just as I'm at his door, the devil on my shoulder whispers in my ear.

Annabelle.

That's his password.

Shit.

I turn my head over my shoulder, staring at the computer on his desk that taunts me.

Am I that unscrupulous that I would use his dead mom's name to get into his things?

Don't do it, Sky.

Don't you dare do it.

Not wanting to feel more like shit than I already do, I don't question it when I rush to his desk and press the keys on his keyboard, spelling out the one name that means something to Noah. When his monitor springs to life, I'm even more disgusted with myself.

"It's done now. No use in turning back," I tell myself out loud, but it doesn't ease the guilt I feel.

There is only one folder on his desktop, and on autopilot, I quickly click on it. My shame and guilt increase tenfold when all I find are articles and pictures of sail boats.

Great.

I just stooped to my very lowest for nothing.

Serves me right.

But just as I close the monitor, the small hairs in the nape of my neck stand on end, and I don't have to turn around to know I've been caught.

"You have exactly one minute to tell me what the fuck you're doing in my room. Start talking."

Shit.

Busted.

Chapter 8

Noah

Sixteen years old

"Talk," I utter curtly into the phone, as I try to balance it on the crook of my neck while simultaneously wiping the oil from my hands.

"Well, hello to you, too," Derrick teases on the other line, and even though I can't see his face, I know the fucker is smiling his all-American toothy grin.

"Kind of busy here, D. If you have something to say, just come out and say it and stop wasting my time. I've got shit to do."

"Yeah, yeah. You're always busy these days."

"What the fuck is that supposed to mean?" I ask after I've thrown my oil rag to the floor to hold the phone closer to my ear.

"It means that you've been slacking off lately. My sister can't shut up about how you're always busy with something or other. Suddenly, you don't have time for your friends anymore? What's that shit all about?"

I let out an irritated exhale, since it seems Stacy let her watch dog off its leash to fight her battles for her. The girl thrives on confrontation, but when it comes to me, she prefers others to do her dirty work for her. Her older brother being her go-to guy for the job. I'm not one bit surprised that Derrick is calling me. I'm just surprised it's taken him this long to do it.

"Do you really care, or is this social call just to get your sister off your back?" I ask outright.

"Both, asshole," Derrick mumbles, aggravated. "Look, I don't know what your problem is these days, but I suggest you get your shit together, pronto. I've had it up to here with my baby sister complaining to me twenty-four seven about how you no longer make any time for her."

"She'll live," I counter, not one bit bothered.

"Yeah, well, I might not," he grumbles, frustrated. "All I'm saying is now that you've got sisters of your own, you should know where I'm coming from."

"They're not my sisters."

My growl is filled with such vehemence that it creates a dead silence on the line. Unbeknownst to him, Derrick just managed to hit a sensitive nerve that has been throbbing nonstop since this whole blended family shit consumed my household. I'm still coming to grips with it, and having people think I'm in any way okay with this altered reality, sets my teeth on edge.

"Is that so?" he rebukes after a long pause, insinuation in his tone.

"It's not like that," I defend, not liking where Derrek's head instantly leaped to.

"Are you sure?"

I bite my inner cheek instead of giving him a reply.

"I mean, I get it. Daisy is something else. Hot doesn't even come close to defining her. Must be hard to have a girl like that walking around your house all the time and not be able to touch her. I'd have a killer time concentrating on my girlfriend with Daisy all up in my business, too."

I'm not sure why I do it, but with the mention of Daisy's name, I let out a relieved sigh, followed by laughter that she's the one that immediately came to his mind.

"First of all, Stacy is my ex-girlfriend. We broke up before summer break, remember? And second, you don't do girlfriends, D, so how would you know? Besides, it's not even like that between me and Daisy. She's cool and all, but not my type. Too high maintenance, that one."

But just as the words leave my mouth, my brow arches in curiosity when I hear Derrick release his own sigh of relief.

"Cool. Glad to hear it." He chuckles, suddenly too fucking upbeat, coaxing my curiosity to heighten further. "Now that that's settled, how about you get your ass over here? I promised Stacy I'd sweet-talk you into having dinner with us tonight."

"Pass," I grumble.

Spending the night with my on-again, off-again girlfriend is not how I want to spend my Friday night. I know how it will go. We'll end up eating some fancy takeout from a restaurant whose name I can't even pronounce and then spend the rest of the night listening to her gossip about people I have no interest in. I'll be bored half to death and end up hooking up with her just to shut her up. As much as my dick would love nothing more than to get some much-needed attention, lately, just the thought of sleeping with Stacy churns my stomach.

She'll want me to say sweet nothings into her ear and stroke her ego by telling her how beautiful she is, when all I want is to get it over with so I can pull on my pants and get the hell out of there. It doesn't bode well for our so-called relationship that I want to bolt the minute I'm done with her. Stacy might be a bitch when she wants to be, but she doesn't deserve being played with. Hence, why I've tried to keep her at arm's length lately. Sooner or later, she'll get the message that we're done. For how long, though, is anyone's guess.

All I know is that right now, I'm not in the right headspace nor do I have the patience to act like the devoted boyfriend she demands me to be. I don't have it in me. Maybe I never did.

"I'll make it worth your while," Derrick counters with a smug tone.

"How?"

"Got a race going tonight. How does a little extra cash sound to you?"

Now this spikes my interest.

"How much are we talking about?"

"The pot should be a couple grand, at the very least. After I get my cut, that is."

I chuckle at that.

Derrick doesn't need the money.

Like Stacy, he's had a silver spoon shoved into his mouth since he was a baby in his crib, but it's no secret that the fucker gets a thrill from hustling. I guess spending his daddy's millions can't compare to the high he gets from his side businesses. If there is an underground fight or illegal drag race taking place on this island, then you can bet your last dollar that it was Derrick Monroe who organized it. There is only so much you can do in Thatcher's Bay, and bored high school kids like us, who need a bit of excitement in their lives before we have to face what undoubtedly will be a pathetic existence the minute we graduate, need this rush of adrenaline just to get by.

It's all about supply and demand.

And like the savvy businessman Derrick is, he saw a need that had to be filled and a way to profit off it. It doesn't matter if you live on the rich side of the island or the poor one, we all need a little something to get us through the day, and Derrick is all too happy to supply that for us. Not that I care how he gets his rocks off. All I care about is how that extra cash will help pay the debt of my mom's hospital expenses that are still hanging over our heads.

"I'm in," I'm quick to reply.

"I thought as much. Come over for dinner, make nice with Stacy for an hour, and then we can get down to business."

"Let me grab a shower and I'll be there in a few."

"I'll be here."

I hang up and start hurriedly cleaning the mess I made in the garage before I head back inside to get ready, my previous solemn mood long forgotten. My father will probably bitch that I'll miss family dinner, but that's just another added bonus for me. Having to sit at the same table with his new wife—the woman he was obviously having an affair with while my mom was on her deathbed—and pretend that everything is hunky-dory just so I can play into his illusion that we are one big happy family, disgusts me.

Not that he gives a shit about how I feel.

He's too preoccupied with how his new family is getting on to care about his old one.

Ever since Clara and her daughters moved in, he's made it a point to be home for every dinner, fully stepping into the role of devoted family man, and turning down jobs that will take him out to sea for days on end.

Funny how he never made that sacrifice when Mom was alive. How money was always an issue back then and staying home was never an option. But I know that this fucking honeymoon phase of his has a ticking clock on it. Sooner or later, the debt collectors will start making noise, and he'll have no choice but to face reality. He'll never truly be able to escape his past, just as I can't escape my future.

But while he's on this delusional trip of his, one of us should have their feet on the ground and do what needs to be done. A few races and fights will get me the money we need to keep our heads above water. The last thing I want is for us to lose our home to the bank just because my father is too busy playing house. He might not think twice about putting my childhood home in jeopardy, but this is the house my mom lived in most of her life, and like hell I'll give it up just because it no longer holds memories he wishes to remember. I guess the point of him having Clara and her daughters move into my home is so that he can create new memories and erase my mom completely.

Fucker.

Hatred starts bleeding through my pores, and instead of tempering it, I do the very opposite and harness it as fuel for tonight's race. Hate can be quite the motivator, and lately it's the only thing that keeps me from losing my shit. And if I want to be a few thousand dollars richer by night's end, I'm going to need all the advantages I can get.

These are the thoughts that run wild in my head as I walk into the house and run up the flight of stairs up to my room. But just as I step into the hall, my brow furrows when I see my bedroom door left ajar. Slowly, I walk toward my room and open the door wider, rage consuming me from within at what I find.

"You have exactly one minute to tell me what the fuck you're doing in my room. Start talking."

My hands curl into fists at my sides as I stare daggers at Skylar's immovable back. She's so still that the only proof I have that she's breathing is the faint sound of her shallow breaths. When she refuses to acknowledge me or tell me why the fuck she's in my room uninvited, I step farther inside and slam my bedroom door so hard I'm surprised it doesn't come off its hinges. Like I expected, the loud thud has her jumping in place, turning around to finally face me. My fury only increases with the way she brazenly looks me dead in the eye, like I'm the one in the wrong here. The only thing that shows her guilt is the way her cheeks flush crimson. Even if I didn't know she was up to no good before I caught her in the act, her pink cheeks are a dead giveaway.

"Are you deaf? I asked you a question," I seethe through gritted teeth, doing my best not to bridge the distance between us and strangle her where she stands. I'd never lay my hands on a woman in anger, but Skylar sure likes to test my fucking restraint. I'd bet she would laugh in my face if I ever even tried to wring her long slender neck. "Well? I don't have all day."

"It's not what it looks like," she stammers, her gaze falling behind me toward the door, hating that I'm standing right between her and her escape. "I was just...I was just—"

"You were what? Snooping around my stuff? Getting off at going through my things without permission?"

"No!" she yells, shaking her head in denial.

"Liar. That's exactly what you were doing!" I shout, my feet suddenly moving closer to her.

"I wasn't. I was just..." she tries to explain, walking a step back with each step I take toward her.

"You were just what, Sky? If you're going to lie to me, at least make it a good one."

"I...um... I..." she stutters, looking around the room for a plausible excuse.

But all her would-be lies die on the tip of her tongue when her ass hits my desk and I'm standing just a hair's breadth away from her.

"You look scared, Sky." I smirk. "Do I scare you?"

"Please," she scoffs, crossing her arms over her chest to put a barrier between us.

"Bullshit. You are. You're fucking terrified."

She widens those big silver eyes of hers, piercing me with all the contempt she holds for me.

Like I fucking care.

"In what world could you ever scare me?" she bites back, pissed, no longer looking guilty for what she's done. I guess facing my wolfish grin does that to her. Not that I mind. I prefer her like this. It will only make breaking her that much sweeter if she puts up a fight.

"Oh, I don't know," I muse, running a finger down her cheek. "I think in the same world where I catch you in my room and when no one is around to help you."

She slaps my hand away, squaring her shoulders and inching her face closer to mine, completely unintimidated.

"Touch me and I'll scream."

I laugh.

"Scream all you want. Go for it. I dare you."

I count the seconds in my head as she continues to glare at me and when she opens her mouth to let out the loudest scream worthy of a Jamie Lee Curtis award, my lips stretch into a smile. When she's done, her chest heaving and panting for breath, I make a show of looking around the empty room to drive the point home.

"See? No one is coming to help you. Because no one gives a fuck about you."

"Fuck you!"

"Is that it? Is that all you got?" I tsk, feigning disappointment. "You have to do much better than that."

"You know what? Just when I start to think that maybe there is a beating heart in here, you remind me that you're nothing but an asshole," she sneers, stabbing my chest with her finger. "Thanks for the reminder."

"Ah, is that what you were looking for? Proof that I was human after all?" I laugh sadistically. "Sorry to disappoint."

"No, you're not. You like it. Actually, no. You *love* people thinking you're a dick. Compensating much?" she taunts with a cocked eyebrow.

"Oh, you want to go there, Sky? Okay, I'll bite. Tell me. Does this feel like I'm compensating for anything?" I say before fully crashing into her just so she can feel my hard mast poke into her stomach.

Her gaze widens in alarm, and her pretty little pink blush turns even redder. I'm not sure why my cock sprung to life like this just by arguing with my stepsister, but right now I don't care. All I care about is watching Sky squirm where she stands.

"Get the fuck off me," she warns softly.

"Make me."

Her nostrils flare as she pushes my shoulders with all her might, thinking that will force me to step back. I laugh in her face as I remain rooted to my spot.

"You're going to have to do better than that." I smirk.

"Is that another dare?"

"If you can handle it."

My hackles rise when she plants on a fake-ass sweet smile just for me. Unfortunately, I'm not quick enough to read her next move, so I never see it coming when her knee jams in between my legs.

"Argh!" I shout, instantly falling to the floor with blinding pain, grabbing my junk in my hands.

Fuck!

Shit!

Goddamn it!

With me cursing in pain laid out on the floor, Sky uses my momentary incapacity to her advantage, turning around to pick up my algebra textbook off my desk and hug it to her chest.

"I left mine in my locker. That's why I came into your room, dipshit. I needed it to study for the test we're going to have next week. Since I know you don't care for such things, I didn't think you'd mind me taking yours," she explains as she steps over my crouched frame. "But thanks. This was entertaining. Let's do it again soon. *Not.*"

I watch through squinted eyes as Skylar leaves my room and slams my door behind her.

Once the excruciating pain starts to subside, I lay flat on my floor, my arms outstretched as I stare at my popcorn ceiling. The girl just rearranged my balls, and yet my cheeks hurt from the big-ass grin on my face.

"Well played, little stalker," I utter into the air. "Well fucking played. But I can play dirty, too. Just wait and see."

Chapter 9

Skylar

Sixteen years old

The day starts off just like any other, with the same stares, the same whispers following me everywhere I go.

Everything's monotonously the same, even in its loathsomeness.

The only thing different is that I've purposely forgotten my textbook in English so that I've no choice but to run back to the classroom to grab it during my free period. It's the only hail mary I could come up with to give myself a reprieve from my abhorrent high school life.

I open the door to slip in, breathing a sigh of relief when I don't see anyone there, grateful to have at least thirty minutes of complete solitude where I don't feel like I'm being judged or ridiculed.

But as I head towards the back of the classroom to get my book, I hear it.

The heavy, familiar panting. One that has been haunting my dreams since the first time I heard it.

My own breath is coming out in gasps, and my cheeks flush as I turn towards the supply closet where the sound is coming from.

I should walk away. I really should.

But listening to Noah get off…makes it impossible.

I tiptoe towards the closet, my heartbeat thumping in my ears. Heat builds in my insides for reasons I don't want to think about.

Whoever he's with must have been in a hurry, because the door's cracked, like they'd thrown it closed in desperation to get their clothes off and not checked to make sure it had actually latched. I know that Noah isn't shy when it comes to flaunting his sexcapades, but not all girls are as adventurous. Curiosity gets the best of me as to who he's with, making me slowly walk closer to the door just to have a better view of what's going on inside the closet. Not that my imagination hasn't planted a pretty picture in my head already.

It doesn't take me too long to see who he's chosen to drag into the only classroom I feel at home in.

Stacy Monroe.

Her face is flushed, and her hair is falling out of its usually perky raven ponytail. He has her bent in half over a lone desk in the closet, his hand on her throat as he slides forward. His teeth are gritted and there's a fine sheen of perspiration on his forehead. But that's not what has my heart in a twist. It's the fact that he looks almost bored. As if he's just going through the motions. His body might be here in this dark room doing all the right things, but Noah is nowhere to be found.

Meanwhile, Stacy is making all sorts of noises fit for a porno audition.

I wonder who came on to who today. Last time I heard they were on the outs. Guess not so much now. Still I can't help but wonder why her? Why Stacy? When there are a million girls available to him, why is she who he always ends up going back to.

I watch for a long moment, my insides writhing. Stacy's hand sweeps out and knocks a stapler off the table and I jump, backing into the desk behind me, filling the room with a loud screech. They both freeze, and I panic, turning and sprinting towards the door. I don't stop sprinting until I get to the bathroom, hearing the door open down the hall as I slip inside.

I don't think he saw me...but what if he had?

What would he do to keep me quiet?

And then there's the fact he's already labeled me as a stalker. If he saw me, actually pulling a Peeping Tom on him, it's sure as shit not going to help my defense.

I feel...hot...and bothered as I slip into a stall, my hands still trembling as I debate perhaps never leaving.

But when the bell rings a half hour later, like the studious person I am, I drag myself out of the stall and back into the real world. Thankfully Noah is nowhere to be seen when I come out to join the stragglers who haven't made it to class yet.

It's going to be fine, he didn't see you, I chant in my head.

The period passes uneventfully, but then it's lunchtime. I've made a habit of bringing my lunch every day so I can disappear into the library in peace. But today of all days, we didn't have any food in the house to make lunch.

And I'm starving.

I think about just not eating, but then that makes me angry because the only reason I wouldn't be eating is because of Noah. And why should I let him keep me from that? I decide I'll slip into the cafeteria and grab some food. And then slip out.

Easy peasy.

I make it to the food line and pay for my food before I see Noah. Or rather...before he accosts me. I've just stepped out of the lunch line when he grabs me by the back of the hair and pushes me against the wall, uncaring who watches.

"Tell me, little stalker. Were you in the English room today?" he murmurs, his eyes locked with mine, one hand still tangled in my hair while the other one is lightly pressing against my neck.

My gaze drags around the room, my eyes begging for someone to help me.

Is anyone going to step in? Where are any of the teachers? Is everyone just going to let Noah manhandle me like this and not say a goddamn word?

"I don't know what you're talking about," I hiss. "Now get off me."

"I don't think you want to know what I'm capable of when I'm really angry," he answers calmly, the burning in his eyes belying his tone.

It's only when I catch a glimpse of a familiar caring face that I smirk right in his face.

"And I think that you should get your hand off my neck before Mr. Evans comes over here and does it for you."

Noah's teeth clench, but he takes a step back, just in time for our Algebra teacher to timidly appear.

"Everything okay over here?" he asks, his gaze bouncing off the both of us in equal measure.

Noah shoots him an annoyed look and stomps off with not so much as a reply, while I stand there shaking in my chucks.

"Everything's fine," I murmur with the fakest of smiles.

"Are you sure?" he questions further, not entirely convinced.

I nod and quickly pass him by, rushing to leave this godforsaken cafeteria, food be damned.

As I pass Noah's table, I distinctly hear the word "stalker", Stacy shooting me an ugly glare.

Looks like things are going to get worse before they can get better.

But they have to get better.

Right?

This can't be how I live the rest of my highschool years. It just can't be.

I won't let it.

* * *

Unfortunately by nightfall, something comes over me and all thoughts of sweet retribution evaporate from my mind.

After finishing one of my smutty romance books, I feel more restless than usual, unable to fall asleep. All I can think about is the sight of Noah today. In that supply closet. The tension in his jaw, in his shoulders...the sound that came out of him. Had he actually been making her feel good, or was he just getting off because he needed the release? Because he was so bored, he needed something... anything... just to feel alive?

I find my hand trailing down my stomach, inside the band of my underwear.

My eyes close as I begin to imagine it was me bent over that desk. That it was me he'd been pushing his punishing dick inside.

I'd never done this before, fumble around to try and ease the ache in my core.

But then again...I'd never had an ache like this before Noah stepped into my life.

My fingers move through my folds, trying to find the sweet spot. And all the while I imagine it's Noah's hands touching me. It's me causing him to make those sounds. A moan slips from my lips as it starts to feel good—

"Well...what do we have here?" murmurs Noah as my door suddenly flings open.

It's late at night, everyone else in the house has long since gone to bed.

I squeak and immediately yank my hand out of my underwear. But that only makes it more obvious what I've been trying to do.

Noah steps into my room and closes the door behind him. I can see his features outlined in the moonlight streaming through my window.

"Get out," I whisper-yell, not wanting to wake anyone else up.

"Not a chance of that." I can see his smirk even in the dim lighting of the room. "I want you to finish what you were doing, little stalker."

My cheeks flush because I've been hoping he somehow missed what I've been doing. He prowls towards my bed, lounging at the foot of it like this is an everyday occurrence.

"Go ahead, Sky. Finish what you started. I dare you."

There's a challenge in his voice, and his words, obviously, and it must do something to my head because...I take his dare.

I slide my covers down so he can clearly see my hand push under my underwear. The heat of his gaze makes it even more obscene. I'm suddenly much more aware of the ache between my legs, my breath, the beating of my heart.

And how much I wish it was his hand making me come.

My fingers begin to press on my clit, the feeling foreign and kind of wrong. Maybe in time I'll be an expert at this...but right now...

"You were picturing me fucking you, weren't you, little stalker?" Noah purrs all of a sudden. And a fucking moan slips from my lips. "You were picturing it was my dick sliding between those legs. I bet your pussy's the tightest I'd ever feel. There's no way anyone's been in there yet."

I should kick him out, slap him in the face for what he's saying. But the sound of his voice and his mean, dirty words are acting as tinder for the fire building inside me.

"Is this the first time you've touched yourself? Or did you come home after that day in the restaurant and make yourself come? You're obsessed with seeing me get off...of imagining it was you...aren't you?"

He purrs the words and a soft moan slips from my lips. "You're delusional if you think you could ever make me come," I whisper, trying to hold on to some sort of dignity.

"Oh really. Then who are you thinking about right now?" he taunts as my fingers start to move faster across my clit.

"Kyle."

His name escapes from my lips. Probably because he's the only one I've actually had an interaction with where I haven't been insulted.

Noah rears back briefly before quickly recovering.

"I don't want to hear that asshole's name come out of your mouth again," he growls.

I would have been thrown off my game, but his thumb has started lightly rubbing my ankle and it's distracting me from the fluent 'asshole' coming out of his mouth.

"Hmm..." I muse, slightly out of breath as I continue to touch myself. It feels good...but I can't quite reach where I'm desperate to get to.

I've crossed the line...no, I've crossed the fucking wall. And there's no way Noah and I are leaving this moment without me getting an orgasm out of it.

Noah would get far too much satisfaction from leaving me wanting.

His hand suddenly grips my ankle tightly and I squeak in surprise. "You think Kyle could make you come? You think he could leave you dripping? Leave you screaming his name?"

The sound of his voice is the sexiest soundtrack I could have playing, quite honestly.

"Answer me!"

"No," I whimper as the heat flares inside me once again.

"Good girl."

Another moan comes out because Noah Fontaine calling me 'good girl' is almost more than I can stand.

"Say it again."

It's official. I've lost my mind. I'm lost in lust, drunk on the feeling of power I have from Noah's attention focused on me like this. And God how I hate him for it.

But I've never wanted anything more.

"Oh...you like being my good girl," Noah murmurs, while his hand slides up my leg. I press on my clit harder. But something's still missing.

His hand keeps going until his fingers are running along the seam of my panties. My breath is literally coming out in gasps with the anticipation of what he'll do. My fingers have stopped playing with my clit.

"Did I say you could stop?"

I write about my characters having 'big dick energy', but I realize at this moment that I've never understood exactly what that even meant before now. The term equalled Noah. I'm quite sure there is no one else that could hold my attention like this. Have my heart beat desperate for every word that comes out of his mouth.

His finger pushes under the edge of my underwear, until he's grazing my sensitive skin. "Admit it," he says softly, his finger moving slightly back and forth.

"What?—" I swear the air is glittering around us. I didn't recognize my surroundings.. or myself. He has me under some kind of spell.

"Admit you wanted it to be you that I was fucking today."

I grit my teeth, shaking my head as his finger surges up and brushes my soaking wet slit.

"I'll give you what you want, little stalker. All you need to do is ask. No. Beg."

"Stop calling me that," I growl, my fingers moving feverishly again. Desperate to get there...before he *makes* me get there.

"Isn't it fitting, though? You always watching me when I'm about to come. Kind of seems fair that I get to watch you right now...doesn't it?"

"It was all by accident...I assure you." My voice is breathless, and I moan again as it starts to feel really, really good.

Noah slips his fingers out from my panties and I pathetically whimper. Which only makes the cocky jerk smile harder. The effect is dazzling, and I find myself taking a mental picture of it and wishing I could keep it forever.

"Don't worry, little stalker. I've got you," he whispers, his gaze focused on my face, an almost confused expression replacing his smug grin.

I want...more. Even though everything inside of me is saying I'm not ready.

"Give me your hand," he growls, and without thinking, I slide my fingers to meet his. He moves my fingers until they're hitting the right spot, feeling far better than my earlier pathetic attempts. His hand stays on top of mine as he slowly moves my fingers over my clit, finding the perfect rhythm, doing his utmost best not to touch me. Leaving it completely up to me. There's nothing but the sound of our breaths in the room.

I'm getting close, far closer than I was before. It's building inside of me, and everything in me hates that it's focused on...him. It's his glittering eyes that I'm staring into, it's his golden hair that I'm wishing my hands could touch. It's his full lips that mine long for.

"That's it, little stalker. Give it to me."

My eyes start to flutter shut as I make it to the precipice. "Look at me," he snaps, and they immediately fly open, like he's the puppet master holding my strings.

His lips are curled arrogantly, and I gasp as I finally fall over the edge, more pleasure than I could ever comprehend coursing through my body. Our eyes are locked the entire time, but as soon as I finish, as soon as my pulse starts to slow, and my breathing regains some dignity, he's off the bed like it's burned him.

"It's a funny thing, Sky," he purrs as he stands by the door, a huge tent in the front of his pants.

"What? What's funny?" I ask, my voice barely above a whisper.

"You've probably never been kissed and yet you're going to think of me every time you get off for the rest of your life because I'm the one who gave you you're first orgasm. Like I said. It's a funny thing to think about."

With that, he winks at me and then strides out of the room like he didn't just carve a hole in my aching chest.

I lay there on the bed, disgust and shame running through me like a river. My panties are wet, and there's a tingly feeling in my veins.

I don't fall asleep that night, dreading every second that will bring me closer to seeing his smug face again.

* * *

It's the afternoon, and the day has actually gone...smoothly. For the most part, I've been ignored, something I'd started to long for, which I used to hate. The bell rings, and I'm walking out of class when I see him.

Kyle.

He strides towards me with a huge black eye. His gaze is locked on mine the entire time.

People are whispering around me, and I find myself frozen in place.

Kyle walks right up to me.

"What happened to you?" I gasp, my hand reaching up tentatively as if I'm actually going to touch his face, before I remember myself and hastily drop it down.

"What do you think happened?" he retorts.

It takes me a second, until my eyes flick over Kyle's shoulder, and I see Noah standing at the end of the hallway, surrounded by his usual adoring crowd.

Noah.

Noah did this. But why?

"I don't understand. I thought you were...friends?"

I guess at least as close as anyone is friends with Noah. When you're a king, I'm not sure you're ever friends with the people you think are beneath you.

"Evidently, Fontaine has a problem with me talking to his stepsister." The word *stepsister* comes out in a mocking tone, and I flinch, thinking of what happened last night. And thinking of what would happen, and what people would say if anyone ever found out what happened in my bedroom last night.

That's all I need. I'm pretty sure that rumor would eventually find its way back to my mother, and I couldn't imagine the look on her face if she heard it.

Thankfully, Kyle continues on as if I'm not having a panic attack in front of him.

"Too bad for him, I recognize gold when it's in front of me," he murmurs. Kyle brushes a piece of hair out of my face and slides it behind my ear, winking at me with his good eye before he strides past like he hasn't just dropped that bomb.

I'm feeling a bit lightheaded when I glance down the hallway, and Noah and I lock stares.

There's a warning in his gaze that should terrify me. But it's offset by the memory of the heat in his eyes last night. The way I held him captive there.

As if he can read my mind, he grabs Stacy next to him, and smashes his lips against hers. She immediately melts against him, and something that suspiciously feels like betrayal shoots down my spine.

I force myself to look away, and I wander down the hallway as if I don't have a care in the world.

And as I slip into class, there's some sick satisfaction inside of me.

Because the entire time Noah was kissing her...he was looking at me.

Chapter 10

Skylar

Sixteen years old

Tonight is homecoming, something that we didn't really care about in our old school, but evidently, here on the island, they're all about celebrating it.

Ironic since most of the people who grow up here never really leave, so what's there to come home to?

The idea of that fills me with dread, and I try to push it away. The countdown of when I can get off this island is like a clock in my head, ticking every hour away as Noah continues to try and make my life as miserable as possible.

It's been months since...the mistake. Or at least that's what I'm calling it in my head. Because I can't really call it anything else.

Since that time, we haven't exchanged more than two words with one another. And that was only me saying 'excuse me' when we almost ran into each other in the hallway as I headed to the bathroom.

He didn't bother to say anything back.

I should be enjoying the silence, enjoying the break. But it feels foreboding in a way, like the silence is just a ruse to get me off guard and he's actually gearing up for something even more sinister than what he'd done to me so far.

Noah is far more intelligent than I've given him credit in the past. Which makes me think that his silence since the debacle in the hallway after he punched Kyle is Noah's way of just lying in wait until he can pounce and do his worst.

As for me, I apparently don't have a self preservation mechanism to speak of since tonight I'm attending the homecoming dance with none other than Kyle.

In my defense, he kind of wore me down.

He started asking a month ago, and I had declined for the first week with a sure no. But that didn't seem to deter him, asking every day the following week too, until my answer switched from a solid 'no, thanks' to something a bit gentler like 'I'm busy' or the not so fool proof 'I have to study.' When the third week came around and he still didn't look to be losing any steam, I finally relented. Or at least I pretended it was his persistence that changed my mind.

I don't want to think too hard on the real reason why I'm going to this godforsaken homecoming dance. Like hell I'll admit that my answer only changed after I overheard Stacy bragging in the school hallway about everything she and Noah have planned for tonight.

Admitting to that means that I care. And I don't care. Not one bit.

Staring at myself through my bedroom's mirror reflection, I smooth down the light pink dress Daisy and I had found at the mall in Falmouth last weekend. The minute Daisy learnt I was going to the dance, she made sure we took a day trip off the island to buy me the perfect dress. In all honesty, I really didn't care what I wore, but the outing was a welcome relief from the tension I constantly experience in our new home.

I was so happy to get out of Thatcher's Bay that I made the rookie mistake of texting my father and telling him both Daisy and I would be on the mainland that day. He replied back saying at one point during the day he would definitely meet up with us to have some father daughter time but neither of us had really expected him to show. In fact, I knew Daisy would have preferred to chew her arm off than have him tag along and ruin our fun with his presence.

It was to both of our surprise when we got off the ferry and there he was, a giant smile on his face like it made his year seeing us.

"Little bird," he bellowed, his arms outstretched like I was still a small child that was going to run towards him and jump into his arms.

It was kinda sad, but for a second, I actually felt like doing it.

I wonder when that faded away completely, the need to feel loved by your parents. It was definitely fading as I got older, but not fast enough. It was my fervent wish that one day I would wake up and truly not care what he did.

One person shouldn't have the power to make or break your day.

My mind immediately flicked to Noah with that thought, but I gritted my teeth and pushed his image out of my head.

My father's grin had dimmed when neither of us made a big deal that he was there, but he quickly recovered, giving both of us tight hugs once we got to him. I was still feeling off from our trip across the water. As much as I longed to get off the island, having to be on the boat for that long had been pure hell. The water was choppy today, the waves licking at the boat and sending it rocking back and forth. One of the deck chairs had almost knocked me over the railing, and I'd finally gone to sit inside on the benches, squeezing my knees to my chest and taking deep breaths.

"Daisy," my father said affectionately as he gave my sister a hug.

"Grant," she drawled disrespectfully, and I elbowed her in the side as soon as he let her go with a frown. She shot me a look and I gave her a begging one in return.

I may have been in a constant state of unhappiness with my father, but that didn't mean I wanted the visits I did get with him to suck. I knew what that was from. It was because a big part of me thought that the more amazing I was, the more interesting I was, the more exciting I was...the more he'd think about me.

And maybe it would get him to want to see me.

I knew it was pathetic, thinking like that.

But I couldn't help it.

It was the part of me I hoped faded in time.

"So I hear we're going to be looking for dresses," he commented as we got into his rusty metal truck that I was always surprised was still running. He'd had it for as long as I could remember. I don't think it actually got that many miles since he preferred to use his motorcycle, so maybe that accounted for the fact that it was somehow still kicking despite him having it since before I was born.

"Who are the lucky guys?"

Daisy made a snorting noise from the front passenger seat and I glared at the back of her head.

"I think Daisy has like three dates," I offered. "One to start the night, one to have dinner with, and one to dance with."

My father shot Daisy a surprised look. "More and more like me every day," he spouted proudly.

Daisy stiffened in her seat, her face paling.

I wish he hadn't said that.

Our father might think that pointing out the obvious, that Daisy is just like him, a free spirit that nothing and no one could chain down, is something that they could bond over, but he'd be wrong. For her, those similarities between them only makes her hate him more.

Or at least that was the theory I had going.

I hadn't been exaggerating though. I was pretty sure Daisy had said yes to at least three guys for Homecoming. And I was pretty positive they all knew about each other, and just didn't care. And why would they? When they could have Daisy.

I couldn't imagine that situation happening to me though.

Not that there was ever any danger something like that ever would.

I'm not my sister.

"Skylar's got a big date too. She's going with the school's basketball star," said Daisy, obviously trying to move the attention from herself and onto me.

My father's eyes widened in shock in the rearview mirror, and a pulse of disgruntlement flashed through me.

"Is that so, little bird? Good for you."

I muttered "thanks", feeling embarrassed by how surprised he'd been. Not that my mother's reaction had been any different.

My father talked the entire way to the mall, not seeming to mind that neither of us were really talking back. Evidently, he'd just gotten back from California. He rode his motorcycle all the way from the northern tip to the southern one, not stopping until he got to the border with Mexico. I listened avidly to all of his tales, trying to picture the things he'd seen.

I wondered if I'd ever get out there.

When we finally got to the mall parking lot, Daisy pushed open her door like the cab was on fire and she was desperate to get out.

I followed at a more leisurely pace. As we walked across the parking lot, my father took the nape of my neck and gave it a gentle squeeze.

"How's your new school going?" he asked, actually sounding genuinely interested.

For a second, I got the insane urge to tell him everything that had happened. To walk him through the almost daily embarrassments I had thanks to Noah. Tell him about the story I was writing, the one with a character who actually took control of her own life.

But that urge immediately disappeared when an attractive woman in a tight skirt walked by, and my dad's attention was immediately redirected.

"It's going great," I finally say with a sigh, knowing he wouldn't hear me now anyway. Not while his attention was on something far more prettier and shiner than me.

Daisy shot me a knowing look at the lie.

She knows I'm not exactly settling in well at Bayshore High. And even though her knee jerk reaction was to go full protective big sister mode and fix it so that I don't feel like such a pariah at our new school, I made sure to nix that in the bud. Having Daisy defend me, because I wasn't doing a good enough job of it myself, only reminds me of my shortcomings. And I've got enough of those.

After the skirt with legs disappeared from his view, my dad finally remembered that we were there too, making up for his distraction by pretending he was actually interested in finding us the perfect dress to take to the dance. As we walked through the mall, going in and out of the stores, he tried his best to keep conversation going by asking us questions about our new home life. Tired of his lame attempts at sounding interested in what was happening in our lives, Daisy eventually turned the conversation back to him. It didn't take much coaxing for him to start going on and on about his own adventures.

We both knew that our father's favorite subject has always been himself.

We'd gone into at least five stores before I found a dress that I liked. It was more on the expensive side, but Daisy forced me to try it on.

I hadn't wanted to look in the mirror in the dressing room, but eventually I had, slightly taken aback by the image of myself in the mirror.

I looked...good. Something I didn't think very often of myself. The pink shade of the dress made my skin look more olive than its usual drab paleness. It also accented the highlights in my hair that I'd gotten from trying to walk my frustrations out every day after school.

"Sky..." My sister gasped as she forced her way past the curtain into the dressing room. I immediately crossed my arms in front of myself self-consciously.

"Don't do that," she commanded. "Don't hide yourself away. It's okay to let people see..."

"Let people see?" I whispered.

"Let people see who's the actual star in our family," she answered back with a shy smile before leaving the room without another word.

I stared after her in shock, a warm, bubbly feeling fizzing up inside of me.

"Little bird, let's see it!" my father called, my sister obviously having said something.

I took a deep breath and pushed the curtain aside with a sigh, walking out of the dressing area, self-consciousness tearing at my skin.

My father took a step back, putting his palms over his heart feigning he was having a heart attack.

"What is this? When did my little girl grow up?" he announced loudly in horror. There were a couple of other shoppers in the store, and they were watching him, amused.

I couldn't help the giggle that slipped out of me, and my father's grin widened.

"You look beautiful, little bird," he said softly, and I had the strange urge to cry.

After I purchased the pink dress, and Daisy had gotten a shiny silver one that reminded me of a disco ball, we'd eaten dinner in the Italian restaurant that was connected to the mall, and then my father dropped us off at the ferry.

I hugged him hard before he left, like I always did, savoring the sight of him as he walked away, because a part of me always wondered if this was the last time. If one day he'd really just disappear somewhere, never to return again.

He didn't wait to see if we got on the ferry. He just waved goodbye from the truck, a wide grin on his face before he drove off.

And immediately, an edge of melancholy coursed through me.

"Chin up, Sky. At least you have a killer dress," said Daisy cheerfully.

Unlike me, she seemed lighter now that my father was gone. I gave her a fake smile that just made her roll her eyes. And we walked on to the ferry.

The water had been better on the way back, but I still kept inside, wanting to be as far away from it as possible.

"Kyle's here," my mom calls out from down the hall, breaking me out of my thoughts. A rush of anxiety floods through me at the thought of what might lay ahead, and I take a few deep breaths.

Daisy's done my hair in loose curls and given me a pair of sparkly fake diamond earrings. Thanks to her, I'm also wearing more makeup than I usually do. Some blush on my cheeks so I don't look so pale. Silvery eyeshadow on my lids and some thick mascara. A swipe of bubblegum pink lip gloss.

On the outside, I'm practically a new woman.

On the inside though...I'm still just me.

"Pull yourself together. You can do this," I whisper to myself as I open the door and head down the hall, only sparing a short glance at Noah's closed door.

Kyle's chatting easily with my mother and Curt as I get to the edge of the living room, and he doesn't notice me standing there.

It gives me one more second to put on a brave face before I walk into the room.

"Oh, honey, you look beautiful," croons my mother a second later.

A blush floods my cheeks at the look on Kyle's face. There's no denying that he's slightly dumbstruck at the sight of me.

Shaking his head a little, he strides forward with a small box in his hand.

"Good thing I had my mom help with these. Wouldn't want anything to ruin the perfection you've got going on tonight."

It's a sweet thing to say, even if corny, but to my disappointment butterflies don't assault my insides at his words. He opens the box to reveal a corsage of sweet white flowers with pale pink ribbon wound around them.

"They're beautiful," I say softly as he slips it on my wrist.

"You're beautiful," he responds meaningfully.

I smile at him shyly and then let my mom take what feels like a hundred different pictures of us before she finally lets us go.

Kyle has an old pickup truck that reminds me of my dad's, and he escorts me to the door.

Daisy had left in a rented limousine with a pack of her friends a little while ago, but I'd refused her offer when she asked if we wanted to ride with them. There was no way I wanted to sit around with her friends for that long, forced to make idle chit chat.

It was going to be hard enough conversing with my date all night.

"Excited for tonight?" Kyle asks as he starts the truck and we begin to drive.

"Yeah," I say with fake excitement, praying he can't see right through me.

Apparently he can't, because he talks about last year's dance and how much fun tonight's going to be. They're having dinner at the dance, so we don't stop anywhere before we get to the school.

The parking lot is completely packed, and you can hear loud music coming from the open gymnasium. Kyle has me wait in the truck while he trots around and proceeds to open the door for me.

He puts out his arm for me to take, and I slide my arm through, noting how strong his arm feels.

We get to the gymnasium doors and my mouth opens in surprise at what they've done to the place. There's thick black drapes covering the sides, and black tulle artfully hangs from the rafters so it doesn't look like a school gym at all, with the exception of the court floor. There's large circle tables set up around the room draped in black table cloths, and silver plate settings and centerpieces are set on top of them. This year's theme is 'starry nights', and they're going all in. There's a dance floor set up in the middle of the room and a stage set up on the far right side. There's only one musician up there playing music on the piano right now, but I know there will be a full band later on.

"Looks pretty good, doesn't it?" Kyle comments as he leads me to a table filled with his friends.

Immediately, I tense up as we approach. I'd done my best to stay as far away from that group of people as possible, since they're also Noah's cronies, but with no sign of Noah, they actually give me polite smiles when we get to the table. Some of them even give me appreciative stares.

Kyle helps me into my seat and then settles down next to me, his arm going along the top of my seat so that his fingers can stroke my shoulder softly. Goosebumps spring up under his touch, and I shift, feeling slightly uncomfortable.

Everyone talks around me, and for a couple of minutes, I almost fool myself into thinking the night won't be that bad.

That is until I feel it.

Him.

As if we're connected by a string, I glance over my shoulder and see him and Stacy walking through the entrance. His gaze is locked on mine.

Meanwhile, Kyle continues to stroke my shoulder. I drag my gaze away from Noah's, who looks unreal in his navy blue fitted suit, something I'm pretty sure most teenage boys would never be able to pull off without looking like a fool.

Instead, he looks like a freaking model. It would be great if just one time he could look terrible.

I study my date. He looks good as well, but younger...softer. I know really nothing about Kyle other than the small details he's mentioned in class, but something just tells me he hasn't experienced the spark of sorrow that Noah has.

Two people at the table abruptly stand up. "We'll see you all later," the guy says somewhat nervously. I'm pretty sure he's on the basketball team as well.

When he and his date walk away, I lean towards Kyle. "What's going on?" I whisper.

Before Kyle can answer, Noah and Stacy are sitting at the table.

Horror clenches my insides. I foolishly thought I was safe. It never occurred to me that someone would sit there until Noah arrived.

I also notice that Noah doesn't help Stacy into her seat.

And he doesn't have his arm around her.

I'm not sure why that fills me with so much satisfaction.

Stacy is beautiful tonight. She looks like she fits with Noah.

And I hate that.

Because I'm sure if I was standing next to Noah in front of a mirror, I wouldn't feel the same.

Not that I would ever be thinking about that when it comes to my tormentor.

"Chicken or steak?" someone asks from behind me. I glance back to see one of the catering staff standing there with a tray full of plates.

"Chicken, please," I say, until I notice there's pecans on the accompanying salad. I glance over at the steak; the salad on that plate is luckily pecan free.

"Sorry, can I have the steak? I'm really allergic to pecans."

The staff member looks annoyed but switches the plates for me.

"I didn't know you're allergic to pecans," comments Kyle.

Of course he doesn't know, I think to myself, because he doesn't know anything about me. But out loud I simply say, "It's the only allergy I have. All the other nuts are fine. But my throat completely closes off with pecans."

"That's too bad," the girl next to me says. "My mom makes the best pecan pie."

I nod, not really knowing what to say, because I doubt that there would be an opportunity for me to try her mom's pecan pie anyway. The staff member gives the rest of the table plates and everyone starts eating.

"I want a drink," Stacy whines. Okay, maybe she doesn't whine, but that's how her voice sounds to me every time I hear it.

"Who's stopping you?" Noah says, taking a bite of steak. "Go get a drink."

Stacy's eyes widen in embarrassment and her face flushes.

"You are such an asshole," she spits, and he just winks at her... which makes her melt.

I should say I'm disgusted that she folded so easily after he was such a jerk, but I kind of get the magic of the wink.

At least a little bit.

She gets up from the table in search of whatever drink she's jonesing for, and I shift uncomfortably in my chair, because Noah's attention seems to be glued to Kyle's hand on my shoulder.

Everyone's talking around us, but Noah's voice cuts through the conversations.

"I seem to recall us having a conversation a while back," Noah says in a soft, dangerous voice.

The girl next to me whimpers a little, like she's either terrified, or she's in heat from the sound of Noah's voice. It really could go either way.

Kyle, for his part, just lifts his chin. "It was a good chat, Fontaine. But I decided I was going to go in a different direction."

It's obvious they're talking about the conversation where Kyle ended up with a black eye. Again, I shift uneasily in my chair.

Everyone's eyes are locked on Noah right now. It's very obvious he hasn't been challenged like this very often...if at all.

"Is that so?" Noah simply responds as Stacy comes back to the table holding two glasses of punch.

She seems unaware of the tension in the air, and instead pulls a small flask from her rose gold pink clutch.

"A little something extra," she gloats as she unscrews the cap and pours a generous portion into the two cups. "Anyone else want some?"

Everyone at the table eagerly pushes their cups forward, none of them even looking to see if a teacher is watching. She adds some to every cup and then glances at me.

"Hey, stalker. Do you want some? Or will Mommy get mad at you?"

I roll my eyes exaggeratedly. "I'm good," I respond sweetly.

I glance over at Daisy who's the reigning queen of her table with the popular kids from her class. As if sensing my stare, she glances over at me and gives me a questioning look. I see a similar flask at their table and hope Daisy will be safe tonight, because I know there's no way that she's missing out on that.

"So tell me, stalker, are you always a stick in the mud, or is that a recent thing since you moved here?"

Hearing Noah's cruel nickname for me coming out of her lips feels like sandpaper on my skin.

Kyle stiffens beside me. "Shut up, Stacy," he snaps, and a flicker of surprise swirls inside me. Kyle definitely has some balls.

"Excuse me?" Stacy says slowly, throwing daggers at my date. "Since when did you become so pussywhipped?"

But then I'm even more surprised by what happens next.

"You heard him. Shut the fuck up," Noah drawls, knocking back some of the punch.

Stacy gapes at him, somehow shocked at what he'd said.

They'd been on and off for years from what I'd heard. . So how is she still so surprised when he acts like this?

Although I don't dwell on that for too long since I'm a little shocked myself. Did Noah defend me just now, or is my imagination playing tricks on me?

Stacy pouts through dinner as everyone else attempts stilted conversations, tiptoeing around Noah because clearly...he's in a mood.

"I can't say I remember Homecoming being like this last year," whispers Kyle, and I giggle...because I imagine not.

Noah's glower deepens when he hears me laugh.

Finally, the miserable dinner is over and the staff come to collect our plates.

Stacy recovers from the fit she's been throwing as soon as it's clear that the Homecoming Kings and Queens are about to be announced. She takes Noah's hand and drags him towards the stage where the principal is making some kind of speech that I'm trying to drown out.

I manage to keep myself from watching them walk away.

"I'm going to go out on a limb and say you probably aren't a dancer," says Kyle, a dimple in his cheek as he smiles that I hadn't noticed before.

My first instinct is to agree with him, to tell him I prefer to watch rather than do...anything. But as soon as I open my mouth, disgust floods through me, because honestly...I'm sick of always being that person.

And maybe tomorrow I'll be back to being that girl, but tonight I'd like to pretend to be someone else.

"I'd actually love to dance," I respond lightly, enjoying the surprise in his eyes just as the principal announces that Noah and Stacy have won King and Queen of our grade.

Kyle's mouth curls up in disgust. "Shocker," he spits. My gaze automatically goes to the stage where Noah's standing next to Stacy, a scowl on his beautiful face, like the win has actually disgusted him.

"He doesn't look happy up there," I murmur absentmindedly, and Kyle hums next to me.

"He's always been an asshole, but he's definitely taken it to another level lately." Kyle's face is thoughtful, and his stare darts from Noah to me, and then back to Noah, his lips pursed in thought. "I wonder..." he murmurs, before his voice trails off.

Whatever he's about to say, I forget, because they've just announced that Daisy's won queen of her grade even though we've just started at this school. I leap from my seat and cheer for her as she ambles up to the stage slowly, not looking the least surprised at her win.

For a second I imagine it's me up there, in a different life, if I was a different girl. I can see the admiration in everyone's face, feel the touch of the fake crown on my hair. I see it all in my mind's eye for just that brief moment.

And then I blink and, of course, it goes away, because there's no chance that something like that would happen to me in this lifetime.

I watch wistfully as one of Daisy's dates twirls her around the dance floor. She throws her head back and laughs with such exuberance that the whole room can hear it. I wonder what that would feel like, to be able to laugh like that, with such abandon.

All eyes are on her...except for one pair.

Noah's.

He's dancing with Stacy, but her back is facing away from me. She's nestled against his chest, and his eyes are locked on mine, like he's not really dancing with her...like he's actually dancing with me.

I realize something then, something I hadn't before. Where everyone else might miss me in the shadows, Noah sees me. He's seen me since that first time I met him.

And I'm not sure what to think about that.

When it's time for everyone else to join the homecoming court on the dance floor, Kyle takes my hand and leads me there, wrapping his arms around my waist, and holding me a little bit closer than I'm comfortable with.

We start dancing, and I try to forget the heat of Noah's gaze. I pretend to listen as Kyle talks about basketball practice, and when his first game starts, but it's only when he mentions the college scouts he hopes will see him this year that gets my attention.

"You want to leave the island?" I ask, surprised.

I had Kyle pegged for a lifelong hometown boy through and through. There's a community college on the other side of town where most of the students end up attending before they begin their lives as fishermen or whatever else people do on this island.

Kyle shrugs. "I mean, what guy who plays basketball doesn't dream of playing pro? And that definitely requires getting out of Thatcher's Bay." He gazes around the room wistfully. "But you're right. I'll miss this place the second I'm gone. I can't imagine leaving it forever."

I stare around the converted gym, trying to see what he sees. I picture the small town, the smell of salt in the air, the waves licking at the rocky shore. I just can't see the magic that he does.

I inhale sharply when I feel the soft stroke of fingertips sliding along my bare back. I quickly glance behind me, only to see Noah passing by, Stacy's hands on the back of his suit coat like a barnacle.

He's turned away from me, but I know it was him that touched me.

The question is...why?

I suddenly feel overheated. "I'm going to take a bathroom break," I murmur as soon as the song ends.

"Do you want me to come with you?" Kyle asks attentively.

"To the girls bathroom?" I tease, scrunching up my nose. Kyle laughs awkwardly. "Oh yeah, right. I'll just be over there when you come back." He points to where some of his friends have sat back down at the table where we ate. I notice that Stacy and Noah have disappeared from the room.

I go out into the dimly lit hallway and make my way into the blissfully empty bathroom. I stall after I finish, standing in front of the mirror noting how...alive I look. Kind of like after that "mistake" with Noah.

Too bad it takes misery for me to feel anything.

Wondering how much longer I have to stay, I make my way out to the hallway, only to be immediately pushed against the wall.

I squeak as a hand slaps across my mouth and stare up into Noah's fiery gaze. I'm caught off guard for a moment, but thankfully my survival instinct kicks in and I start to struggle. But all Noah does is laugh cruelly at my poor attempts to go free. When he loosens his grip, I freeze as his hand moves away from my mouth and he softly trails a finger from my lips, down my neck, to my collarbone. He traces along it, almost absentmindedly.

"What do you want?" I growl.

"Why does he look like that?" Noah answers instead.

"What are you talking about?"

"Kyle. Why does he look like that?"

"Look like what?" I counter confused.

"Like he knows what it feels like to be inside of you."

I gasp, my eyes wide and my cheeks darkening. I honestly had never gone there in my head with Kyle. For heaven sakes, I hadn't even kissed him. I haven't even been kissed.

Before I can say anything in my defense, Noah leans forward, his lips brushing against the edge of my ear, goosebumps trailing down my skin. "The only person who's going to know what that feels like is me," he whispers, the threat hanging between us. "Remember that."

I'm frozen as he abruptly pushes away from me and ambles down the hall like he hasn't just rocked my world.

I'm achy...hungry. My breath is coming out in gasps. I'm still leaning against that wall when Kyle comes out to look for me. He stares at me questioningly. "Everything okay?"

I force myself to move off from the wall.

"Everything's fine," I murmur, and I let him grab my hand to lead me back into the gym where the dancing is still going.

For the rest of the night I try to have fun on the dance floor. Emphasis on try. With Kyle's friends actually being nice to me, and Noah and Stacy rooted on the other side of the room, after a while, it doesn't feel too hard to pretend that I am.

The only thing that prevents me from actually enjoying this rite of passage that is Homecoming is the constant flashbacks of what happened in the hallway with my stepbrother. I can't stop thinking about what Noah said. I can't stop thinking of his lips brushing against my skin, the hard weight of his body against mine.

I just can't stop thinking about...him.

I'm so consumed in my own thoughts that when something cold and wet falls on my head as Kyle and I are slow dancing to some song, it takes me a while to register it. I let out a small scream and turn, just as more cold punch is splashed right at my face. Stacy and three of her friends are gathered around me, and before I can move, the rest of their cups are dumped all over my head. I stand there, dripping wet, my beautiful pink dress completely ruined, my mascara streaking down my face, and my hair plastered against my head. The music is cut off and everyone's just staring at me before they start laughing.

I gape at the three of them.

"Why?" I stammer.

"Because Cinderella always has to return back to her place at midnight. We just wanted to make sure that you remembered that," says Stacy sweetly.

Just beyond her shoulder is Noah, leaning against a column with some of his friends, laughing just as hard as everyone else.

Betrayal sparks through me. To see him standing like that laughing at me, right after that moment we just shared in the hallway. He truly is the devil.

Someone pushes past me and then Daisy's there, her arm reared back. She punches Stacy right in the face, and blood explodes from her nose.

Stacy screams loudly and the laughing abruptly stops. Daisy looks like some kind of avenging angel as she stands there, glaring furiously at Stacy and her friends.

"Don't ever touch my sister again, bitch," she growls, rearing back her arm to hit her again.

Stacy cowers and Daisy's date grabs her arm before she can do any more damage. There are teachers pushing through from the edges of the room, the worst chaperones of all time if you ask me. Kyle's put his arm around me comfortingly, but it's the way he's staring down at me that really gets under my skin—pity.

He reeks of it and how I hate it.

I rip myself away from his grip and walk out of the gymnasium as slowly and confidently as you can when you look like a drowned rat.

The cold air assaults my senses the second I step outside, and angry tears burn my eyes. When someone bursts through the door behind me, I don't have to turn around to know that it's Daisy, ever my hero.

Thankfully, she doesn't say a word. She just takes my hand and squeezes it, standing next to me as I stare out into the darkness.

I try my best, but the tears I'm trying so hard to hold in finally come streaming down my face.

"I hate this place," I whisper, and she squeezes my hand again.

"I know."

She allows me to sit there in my sorrow for a few more minutes.

"Come on, squirt. Let's go home," she says softly after a while. "I'll call us an Uber."

But just as she says it, a flashy red convertible drives right up to us and stops abruptly. I feel Daisy stiffen beside me, almost as if she's getting ready for another fight tonight.

My eyes are still blurry from my unshed tears, as I try to make out the dark haired boy, with a little too much swagger to his step, walk towards us.

"Don't start," I hear my sister call out, stopping the boy in his tracks.

"I wasn't going to," he replies with a smirk.

"Sure you weren't." Daisy scoffs. "Just go away, Derrick. I'm not in the mood for you to give me shit about your sister. She fucking deserved the shiner she got," Daisy adds with venom in her tone.

"I'm not here for my sister. It's yours I'm worried about," he says sympathetically, eyeing my drenched state up and down. "Stacy really did a number on you, didn't she?"

I'm still too raw of the sheer embarrassment that I just experienced to answer him.

"Yeah. My sister sometimes goes a little overboard when she's in one of her moods. Sorry about that," he mumbles disappointingly.

Sister?

Does he mean Stacy is his sister? How come I didn't know she had a brother? Or how Daisy is somehow friends with him? Even though by the loathing way she's staring at him, I'm not sure they'll stay friends for long.

"How about I give you two a ride home?" he asks in earnest.

"Pass," Daisy replies coldly, digging her heels in. "One of my dates will take us," she lies.

"Get in the car, petal," he retorts evenly, only this time it doesn't sound like it's a request anymore. More like an order.

I stand there watching this unexpected interaction, mouth agape as they continue their deadlock stare. It's only when I start to shiver from the cold air hitting my drenched frame that Daisy relents.

"Fine. You win. This time," she tells him, after wrapping her arm protectively over me to warm me up.

Not missing a beat, Derrick opens the passenger door while Daisy ushers me into the car, but I hesitate climbing in, knowing that I'll end up staining the expensive white leather seats.

"It's okay. I'll make sure the dry cleaning comes out of Stacy's allowance." Derrick winks at me.

Unlike his sister, he's got kind playful eyes. Eyes that make me trust that he's telling me the truth. That he actually cares what his sister did to me and that he will make sure she pays some kind of penance for her crimes.

Not that it matters.

She's made sure to paint a scarlet letter on my chest for all of Thatcher Bay to see.

The damage is done.

I wallow in my misery in the back seat, while Derrick and Daisy whisper in the front. I don't even try to listen in. Thankfully mom and Curt are already asleep by the time we get home. Just imagining my mom's face if she saw me this way, churns my stomach.

Daisy tries to distract me by spending the rest of the night in my room, stuffing me with junk food while we watch trash reality television.

But no matter how hard she tries, she can't remedy what happened tonight.

Stacy might have made me the laughing stock of all of Bayshore High.

But that's not why I'm hurting.

It's the fact that I know it was Noah who planned it all.

Down to the very last detail.

Chapter 11

Skylar

Seventeen years old

One year later

"You're coming and that's the end of it," Daisy commands after stealing my laptop off my bed in front of me and holding it hostage behind her back.

"Fat chance that's happening. Give it to me!" I order just as loud, going up to my knees on the mattress and swinging my arms aimlessly about in the hopes I'll grab hold of my irritating big sister and rescue my laptop.

"Fat chance that's happening," she parrots, stepping farther away from my grasp.

"Damn it, Daisy. I told you before that I don't want to go to a stupid party."

"Too bad. You're going."

Nope.

Not happening.

"Give me one good reason why I shouldn't stay home tonight?" I exclaim, annoyed.

"Because!" she shouts out, just as irritated.

"That isn't a reason."

"Fine! You want a reason? Then how is this one for size? We've been living in Thatcher's Bay for over a year now and you still haven't made one friend. One friend, Sky," she repeats, frustrated.

"Kyle is my friend," I defend, even though we've hardly spoken to one another all summer. In fact after the Homecoming debacle, he's kept me at arm's length. Not that I blame him.

"No, Kyle is a fuck boy who wants to get into your pants. There's a difference," she deadpans. "Enough is enough, Sky. You've spent most of our summer vacation locked inside this house like some kind of hermit. If you refuse to put yourself out there willingly, then you best believe I'll force you to."

"Argh! I hate it when you start babbling and it actually starts making sense. You are not my favorite person right now, I can tell you that much," I mumble, falling back to sit on my haunches in defeat.

"Yeah, I am." She smiles triumphantly. "Come on, sis. You have to admit you need a bit of fun, and what better way to get it than going to a back-to-school party?"

"I think you must have me confused with another sister I don't know about. I'm not a big partier. That's you. Not me." I pout, loathing the idea of going to some stranger's house filled with kids who hate me on mere principle alone.

Whoever will be at that party will undoubtedly be from Bayshore High, and we all know I didn't exactly make a big splash when I dipped my toes in that cesspool.

I have Noah to thank for that.

Just the thought of having to interact with actual people has me cringing and hugging my pillow tightly to my chest.

Knowing the reason behind my reluctance, Daisy places my laptop on my desk and then crawls over to me on the bed until she's sitting cross-legged right beside me.

"It's one party, Sky. Not a death sentence," she says softly, running her fingers soothingly through my hair. "You can't stay cooped inside this house all the time. It isn't healthy."

"And getting groped by drunk football players is?" I raise my brows to my hairline.

"You're exaggerating. Hooking up or getting drunk aren't the only things that happen at parties. There's dancing, music—"

"Beer pong," I add with a roll of the eye.

"Probably." She laughs, amused. "But it beats staying locked away in this room all the time. Or did you plan on being a shut-in until you graduated high school?"

"The thought did cross my mind," I snicker. "Besides, I'll have more fun on my own here than I will at some lame-ass party anyway."

"How can you say that when you haven't even tried?" she counters with a tender smile. "Okay, let me put this in a way you'll understand. Do you want to be a great writer or not?" My forehead instantly wrinkles, wondering where she's going with this. "Aren't you always saying that you need to experience life in order to be a great writer? Don't you want to be the next Hemingway, or Plath, or even the next Virginia Woolf? Well, guess what, squirt? They lived a full life, which means you'll have to, too. You're only delaying the inevitable."

"All those writers committed suicide in the end, so you're not making a very good point, Daisy." I shrug with a smug grin.

"Jesus, give me strength!" she blurts out, hands pressed together in prayer and raising her sights to the ceiling to the Almighty himself before laying her eyes on me again. When she finds that all her pleas and prayers are going unheard, Daisy takes a different approach to her dilemma.

"You know what?" she starts, dead serious. "Enough with the pep talk. Just get your ass up and get dressed. I'm not moving an inch until you're ready to leave with me."

"Then I guess no one is going anywhere tonight and you're stuck spending your Saturday night at home with me." I smirk.

"Oh no, I'm not. And neither are you," she says before trying to push me off the bed with her bare feet.

"Daisy, stop!" I giggle, clutching the duvet underneath me to keep my balance.

"I'll stop when your ass is up," she heaves out, doing her best to push me to the floor.

When she successfully gets her way and I fall to the floor, she lets out a victorious cry.

I should have remembered that Daisy doesn't like people telling her no. She's more stubborn than I am, and that's saying something.

"Fine," I relent, brushing off my knees as I get up from the floor. "I'll go to this stupid party with you, but on one condition. If I'm not having a good time, then we leave. No questions asked. I'm not going to stay alone in some corner somewhere while you suck face with some rando. Deal?"

"Deal." She grins widely, outstretching her hand so we can shake on it. I give her hand a little jiggle, unable to be mad at her for forcibly pushing me out of my comfort zone. "Now what should you wear?" She masticates her lip before jumping off the bed to rush toward my closet.

"What's wrong with what I've got on now?" I look down at my clothes, wondering why I can't go with what I'm wearing now.

"You are not going to the last party of the summer in raggedy old shorts and a hoodie that has seen better days," she scoffs, scrolling through the hangers in my closet.

"Why not?"

"First of all, it's August and hot as hell outside, and secondly, if you wear something cute, you'll feel more confident in actually partaking in conversation with someone. Trust me. I know what I'm talking about."

"Whatever," I mumble, but when Daisy picks out a skirt that's short enough for everyone to see my underwear when I bend down, I quickly nix that idea.

"Nope. I'm not wearing that. Nuh-uh." I shake my head, arms crossed on my chest to show I mean business.

"Why not? I love this skirt," she sulks.

"Then you wear it. It's yours, anyway. Mom must have put it in my closet by mistake."

"Fine, then I will," she says unbothered, flinging it on the bed before she continues to rummage through my clothes to find me something to wear.

"Oh, this is perfect!" she shrieks excitedly, taking out a hanger with a cute little white dress hanging from it.

"Daisy, I haven't worn that dress in years. I doubt it even fits me anymore."

"Try it on and see," she retorts with a twinkle in her blue eyes.

Since I know my sister won't let up until I try it on, I snatch the dress out of her hands and put it on. Once I've slithered into it, to my astonishment I realize that the simple summer dress does in fact fit me like a glove, even if a little tight on my chest area. Wanting to make sure that my boobs won't spill out from the top of the damn thing, I walk over to the full-length mirror in my room for a full inspection.

Hmm.

It is pretty, even if it is a little short.

Still, it's better than Daisy's miniskirt. I won't run the risk of flashing anyone in this dress and my cleavage actually looks really good in it. Almost as if the twins are ready for this party too.

I pat the dress down my midriff as I continue to stare at my reflection.

I know the girl staring back is me, but she doesn't look like me at all.

The girl in the mirror looks like she's been *seen* all her life and knows exactly who she is.

She looks like someone who actually has her shit together.

And Lord knows, I don't.

The reflection is a beautiful lie of someone that doesn't exist.

And might never exist.

"Perfect!" Daisy claps enthusiastically, unaware of the somber thoughts strolling in my head. "All you need now is just a little touch-up. I'll go grab my stuff to do your hair and makeup."

"No makeup!" I yell nervously.

"Yes, makeup!"

"No!"

"Yes!"

"Daisy!"

"Skylar!"

Suddenly, we find ourselves in a standoff, neither one of us wanting to budge, but as usual, after a long, insufferable pause, I'm the first to concede.

"You're impossible, you know that?"

"Part of my charm." She grins.

"Yeah, keep telling yourself that. Fine, but only very light makeup. Don't make me look like a clown."

"Like I'd ever do that." She scoffs, insulted, as she rushes out the door before I have time to change my mind.

I sit anxiously in front of the vanity, waiting for my sister to return with her hellish makeup kit. As the seconds pass by, my knee bounces nervously as I try to think of any excuse I can come up with that can get me out of this mess. Unfortunately, when Daisy walks back into my room, her proud smile is so widely stretched on her face, I don't have the heart to steal it away from her.

True to her word, Daisy uses a very light blush to color my cheeks and a pretty shade of pink lip gloss on my lips. She does go a little overboard on the eyes, though, but I actually don't mind the smokey eyeshadow since it makes my silver eyes pop.

Like she forewarned, Daisy ends up using the tiny-ass miniskirt paired with a crop top that shows off her flat stomach. Like my mother, my sister's long blonde hair is sleekly brushed back to perfection, making her look graceful even in skimpy clothes.

When I venture another look in the mirror, it pains me that I don't see any resemblance to either my sister or mother.

All I see is my dad—my deadbeat father.

I have his light gray eyes.

His wild dark brown hair.

Even the cheekbones Daisy raved about when she was adding color to them are his.

But that's where our similarities end.

His loud personality to live life by the edge of his seat was solely inherited by Daisy.

I'm more like Mom.

Reserved.

Private.

But while I always felt that my mom was sometimes too quiet for her own good, my self-imposed silence was due to not wanting people to know just how fucked up I truly am. How restless and angry I am all the time. I should chuck that irksome quality in the short list of things my sperm donor of a father gave me.

It's one of life's great mysteries on how my mom and dad ever got married and stayed together long enough for them to have me and Daisy. Maybe my dad thought he could change his rolling stone ways if he settled down with a good girl like my mom.

But people don't change.

They are what they are, and no outside forces will ever change that.

And in my father's case, he would rather sweet-talk a stranger half his age into his bed than remember to call his daughters on their birthday.

Yeah.

Mom picked a real loser with dear old Dad.

Luckily, I think she finally found a winner with Curt. He treats her like a queen. Always making sure she's happy and feels loved. Doing small things like giving her a foot massage on the couch after a long day's work, or surprising her with flowers and planning romantic date nights for her. His kind heart and affection doesn't end there. It has trickled over to me and my sister too. He always has a kind word for me and Daisy, and tries his best to be present in our lives. He's like Mom in that way, easy-tempered and level-headed. I have yet to hear him lose his shit with anyone.

And when I say anyone, I mean Noah.

Noah is always pushing his buttons.

Always trying to get a rise from him.

And although I have witnessed Curt being cross with his son, I have never seen him being mean just for the sake of it. All I see is sadness in his eyes when Noah rebels against him. What happened between them before we three came into the picture left some deep, ugly scars, and neither one is willing to let them go anytime soon.

"You look hot!" Daisy squeals after she finishes curling my hair into large, long waves.

"You look pretty, too," I state with a meek smile, hating that my thoughts always end up on my in-house bully.

"Fuck pretty. Tell me I look like something you want to eat and devour." She bats her eyelashes seductively at me.

"Ew. God, you're gross," I reply with a giggle. "How about you take it down a notch tonight?"

"No can do, lil' sis. Life is too short for us to be anything but our authentic selves. I might be an acquired taste, but I'd rather be me than anyone else," she says lightheartedly.

But her light features turn serious as she places her chin on my shoulder, hugging my stomach from behind and staring at our combined reflection in the mirror, her gaze locking with mine.

"If you only learn one thing from your big sister, then let it be that. Treasure your uniqueness, Sky. You are one of a kind. There is no one in this world quite like you. And there never will be," she adds the last part with such affection and certainty, that she almost has me believing it.

Again, I can't help but envy my sister. She is her true self twenty-four seven, while I'm still grasping at straws trying to figure out who I am.

It's easier for Daisy.

She is a glorious force of nature while I'm a mild bitter wind.

"Okay, let's go," she urges, giving me a nudge to get out of my seat. "The night awaits."

"Great," I grumble under my breath, already dreading going to this party.

Of course, it's only when we arrive on the other side of the island twenty minutes later where this so-called last summer bash is being held, that my true panic sets in.

"Daisy, whose house is this?" I ask as we drive through an iron gate with the letter M on it.

"Hmm, I forget," she replies aloofly.

"You're lying! I can tell," I shout.

"Fine," she says exasperated. "It's the Monroes."

Shit on a stick.

"The Monroes'? As in Stacy Monroe's house? Noah's girlfriend? Jesus H. Christ, Daisy! Why didn't you tell me this was Stacy's party?!"

"Why would it matter?"

"Hello? Because last time I was at a party with her, she made sure to embarrass me in front of the whole school!"

"That's last year's news. No one remembers that shit anymore."

I remember, I think to myself.

"It's just a party, Sky. Besides, there will be so many people here, I'm sure you won't even run into her anyway. Chillax, will ya?"

It's not her I don't want to run into.

It's Noah.

But I keep that comment to myself too.

I've done my best to not put myself in my stepbrother's path all summer. It hadn't been as hard as I thought it would be either, since he worked with his father for most of it. Like most fishermen in Thatcher's Bay, they would leave the house in the early hours of the morning before anyone else was up and only returned home late mid-afternoon. Like clockwork, the minute Noah came home, he would grab a shower and be out the door again to go God knows where until all hours of the night. The only days that I had to be extra cautious to stick to my room were on the weekends, and even then, he would spend most of his time in the garage fiddling with his bike.

I know when school starts back up again next week, this peaceful reprieve between us is going to end. I just thought I'd still have one last weekend where I could pretend he didn't exist. But now that Daisy has forced me to walk into this lion's den, aka his girlfriend's party, all those hopes are tossed out the window.

Completely oblivious to my troubles, Daisy parks our car among a slew of others and jumps out of it, eager to get her party on. I stew in my seat, wondering if she would even notice if I ran home right now.

As if reading my thoughts, Daisy presses her palms flat on the hood of the car and stares at me.

"Don't even think about it, squirt. Get your ass out of the car. Now, before I drag you out."

I throw her my meanest glower, but it doesn't affect her resolve in the slightest. Instead, she just hikes up her brow, crosses her arms over her chest, and taps her foot on the concrete.

"Don't make me haul your ass out myself."

Shit.

She's not bluffing.

Unlike me, Daisy isn't embarrassed lightly and is all too happy to make a scene if it means getting her way.

Fuming, I get out of the car, making sure to slam the door as I go about it.

"You have one hour. That's it," I warn, pointing a menacing finger at her as I bridge the gap between us.

"Three hours," she negotiates with a mischievous grin on her face.

"Two. Or I'll walk home right now."

"In those heels?" She giggles, pointing to the five-inch heels she insisted I wear tonight. "Good luck with that. Three hours won't kill you. And besides, what's the worst thing that could happen? You having fun? Oh no! The horror!" she teases, linking her arm through mine.

"I really hate you right now," I seethe through gritted teeth.

"No, you don't." She continues to cackle.

Rocks sling to the pit of my stomach as we walk into the large mansion filled to the brim with Bayshore High kids. In true Daisy fashion, all eyes are on her the minute she steps one foot through the door. I try not to notice how everyone greets her with open smiles, only to frown and gawk at me walking at her side. I read the question in their perplexed glances well enough, though—what the hell is *she* doing here?

I don't know, dude. I'm at a loss, too.

I feel you. I don't want to be here either.

Would you believe me if I said I was tricked?

"Let's grab a drink," Daisy utters, unaware of the silent conversations I'm having with the other partygoers that can't stop staring at us.

"You're driving," I protest on a huff, hating that I ever let her convince me to come to this thing.

"Hmm. You're right. Then I guess you'll just have to do my drinking for me," she jokes, nudging my shoulder with hers.

"Sure. I'll get right on that," I retort sarcastically.

The only thing I'll be drinking tonight is water. I'll nurse a red Solo cup and pretend it's vodka for the rest of the night if I have to. No way am I drinking and risk making a fool of myself with all these vultures about.

"Oh, let's go outside! I think that's where the real fun is happening."

"Whatever you say," I grumble, already looking at my watch and counting down the minutes until we can leave.

We walk out to the Monroes' backyard, and instantly, I realize that this shit show just got a whole lot worse.

"POOL PARTY!" Daisy screams at the top of her lungs like she's never seen water before.

Everyone is having a ball, dancing to loud hip-hop music on the green while a bunch of kids are in the pool playing their own version of Marco Polo. To anyone else, this would in fact look like an unmissable party. To me, however, this is my worst nightmare come true. Parties aren't my thing, but add a pool to the equation and my anxiety spikes up to new dimensions.

It's only when Daisy starts stripping off her clothes that it dawns on me what she's about to do.

"What are you doing?" I stammer anxiously.

"What does it look like? I'm going for a swim. Duh."

"But you didn't bring your bikini?"

"So?" She wiggles her brows while taking off her top and shimmying out of her skirt. "Remember what I told you about only living once? This is it. Seize the day, sis. Carpe fucking diem! No fear!"

And with those words still hanging in the air between us, she runs to the pool in her underwear and cannonballs her way in. Everyone cheers her along when she rises to the surface, looking like a mermaid right out of an R-rated teenage movie.

Unable to keep still, I grab her clothes before someone swipes them away, biting my lower lip as I watch her laugh and have the time of her life.

"Come on in, Sky! The water is amazing!" she calls out animatedly, yet I stay rooted to my spot. "No fear," she mouths so that I'm the only one to hear her secret message.

Right.

No fear.

Like that shit is easy.

It is hot, though.

Although the sun has already set, the night's heat is still unbearable. I shift from one foot to another, my gaze falling on the kids inside the pool who are having a blast with my sister in their midst. If I didn't have a deathly fear of water, I might have said fuck it and just took a page out of Daisy's handbook. Unfortunately, I can't swim to save my life, and I doubt anyone here would save me from drowning if I so much as tried to follow my sister's command.

Still...

The water does look tempting.

No fear.

Screw it.

When in Rome, I guess.

Ever so carefully, I lower myself to the edge of the pool and sit down, raising my dress just enough to get my legs wet. I close my eyes and hum in delight.

This isn't so bad.

Not bad at all.

I can do this.

I *am* doing this.

When I open my lids back up, I see that Daisy is on the other side of the pool, being pulled up by her arms by none other than Stacy's older brother, Derrick. When she's fully out of the pool, he wraps her up in a beach towel, and then presses his hand on her lower back, urging her into the house.

The conspiring looks they give each other tell me and everyone else in the near vicinity that Stacy's big brother is Daisy's pick of the night. I chuckle under my breath and promise myself I won't hurt her game by ending her fun for at least a few hours. Three hours is plenty of time for Daisy to do whatever she does at these things. And it's also enough time to appease her sisterly duty of trying to get me to have the full teenage experience of going to my first high school party.

Three hours.

I can survive three hours.

But just as I think this, I feel two delicate hands grip my shoulders, nails sinking into my skin.

I turn my head over my shoulder and come face to face with the hostess of this godforsaken party.

"I don't remember inviting your skanky ass to my party. But now that you're here..." Stacy smiles menacingly at me, and before I can prevent it, she pushes me into the pool.

As my whole body becomes submerged underwater, and my chest burns for breath, the last thought that runs through my head is how anticlimactic it is that this is how I die—at a fucking high school party.

Fuck my life.

Chapter 12

Noah

Seventeen years old

I'm lying bored in a pool chair, aimlessly scrolling through my phone, when Daisy's loud voice reaches my ears.

"POOL PARTY!" she shouts, before jumping into the pool, making everyone cheer her on.

"That girl has too much energy for her own good." I smirk, watching her put on a show.

"God, your sisters are so weird," Stacy mumbles in irritation beside me.

"They're not my sisters," I retort evenly.

"Your dad married their mom, didn't he? Then they are your sisters," she snarls, nostrils flaring. "I have no idea why Derrick even invited her. She's so...so...extra."

He invited Daisy because, like the rest of the guys at our school, he wants to get into her panties, but I keep that remark to myself or risk pissing Stacy off more than she already is. As much as my girlfriend hates it, not only is Daisy a total knockout but she's also cool as fuck. Is it any wonder that all of Bayshore High fell head over heels in love with her the minute she stepped foot into its halls? I think not. Stacy has to get over it already and just deal.

"Oh God, she brought the reject with her," Stacy groans. "I'm going to kill my brother. Argh!"

While Stacy is having a total meltdown, my gaze discreetly falls to the jittery figure standing by the pool watching her big sister be the life of the party. Sky looks like a deer caught in the headlights.

"That's it. I have to get something to drink if I have to put up with those two being in my house. You want anything, babe?"

I shake my head.

She pecks my cheek with a kiss and then sashays her way back into her house. But my eyes aren't on my girlfriend as they should be. They're on Sky. Daisy splashes in the water, urging her sister to join her.

"Don't do it, Sky," I order her in my head, and I let out a sigh of relief when she makes no move to take off her dress to join her sister.

Instead, she hurries to pick up Daisy's discarded clothes for safe keeping. My forehead creases, wondering why she looks petrified as she slowly lowers herself onto the pool's edge to sit down. But just as my curiosity is piqued by the look of fear in her eyes, it vanishes completely when she starts pulling her dress up over her thighs in order to prevent it from getting wet. She dips her long legs into the pool, coaxing my mouth to run dry as she runs her hands up those tanned thighs. When she dunks her hand into the pool and then sprinkles droplets of water over them, making her thighs glisten, my chest tightens. Sky closes her eyes, her head falling back as she enjoys how the water cools her down. Which is fucking ironic since suddenly my skin feels like it's too hot to bear.

Fuck.

Stacy was right.

Sky had no business coming to this party.

But just as the thought crosses my mind, I see my girlfriend go to her haunches just behind Sky. I'm not sure what she whispers in her ear, but what she does next has me standing up from my seat in an instant. Stacy pushes Sky into the water, the look of terror back in her silver eyes before the water takes her under. I look around and curse when no one even registers what Stacy just did, too preoccupied in getting drunk and hooking up. I start counting down my heartbeats, waiting for Sky to swim to the surface, my hands balling into fists beside me.

"Come on, Skylar," I whisper through gritted teeth, while everyone continues to have a grand old time.

Unable to take it any longer, I step closer to the pool, trying to see if I can catch a glimpse of her. Each second that passes where she doesn't come up feels like a fucking eternity. And then finally, I see her, struggling under the water, trying to pull herself up and failing miserably at it.

I don't think.

I just act.

Flinging myself into the pool, I dive in, the loud burst of cheers from my idiot friends the last thing I hear before I hit the water. My calves and hamstrings begin to burn as I kick and swim toward the other side of the pool, panic setting in as I find Sky at the very bottom. The deathly fear in her eyes when she sees me approaching will haunt me for all my days.

Fuck.

Instead of believing I came to her rescue, it's clear as day she thinks I'm here to end her for good. My suspicion is confirmed when she starts shaking her head, water filling her mouth as she screams for help. She slaps my hands away when I try to grab her waist, but luckily, I'm faster and stronger, wrapping my arm around her and pulling us up to the surface. Sky gasps for air, coughing up the water that made it into her lungs, as she holds onto my shoulders with all the strength she has. I swim us to the pool's ladder, hoisting her up with brutish force.

"Get out," I bark at her.

Trembling, she does as she's told, shock making her moves so uncoordinated, it takes her a minute to grab onto the rail. When she finally has a good grip on the ladder, she begins to pull herself up, her golden body glistening under the white soaked fabric of her dress. The material clings to her body in a way that I can see every nook and cranny, leaving absolutely nothing to the imagination. The guttural sound that rips through my chest must have been loud enough to catch her attention, because she suddenly stops mid-step, throwing her head over her shoulder to look at me. The furious expression on my face must chill her to the bone because she finds her footing again and quickly picks up the pace. When her feet are back on solid ground, I hold on to the bars and lift myself up behind her.

Sky is still gasping for breath, her body and hair dripping wet on the floor. The growl I let out when we're toe to toe facing each other sends a cold shiver down her spine.

Or maybe it's not you at all, dipshit.

Maybe she's trembling because she thought you were about to make sure she drowned.

Fuck.

Infuriated, I grab her by the elbow and march her into the house, looking for the closest free bathroom I can find.

"Where are we going?" she stammers, her voice coming out throaty from all the coughing she did a few seconds ago.

I don't answer her, too angry to say one goddamn word.

"Noah, stop. You're hurting me," she croaks, staring at where my fingers are digging into her flesh.

I ease my grip on her immediately, cursing myself for not knowing my own strength. But that's what Sky does to me. She gets under my skin and makes me lose all composure. When I can't find a single unlocked bathroom, I walk up the stairs to the second floor toward Derrick's room, hoping I'll find Daisy in there with him and let her handle this fucking mess. To my bitter disappointment, when we step inside his room, it's completely empty.

Goddamn it!

Can't I catch one break?

Just one, for fuck's sake!

I release my grip on her to pull open one of Derrick's drawers and grab something for us both to wear, since my clothes are also soaked. I toss the first thing I see at her, a Bayshore High sweatshirt, and then rush to his bathroom to grab us some towels.

When I return back into the room, Sky remains completely still, glued to the spot I left her, leaving a pool of water on the carpet.

"Dry up and get dressed!" I yell at her, unable to keep my temper under control as I throw her a towel.

She picks the towel and the sweatshirt from the floor, heading toward the bathroom, but before she's able to bypass me, she stops, throwing me daggers with her fucking gorgeous eyes.

"Why are you being such an asshole?"

"Why? Why?! Take a fucking guess, sweetheart!"

She stares at me perplexed for a full ten seconds, and then she sneers at me.

"As if I could ever know what goes on in that psychotic mind of yours."

"Oh, I'm the psycho? Is that why you thought I dove into the pool not to save your sorry ass but to make sure you'd never reach the surface?"

When her face falls, my heart drops to the pit of my stomach.

The fuck.

She really thought I could be that ruthless. That fucking cruel. That...psychotic.

But before I'm able to curse her out, she beats me to the punch.

"You never cease to amaze me. Your girlfriend almost drowned me and yet somehow you make this all about you. Conceited much?" she yells in my face before she nudges my shoulder with hers and struts to the bathroom behind me.

Before she has a chance of slamming the door in my face, I place my hand on it and walk right in with her.

"How was Stacy supposed to know you couldn't swim?" I bark out, pulling my wet t-shirt off me and hurling it to the floor.

She lets out a high-pitched laugh, before pulling her own wet dress off and throwing it to my bare chest.

"That's your excuse for her behavior? That it was totally okay for her to shove me in the deep end as long as I knew how to swim?"

My jaw tics and my back molars grind when I see her in a white bra and panty set that showcases her perfect round pink nipples and just a dust of hair on top of her mound. Sky is so furious at me that she doesn't even realize that she's as good as naked before me.

"I couldn't give a fuck why Stacy does the shit she does. All I care about is that if you have this incessant need to embarrass yourself, then do it where I don't have to watch," I rebuke, kicking off my sneakers and socks before unzipping my jeans and pulling them off.

The blood in my veins turns to liquid lava when Sky's eyes fall from my face, trailing slowly down my chest, abs, and taut muscles, only to stop when they reach the bulge in my wet boxers. Unable to help myself, I pull them down and kick them toward her feet, before grabbing a towel to dry myself off.

"You're such a prick, you know that?"

"Stare at my dick any longer and I'll show you just how *big* a prick I can be." I smirk victoriously, but my triumph is short-lived when her hands snake behind her back to unclip her bra.

"You think that shit fazes me? Think again," she snaps, making me swallow hard when she discards her bra onto our shared pile of clothes, giving me a full view of her breasts. "What? No comeback? No snarky reply?" she asks sarcastically, placing her hands on her hips, taunting me with her luscious curves.

"Nothing I haven't seen before," I grumble, turning my sights away from her before I do something stupid—like lick every last droplet of water that's clinging to her body.

I shouldn't be turned on right now. I should be fucking livid with her. She really thought I could hurt her. Leave her there to drown. That shit has no excuse. I know I've always acted like a jerk to her, but I'd never let real harm come to Sky. Embarrass her, humiliate her, sure. Hurt her though? Just the thought has me blinded with rage.

Needing to tap into that fury instead of the building lust inside of me, I give Sky another menacing glower.

"Also, from what I saw downstairs, nothing the rest of the school hasn't seen either. School hasn't even started, and already you'll have everyone talking about you on Monday."

"Please," she sneers, unbothered that the only garment left on her body is a piece of flimsy lace fabric covering her pussy that I could rip off with my teeth with one hard pull. "There were girls downstairs with less on than me. Even Daisy went into the pool in her underwear."

"That's because Daisy knows no one will fuck with her. You're not your sister, Sky, so stop trying to be."

The flash of hurt in her gray eyes pierces my chest like someone just threw a damn ax to it.

"Fuck you, Noah. Fuck you!" she cries, lunging herself at me and punching my bare chest. I grab her wrists, binding them behind her back, as her chest violently heaves up and down.

"What? You're okay dishing it out but not strong enough to take it?"

"I hate you," she seethes, her face so close to mine we're practically breathing the same air.

"I couldn't give a fuck. Stay in your fucking lane, Sky, if you know what's good for you."

"No."

"No?" I cock a brow, pretending that her hard nipples rubbing up against me isn't driving me insane.

"You heard me. You can't bully me around. I can do what I want when I want."

"You have no idea what you want," I breathe out, my eyes scanning her gorgeous face, finding a flicker of vulnerability in her gaze. "I'm not wrong, am I?" I add, my voice dropping an octave when I don't feel her resist my hold on her wrists. "You haven't a clue what you want and that fucking scares the shit out of you."

"I know what I want," she whispers, her eyes turning just as hooded as mine must be.

"Yeah? You sure about that?" I groan, my cock so hard it's stabbing her stomach.

"Hmm," she hums with a nod, the melodic sound making my mushroom head leak with approval.

"Prove it," I goad, licking my parched lips.

When her eyes fall from mine to my mouth, my heart rattles beneath my rib cage.

"Sky, wait—"

But it's too late.

Before I can do anything about it, her lips crash to mine in the hungriest of kisses, making sure that all my protests are in vain.

Just like the rest of her, Sky's lips are soft and inviting. Whatever restraint I had left breaks when she tentatively peeks her tongue out to taste the seam of my lips, her body melting to mine. My cock rubs against her pussy, needing the friction, as I give way to our kiss. I release my hold on her, and without missing a beat, Sky wraps her arms around my neck, pleading for more. And against my better judgment, I give it to her. My hands grip her warm hips, her hot flesh singeing mine. My tongue plunges into her mouth, needing to learn every secret she's been keeping from me. When she starts rocking her hips, the tip of my cock hits her swollen clit, making her moan out in pleasure. With each wail she lets out, I swallow them whole, my fingers leaving their mark on her flawless skin.

Fuck.

I've never been more turned on by a kiss, and all I want to do is slide her panties to the side and fuck her right here in my girlfriend's brother's bathroom.

Girlfriend.

Stacy.

Jolted, I pull away, shoving her off me. I wipe my lips with my forearm, hating this girl in front of me with every fiber of my being.

"Don't you fucking ever do that again!" I shout, my whole body shaking with fury. "I should have known," I seethe, disgusted with myself as well as her. "The apple doesn't fall far from the tree, now does it? I'm with Stacy. I know your mother never taught you this shit, but don't you ever go after something that isn't yours to begin with. Ever!"

With each belt I let out in the small room, the confused expression on her face morphs into shame and then ultimately...hurt.

I turn around and leave, not wanting to spend another second in her presence. I slam the bathroom door behind me and hurriedly grab a t-shirt and some sweatpants from Derrick's dresser. Once I've found a pair of clean socks and some sneakers lying around on the floor, I put that shit on too, rushing out the door to seek out some goddamn clarity. But since I doubt I'll find that anytime soon, looking for Stacy will have to do. It doesn't take me long to catch sight of her downstairs, sitting in the living room with her crew, laughing away, completely oblivious that I was seconds away from cheating on her.

"Hey, babe. Where...have you...been hiding...all night?" she hiccups, showing she's spent most of the time I wasn't with her drinking like a fish.

I don't let her say anything else, dropping to sit right beside her on the couch, and palm her face in my hands, pulling her to me. I kiss her hard, hoping she can erase the lingering heat Sky's lips left on mine. But to my bitter dismay, Stacy's kiss does nothing for me.

Absolutely fucking nothing.

All I can taste is Sky.

All I can see is Sky.

Even my skin aches for her touch.

I break this poor excuse of a kiss, spiders instantly crawling up the nape of my neck when Stacy's half-mast eyes shine brightly at me.

"What was that for?" she coos, nestling her head on my shoulder.

"Just wanted to check something out." I fake a grin.

"Well, whenever you want to do that again, you know where to find me."

I grab the Solo cup of vodka out of her hand and drink the whole thing down in one gulp. Stacy threads her fingers through mine, her attention now back on her friends. My body continues to be stiff as a board, as if it's on high alert to all the dangers that might come at me. And when I see Sky walk down the flight of stairs, now dressed in Derrick's hoodie, and with her sister at her side, I realize that the only real danger to me is the one that sleeps right under my own fucking roof. My body only manages to relax when I see the two of them leave.

Skylar needs to keep the hell away from me.

But most importantly, she needs to learn not to mess with me.

And I know just the person who will be up for the task.

"Hey, babe?" I ask, pulling my girlfriend's focus off her friends and back on me. "Do you think it's weird my sister just tried to shove her tongue down my throat?"

"WHAT?!" she shrieks, turning every shade in the crayon case.

Yep, I found the perfect person to teach Skylar a lesson.

* * *

All through Sunday, Sky hardly leaves her room, too embarrassed to come out.

Not that I care.

The only thing that gets me through living with her another fucking second is knowing that when school starts, she'll never dare provoke me again. When Monday finally arrives, I lean against my locker, counting down the seconds for the showdown to begin.

Like clockwork, Stacy and her army of minions storm through the halls with one sole purpose in mind. As if knowing shit is about to go down, everyone loitering the hall parts like the Red Sea for the queen bee to take center stage.

Completely oblivious to the karma that's coming to her, Sky doesn't even register the predator that's fast approaching behind her. Sky retrieves some book out of her locker and closes it when, without even a hint of warning, Stacy grabs her by her hair and slams her head right on the locker, leaving a nasty cut and bruise on her forehead.

My jaw clenches when I see blood beginning to drip down Sky's shirt. I shove the guilt down my throat, repeating in my head how she brought this all on herself. She shouldn't have looked at me the way she did back at the party. She shouldn't have gotten half naked in front of me. And she sure as shit shouldn't have kissed me.

You kissed her back.

You liked it.

I push those thoughts down to the darkest confinements of my soul and keep my attention strictly on what Stacy does next. If she tries to hit Sky again, I'll have no choice but to jump in. I wanted Stacy to cuss Sky out, embarrass and belittle her, not physically harm her. Not make her bleed.

"Bitch!" Stacy shouts at the top of her lungs.

"What the hell is your damage?!" Sky yells back, pushing Stacy away from her.

"Don't you dare touch me, skank!" Stacy shrieks.

A little unoriginal there, Stace, but it will do.

"Who do you think you're calling a skank?" I hear a familiar voice call out. The crowd centered around the two girls disperses just wide enough for Daisy to pass through. "You better not be talking about my sister or you best believe that nose job your daddy got you for your sweet sixteen is money down the drain. I'll rearrange your face so good the best plastic surgeons won't be able to fix it."

To her credit, Stacy stands strong, even if a smarter person would back the fuck down facing such wrath.

"She's more than a skank. Your sister is a total freak show. You disgust me," Stacy yells, scrunching her face like she just smelled spoilt milk.

"Don't test me, Monroe. Walk away. You're getting on my last nerve," Daisy threatens while Sky continues to remain mute.

"Ah! You don't know, do you? The freak didn't have the guts to tell you, did she?" Stacy announces, a gleam of victory in her eye. "Well, let me be the one to tell you why your sister is disgusting. Sky kissed Noah at my party. Yup. Her own brother! Who does that if not a total freak?!"

Everyone bursts into laughter, while Sky's gaze falls to the floor in utter shame. Like everyone else, I catch the stunned look on Daisy's face. But if Stacy thought Daisy would join her fan club and debase her own sister, then she doesn't know Daisy as well as I do.

"You're done here, Stacy. Now jump back on whatever broomstick you flew in on and leave my sister alone. I'm not asking. I'm telling. Go!"

"Fine. I'll go. But if the incestuous freak touches my boyfriend ever again, I'll be back. And next time, I won't play nice."

"I swear to bloody God—" Daisy warns through clenched teeth and closed fists.

Stacy lifts her hands up and steps back from both sisters, a cunning smirk to her lips.

She accomplished her mission.

Everyone in the hallway heard her loud and clear. By noon, there won't be a person at Bayshore High who won't know what happened here.

The job is done.

Sky will think twice before she fucks with my life again.

That much I'm sure.

When the bell rings, I pull away from my locker and walk past them, head held high and a spring to my step, while Daisy side-eyes me all the way. But as I turn the corner, curiosity takes the best of me. Now hidden, I stand rooted to my spot and eavesdrop on the two girls.

"Is what Stacy said true? Daisy asks, confused. "Is that why we had to leave the party so quickly? Not because someone threw you in the pool but because you kissed Noah?"

"Yes," Sky answers, tears in her voice.

"Oh, Sky. Why did you go and do that?"

"I...I don't know. One minute he was yelling at me and the next... the next I wanted to kiss him. It all happened so fast. I'm not sure why I even did it."

"You're not sure?" Daisy asks, her tone incredulous. "Could it be," Daisy pauses, her tone turning gentle. "Could it be because you might like him? Like Noah?"

I hold my breath, my lungs burning with the lack of oxygen waiting for Sky to say something. But when Daisy's question is answered in silence, I suddenly feel like someone just punched me in the gut.

"Do you agree with her? Do you think I'm a freak?" Sky whispers on a sob, the silent sound of her tears making my skin itch.

"No, Sky," Daisy comforts. "You did something impulsive in the moment. You acted on instinct. It took courage to put yourself out there. I'll never reprimand you for being brave, sis. Never."

"Not even if the whole school thinks I'm a perv now?"

"It will die down. That's the good thing about high school. By the end of the week, there will be a new fuckup for everyone to gossip about."

"Do you really think so?" Sky asks, sounding hopeful, coaxing a fist to twist my insides out.

"I do," Daisy says assuredly. "And even if Stacy and her Barbie bitch crew give you a hard time, I got your back. Always."

"You can't fight my battles for me," Sky mumbles.

"Oh, I know. And I won't. But that doesn't mean you have to go at it alone."

"Thanks."

"You got it," Daisy replies lovingly.

The instant I hear their footsteps drawing near, I know that's my cue to leave. My steps only falter when I hear Daisy's last remark.

"Sky, just stay away from Noah from now on, okay? He's not good for you. He's broken, and broken things are only happy when everything else around them is just as broken as they are."

Chapter 13

Skylar

Seventeen years old

Daisy's wrong though. The school doesn't forget. Although the taunts slow a bit, for the next few months, the life I already thought was hell, is even worse. Notes are slipped into my locker calling me an "incest whore". One day, I came to find that someone had plastered pictures in the hallway of me getting out of the pool that night, and you can see almost every inch of my body through my waterlogged clothes. Guys and girls cough "slut" as I walk by, and I'm sure that I've never been so humiliated in my life.

Soon, the taunts get so bad that I can't take it anymore. I leave school in the middle of the day and take a cab to the ferry. I get on, no one questioning why a high schooler isn't in class, and I take it all the way across the bay.

When I get there, it only makes me feel worse. Because unlike Daisy, who would have a million people to call when she visited home, I have no one. Just a few acquaintances that certainly wouldn't leave school to come get me. I take another cab to the mall and walk aimlessly around the stores, remembering the day I bought my homecoming dress. More despair floods my veins, because I can't even call my dad. He's disappeared again, on some trip, somewhere. No surprise there. He's never been around when I needed him. Except for my sister, no one ever is.

I've never felt so alone.

I decide to catch a movie even as my phone rings with a call from Daisy.

I don't pick up.

I buy a ticket to whatever movie is next, and then a large popcorn, and then I sit in the theater for the next hour and a half, staring blankly at the screen as tears stream down my face. There's only a couple of other people there, some alone, some with one other person. There's a woman in her fifties a few rows down from me. She's calmly drinking her soda as she watches the show. She's drab, dressed in a pair of oversized gray sweats, her mousy chestnut hair in a ponytail. Like me, she's also alone but she looks like she's okay with that. Content even.

Is that my future, I wonder. Am I going to find myself alone? Always going to the movies alone, going out to eat alone, sitting at home with my cat alone.

It all feels...hopeless.

Someone's head explodes on the screen, and I think, for the first time, that maybe...the world would be better off without me.

My mind starts to spiral. I start to think about how I could do it. I could slip away like this, take some prescription drugs and then let myself sink into the water. Just drift away like I feel I'm drifting through life.

But then Daisy's face fills my head, and I see her standing at my grave side, tears streaming down her face, her spirit broken. I see my mother sobbing into Curt's chest. A snarky voice inside tells me "they'll recover, maybe they'd be even better off without my baggage", but I try to push the thought away.

By the end of the movie, I'm disgusted with myself...and I've realized...I might need some help.

It's midnight by the time I get home. I've walked all the way from the ferry stop in the rain, and I'm completely soaked. There's a police car in the front of my house, and I brace for what's to come. All the lights in the house are on.

Taking a deep breath, I walk up to the front door and knock, because I left my keys in my backpack at school. The door flies open and there's my mother, looking at least ten years older than she had this morning.

"Skylar! Oh my God!" she cries as she flings herself towards me, throwing her arms around me.

I can see inside the house. There's a policeman standing there next to Curt, both of them staring at me with frowns on their faces. Noah is also hovering in the back of the room, his lips pursed and his arms crossed in front of him.

Daisy comes flying down the hallway, practically pushing my mom to the ground in her hurry to get to me.

"Where the fuck have you been?" she growls, squeezing me so tightly, I'm finding it hard to breathe.

I realize I'm shaking then, and the tears that have been on and off all day are streaming down my face. Again.

I'm dragged inside, everyone staring at me incredulously when I tell them I had gone to the mainland all afternoon and that I just lost track of time.

My mom and Curt apologize to the police officer and thank him for coming, and he gives me some sort of lecture about never doing this again before he disappears into the night.

I'm still feeling numb though, still trying to fight off the blanket of melancholy draped across my shoulders since that moment in the theater when I first started thinking about ending my misery.

"What were you thinking?" my mother shrieks as soon as the door's closed. "You realize how worried we've all been? I would've never expected this type of behavior from you." She's ranting and raving, her face turning red as she gestures, and I just sit there, like a lump on a log.

Finally, my mother realizes that her screaming isn't getting through to me. She murmurs something to Curt and he leaves the room, snapping at Noah to follow him. Noah reluctantly follows him, and I feel the loss of his gaze the second he's gone.

Daisy refuses to leave though. She's standing there with her arms crossed, her hair uncharacteristically unkempt like she's been running her hands through it all evening.

My mother sits down on the couch next to me and takes one of my hands in hers. "Skylar, help me to understand."

"She's being bullied," Daisy blurts out, finally shocking me out of the fog that I've been wrapped in.

My mother's mouth drops. "Bullied?" She stares at me, concerned. "Why haven't you said anything?"

Again, Daisy inserts herself before I can say anything, not that I have anything to say.

"Would you even have cared if she did?" Daisy spits sarcastically. "When was the last time that you even spent some quality time with us and asked what was going on in our lives? Sorry to burst your bubble, Mom, but since we move here you've been so far up Curt's ass you've forgotten about us completely. You've been acting like Grant and that shit is saying something."

Shock and guilt is written all over my mother's face as she stares incredulously at the both of us. She opens her mouth, to defend herself I'm sure, but Daisy waves her away, not wanting to hear it.

"Sky, you should've said something to *me*. You scared me. Not knowing where you were all day, scared me. If all you wanted was a break, I could've gone with you to Falmouth."

That does get my mom speaking again, because she starts lecturing us both on the fact that we are, under no circumstances, allowed to play hooky from school, and how this whole instance has damaged her trust in me.

She seems to skip right over what Daisy's told her, or the accusation that Daisy's levied about just how interested in her daughters' lives she's been over the last year.

After another thirty minutes of lecturing, I'm sent to my room, grounded for the foreseeable future. Daisy tries to follow me inside, but I tell her I just need some space, and reluctantly she gives it to me.

* * *

I'm lying listlessly on my bed, staring up at the ceiling when the door opens, and I don't have to look over to see who it is this time.

Noah walks inside and closes the door behind him, clicking the lock. He stands there by the door, so long that I have no choice but to glance over at him. The look on his face is inscrutable. He's just staring at me...almost blankly.

Finally, he walks over to the bed and sits at the foot, reminding me of that moment we shared. It almost feels like another lifetime at this point.

"Where did you go?" he finally asks.

I don't bother answering him.

I don't owe him anything.

In this moment, it feels like he's won, like all the fight's been wiped out of me. Who was I to think that I had enough in me to go up against someone like him?

I was a fool, that's what I was.

"Skylar!" he snaps, frustration thick in his voice.

I stare at him.

He looks...wrecked. There are dark circles under his eyes and his hair is all over the place.

"I hate you," I whisper to him, and he leans back, his face stunned.

"What?—"

"I hate you."

He shakes himself out of his momentary stupor and leans forward.

"Is that what you've been doing? Going out to God knows where and blaming me for all of your problems?" he taunts.

I jerk up, adrenaline spiking through my veins for the first time in maybe...weeks.

"Excuse me...are you actually asking that? You are the cause of all my problems!"

"I'm not the cause of any of your problems. I'm just the one that points out you're too scared to do anything about them!"

"You told the entire school that I kissed you," I hiss, my heartbeat so rapid it feels like it could explode out of my chest and fly away any moment now. "Everyone thinks that I'm some kind of sick freak now. I hear about it all day, every day. My life is ruined until I get out of this place. You've made my life...unbearable."

The word 'unbearable' slips out, more honesty than I ever would have wanted to give him.

"This is on you," he mumbles under his breath.

"On me? Really? All this is on me?!" I question in outrage.

"Isn't it?" he counters looking me dead in the eye. "You're wasting time blaming me when you should be asking yourself one very important question."

"And what's that?" I seethe.

"Why you never told anyone that I. Kissed. You. Back!" he spits.

Now it's my turn to rear back, like I've been physically hit. I stare at him incredulously.

"You think anyone would have believed me? Those idiots worship the ground you walk on. You could tell them to get on the floor and lick it, and they would do it without a second thought," I explain frantically.

"So what? You could have still told the truth."

"Like they would ever believe me over you." I scoff.

He gets up from the bed and shakes his head before tossing one last remark over his shoulder.

"What makes you think I would have denied it?"

When he starts walking out of the room without saying another word, my apathetic heart begins to faintly beat in my chest, needing this exchange to remind itself that it still has life in it. So much life in it.

"Is that your way of telling me that the truth is my friend?" I ask before he has a chance to leave.

"Probably the only one you have," he quips, his back still towards me.

"That was my first kiss. My very first kiss. And you ruined it. How's that for some truth?"

With my heartbeat drumming a mile a minute, I watch as Noah's back stiffens, his hand white knuckling the knob of my door. I wait with bated breath for him to turn around. For him to confront me. To call me a liar. To say something.

But he doesn't. Instead he just leaves.

He's said enough for one night.

We both have.

Chapter 14

Skylar

Seventeen years old

I'm determined to be a new girl when I return to school the following week. I hold my head high as I walk through the halls, ignoring the whispers around me. None of them are about me ducking out early on Friday. Obviously, you would have to care to notice that. Everyone's still far more interested in all the rumors floating around about me and my stepbrother.

I walk into English and see Kyle sitting there, doodling on a notepad.

"Hi," I say brightly, or as brightly as I'm capable of. His head shoots up and he stares at me, confused, something I don't blame him for.

I'm not sure that I've ever actually initiated a conversation between the two of us as of late. I've always made him talk to me first.

"Hi," he says carefully. "How was your weekend?"

"Not bad," I lie. "Yours?"

It's really impressive how bad I am at this—small talk and all of that. But he doesn't seem to notice that.

He takes a deep breath and leans forward. "There's a party after my basketball game on Friday. Would you want to come with me... And maybe watch the game beforehand?"

"No," is on the tip of my tongue, because there's very little that I would want to do less.

But last Friday's lessons are buzzing around my head, and I know what my answer has to be.

"Sounds good," I say casually as the teacher stands up to take roll.

Kyle pretends to almost fall out of his seat, catching himself on the edge of his desk. "I'm sorry, did you say...yes to me?" he teases.

I roll my eyes. "Don't push your luck," I flirt, butterflies zinging around inside of me not because of any emotions he's making me feel, but because I'm impressed...with myself.

"It's a date."

The butterflies flare up at the word 'date', but if I'm going to go out with anyone, it's going to be him. For some reason, this handsome, popular guy hasn't joined the ranks of the students in this school desperate to make my life hell. And he's actually stuck up for me a few times.

It's not the worst I could do.

"It's a date," I repeat, ignoring the huge smile that blossoms on his face.

Friday night's social event hangs over my head for the rest of the week. Daisy's absolutely over the moon that I'm going to the game and the after party as she's already made plans to be there.

Although I'm supposed to be grounded, Daisy convinces our mom that this is what I need, using the 'bullying story' to wheedle her into letting me get out of the house, even though my mother's doing her best to ignore the reality of it. I think her letting me go also has a lot to do with what Daisy accused her of. Guilt has a way of making my mother more lenient it seems.

But while my mother is all too happy to sweep things under the rug, Daisy isn't as forgiving.

She's tried numerous times to coax the truth out of what really happened last Friday, but so far I've managed to evade her probing questions. So even though it must drive her mad, we still haven't had the talk on why I just packed up my stuff and got on the first ferry out of Thatcher's Bay. And if I have it my way, we never will. Admitting to Daisy how low I actually was that day will only serve as a reminder of how dark my thoughts can take me. I don't ever want to go there again. Not if I can help it.

"You can sit with me for the game and then go with Kyle to the after party. And I can save you the second you say so," Daisy promises, obviously still concerned.

I nod determinedly, keeping my mind away from what happened at the last party I attended. At least I know I'm never going to repeat that particular mistake again.

* * *

It's Friday and Kyle's followed me down the hallway after class. As we pass Noah, he slips his arm around my shoulder. I stiffen and do my best not to give him the side eye. This is what I want, right?

It's healthy to have relationships.

But even as I think it, my gaze flicks to Noah who's leaning back against the lockers, his eyes locked on me as his band of admirers hover around him like flies around spoiling meat.

I tear my gaze from his and turn and flash Kyle a smile.

"So...I may have another request, just because I can't help but push my luck," he says, nerves evident in his voice.

It's that sound that finally allows me to relax.

Assholes don't get nervous...right?

"What's that?"

"I have an extra jersey with my number on it...think I could get you to wear it for the game?" he asks hopefully.

It is too much, but I find myself saying yes, especially when Stacy walks by, hitting my shoulder as she passes.

And that's how I end up here, sitting in the stands with a giant number twenty-two on my jersey while the raucous crowd around me screams and cheers for my date.

"Isn't this great?" yells Daisy, trying to be heard over the crowd.

"Yeah. Great," I respond, attempting to not sound too sarcastic.

What is wrong with me?

I mean, I know I'm different. But there just has to be someone else in this school that has the overwhelming desire to stay home and curl up in a comfy armchair with a book instead of being at a high school basketball game, cheering on a bunch of jocks?

The crowd cheers when Kyle makes another basket and this time, he points to where I'm sitting, like he's dedicating the score to me. Even though it's a sweet gesture, I can't help but wish I was anywhere else than here. Still, I plant a fake smile, not wanting to hurt his feelings.

As the game continues, one thing becomes crystal clear.

The school loves Kyle.

I've learned that the school's basketball team is kind of a big deal. We suck at football, but the basketball team can actually hold its weight against the bigger schools on the mainland. And with Kyle on our team, there is no question that we're winning tonight.

When the other team gets the ball and makes their way to the other side of the court, I decide now is the perfect time for a little break. .

"I'm going to go get a Diet Coke," I say to Daisy.

She nods, even though I'm not sure she actually heard me, too consumed with watching the game play out. I stand up and start to make my way down the steps, praying that I don't trip and give the school another thing to talk about.

It's much quieter in the hallway, and I let out a sigh of relief that I can enjoy some peace and quiet. I decide to go to the bathroom before I find the concession stand, but the line for the main ladies room is thirty people long... And I suddenly really need to pee.

I decide to try the one farther down the hallway, on the other side of the gym, even though the lights aren't on over there. I can still hear the faint roar of the crowd, but it is a bit creepy walking down the empty dark hallway.

A girl's gotta do what she's gotta do though.

I walk into the empty bathroom and choose a stall to use. I've just begun to pee when I think I hear the main door open, another smart person deciding to avoid the line.

After I flush and open up the door...I realize it's not another girl that's come in.

It's Noah.

He smirks at the obvious shock on my face, but I quickly recover and try to look nonchalant as I walk to the sink to wash my hands.

"I wasn't aware that you're a lady, Noah, although I guess you do have a penchant for visiting our bathrooms." I'm referring of course to the memorable bathroom experience with our waitress when our parents got married.

He's leaning against the wall, his arms crossed in front of his chest, a tendril of golden hair falling in his face. He's of course not wearing a school T-shirt, because he's far too cool for that. Instead, his tight black shirt is stretched across a chest that seems to have bulked up over the last year.

He's gorgeous, and the scowl on his face only adds to the yearning in my chest, because I'm nothing if not a masochist.

I dry my hands and move towards the door, but I'm stopped with a single word from his lips.

"Skylar," he purrs, and it's amazing how he can make my name sound so dangerous.

I slowly turn towards him, anticipation and dread singing through my veins. It feels like even though he's hell-bent on destroying me, he's also giving me life. Evidently, the pain of our interactions is what I need to keep going.

"Noah," I respond breathily.

He moves forward, his movements smooth and almost sensual as he stalks towards me. I can't help but back up, until I'm pressed against the cold tile wall as he hovers over me.

"This seems to be a thing for you, pushing me up against walls," I say softly, even as my chest rises and falls with a staccato breath.

"What's your plan, little stalker?"

"My plan...?" I ask, confused.

"You going to pretend to cheer for him throughout the entire game? Then when you go to his big mansion for the after party, are you going to hang on his arm like you actually give a shit?"

My eyes widen. "I—"

"You what? Are you going to let him take you upstairs to his room?" he asks, and I realize how close he's gotten to me. Every time I breathe, my breasts rub against him. He has one hand against the wall above my head, and his other one is by my waist, effectively caging me in.

"I'm going to leave now," I tell him, wishing that the words came out resolute instead of so breathy.

His hand moves from the wall to my waist, slipping under Kyle's jersey and softly tracing my skin.

"What are you doing?" I whisper. His eyes are fastened on my face, his expression almost...puzzled. Like he's not quite sure what he's doing right now. His fingers slide past the waistband of my leggings, and then under the top of my underwear.

"Noah–"

I shiver when his lips brush against my ear, but at least I've escaped his far too intense gaze.

"Are you going to let him touch you like this, to feel how soft and smooth your skin is?" He says the words as his fingers push farther down, until he's tracing the crease between my leg and my core.

"Do you think he'll know what he's doing when he gets his hand down here? Or do you think he'll fumble around like it's his first time because he's a selfish prick who's never bothered to learn what gets a girl off?"

"Selfish prick," I laugh softly, "that's rich coming from you."

I squeak as his fingertips are suddenly brushing through my embarrassingly wet folds.

"Do you think you'll be this wet for him? Or will you have to think of me the whole time and fake getting off?" His thumb finds my sweet spot and he presses firmly down, pleasure building up inside of me as he does so. It's not even just his touch that's doing it, although that's obviously helping. It's him. The way he's completely enveloped my body. It's the smell of his musk, how every time he talks, the tip of his tongue brushes against my ear.

Like everything about him was designed to make me want him. He's my foil. The enemy of my story that at the same time feels like my other half.

His thumb is lazy as he takes his time circling my clit, adjusting where and how he presses depending on the sound of my breath.

There's a sudden scream in the hallway and I jerk, my head banging into the wall behind me. Noah takes his time pulling his hand from my pants. My insides are on fire, everything inside of me begging that he finish the job.

My pride won't let that happen though. I stare at him in shock as he slips two fingers into his mouth and slowly savors my taste, groaning softly like it's his favorite thing.

"Have a fun rest of the night," he says with a wink as he strolls towards the door, whistling a song that will either play in my nightmares...or my darkest fantasies.

I'm a mess as I watch the door swing closed behind him.

* * *

I go back to the gym as if I'm in a trance. Daisy searches my face when I sit down. "What's wrong with you?" she asks, concerned.

"Nothing," I quickly reply, and she studies my face, looking for the cracks that will tell her what I'm hiding.

I turn to the game, ignoring her eyes boring into the side of my head. I let out a sigh of relief when one of her friends finally manages to pull her attention away from me.

Just like he predicted, it feels like another person who cheers for Kyle for the rest of the game.

It feels like another person who lets Kyle hold her in his arms.

It feels like another person who goes to the party and tries to smile.

And it feels like another person who kisses Kyle in a dark hallway while loud music blares around us.

Because I don't feel a thing.

Just like he knew I wouldn't.

Chapter 15

Noah

Seventeen years old

The minute my father opens the front door and finds me standing beside our little island's sheriff, his face turns to stone.

"What did he do this time?" he questions with a scowl.

"We caught him drag racing through Main Street this time," Sheriff Boyd explains on a frustrated exhale as my father ushers him into our home with me in tow. "It's starting to get out of hand, Curt. You're going to have to do something about your boy. Sooner or later, he'll get himself in a world of trouble that even *I* can't get him out of."

"Yeah, I know," my father retorts, running his hand over his face in disgruntlement. "Did anyone get hurt?" he asks apprehensively.

"No. Not this time. But between the fights he gets into and pulling reckless stunts like this, it's only a matter of time before someone does," Boyd rants on, looking just as disappointed in my behavior as my father does. "I swear, if he wasn't Annabelle's kid, I would have locked him up years ago to teach him a lesson. I must admit, I'm still of two minds about it. Maybe the best thing I could do for your boy is give him a good scare and press charges against him. Maybe that would set him straight."

Instead of the imposing threat of imprisonment that Sheriff Boyd just laid out at our feet, it's the mention of my mother's name that really sucks all the air out of the room. As I glance over at my father and witness his crestfallen features pale a sickly shade of white, acting as if he has just been sucker punched in the gut by his childhood friend with the reminder of his late wife, my hands instinctively curl into fists, my throat burning with hatred for the man standing in front of me.

It's been so fucking easy for him to erase my mother from his life that anytime he's confronted with the fact that not everyone on this island has such a fickle and selective memory, he acts like it's a backward slap to his current happiness.

"Do you have anything to say for yourself?" my father demands, pulling his attention off the sheriff to direct his resentful gaze on me, making sure to bypass his friend's comment about my mother as well as the threat of locking me up.

We both know Boyd won't do shit to me. Not while I'm a minor, at least. When I age out in a few months, then that's a different story. Not that my asshole of a father really gives two shits what happens to me then. Especially after graduation. All he'll care about is that he'll no longer have the living, breathing reminder of my mother walking around his happy home anymore. I'm only halfway done with my junior year in high school, yet I bet the fucker is anxiously counting down the days for me to get my diploma and move out.

"Well, Noah? Do you?" he insists, his tone becoming more aggravated.

"Yeah." I pull out the wad of cash inside my pocket and slap it on the kitchen counter. "I won."

On that note, I brush past him, purposely knocking his shoulder with mine before heading upstairs, uncaring that I just added gambling to my long list of felonies in front of Thatcher's Bay's finest, no less. Not that I'm worried. Even though the good sheriff just insinuated he'd love to lock me up for my own good, he hasn't done it yet, and even though he might have his reservations about it, I very much doubt he'll do it tonight after he went through all the trouble of bringing me home safely without filing a report.

Just as I'm leaving the two men alone in the kitchen to discuss what a little shit I am, I catch a shadowy figure quickly hiding from my view at the top of the stairs. Even as she hurries on featherlight feet back to her bedroom, doing her utmost best to not alert anyone of her presence, I catch her retreating form anyway. It doesn't take a genius to figure out who could possibly be up this late, eavesdropping on our conversation.

My stepsister is the worst Peeping Tom there is.

No matter how discreet she tries to be with her stalking tendencies, I always end up catching her in the act. I usually shrug that shit off my shoulders, but unfortunately for her, tonight I'm not as lenient.

Instead of marching to my room, I rush toward hers and kick the door in for good measure. A sinister smile immediately crests my lips when I realize in her haste, she forgot to lock her door behind her, making the little love tap I do with my boot swing her bedroom door wide open with ease.

She should know better.

But after tonight, I'm sure she'll think twice before leaving it open again.

"The hell are you doing?! Are you insane? Get out!" she whisper-yells from across the room, her indignant tone grating on my every nerve.

I don't let her say another word, preferring to take advantage of her surprise to pounce on her instead. My hand is quick to cover her mouth as I walk us both back into a corner of her room until her spine is flush against the wall.

"Why the fuck are you always spying on me?" I growl in her face.

Her eyes widen in fear before she vehemently shakes her head, lying through her teeth even when I have her mouth forcefully muzzled.

"Don't fucking lie to me, Sky," I seethe through my clenched jaw near her ear. "I feel your fucking eyes on me everywhere I go. It's fucking unnerving. How would you like it if I did the same shit to you, huh?"

Her eyelids slant in pure hatred, sparking up an idea that will only kindle those furious flames I see burning in her eyes a little brighter.

"You know what?" I chuckle sardonically. "I think you fucking owe me a show. I've given you plenty of my own, after all. It's about time you fucking pay up and return the favor."

"Fuck you," she curses through my fingers.

"You fucking wish I would. Nah, Sky. You haven't earned my dick yet."

When her nostrils flare with contempt, my cock disagrees with my comment, stirring awake and making the small, titillating idea of revenge in my mind blossom to new and unexpected heights.

"You want to watch me, Sky? Then pay the fuck up. It's about time you got a taste of your own medicine." Seeing the resolve in my glare, she starts wrestling under my grip to break free, but I'm not having it. "Tsk, tsk," I taunt, my adrenaline spiking higher than racing my bike down a deserted street ever did. "I'm not fucking leaving here until you give me what I want. Those are the rules."

"Fuck your rules," she mouths, her loathsome stare piercing through mine.

"Fine," I relent, taking my hands off her while stepping away from her just an inch, enough for my face to align with hers. "Don't give me a show then." I shrug nonchalantly. "However, I'm not sure what your mother and my asshole of a father will think when they find out you asked me into your bedroom in the dead of night."

"I didn't ask you to come here! You barged in!" she hollers, pushing my shoulders so I can give her more room to breathe.

I stay rooted to my spot, inclining my head to the side, licking my lips before throwing her a devilish smirk.

"That's not the story I'll tell them. My memory might not be all that sharp, but I expressly remember you waiting up for me to get home, and then making sure I followed you back into your bedroom. Alone."

"That's not what happened at all," she blurts out, appalled.

"Are you saying you didn't wait up for me?" I arch a brow, taking a further step back. "Or that you weren't hiding at the top of the stairs just waiting for me to come up?"

"I wasn't waiting for you."

"No. You weren't." I glower, crossing my arms over my chest. "You were just getting your kicks by eavesdropping on other people's private conversations. I'm not sure that Mommy Dearest is going to like learning how her precious girl is a freak who gets off on other people's misery."

"Please," she states sarcastically with an eye roll while mimicking my form by crossing her arms over her chest, her futile attempt at trying to look intimidating. "You're not miserable. You're just bored."

"Is that what you think I am? Bored?" I laugh menacingly.

"Yes," she deadpans unapologetically.

With our gazes still fixed on one another, I walk over to her bed and fall flat on my back, crossing my arms behind my head on her pillow.

"You think you know me that well, don't you, Sky? Please enlighten me then. Why do you think I'm bored?"

She chews on her fat bottom lip, her gaze bouncing from me over to the wide open door I kicked in, wondering if she's fast enough to close it before someone catches us in here together. Her mom and sister might be sound asleep, but she knows as well as I do that my father is still downstairs with the sheriff and that at any minute, he'll make his way upstairs and pass by her bedroom door.

It's no secret that Sky and I have hated each other since the moment we met, but if my father were to catch me in my stepsister's bedroom like this, sprawled comfortably on her bed like I've done this a million times before, it would be enough to plant the seed of doubt in his mind. He might not like the fact that we never got along, but he would hate it even more if he thought we had been fucking like bunnies under his roof all this time without anyone being the wiser. The idea that I could piss him off and rattle Sky's cage in the same breath has me doubling down on my resolve to see her squirm.

"If that's bothering you, feel free to close it. I'm in no hurry," I retort, throwing a glance at the open door while making myself even more comfortable in her bed by kicking off my boots and letting them drop with a loud thud on her floor.

It's not like a locked door will stop my father from getting in if he feels something is amiss. I know that much. He's barged in enough times over the years when he thought I was up to no good. Little Miss Perfect here won't deter him from doing the same to her if he feels she's pulling a fast one on him.

Sky throws me an icy glare before hurrying to close her door, locking it this time just to be safe. I can't help but smile widely at her poor survival instincts, since it's fucking ironic she feels the true threat lies outside her bedroom walls and not within them.

"Now that's done, how about you tell me just how bored I am? I'm dying to see how fucking insightful you think you are."

Her upper lip curls at the corner of her mouth to show her discontent, but like a moth drawn to a flame, she pushes herself away from the door and slowly walks toward me until she's standing halfway in front of me. I try my best to keep my triumphant grin in check, but she sure doesn't make it easy with the way her bravado has increased tenfold now that she feels no one will discover us alone in here together.

A fool's bravery if I ever saw one.

"You get off on being reckless because that's the only thing that makes you feel alive," she starts to explain, unimpressed. "You surround yourself with friends that think you're some kind of god, so you can't count on them to give it to you straight or even challenge you in the least. You hate school because you're mostly bad at it, so academics don't bring you any kind of joy. And since you think you're too cool for sports, any athletic ventures constitute a waste of time in your book."

My arrogant smile remains intact as she goes through her list of reasons, acting as if she has a direct line to my inner thoughts, when I never gave her such a privilege.

"You think you're above everyone else, so no matter how hard you try to connect with anyone, you end up being disappointed because no one measures up to your high expectations. And don't even get me started on your vapid and shallow girlfriend, whose only purpose is to look pretty hanging on your arm."

"Don't forget she has to look pretty good on her knees too," I interject with a mocking grin, knowing exactly how to ruffle my nemesis's feathers.

Sky's face turns lethal as she eats the small distance between us until her knees hit the mattress. What I don't tell her is that Stacy and I broke up again a few days ago right after that stupid ass basketball game that dipshit Kyle manipulated Sky into attending. It's too much fun letting Sky think otherwise anyway. Almost makes putting up with Stacy's shit for so long worth it.

"Your very existence is pathetic," she snarls. "You have nothing going for you and you know it. You are the perfect example of someone peaking in high school. If that isn't a sign of a life filled with complete and utter boredom, I don't know what is."

My victorious smirk immediately falls from my face with the remark.

"You're a real piece of work, you know that?"

"Is that supposed to hurt me? You've called me worse." She smiles widely, pleased she's gotten to me.

Fuck that.

And fuck her.

She wants to play?

Then we're going to fucking play.

Before she's able to stop me, I fly off the bed and pull her down on top of me. She lets out a surprised shriek, making me have to clamp my hand over her mouth. I roll her over on the bed and cover her body with mine to keep her still and pinned down beneath me.

"You think you know me so well, don't you, little stalker?" I grunt in her ear as she thrashes away under me. "So fucking perceptive. Watching everyone from the corner of a room and dissecting all their flaws and vulnerabilities. Must make you feel so fucking proud of yourself. But news flash, Skylar. No one gives a shit what you think about them. Because to them, you don't even exist. You're nothing. Nothing. You don't even register. And that must make you sick to your stomach. Knowing that you could disappear at any given moment, and no one would even bat an eye."

I'd know.

I'd always know.

"Get off of me!" she tries to shout from beneath my grip but her wails don't deter me.

"Not going to happen," I grunt, my body suddenly feeling electrified with the way hers rubs against it. I swallow dryly, trying desperately to tap back into my rage. I imprison her wrists together, her arms up over her head while my thighs lock hers in.

"You know, for someone who is so fucking clever, you can be downright stupid when you want to be." Her brows pinch together in confusion, her eyes locked on mine. "If you don't shut the fuck up and do as I say, then sooner or later, my father will come into this room and find me on top of you. Maybe that's what you want. Is it, Sky? Do you want the world to know that you let the guy you think is so fucking pathetic paw all over you?"

At this, she quiets down, her body finally melting into the mattress in total submission.

"Yeah, I didn't think so," I scoff, eyeing every curve of her beautiful face and inwardly cursing every flawless feature. "You've had your fun, now it's time I had mine. Put your hand down your shorts," I order, loosening my grip on her wrists.

"No," she blanches, her gaze bouncing off of my face and over my shoulder, staring at her locked bedroom door.

"I told you I wanted a show, and now you're going to fucking give it to me. Fuck knows I've given you more than you deserve. So, as I see it, it's time to pay the piper. Put your hand down your shorts, Sky. It's either your hand that goes down there or mine. Your choice."

"I hate you," she seethes, but starts to do as she's told.

I sit back on my haunches and watch as her hand begins to tremble and sneak down her chest toward her shorts.

"Put it inside your panties. No cheating," I demand when I see she's trying to rob me of my vengeful show.

"I am," she lies.

"You're not."

"How do you know?" She throws daggers at me.

"Because I can't smell that dripping cunt yet."

A pretty shade of pink crawls up her neck all the way to her cheeks, coaxing my cock to strain in my jeans again. The fucker doesn't realize that this isn't about me getting off. It's about wanting her to feel just as fucking humiliated as she's managed to make me with her little rant. I want her to hurt. I want her to feel just as pathetic as she has proclaimed me to be.

"Fuck this," I growl impatiently before grabbing her waistband and pulling her shorts off her legs in one menacing tug. I throw them over my shoulder and grip her ankles in place.

"You want to play hardball, then this is what you get. Now do as I say or suffer the consequences."

"You are so unhinged, you know that?" she spews, but I don't miss how her legs relax under my hold.

"Less talking and more doing, or your panties are the next thing to go."

This time she holds her protests on the tip of her tongue, and slowly shoves her hand inside her panties.

"There. It's done. Now what, you lunatic?"

"Aw, baby. Giving me pet names already? I think you can come up with better than that."

"How about psycho? I think it fits you perfectly," she rebukes with a fake-ass smile.

"If I'm a psycho then that officially makes you my little stalker. Not sure which one of us comes off better. Speaking of coming..." I taunt, eyeing her white cotton panties and smiling when I see there is a little wet spot already imprinted on them.

A sick sense of triumph runs through my veins when I see that my little freak gets off on these games of ours just like I do. My hold on her ankles tightens when she takes longer than I want her to.

"You're hurting me," she proclaims in a hushed whisper.

"I haven't even begun to hurt you, Sky. If you continue to stall your ass, then trust me, I will," I growl back at her, but ease my grip just the same.

Her shoulders slump, and her expression morphs from one of hatred to embarrassment.

"I don't know what you want me to do."

"Isn't it fucking obvious?" I chuckle sinisterly.

"Yeah, asshole. It is. I'm just not used to doing this type of thing, okay?!" she bites back, trying to keep her voice strong, but I hear the trace of resentment in her tone for having to confess her inexperience, especially to me.

I remember a night where I forced her to play with herself and come for me. I wanted the first time for her to be tainted with the knowledge that I was the one who got her off. Looks like she hasn't tried to come on her own since then. My knee-jerk reaction is to press my thumb in her wound and make her bleed. But to my utter shock, I do the opposite.

"Close your eyes," I tell her.

"No. I don't trust you."

"Yeah, well, that makes two of us. Now close your fucking eyes, Sky."

She takes a second to stare me down, but in the end her lids close just like I ordered them to. I take one hand off her ankle and run my fingers through my hair, wondering if I should just take her embarrassing admission that she's still so green when it comes to sex as a win and get the fuck out of here.

No.

I want more than just her embarrassment.

I want her fucking submission.

"What's taking so long?" she stammers nervously.

"Are you that anxious to come in front of me?"

"More like I want to get this over with so you can get the hell out of my room."

With her eyes closed, I let myself smile at her sass. For all the time we've lived together, Sky has never once shied away from fighting me. And right now, the battle I've instigated between us is one I am determined to win.

I take in all her curves, noticing for the first time that she's not wearing a bra under her flimsy tank top.

That's the thing about hate.

Sometimes it blinds you from seeing what's right in front of your eyes.

Sky has grown into her body. When I first met her, she was just this skinny-ass girl, bland and boring.

No.

That's a lie.

Sky was never bland to me.

And she sure as fuck was never boring.

Even compared to other girls I've hooked up with in the past, Sky always managed to dampen their beauty any time she came into view. They could have been hot as fuck, and my gaze would still try and find the shy girl who hid her scarecrow frame under large hoodies.

But now that I have her all sprawled up on her bed in nothing but a short tank top and panties, I can see she's coming into her womanhood—her power.

And Skylar's power is fucking blinding.

Two full breasts taunt me with how perfect they would fit in my palms. Her long legs wrapped around me and her hand-gripping hips doing nothing to settle my hard-on either. I watch in silence as her chest begins to heave up and down, her lids still closed, waiting for my next move.

Fuck.

I should leave.

I should bolt out the door and leave her here wanting.

I should.

I fucking should.

But instead, my hands begin to slowly creep up her long legs, leaving a trail of goosebumps in their wake. My heart jackhammers in my chest as I watch her lips part for breath, her tongue peeking out just enough to lick her parched lips. When my fingers dig into her skin just above her thigh, she lets out a sigh, only to swallow it back, not wanting to give me the satisfaction of hearing how much she's loving my hands on her. But it's too late for such futile efforts. Sky is fucking turned on, and the worst part of this shit show is that so am I.

The way my heart keeps drumming loud in my ears has me taking a beat just to stare at her. I take all of it in. How her eyes remain closed in both fear and anticipation. How her hands clutch the duvet beneath her, her shallow breathing coming out in spurts.

She's never looked more beautiful to me than she does right now.

Waiting for me.

Needing me to make her feel alive.

It's all fucking intoxicating.

And before logic or reason can raise its ugly head, and kick me out of her bed, I slide her panties to the side. Her breath catches, hissing at the cold air kissing her pussy. The urge to crawl down her body, just to take a long whiff of her arousal, has my own breathing stalling. I know if I even attempt to glide down her body and breathe her in, I'll end up eating her out. No question about it. The thought alone has my thumb going right to her core, stroking her slit, before lightly grazing her clit.

Her eyelids fly open in astonishment, her hands fisting her

bedsheets. She stares at me in bewilderment, while I keep my expression hard as stone.

"Touch me," I order, the lust-filled husky tone of my voice betraying me.

Sky doesn't fight me and complies with my command effortlessly. Her quivering fingers run up my chest, but when I let out a frustrated growl, slanting my gaze at her, she rectifies her error, slipping her hands underneath my t-shirt. My chest constricts with just the touch of her fingertips on my bare feverish skin.

We're trapped now.

Consumed by this thing between us, urging us to be burned alive by these flames.

Unable to find one thing to pull us out of this moment.

When her nails trail down my abs and the stars in her gray eyes twinkle at me, I realize the stakes in this game just got a whole lot steeper. My cock strains in my jeans, as I toy with her clit, rubbing at it in a way that has those same stars in her gaze taking flight. It's only when I insert a digit into her tight cunt that we both lose our minds.

"Noah," she pants out, digging her nails into my chest, leaving half-crescent moons on my skin.

My name on the tip of her tongue coaxes me further, and before I know what I'm doing, I lean down and pluck one of her diamond shaped nipples into my mouth and suck on it through her tank top.

"God. Noah!" she sobs, pulling one hand off my chest so she can grab onto my hair.

Every pull has me ravenous, and when my finger glides easily in and out of her wet pussy, I slip in another finger, fully fucking her now.

"Oh my God. Oh my God," she repeats on a loop, her head thrashing every which way.

I pull my teeth off her little bud and lift up just to look at her.

Beautiful.

So fucking beautiful.

I hide my face in the crook of her neck, groaning when her arms wrap themselves around my shoulders, her fingernails running up the nape of my neck. Her body continues to sing for me, her hips rocking to the tempo of my fingers. My teeth latch onto her earlobe, biting hard on her flesh before releasing it from my grip just to lick the sweat off her hot skin.

Sky is so enraptured with how her body has sprung to life, she doesn't even register my father's footsteps walking up the stairs, approaching the hall just outside her room. She's so fucking primed to coming undone that all it's going to take is one flick of the wrist to get her there. The devil on my shoulder screams for me to push her over the cliff, let her scream out her bliss and have my father hear her come on my fingers. She would never live it down and he'd blow a fucking casket—two birds, one stone.

But in the end, it's not the devil in me that pulls my strings. It's something else. Something that I refuse to acknowledge but fall prey to its wants anyway. Just as I add more pressure to her clit and she gasps out in ecstasy, her big silver eyes widening and meeting mine, I crash on top of her and catch her orgasmic cry with my mouth. I swallow it whole as her body shakes and trembles with the almighty orgasm I ripped out of her. I groan with how sweet she tastes as she continues to convulse underneath me, chasing the high I gifted her for all its extent. Her perky nipples stab my chest, her hot core scorching the tip of my fingers, making me hallucinate with images of licking her clean with my tongue.

It's only the faraway sound of my father's bedroom door closing that snaps me awake from the lurid fantasy. As if someone turned the lights on in my chaotic brain, I jump off her, my hands twitching at my sides.

My Adam's apple bobs as I stare at the beautiful mess I've made of her, wishing I could do it all over again. Sky struggles for breath as she stares at me in confusion, her legs wide open and so fucking inviting that it takes inhumane effort to walk away from her like this.

"Noah—"

"And I'm the one who's pathetic, huh? You came like a fucking

Fourth of July fireworks show, and I barely touched you. Next time, look in the fucking mirror before you ever judge me again, Sky. Girls in glass houses should think twice before throwing stones."

The hurt in her eyes should make me ecstatic, but all it does is make me feel like shit. Without another word, I turn around and rush out her room, not sparing her a second look. When I'm finally in the safety of my bedroom, I lean against the door, grabbing my chest to try and slow my rapid heartbeat. But as I look down at the hand grasping my t-shirt, I see and smell her juices still glistening all over my fingers.

Call it a moment of weakness.

Call it fucking insanity.

Call it whatever the fuck you want, but I'm too on edge to make sense of what I do next.

I shove the hand that just toyed with her most sacred of places into my mouth and suck my fingers clean, all the while using my other hand to free my hard cock from its restraints. Images of Sky on her back, riding my hand, assault me as I thrust into my closed fist.

I see it all in my mind's eye so fucking clearly—as if she used a jagged blade to carve it into my memory, making sure it filled all the dark and empty corners of my brain.

I remember everything.

Every fucking detail.

The way I licked the bead of sweat that fell from her brow as she let me have my way with her. I can still hear the sound of her soft sighs of elation as her body eagerly responded to my forbidden touch, almost as if it was fucking built for me and me alone. My chest tightens as I relish in the way her spine arched up to meet my fingers, her greedy little cunt riding them like a pro. I pump myself faster with the memory playing on a loop in my head, and before I know it, I'm coming with her name on my lips.

Sky.

Sky.

Sky.

I look at the mess I've made on my hand and slam my head back repeatedly on the door, forcefully shutting my eyes closed, wishing I could shut her out as easily.

Fuck.

She's right.

I am fucking pathetic.

Because in this very minute, I realize what was in front of me all along.

It's not using my fists on some jackass's jaw that gives me a rush like this.

It's not racing my bike or winning money from those rich fuckers that I go to school with that has blood pumping through my veins.

The only times I've ever felt truly alive is when she's near.

Fighting me.

Hating me.

Coming for me.

And that epiphany is too much for me to take.

I'll fucking cut my heart out of my chest before I ever let her realize the hold she has on me.

She's taken too much as it is.

Like hell I'll let her have my heart too.

Chapter 16

Skylar

Seventeen years old

I flip the page of my book, pretending to read, when in reality, I can't stop staring at my mother and Curt on the other side of the porch from under my eyelashes. I lower my head to hide my smile as they continue to send sweet discreet glances to one another, whispering sweet nothings in each other's ears as if they were the only two people on earth. My insides warm, witnessing how acutely in tune they are to each other, even when doing something as trivial as my mother cutting her husband's hair on a Sunday afternoon.

After all this time together, they still act like they're on their first date, completely smitten and in awe of how they got to be so lucky to find each other. No matter the hardships we've had to overcome, I've never questioned the sincerity of their love. It's as clear as day how devoted they are to one another, and only a blind fool would think otherwise.

My mother is happy.

Truly and unequivocally so.

Just as that fleeting joyful thought crosses my mind, there is a pang in my chest as I recall how that wasn't always the case. How she suffered at the hands of my cheating father and all the tears she shed over not being able to save her first marriage and keep her little family together. As if her first heartbreak wasn't enough to cause some serious damage to her heart, then the loser boyfriends who came after my deadbeat father made sure to shatter her already fragile self-esteem. It's no surprise that most of them didn't stay long enough for me and Daisy to even remember their names. Not that Mom went out of her way to introduce us to many of them, though. It's almost as if she already knew that they wouldn't stick around since none of them wanted to be settled down with a woman who had two young children and was living paycheck to paycheck. To them, Mom came with too much baggage to be worth the trouble. She might have been good for a few laughs and worth a night or two of fun, but that was about it.

It's a damn miracle Curt came into her life when he did, considering his own broken heart.

Maybe that's why they were always fated to find each other.

But if that's the case, what was the point of having them suffer such loss and misery before getting their happily ever after? Was it a test? Was such heartache inserted into their lives just so they wouldn't take the real thing for granted when they found it?

If I were an expert in the rules of love, then maybe I would venture a guess to answer that question. But since I'm clueless to all matters of the heart, I wouldn't be able to tell you. I'm just happy they found each other, even if it had to be later in life.

Still, I can't help wondering what it would have been like if my mom met Curt first before she ever met my father. But just as I imagine that alternative universe, my lips flip into frown. If that had been the case, then maybe I wouldn't exist, or at least not this version of myself.

Or worse, I would and so would Noah, making him my full-fledged brother.

A sick shiver runs down my spine at the thought.

I couldn't live in a world where he was my brother.

That would be all sorts of messed up.

Especially considering last weekend's events when he barged into my room to play his latest game on me. I close my eyes and let another shudder run through my body at the memory of how his breath stalled and his blue eyes darkened with the way my body responded to his forbidden caress.

A brother couldn't touch me like that.

I'm not sure a stepbrother should touch me like that either.

In fact, I know he shouldn't have.

But even though sense and logic tell me otherwise, ever since that night, I've lied in bed anxiously staring at my bedroom door, trying to manifest Noah walking through it just to punish me again. His brand of wrath is the most delicious thing I've ever tasted, and I, for one, would be totally okay with having seconds.

"Are you getting a chill, Skylar? My sweater is right there if you need it," Curt says worriedly, successfully pulling me out of my illicit thoughts. He points his chin to his discarded wool sweater hanging on the back of a nearby chair, while my cheeks instantly heat up, as if I was just caught doing something I shouldn't have.

Wasn't I, though?

Imagining my stepbrother's fingers making me come isn't exactly what I'd call me being on my best behavior.

"Are you getting sick, sweetheart? You look flushed. Come here so I can check your forehead for a fever," my mother orders, concerned, putting her scissors down in favor of seeing if I'm getting sick.

I am sick, Mom.

Very sick.

Just not in the way you think.

"I'm fine, Mom. Just a cold wind that must have passed," I lie, unwilling to tell either one of them the truth of why my body can't stop shivering.

"Put Curt's sweater on just the same. I don't want you to catch a cold."

Not wanting to fight her on this, I get off the bench swing to grab Curt's sweater just to ease her worry. But just as I'm reaching it, the familiar sound of a motor bike approaching stops me in my tracks. My heart pounds in my chest as Noah pulls up our driveaway, his long blond hair flying in the wind, making him look almost ethereal in his rebellion.

"I told that boy a million times to wear a helmet. I swear he doesn't use one just to spite me," Curt grumbles under his breath.

"I'm sure that's not the reason why. You must be patient with him, love," I hear my mother reply softly. "Or you'll just end up pushing him away even more."

"I've been nothing but patient, Clara. Something's got to give. I'm at my wits' end where Noah's concerned. Maybe I should let Boyd lock him up and spend a few nights in a jail cell just so he realizes his actions have consequences."

My mother's shoulders slump at that remark, but she quickly recovers to put on a bright smile when Noah gets off his bike and starts strutting up the stairs to the porch.

"Hi, Noah. Did you have a nice ride?"

"Hmm," he mumbles in response to her, preferring to place his sole attention on his father. "What's all this?"

"What does it look like?" Curt snaps, annoyed, and I don't miss the light squeeze my mother gives her husband's shoulder to keep him calm. Curt lets out an exhale and relaxes his tense form. "Clara thought I would benefit from a cut, so she volunteered to do it for me."

"Isn't that what barbershops are for? Are we that broke, we can't afford to let a professional do it for you? Can't be that expensive," Noah retorts, leaning against a pillar and crossing his arms over his majestic chest.

A chest that I know holds nothing but strong, hard abs hidden way underneath his black Henley. Abs that he let me fondle with my fingertips just a week ago and have been taunting me ever since.

"How would you know?" Curt chuckles sarcastically, pulling me out of my perverse reverie. "You haven't cut your hair in years."

I watch Noah's face scrunch up, hatred burning in his gaze toward his father.

My mother catches the look, too, and quickly tries to do damage control before Noah says something that will dampen the good mood we've enjoyed for the better part of the day.

"If you'd like, I could trim it for you? I'm not a professional like you said, but I've cut my girls' hair all their lives. If you'd let me, I'm sure I could trim yours."

The hope in my mother's voice guts me. She's always trying to climb over Noah's fortress walls, hoping that one day she'll be able to live in his heart as he lives in hers. My mother's love for Curt immediately extended to Noah and she's been on a futile mission to win him over since she and my stepfather exchanged *I do*s. It saddens me that Noah is unable to see just how wonderful my mother could be to him if only he gave her half the chance.

"Don't waste your time, Clara," Curt grumbles, throwing a disappointed side-eye to his only son.

Just as it pains me to see how dismissive Noah is of my mother, it also pisses me off how Curt never gives him the benefit of the doubt. Sure, he's an asshole, but Noah is still his son. He should be in his corner as my mom is for me and Daisy. But since the first day we stepped into this house, I have yet to see Curt have Noah's back on anything.

As if hearing my thoughts, Noah's lips slant into a roguish smile that tells me he's up to no good.

I should know, since I've been at the receiving end of that smile a million times before.

"You know what? Why not?" Noah's grin stretches further.

My mom's face lights up, while Curt's forehead wrinkles in apprehension, clearly knowing his son as well as I do.

"Take a seat then. Just give me a few minutes to finish up with your father's hair first."

"Take as long as you need. I'm not going anywhere." Noah throws her another one of his ominous smiles, making me just as worried with what he's got up his sleeve as his father is.

Noah starts to walk to a side bench, bypassing me without so much as a hello my way, when I remember why I got up from my seat in the first place.

"What are you doing?" he suddenly asks me, his tone no longer upbeat with mischief when he sees me picking up his father's sweater to put on.

"I'm cold," I explain, fully committing to the lie.

But just as the explanation has left my lips, Noah takes off his leather jacket and throws it at me.

"Put that on."

Since I feel our parents' curious stare on us, I quickly put on his jacket and walk back to the bench swing, acting as if this is no big deal. As if Noah lending me one of his most prized possessions holds no significance whatsoever.

Nothing to see here, people.

Nope.

Nothing at all.

The fist around my heart tightens as I shove my hands into the jacket's pockets, feeling warm all over. It takes everything in me not to lower my nose to the lapel just to relish in his scent.

And I called *him* pathetic.

Sigh.

Noah starts scrolling through his phone, while I watch my mom continue on with her task of cutting her husband's hair. Whatever tension ensued with Noah's arrival is now forgotten as both of them start to tease each other, back to their love bubble. Every once in a while, my mother giggles like a lovesick schoolgirl, while Curt chuckles softly, his hands always finding excuses to touch her.

Between being enveloped with the heat of Noah's jacket and

watching my mother's happiness in full display, my own heart pitter-patters, wondering if that type of love will ever be in the cards for me. But just as I think this, my heart dips into my stomach when my eyes land on the boy sitting across from me.

Like me, Noah is also mesmerized by our parents.

But while their love gives me a sliver of hope for what life has in store for me in the love department, Noah's cold expression says he feels something different completely.

Resentment.

Pure and unadulterated resentment of their happiness.

My frown is immediate, and all the blissful warmth I had been momentarily spoiled with morphs into something cold and ugly, chilling me to the bone.

"There," my mom says gleefully, satisfied with her handywork. "Now you look like the man I fell in love with."

"Glad to hear it. I wouldn't want to be anyone else." Curt chuckles, getting up from his seat and placing a tender kiss to her lips.

My mother's cheeks turn crimson at the small display of affection.

"You're up, Noah," my mother says, turning to Noah with a genuine smile once she's collected herself, but her grin quickly falls to the floor when she sees the same disgusted look on Noah's face that I do.

She opens her mouth to say something to him, but then is interrupted when her phone decides to ring. My mother is quick to answer the call, making sure to divert her attention off of Noah and stare into the distance, since it's obvious his glower is unsettling her. When she hangs up the phone, there is a look of relief on her face.

"I'm so sorry, Noah. That was Mrs. Henderson. Seems like Mr. Henderson had a bad fall off their roof and she wants me to come over to have a quick look at him to see if it warrants him going to the hospital."

"Damn it. I bet the old fool was trying to clean his gutters without me," Curt adds, shaking his head in dismay. "I'll drive you. While you check up on him, I'll clean the gutters, so he's not tempted to do it by himself again."

Curt grabs his sweater and pulls it over his head before going inside the house to grab his car keys. But as my mother waits for his return, she stares at me and Noah in a way that I'm not exactly comfortable with.

"You know what? Skylar could cut your hair if you want. She's done mine plenty of times, so you're in good hands if you're still up for it."

"I don't think that's such a good idea," I quickly interject, not liking the alternative solution she came up with.

"Nonsense." My mom grins widely, dismissing my hesitation. "You can do it, Skylar. I know you can."

"What can Skylar do?" Curt questions absentmindedly when he steps back onto the porch with my mom's coat in hand.

"I was just saying that Skylar could be the one who gives Noah a little trim if he wants one," she explains while she lets her husband help her put her coat on.

"Maybe the boy should go to a barber like he said," Curt adds his two cents, not liking the idea of having me anywhere near his son with sharp objects.

Not that I'm surprised.

Curt and Noah might have a difficult relationship, but no father wants to see his son hurt. He probably thinks I'd cut Noah on purpose. Even I have to admit that the idea is oddly appealing. Especially with how Noah was making my mom feel less than not a second ago. A little nick won't kill him, but it sure as hell will make him think twice before he acts like a dipshit to my mom again on my watch.

"Actually, I'm up for it if Noah is," I say a little too eagerly, surprising everyone.

Noah runs his thumb over his lower lip, looking intrigued. He then surprises us all when he offers a clipped nod in consent.

"There. It's settled," my mom quips with a pleased smile, stretching her hand out with the pair of scissors to me.

I stand up from my seat and walk over to grab them from her and then turn to Noah, who is still staring at me like he's trying to unravel what my game plan is.

"Well? Have a seat." I pat the chair.

He rolls his tongue over his front teeth before standing up and taking the seat in front of me.

"Brilliant," my mom coos, satisfied with the scene. "We shouldn't be long, unless, of course, Mr. Henderson's injuries are more severe than his wife led me to believe. I'll call you either way, Skylar."

Noah and I both stay silent as we watch our parents get into the truck and pull out in the direction of the Hendersons' home.

"So? Are we going to do this or what?" Noah grunts, looking suddenly uncomfortable with sitting helplessly while I have a weapon in my hands.

I lean down to his ear, and smile when a shudder runs through his spine with just my breath fanning his neck.

"So eager," I mock. "You didn't look so enthusiastic a few seconds ago."

He tilts his head to the side, my breath catching in my throat with how close his lips are suddenly next to mine.

"Oh, that's right. I forgot you know every little thing about me. Even what thoughts run through my head. Or at least that's what you tell yourself."

"I know enough." I frown, straightening up.

"Sure you do." He smirks, turning his face away from me. "Keep thinking that."

I square my shoulders and start combing his long hair, trying desperately not to marvel at how soft and silky it feels between my fingers.

"How short of a trim do you want it? An inch? Two?" I ask with as little emotion as I can.

"Cut it all off."

"What?!" I blurt in outrage, taking a step back, offended he would suggest such a thing as cutting off such beautiful hair. "You're kidding, right?"

He shakes his head, not looking at me.

"This is a joke. You can't be serious," I continue to protest.

"It's time," he deadpans, steel resolve in his tone.

I chew on my lower lip, unable to find the right words to say that can persuade him to change his mind even if only for my sanity's sake.

"Are you sure?" I question after an excruciating pause.

He nods.

I swallow dryly, feeling completely unequipped to do what he wants. I was all prepared to make him squirm a little while I pretended his hair wasn't safe in my hands, or even hint that if he didn't sit remotely still that there was a good chance the scissors would slip through my fingers and nick his precious neck, but not once did I ever consider following through with the threat.

And now here he is, giving me permission to cut away a piece of his essence.

Like it's nothing.

Like his golden halo hasn't haunted my dreams.

"I don't think I can do it," I tell him truthfully.

My very first memory of Noah was of how awestruck I was with his ocean eyes hiding beneath such stunning long hair, and over the years, his glorious mane just grew as wild and untameable as the boy himself.

It's one of the things that make Noah, Noah.

No matter how much I've hated him in the past, I couldn't be responsible for destroying such a significant part of him. I'd feel like Delilah stealing Samson's strength away. Noah's long, luxurious blond locks are part of his identity. Cutting them away might change him somehow, and I'm not sure how I would feel about that.

I'm still struggling with what to do when I feel his arm snake around my waist and pull me closer to his side. I lower my gaze to his and stop breathing. There is such a vulnerability in his gaze, a rawness I've only seen once before. In my room, just seconds away before he kissed me.

"I want *you* to do it. You, Sky."

With another dry swallow, I offer him a meek nod and try to tap into all the courage I have.

This is his choice.

It's what he wants.

The least I can do is respect it.

I don't owe him anything, but my heart says I owe him this much.

When he drops his arm from around my waist, I walk behind him, praying that I don't fuck this up. With trembling hands, I brush his hair again with a comb and position the scissors right at the base of his neck. I close my eyes and take in a deep breath before opening them up again and performing the first cut. When a quarter of his hair falls to my feet, the corner of my eyes start to sting with unshed tears. I bite into my inner cheek to keep my sobs at bay as I go back to repeat the action. A tear falls down my cheek when another batch of hair falls to the floor, pooling at my feet.

It's on the second cut that I feel his hands fall back and hold on to my calves as if he needs to be tethered to the ground, too, and not give in to this unexpected feeling of loss that is consuming me and threatening to eat me whole. My body trembles as I grab the last string of long locks. My tears are free-falling now, making my vision too blurry to see straight. I wipe my tears away with my forearm, seeing them drench the sleeve of his leather jacket. I lean into him and take a whiff of his scent, giving me the courage to finish this once and for all. It's only when I cut the last batch of hair, that I step back and drop the scissors from my hand on a loud thud as if they had been burning me all throughout.

"It's done. It's done," I cry.

When Noah turns around in his chair, that's when I see that he's crying too.

"Come here, Sky."

I don't question his command; I just throw myself at him, sitting on his lap and cradling my head in the crook of his neck, letting my tears fall on his shoulder.

"I'm sorry. I'm so sorry," I sob.

"Shh. It's okay, baby. It's okay. It was time. It was time," he repeats on a loop, rubbing my back soothingly with his hand.

He lets me cry my fill, while I try to comprehend why I'm feeling like this. Like I just forced him to lose a part of himself. A part that he had been desperately trying to keep a hold on to.

"I'm glad it was you," he whispers in my ear, before tilting my chin up to look at him. "It had to be you."

"Why?" I croak, licking the tears from my lips.

"Because," he starts softly, wiping my tears with his thumbs, "it's just like you said. You might be the only one who truly knows me, Sky. Knows how significant this was to me."

"Will you tell me why?"

His saddened expression transforms to one of misery.

"It's okay. You don't have to tell me." I start to shake my head, not wanting to force him to divulge the reason for such pain.

Noah continues to gently caress my cheeks, his watery eyes killing me from within.

"The last person who cut my hair was my mom," he explains, softly making my aching heart cry even more for the lost boy in front of me. "She was probably the only person that ever loved me, and I loved her with all my heart. I still do. I always will even if everyone else has forgotten her." I hiccup on a pained sob as he tightens his hold on me. He gently presses his temple on my forehead, his nose running through the length of mine. "I guess it's only fitting it was you who cut it off now."

"Why? Why me?"

He pulls away just an inch to pierce me with the eyes that hold the key to my locked heart. My chest heaves up and down, unable to bring oxygen into my lungs as he stares at me with such intensity that my toes curl. I can see the answer to my question in his eyes. It's right there for me to grab it and store it safe in my heart. All I have to do is be brave enough to reach out for it. And when his gaze falls to my lips, I wait on bated breath for the kiss that will undoubtedly change my reality forever.

But just as my heart leaps to my throat, ready for him to steal it away from me, we hear a car turn into our driveaway. As quickly as I can, I jump off his lap, just as my sister swings the front door open.

"Dude! You cut your hair!" she exclaims in shock, ignoring the boy who is honking in his Porsche for her.

"Hmm," Noah mumbles. "Where are you and Derrick heading to?" Noah asks, dismissing her shock and getting up from the torture chair.

"We're heading into town," she replies, still eyeing the butchered job I did on him.

"Mind if I tag along? I need to get this sorted."

"I don't blame you," she teases, but then her brow furrows when she sees me shift uncomfortably from left to right. "You want to come, sis?"

I shake my head.

"Okay, then." She shrugs, bouncing off toward her date.

"I'm going to need that," Noah says, his voice stern.

It takes me a few minutes to realize he's staring at the leather jacket I'm still wearing.

"Oh, right," I stammer, hurriedly taking it off me and feeling instantly cold when I hand it to him.

He grabs his jacket right where my hand is gripping it, my heart doing a stupid backflip when his thumb discreetly brushes my fingers.

"Thank you," he whispers, making me realize that his gratitude isn't for having his jacket back.

I lick my lips and nod, too overwhelmed to utter a word.

He turns around and heads toward my sister and Derrick, while my feet remain planted to the spot. I'm unable to move long after they've left.

All because it's at this moment that I'm hit with the stark truth that my subconscious has been desperate to keep hidden away from me.

I'm in love with my stepbrother.

And the worst part...

There is a small part of me that believes he might be in love with me too.

Chapter 17

Skylar

Eighteen years old

One year later

It's raining, as it often is on this island.

And for some reason, instead of crabbing a cab or calling an Uber, I'm walking down this road home, completely dripping wet.

Or maybe I do know why I'm out here walking in the rain. It's a walk born of frustration, of disappointment with the trajectory of my life.

My senior year has been one grueling disappointment after another lately.

There's the fact that my father convinced me to go to the mainland to meet him for dinner last night, and forced me to take the ferry, which he knows damn well I hate. When I got to the restaurant, he wasn't even there, never even bothering to pick up his phone when I called.

There have been lots of times where my father has disappointed me. But for the most part, those were done from the safety of my home. So I could stand with my nose pressed against the glass, waiting for his truck to appear. And when it didn't, I was at home so at least I had my mother to comfort me.

This was the first time that I hadn't been at home when he hadn't shown up. I'd stood by the dock just watching. Finally, I tried to call him, and then it was like I couldn't stop. I kept calling and calling and calling...and he never picked up. Didn't even bother sending me a text to explain his no show. I'd had to take the ferry all the way back to the island, his rejection a living, breathing thing under my skin for the entire trip.

Then there's also the fact that somehow I've become Kyle's girlfriend. I don't know how it happened, only that he's gotten into his head when school started that I'm somehow his. Not that we're having sex, or doing anything besides the occasional kissing. But he's everywhere, suffocating me with his nearness. With his mere presence.

It's not supposed to feel like this. I'm confident of that. Even though everyone tells me that I'm so lucky to have such a good looking, popular, nice guy by my side, for the life of me, I can't see the benefits to it.

Sometimes I wonder if watching my parents' marriage fall apart broke me in a way, that those important younger years that form the basis of your personality were skewed because the one person in the world that was supposed to love us no matter what, never loved us enough.

Regardless of the reason, I'm walking in the rain, the mud sloshing on my boots. I'm not exactly sure where I'm going, but I know I just need to get away.

Some writers talk about the rain being cleansing, and I try to imagine all of my inner angst sliding down my body and onto the ground, fluttering away so it can't burden me anymore.

It doesn't seem to be working.

A flash of gold catches my attention, and I glance over to the right to see that I'm passing the island's cemetery. The gold flashes again and I pause, trying to see what it is, only for the rain to let up a little and reveal Noah on his knees in front of a small gravestone.

Maybe I'll look back at this moment and wonder if it was when I truly lost my mind, but I find myself walking towards the opening in the fence line, towards where he kneels.

Maybe it's his sadness calling to me, causing an inexplicable pull that I can't ignore.

He doesn't look up as I approach, even though my feet are sloshing in the puddles made by the falling rain. He's the only one here that I can see, and for a second, a morose thought crosses my mind—would anyone fall on their knees in sorrow for me if I was buried here?

I don't stop walking until I'm right next to him. The stone has his mother's name engraved on it, and Noah doesn't shy away from the fact that his body is trembling as racking sobs fill the air, joining the gentle patter of the rain.

The rain doesn't feel cleansing right now; it feels like the earth has joined him in mourning his mother. It's a terrible thing to see this beautiful boy pouring out his sorrow for someone who is no longer here.

"Noah," I finally whisper, so quietly that I'm surprised he can even hear it. But as soon as I say his name, he glances up at me, his tears sliding down his face, mixing in with the rain streaking across his skin.

"It's her birthday," he murmurs. "She was always big on birthdays. When I was little, I promised her that she would never spend a birthday alone. That I would always spend the day with her. I promised." He shifts from his knees and sits cross legged on the cold, wet ground.

I want to offer some words of comfort. Anything, really. But before I can get anything out, he starts to talk.

"My dad was gone a lot growing up. Your mom was able to do

what my mother never could— keep him around. He would go fishing for days, but one particular year he promised he would be back in time to celebrate her birthday. I remember walking down the hallway and seeing her standing in the kitchen, her hair all done and makeup on her face, a slight glow to her cheeks. She was so excited for him to come home."

He rips out some of the grass in front of him.

"Then the hours passed. They passed and they passed, and he never walked through the door. I remember someone knocking, and her jumping up from the couch, just in case, I guess, my dad had lost his keys or something like that. And when she opened it up, it was just to see that a package had been delivered. It wasn't even a package for her. It was some fishing line my dad must've ordered before he left. She looked so fucking sad sitting on the couch."

He shakes his head, biting down on his bottom lip so hard he breaks through the skin. Drops of blood drip down the front of his face. I find myself reaching up, rubbing at the crimson drops with my thumb.

"She went to take a nap finally, I guess hoping she could just sleep away the day. And even though I was only nine, I still went into the kitchen and tried to make her a cake. It was a complete failure, of course. I burned myself at least twenty times, and it was burnt to absolute shit when I pulled it out. But you should've seen her face, Sky," he whispers, his eyes wide and staring unseeingly, like he's back in the kitchen right that very second. "She looked at that cake like it was a work of art. Like it was the best thing she'd ever seen. I had one candle on there and she let me light it, and then listened as I sang to her with tears streaming down her face. And I promised her that day that as she ate my terrible cake, that she'd never be alone on her birthday."

His fingers trace her etched name on the stone. "So here I am."

By this time, tears are falling down my face, because I can just imagine a little golden haired boy making a mess of the kitchen in order to bring a smile to his mother's face.

"Did your dad ever come home that day?" I ask hoarsely.

He stiffens, and then slowly shakes his head. "He was always doing things like that to her. Taking her for granted and making her feel like she was never enough. I watch him now with your mom, and I just wonder if that was my mom's curse, thinking that she'd fallen for her soulmate, when he was never that to begin with. My father never felt that way about her. He never looked at her like she was his beginning and the end. He didn't look at her the way he looks at your mom. Funny thing is that I actually believed he loved my mom growing up. He probably thought he did too. But now...with your mom in the picture, we both know that's a lie."

His fingers dig into the grass around him frantically, like he wants to unearth the coffin lying six feet under him.

"I think that's probably one of the worst things in life, falling for someone who can never love you the way they should. The way they deserve," he says hoarsely.

Noah rarely, if ever, has talked so openly like this...and it's almost too much. Him showing me this version of himself, the one that feels so deeply and sees the world almost as a romantic. I would've never expected the words 'soulmate' to come from his lips, and it's completely heartbreaking thinking about what he's just said.

"I'm sorry," I whisper. And I'm not exactly sure what I'm apologizing for.

Am I apologizing for her death...or the fact that my mom is his dad's true soulmate?

Things would have been simpler if the opposite was true. But there is a visceral part of me that can't imagine a world where Noah wasn't in my life, no matter how he got here.

Thunder breaks the silence around us and it sparks an idea in my head.

"I'll be right back," I say, springing to my feet. He stares at me like I've lost my mind, but I start to back away nevertheless.

"Don't go anywhere!" I call out inanely, like it makes sense for him to continue sitting in the mud in the cemetery.

It takes me a couple of steps to drag my gaze away from his, but then I turn and start sprinting, out of the cemetery, and down the sidewalk towards where some of the stores are. I'm puffing by the time I get to the small grocery store, and judging by the looks I'm getting, I'm a mess. Water and mud are puddling on the floor beneath me. I ignore all of their looks and make my way towards the bakery located on the left of the store.

I see it immediately, what I've come in here for. A chocolate cupcake with a cherry on top.

"That one, please," I tell the employee standing behind the glass counter. He eyes me dubiously, but reaches in and grabs the one I've pointed to.

I fidget as I watch him place the cupcake in a small cardboard box, and I practically yank it out of his hands when he holds it out to me.

"Thank you!" I remember to call out as I rush towards another aisle, searching for a birthday candle.

By the time I've left the store, I have a cupcake, a candle, and a lighter tucked away in a small plastic sack. I hustle back towards the cemetery, urgency threading through my veins.

Will he still be there? I wonder as I make my way down the sidewalk.

I hesitate once I get to the entrance of the cemetery and see him in the same spot I left him.

What the hell am I doing? The idea suddenly seems stupid, but as if he can feel my presence, Noah turns in my direction and sees me, and I have no choice but to walk towards him.

I stand in front of him, fumbling with the sack in my hand. His gaze dips curiously towards it.

"Where did you go?" he asks.

I think about lying for a second, telling him something ridiculous like I had to go grab some tampons, but the sight of him sitting there, his shoulders drooped, and his shirt plastered to his skin gets me going.

I plop myself to the ground and pull out the cardboard box, which immediately gets soaked.

He's still staring at me curiously, so I flip open the lid of the box to showcase the cupcake.

"I thought...we could celebrate her birthday properly," I whisper nervously.

His gaze widens, those incredible eyes of his searching my face, and I can't read at all what he's thinking, his face is perfectly blank.

His hand finally reaches out to grab the cupcake and he stares at it for another long while.

"I got candles too," I say, before realizing how ridiculous that was. How am I going to light a fire when it's pouring buckets out here?

He doesn't make fun of me though. He just continues to stare at the cupcake, his thoughts a million miles away.

Finally, when I almost can't take the silence anymore, he speaks. "I like it," he murmurs, taking the lid all the way off the cupcake even though it's now getting soaked. I pull the candle and the lighter out with trembling hands, and he sets down the box and the cupcake on the ground, holding his hand over it as I push a bright pink candle into the spongy cake. I try to light it, but I'm shaking too bad, either from the cold or my nerves about the situation.

Noah grabs it from me and uses his one hand to block the cake as he lights the flame. We both stare at it.

"I think I would've liked to have met your mother," I say.

His eyes hold mine. "She would've liked to have met you, too. She always had a gift of being able to see the best in people. It wouldn't have been too hard for her to find the good in you. She would have loved you."

My cheeks flush at the inference that his mom would have loved me in any capacity. If she was still alive, I know that I would have wanted her approval. I'm not entirely sure why it's important to me, but it is.

"Should we sing?" I ask, trying to divert his attention.

Finally, the corner of his mouth tips up, the first semblance of a smile I've seen since I first came across him here.

"Yeah, let's do it."

We both begin to sing softly, our voices getting louder as we get through the song, until we're belting happy birthday at the top of our lungs by the end.

He moves his hand from covering the candle and the light immediately extinguishes. But before I can say anything, he grabs my face, cradling it with both hands as he stares at me. His chest is rising and falling heavily, and he moves forward until his lips are just a breath away.

"What are you doing to me, little stalker?" he whispers, and a tear trickles from my eye and slides down my face. He watches it, fascinated, rubbing the path where it's fallen, and then he leans forward that last little inch, and his lips softly brush against mine.

The world around us fades with just that small touch. Fire lights in my veins, spreading warmth and working away the chill settled into my skin. If magic were real, the soft brush of his lips on mine would be what convinces me. There's a pulse of electricity between us, a feeling that his lips were always meant to be on mine.

I wonder if in a different life, a different world, he maybe... would've been... *my* soulmate.

Maybe it's the writer in me, seeing magic where there isn't, but the moment feels far deeper than the soft, comforting, grateful kiss that I'm sure Noah imagines it to be.

He doesn't try to deepen it. Instead, he continues to hold his mouth there, until we're just breathing in each other's breaths. I feel... immeasurably precious in this moment. Something I've never felt before in my life. I wish there was a way to take a screenshot of the moment, so that you truly could hold it with you as it really was. Because there's no way that my faded memory of this could surpass how it actually is.

When he finally moves away, I swear he takes a piece of me with him, and I almost cry out from the loss of it.

"The cupcake is ruined," he remarks in a rough voice, his gaze flicking to the pile of sodden cake below us.

I reach down and take a dollop of the frosting on my finger and then streak it against his cheek.

He rolls his eyes but makes no move to get it off...then again, I guess the falling rain will take care of that.

"Thank you," he says softly, and my cheeks flush again at the depth of emotion in his voice.

I know when we leave the cemetery, it will go back to usual. The bubble we've created for ourselves will pop and disappear.

But at least for a moment, I had this with him.

Chapter 18

Skylar

Eighteen years old

It feels wrong to be eating lunch with Kyle the following day. He takes every chance he gets to move in on me more. It's felt like a cat and mouse game with him since school started, and with every passing day, his frustration with me grows.

We're seated with some different friends than he usually sits with, ones that Noah isn't going to commandeer and want to sit by. Not that it matters. I can still feel the weight of Noah's glare for the entire lunch though.

We've just started lunch when I realize I have a couple of science problems I still need to do before class. I try to make an excuse to go to the library to study, but Kyle somehow guilts me into grabbing my notebook from my locker, so that I can work on it here with him at the lunch table. Not wanting to start a fight with all his friends watching over us, I just nod and accept defeat. I dash to my locker and grab what I need, and then take a much slower walk back to the cafeteria.

Everyone's chatting about Friday night's game when I sit down, and I halfheartedly listen as I shovel some of my salad into my mouth so I can finish eating before I start my science problems.

It takes me a couple of bites to realize something's wrong.

Really wrong.

I start to cough, my throat closing up at rapid speed, making it hard to intake air into my lungs. I stare down at my salad in horror, moving some of the leaves around when I realize that there's flakes of pecans all over it. Something that definitely wasn't there when I'd left to go to my locker.

I gasp for breath, and I can feel my face going red.

It takes forever and a day for Kyle to finally realize that something's wrong.

"Sky?" he asks, concerned.

I can't answer him. My hands are wrapped around my throat and it's almost impossible to breathe. Unable to keep my balance, I abruptly fall out of my chair to the ground.

“Skylar!" he calls out frantically.

The world's turning fuzzy around the edges, and all of a sudden, Noah is hovering over me. His mouth moves, but I can't hear the words coming out. He screams at someone, and then the world completely fades to black.

* * *

There's an annoying beeping sound in my ears when I come back to consciousness. My eyelids feel like they've been glued together, and it takes what feels like forever to finally get them open, revealing a white, sterile, unrecognizable room. I move my arm and feel a sharp splash of pain. Sluggishly, I stare down at the offending limb, finding an I.V. hooked up to it.

A second later, something collapses against me.

"Sky!" Daisy says frantically. "You're awake!"

My head feels like there's a fifty pound weight attached to it, but I finally get it turned so I can look at her. There are dark circles under her eyes, but her smile is bright and relieved.

"Where am I?" I ask, my voice coming out in a rasp.

"You're at the hospital. You scared us to fucking death." She shakes her head and wraps her arms around herself, looking uncharacteristically unsure for perhaps the first time in her life.

The hospital?

I try to recall how I could possibly have gotten here. I remember I was at school...I had run to get an assignment and then I was seated at the table...

My salad! The mysterious pecans!

"I ate some pecans," I say slowly. Daisy nods her head in agreement.

"Sky, I'm honestly shocked. You always do a much better job of making sure you're okay to eat something."

"I swear there weren't any before I left..." I whisper, half to myself, trying to really remember how careful I had been.

I remember asking the lunch lady if there were any pecans in the salad, and have a very clear memory of her saying there weren't. I also had at least a few bites of it before I left for my locker, so there was no way my allergic reaction wouldn't have set off at the first bite. My nut allergy was so severe, it was basically instantaneous. So I obviously hadn't been exposed to them prior to leaving.

But surely someone at the table would have noticed if someone had dropped by and sprinkled some nuts on my salad while I was gone.

The idea of them not noticing, and not saying anything to me... sounds insane.

"What happened?" I croak.

"You were just eating and then..." She closes her eyes as if in pain. And that's when I realize how pale my sister looks, her normally perfect hair all over the place, the chaos of it matching the emotions in her eyes. "You passed out, and fell from your chair onto the floor...

And then you started to have some sort of seizure and..." She shakes her head, her voice trailing off again.

"Noah had to give you CPR until the medics got there."

"Noah gave me CPR?" I croak out.

She nods and raises a trembling hand to her face to brush some hair out of her eyes. "I know you want me to be firmly on the hate train with him after everything he's done, squirt, but I'm not sure that I can pretend to hate him after he saved *my* person's life."

I'm still reeling with the image of Noah performing mouth-to-mouth on me in front of the whole school in my head, but her words bring me right back.

"Your person?" I ask, staring at her a little bit...awestruck.

I've always known that my sister loves me. It's been the two of us through all the crazy things that have happened with our parents, but a part of me, the part of me that always says I'm not good enough, never imagined how important I could be to anyone. Not even my own flesh and blood.

Daisy seems most of the time to be larger than life. The main character of every book you're going to read. I guess I'd always thought of myself as a small side character in her story, certainly not... her person.

And when Daisy abruptly bursts into tears, I'm even more shocked.

Because Daisy doesn't cry. Ever.

"Of course you're my person. I wouldn't even know what to do without you," she sobs. "Don't you ever, ever scare me like that again." Her hands grip onto the hospital bed, jostling it as she makes her point. "Promise me," she practically growls.

And I mean, it's a hard thing to promise someone that you're not going to accidentally eat something you had no knowledge of in the first place...but obviously, I'll say whatever I have to, if only to wipe the fear off my beautiful strong sister's face.

"I promise," I murmur softly.

She reaches up to her cheeks and wipes at her tears almost

angrily, like they've betrayed her or something. My heart hurts seeing her this way. So fragile. So uncertain. This is not the girl who acts like she couldnt give a flying fuck about anything. This is the big sister who would go to the ends of the earth to protect me. To hell itself if need be.

"How are you feeling though?" she asks, once she's gathered her composure.

I try stretching my arms and I wince at how sore my insides feel for some reason, like I've thrown up a million times and they're sore from the effort. I also feel exhausted, like I've run a marathon with no training, not that I'd do something like run a marathon though, obviously.

"Tired," I finally answer.

My stomach chooses that moment to growl. "And apparently...hungry."

She looks happy about that.

"That's a good sign. The doctor said that was a good sign." She leaps up from her chair. "I'm going to try to find someone and get you something to eat. Just stay right there."

Like I have a choice.

Daisy darts out of the room and I settle back against my pillows, staring around at the stark whiteness around me. I think I read somewhere that they did most hospital rooms in white because it was supposed to be a calming experience for a sick person. But I could do with a splash color at the moment.

"You're awake," says a very relieved voice from the doorway. Noah's very relieved voice.

I glance towards the sound and find him leaning against the doorway. It's impossible to miss how exhausted he looks, just like Daisy.

"I'm up," I confirm, feeling shy. The last thing I can remember is him hovering over me, and now knowing that he saved my life....

He takes a few steps into the room, tentative ones.

"I —" Noah starts before trailing off and sighing as he looks down, unable to meet my eyes. "I thought you were going to die," he finally finishes.

I don't answer him. I'm too busy just staring at him, caught in his web like I always am when he's around. Like he's the sun and I'm a solitary planet, caught in his orbit.

"I thought you were going to die," he repeats again, and this time a tremble travels all the way through his body.

"I'm here," I soothe, wishing I could just gather him into my arms. "I'm not going anywhere."

He turns towards me, and our gazes lock. There's so much unsaid in his blue depths. Things that I long for him to say, but of course he doesn't.

He clears his throat and the moment is broken. "They're doing an investigation at the school. There weren't any pecans in that salad."

"So someone put them in there," I say the words he's left unsaid. I should feel shocked, or maybe terrified...but instead, I just feel tired.

He opens his mouth to say something else, but then there's a knock at the door, and a nervous looking Kyle is standing there.

"What are you doing here, you piece of shit?" Noah growls, baring his teeth and taking a step towards him with a clenched fist like he is going to knock him out.

Kyle's eyes widen at Noah's ferocity and he holds up both hands in front of him. "Whoa, Noah I'm just here to check on your sister. I don't want to start anything."

"Oh, we're going to be starting something alright," Noah spits before he lunges forward and tackles Kyle back out into the hallway.

The familiar sound of flesh pounding flesh tells me that they're exchanging hits. I hear someone yell in the hallway for them to stop as I scramble to sit up to see what's happening. When I finally manage to do so, I catch a glimpse of them through the doorway, Noah relentless with each punishing punch. Kyle rears back and catches Noah in the eye...a hit I'm sure is going to leave a mark. Before Noah can retaliate, the security guards arrive, pulling the fumbling boys off of each other.

"Noah! What the hell are you doing!" I hear Curt bark, even though I can see him from where I'm sitting.

As if Curt's voice is a pin, and Noah is a balloon, Noah's body deflates at the sound of his father's voice.

Kyle's face is red and pinched as he stands there, his arms still held by a security guard in a beige uniform. He's telling everyone about how Noah attacked him out of the blue.

My mother appears in the doorway. "What's going on?" she says sharply, eyeing the scene in front of her before her gaze dips to my bed.

"Skylar! Oh, sweetheart. You're awake!" she cries, hustling into the room, completely forgetting the scene behind her. Coffee sloshes out of her too full cup as she walks.

I smile at her, but I'm distracted, my gaze captured on Noah. I can't hear what everyone's saying, but finally, the security guard lets Noah go. Noah strides away without a look back, ignoring Curt calling out for him. Kyle heads in the opposite direction once he's released, apparently no longer wanting to check up on me. Not that it bothers me. In fact, I feel relieved that he's decided to go home instead of extending his hospital visit.

Mom is at my side, holding my hand when Curt walks into the room, his gaze widening when he sees me.

"Skylar! I'm so glad you're awake."

"Is everything okay?" I ask, ignoring his relieved remark. "With Noah? Is everything okay with Noah?"

"Everything's fine," Curt says defeated. "Noah can handle himself just fine. He doesn't need you to worry about him. Like he likes to remind me, he doesnt need anyone," he adds sullenly, brushing his son away like he always does.

Curt misses the magic I see in Noah. And in that moment, I feel bad for him.

I feel bad for them both.

I'm saved from further conversation by the arrival of the doctor and a still harried looking Daisy.

The doctor examines me and decides he wants to keep me in the hospital for just a few more hours for observation, and then I'll be able to go home. All the while, I stare at the door counting down the seconds until Noah comes to see me again.

But he never returns.

* * *

It's midnight, and I can't sleep. Considering that's all I've been doing since my pecan incident, my lack of sleeplessness feels warranted.

Daisy wanted to sleep in my room tonight, but I sent her away. I'm not even sure why.

Or maybe I do know.

Maybe it's because I'm hoping that *he'll* come to my room.

Noah.

Everyone else in the house has gone to bed, and as far as I know, he hasn't even come home from wherever he went after the hospital.

Maybe I imagined it all. Maybe I imagined the pain in his gaze, the worry etched in his features. Maybe I'm trying to read into something that doesn't actually exist.

But just as the somber thought begins to take root, there's a soft knock on the door. Immediately, anticipation rushes through me.

"Come in," I whisper, not bothering to ask who it is.

My body knows who it is. I think I could sense him anywhere now.

Sure enough, when the door opens, it's Noah's large form slipping into the room. He hovers by the door, not saying anything.

Until finally, the darkness allows me to be brave.

"Come here," I murmur, and without delay, he walks over like he's been waiting for my invitation. He stands next to the bed and I scoot over, pushing my covers aside wordlessly, an invitation for him to slip in.

He hesitates for a brief second before sliding into bed with me, his face turned towards mine. A deep breath reveals his delicious scent...but also the smell of alcohol. Evidently Noah's been out drinking.

"Where have you been?" I ask.

He shrugs, as if he doesn't know, or maybe he doesn't think it really matters. I inhale again, part of me sniffing for the smell of perfume, of Stacy's perfume to be exact, but there's no hint of any of that.

"I'm sorry about what happened," he tells me. "I didn't mean to make a scene at the hospital, but when I think about the fact that he was seated right next to you...at the table... and he just... Either he didn't give a fuck to pay attention or just didn't care that someone put something in your food. So when I saw his fucking face there at the hospital, looking all fucking concerned, I just lost it. I just... couldn't take it."

"We don't know that someone put something in my food. It could have been a mistake in the kitchen," I say, although neither of us really believes that.

"I—I don't think I could survive if something happened to you, little stalker," he whispers, his words causing a tingling in my veins.

"Nothing's going to happen to me," I promise.

He nods, but his hand reaches between us and grabs mine, bringing it to his heart. I can feel the rapid beat of it through his chest, but his features don't match the anxiety I'm sensing.

"You were lying there on the ground, and you were so pale. There was even a tinge of blue around your lips."

"You saved me," I remind him, sensing that he's caught back in that moment, and needing to get him out of it. "Not only that, but you also gave the school lots to talk about," I chuckle darkly. "By this time tomorrow, I wouldn't be surprised if they started to build a statue in honor of your heroics."

"Fuck them," he says lazily. And I know he really couldn't care less.

"Can I sleep in here?" he asks, and there's a funny feeling behind my eyes, like I'm about to burst into tears at his question.

It seems like only seconds before he falls asleep, my hand still held tight against his chest, but it takes far longer for me to fall asleep, because like the creep I am, I'm savoring this moment with him, as usual, not sure that I'll get another one.

And sure enough, after a couple hours of laying there, I fall asleep. And when I wake up...he's gone.

* * *

It's my first day back at school and I'm trying to play it cool, but I feel just as nervous as I ever do. Is anyone going to comment about what happened?

To my surprise, for the most part, people ignore my presence as I walk down the hall. Including Noah, who's talking to a group of friends and doesn't look over as I pass by. When I get into class, Kyle's sitting there though, and it's obvious he has no intention of ignoring me. He smiles awkwardly as I sit down.

It's funny how things can change. I've always thought that Kyle was attractive, but right now, there is nothing I deem desirable in him.

"I'm glad you're okay," he comments lamely, and I shoot him a bland smile, nodding as I get my books and place them on my desk.

"You're not mad at me, right?" he asks.

"What would I be mad at you for?" I ask, straightening my pencils.

"For what happened at the hospital. I didn't mean to start something with your brother."

"He's not my brother," I snap, too quickly.

"Right... I mean...your stepbrother," Kyle says slowly.

I'm screaming at myself for giving too much away, but luckily I'm saved from any further conversation by the teacher starting her lecture, and when class ends, I hustle out, doing my best to get away when usually I would walk with Kyle.

Needing a break, I slip into the bathroom and lock myself in one of the stalls, wondering how life has gotten so complicated since I moved here. The bathroom door opens and I hear familiar voices chatting. It's Stacy and her friends.

"No one told me she was *that* allergic. My gosh, I wouldn't try to kill her," she jokes, and her friends titter away.

Of course, I immediately know what she's talking about.

It was Stacy all along.

The fucking bitch put the pecans in my salad.

Rage that I don't usually feel courses through me, and I slam open the door, only to be met by Stacy and her friend's surprised faces.

"It was you! You did this to me! You could've killed me!" I shout in outrage.

To her credit, Stacy quickly wipes the look of shock from her face at being caught red handed.

"I don't know what you're talking about," she has the audacity to say.

"Yes, you do!" I yell. "I heard you, Stacy. Don't try and deny it."

Even though her minions shrink behind her, Stacy holds out strong, schooling her features to show absolutely nothing.

Fury boils inside me, that even now, even when she's been caught, she refuses to acknowledge what she's done. Refuses to even consider the real repercussions of her action. If Noah hadn't been there...if the paramedics hadn't arrived in time...I would no longer be here. Because of her. And she doesn't even care.

"I knew you were a bitch, Stacy. You've had it for me since I came to this school. But I had no idea that you could be this soulless."

There's a flash of shame in her green eyes, but all too soon does it disappear, proving to me that my suspicions of her are correct. She really doesn't care that because of her little prank, someone's daughter, sister, could have died. That the little joke she played didn't only hurt me, but also the people I love.

Shaking my head in disgust, I push past her, knocking her shoulder on the way out of the bathroom. Right as I open the door, she yells behind me, "It's not like you died. Drama queen much?"

But to both of our surprises, Noah is standing right outside the door and hears Stacy's comment perfectly. An icy anger spreads across his features. Noah stalks towards the door.

"What did you just say?" he growls pulling Stacy out of the doorway.

She gulps.

"Nothing, Noah. I was just saying I was glad that your sister didn't die."

"Stepsister," he and I both correct in tandem, causing Stacy to give us a curious look.

"That's not what you said. You said, 'it's not like you died.' Was it you? Did you put the pecans in her salad? Was this your fucking handiwork? Answer me, Stacy!"

Noah's furious, and it's honestly terrifying.

Stacy's shaking in her boots.

I decide to defuse the situation by answering his question.

"I overheard her and her friends talking about it. She *is* the one that did it."

Stacy shoots me a death glare, but it disappears in an instant when Noah slams his hand against the wall.

"We're done, Stacy. You're done... And I'll be urging Skylar to report you to Sheriff Boyd as well as the school."

Stacy's features immediately transform to panic.

"Wait, Noah. It was just a little prank. I thought maybe she would break into hives or something. I didn't know she would get so sick. I promise. I didn't know," she cries, her hands clasped in front of her like she's begging before an altar.

He looks down at her like she's vermin at his feet.

"Listen closely, Stacy. Don't ever talk to me again. Don't look at me. Don't even come near me. And if I catch you giving Skylar anymore shit, you'll be sorry."

"Noah, please," she stammers through her now flowing tears.

"Fuck your pleases. You're done," he says coolly before placing his hand on my back and pushing me out of the bathroom right as the bell rings, signaling the next class is about to start.

We leave a sobbing Stacy behind us as we walk down the hallway.

"You should destroy her," Noah tells me seriously, his lips still scrunched with anger.

"I think you just destroyed her yourself."

Whereas a second ago, it probably would have felt good to get Stacy into a lot of trouble, at the moment, I still feel like I'm walking on air over how he just defended me.

Noah opens his mouth, like he's about to say something, but then he closes it and shakes his head, beginning to turn away. "Get to class, little stalker," he says before striding away.

"Did you mean it?" I call after him and he stops mid-stride.

"Mean what?" he asks without turning around.

"That you're done with her?"

He pauses for a moment to brush the back of his knuckles on my cheek.

"I've been done with her for a long time, Skylar. You're the one who hasn't been paying attention. You're slipping, little stalker," he finally answers with a wink, before continuing to walk away.

I stand there watching his retreating form, fully knowing that he just took a little bit more of my heart from me, and that I'm powerless to stop him from taking it all.

And I can't help but wonder...if it's safe in his hands?

Chapter 19

Skylar

Eighteen years old

"What? No hot date tonight?" Noah asks my sister when he struts into the living room and sees Daisy in oversized sweats.

"Slim pickings with this godforsaken storm, unfortunately," my sister mopes, snuggling into her seat by hugging her pillow under her head. "What about you? Couldn't convince Stacy to go out tonight?"

"Haven't you heard? We broke up," he explains with an exaggerated yawn.

"Again?" My sister laughs. "God, you guys are so boringly predictable. How long is this breakup going to last for this time?"

"I think this one is going to stick." He lets out a chuckle.

"Yeah, right. I'll believe it when I see it."

"You and everyone else," he retorts, his eyes discreetly fluttering to me.

I quickly snap my gaze away from him and pretend the television screen is way more interesting than the bomb he just dropped on my sister. With Daisy graduating last year, it's normal that she no longer knows the ins and outs of Bayshore High gossip, but everyone else at school is fully aware that Noah and Stacy are no longer a thing. The only thing they don't know is the reason why.

But then again, no one knows that her prank almost killed me either.

Before I could go to the school board or the police to point a finger at her, some lunch lady copped to her crime, saying that she mistakenly added pecans to my salad, completely unaware of my allergy. Noah was furious when he found out. And when he confronted Stacy's brother, Derrick about it, telling him that she was the one behind all of it, he already knew. Seems like Stacy's father is a big deal on the island, with even deeper pockets to pay for his daughter's mistakes.

I guess I should take comfort in knowing that at least Noah is on my side.

But deep down I know my sister is right. Noah and Stacy have been off and on again for years now. It's just a question of time before Stacy finds a way to lure him back into her clutches.

"What are you guys watching?" he asks, apparently done with the whole ex-girlfriend topic.

"Just some slasher flick. Scaredy-cat over here didn't want to watch the movie alone," Daisy teases me with a wink.

"I didn't want to see it at all. You're the one who changed the channel on me," I mumble, pulling my blanket up to my chin.

"Let me guess? Sky was watching some lame-ass documentary again," he mocks with that crooked smile playing on his lips that always sends a shiver down my spine.

God, how I hate that he knows me so well.

More so than what his smile does to my body.

"What else?" My sister snorts. "This one was about suffragettes. I tried to watch it with her, but when I almost fell into a deep coma within the first five minutes of it, I switched the channel fast. No way was I going to spend my Friday night being bored to death when I could be easily enjoying myself watching some serial killer cut up his victims into tiny little pieces."

"Feminists all around the world applaud your priorities, sis," I grumble, my shoulders slumping in defeat.

"Hey, do you want to stay and watch it with us? It just started," Daisy asks Noah.

"Sure, why not? Don't have anything better to do." He shrugs.

Since my sister is sitting in the only recliner in the room, Noah has no choice but to sit on the couch with me. Thankfully, he sits on the other end of it. Far at the other end, making sure there is a huge gap between us.

"Where's your mom?" he asks curiously after the killer on the screen kidnaps his first victim.

"Working the night shift. Only us here," Daisy explains absent-mindedly, snuggling under her fleece blanket, completely mesmerized by how the killer is sharpening his knives.

Even though this is not the type of movie I'd normally watch, my gaze continues to stay glued to the TV just so I'm not tempted to stare at the boy sitting on the other side of the couch. My attention only breaks from the screen when a loud crash of thunder erupts, making me jump from my seat. All three of us stare out the living room window, watching the violent wind thrash the leaves off the oak trees in the front yard. The storm is so bad that the window shutters bang furiously on the wall in tandem with the heavy rain hitting the porch, creating its own somber symphony to accompany the deafening sound of thunder.

"Are you worried about your dad?" Daisy asks, concerned, pulling her lower lip with her teeth. "It's looking like it's a big one tonight," she adds, and as if the storm heard her concern, the wind starts howling even louder.

"Nothing he isn't used to. He'll be fine," Noah dismisses, but I see a small flash of fear in his eyes.

"Hope so. I can't wait until he comes home," she replies in earnest.

"Since when have you ever been worried about my old man being out at sea during a storm?" Noah teases, trying to lighten the heavy atmosphere in the room.

Daisy takes his attempt in easing her worry and runs with it.

"Since he promised we would get a new heating system added to the house. That's when. This winter has been a bitch and it's only November."

"Ah. I should have known you'd have your own selfish reasons for wanting him to come home safe and sound." He snickers with a full-blown smile to his face.

"But, of course. Why else would I be worried?" She laughs.

The way they both smile at each other has my stomach in knots. Noah and Daisy have always acted like normal siblings would from day one. Their comradery and playful banter comes effortlessly to them. I can't help but feel a tinge of jealousy with how easily Daisy seems to know exactly what to say to keep Noah relaxed and completely at ease with her.

I've always had the opposite effect on him.

But then again, he doesn't inspire any calm in me either.

Noah is like the storm outside.

Loud, cruel, and catastrophic.

How I wish I hated it.

They start talking about something or other, but I'm not paying any attention. Instead, I just sit here quietly, too afraid that if I do open my mouth, I'll end up saying the wrong thing.

"Dude, you're shivering," Daisy reprimands suddenly, pulling me out of my reverie. "Skylar, don't be stingy and share your blanket with Noah before he freezes to death."

"I'm good," he retorts, clipped.

"Don't be a hero, Noah. It's fucking cold and you know it. Just scoot on over to Sky and get under the blanket with her. You'll thank me for it."

At first, I think he's going to come up with another excuse to not sit right next to me, but hell must have frozen over, because he takes my sister's advice to heart and eats the distance between us, until he's right there beside me. I don't even look at his face when I lift the blanket so he can cover himself up with it.

"Thanks," he mumbles under his breath.

"No problem," I reply in the same low tone.

Although he was shivering just seconds before, the heat of his body begins to scorch the side of mine. I keep my mouth sealed shut even when he starts taking some popcorn out of the bowl on my lap.

"I can't watch a scary movie like this," Daisy says out of the blue, jumping out of her seat to turn off the overhead light. "There. Much better," she singsongs, plopping back to her seat when she's made sure that the whole living room is almost pitch black.

Any other night I would have told her to turn the lights back on, but not tonight. I'd rather prefer the darkness hiding the effects Noah is having on me just with his close proximity alone. We all turn our attention to the movie again, which takes great effort on my part, since all I can focus on is the way his body melts into the couch. How his chest slowly heaves up and down with each intake of breath. Or how his knee rubs against mine. Thankfully, I'm able to snap out of it and concentrate on the horror movie taking place in front of me. But when a frightening scene occurs that I wasn't expecting, I let out a terror-stricken scream, only to gasp when I feel Noah's hand squeeze my thigh.

"Jesus, Skylar. That wasn't even that scary." Daisy laughs.

"Tell that to my beating heart, why don't you? I almost had a heart attack," I exclaim, removing the bowl of popcorn from my lap and placing it on the side table.

"Such a scaredy-cat." My sister continues to chuckle, but I'm unable to give her the comeback she deserves since my heart is drumming madly inside my chest for a whole different reason now.

Noah loosens his grip on my bare thigh lightly and begins to caress the inside of it with his thumb. My breathing grows shallow as he draws circles on my leg, coaxing my heart to jump up to my throat with each light caress. Under such dark surroundings, with only the television offering a flicker of light into the room, we're nothing but shadows. Add in the blanket on top of us, and his illicit touch is completely missed by my sister.

Slowly, I tilt my head to the side just enough to look at him, but his focus stays purely on the bad guy chopping his victim up, instead of the goosebumps he's inflicting on me.

How can he act this unbothered while I'm burning up?

Nah.

Two can play this game.

I gather up all my foolish bravery and place my hand on his leg, mimicking his move. A hint of a smile crosses his lips, but it quickly disappears. I look over at Daisy whose lids seem to be struggling to stay awake, even with the sound of the chainsaw coming from the screen.

Noah's fingers inch higher up on my leg, and then dives slowly in between my thighs, right at my apex. I have to bite my tongue just to keep silent.

He's playing with me.

Seeing how far I'm able to take this without getting caught.

Oh, buddy. I'm all in.

In true form, I repeat his move, my hand going a little bit higher on his leg, and then diving right where his crotch is, a tangible bulge awaiting me there. His teasing smile disappears, while mine surfaces on my face. Gently, I caress my knuckles on his bulge, a soft moan escaping his lips. Empowered by his reaction, I palm his hard-on, softly at first, then tightening my hold.

He snaps his hooded eyes at me, his tongue peeking out to wet his lips. I cock a mischievous brow, calling checkmate on this game. But I should have remembered who I was playing with.

Noah doesn't like losing.

Especially to me.

When a devious smile reveals itself on his lips, I know I've bitten off more than I can chew. His hand covers mine on his dick, making sure I can't pull away, adding pressure to it. The hand that had been just teasing me with its heat suddenly spurs to life, his thumb lightly stroking my core over my shorts. We're both still fully clothed, me in my pajama shorts and top and Noah in his simple white t-shirt and gray sweatpants. But we could be naked for all I care, since every caress feels like it has a direct line to my core. The loud thumping of my heartbeat is even louder in my ears than the soundtrack of a chainsaw hacking away on the TV, the thunder wreaking havoc outside, or my sister's soft snoring.

Noah surprises me still, taking my very breath away, when he tilts his head to the side to face me.

He couldn't look more beautiful to me if he tried.

His blue eyes lock with mine as he continues to tease me with his light strokes. I try not to squirm under his penetrating gaze, but my body has other plans. My legs spread a little more, giving him ample space to work his magic on me. His ocean eyes look even more thunderous than the weather outside when I hike my ass up just so I don't miss a single touch.

Unable to prevent it, I gasp a little too loudly when he leaves my core to shove his hand down my shorts and inside my panties. The hand that had been keeping mine prisoner on his cock lifts from the blanket only for it to slam over my mouth. Noah shakes his head, his way of telling me to stay silent. I blink twice and nod. Once he's made sure I won't make a sound, he removes his hand from my mouth, but not before he lightly runs his thumb over my bottom lip. His half-mast eyes squint further when my tongue instinctively peeks out and licks the pad of his thumb. I watch his Adam's apple bob, his gaze falling to my hungry lips. He snatches his thumb away and snaps his head away from me, pretending to watch the movie again. I follow his lead, biting my inner cheek when his strong hand pulls my leg over his, spreading me wide open for him.

My chest heaves when I feel his fingers gently play with my slit, feeling my wetness coat them. My own hand remains paralyzed as his bulge gets bigger in my grasp. When he realizes that I'm not moving, he stops his delicious assault on me and lowers his sweats, just enough to spring his hard cock free under our shared blanket. It takes everything in me not to make a sound and wake my sister up.

Carefully, I grab his length in my hand, feeling the weight of it. The velvet smoothness. His soft exhale tells me he likes my touch, and when I feel his digit once again rubbing at my clit, I realize this game has stakes. He'll only show me pleasure if I show him the same. Crap. Noah is an expert, while I'm just a novice. I've never done this sort of thing before, while Noah has years of experience.

I try not to think about that and just enjoy his touch on me. My swollen breasts ache, as his cock swells in my untrained hand. I add more pressure, sliding up and down from his tip to his balls, observing his light blue eyes darken.

It's so intense.

All of it.

His eyes.

His body radiating energy.

Mine threatening to combust just with the way his fingers graze my clit.

Suddenly, something takes over my body, and I feel a familiar bolt of energy strike me down, making my legs quiver. I can see him staring at me through his periphery as a myriad of sensations take over my body.

I wonder how I must look to him.

But just as I'm thinking this, Noah adds more pressure to my nub, creating a spark that sends electricity to pulse through my veins. My jaw slacks as a tiny wail escapes me before I have time to slap my hand over my mouth. I'm panting when my soul returns to my body. I glance over at Noah, his jaw ticking, his brow furrowed in agony. Licking my parched lips, I lightly squeeze his cock before pulling the skin back down in one smooth move. When I reach the head, my thumb finds the crown slick and wet with pre-cum. Just as I'm about to pump his cock in my clenched fingers, Noah grabs hold of my hand, halting my next move. I don't know why him stopping my caress feels like a rejection, but it does, instantly dimming my euphoria.

"Damn it," Daisy yawns. "I totally fell asleep, didn't I? Did I snore much?" she asks, still rubbing her eyes with her fists.

"Just the usual," Noah retorts evenly, like him giving me an orgasm was no big deal.

"Hardy har har. I'm going to bed," she states drowsily. "Are you coming, Sky?"

"She already has," Noah whispers under his breath with a smirk, making me thankful it's too dark for my sister to see the flush that is coloring my cheeks.

"In a bit. Just want to finish the movie," I reply with all the nonchalance I can muster.

"Suit yourself, but don't wake me up in the middle of the night if you have a nightmare. Nighty night, kids."

I sit still and wait for her to walk up the stairs, only relaxing when I hear her bedroom door close. I then turn over to Noah, whose gaze is already fixed on my face.

There are a million things I want to say right about now, yet I focus on the one that I'm still hurt by.

"Why did you stop me? Was I hurting you?"

"Yes," he groans huskily.

"Oh," I reply, my head falling to my chest.

I knew it. I really do suck at this.

But then Noah surprises me by tilting my chin up gently with two fingers.

"You didn't hurt me like that, Sky. When I saw Daisy starting to wake up, I had to stop you. I doubt you'd want to explain to her why you were ten seconds away from having me come all over you."

"Oh." My cheeks blush profusely.

"Yeah, oh." He smiles with a hooded gaze.

We then sit there and just stare at each other. My eyes take him in as his memorize mine. When my gaze falls to his lips, I silently beg them to kiss me.

"I'm going to kiss you now, Sky," he says as if reading my thoughts.

I close my eyelids, waiting for him to kiss me, but then open them when I hear him shuffle from his seat beside me to go on his knees in front of me.

"What...what are you doing?" I stammer, eyes wide.

Instead of answering me, he throws the blanket off me and pulls my shorts and panties down my legs.

"Noah?" I gasp when he pulls my ass to the edge of the couch, curling my legs around his broad shoulders.

"Shut up, little stalker, and just let me kiss you. Please," he growls in utter desperation.

And before I'm able to stop him, his flat tongue swipes leisurely from the bottom of my slit right up to my clit.

"Oh God!" I sob out, my hands clenching at my sides as my ass arches off the edge of the couch.

He pulls away, his sea of blue in flames. He grabs a discarded pillow from the couch and lays it on my lap.

"Bite down on this, baby. Or don't. I really couldn't give a shit right now," he threatens, his head going back to hiding in between my legs.

Not wanting Daisy to come back down, I grab the pillow and bite down on it, just as Noah sinks his teeth into my inner thigh. My eyes roll to the back of my head as he sucks at my flesh, leaving his mark before he attacks my pussy with his mouth again. The pillow muffles the loud wails that are ripped from my throat as his tongue lashes at my most private area, owning it completely. The pulse in my clit beats to the song his tongue is singing to it. His brow glistens with sweat, his eyes staring at me while he eats me out. It's the most erotic thing I've ever experienced. When he sucks and nibbles at my clit, my back arches up again, only this time, Noah plants his hand on my stomach, preventing me from moving an inch. His fingers on my heated flesh feel incredible, but like this, his tongue's ministrations are too much for me to bear.

"Noah!" I cry into the pillow.

This is what Icarus must have felt when he flew up into the heavens and touched the sun's golden rays for the first time. My whole body explodes into a ball of light, feeling like I'll never be able to go back after this. It takes forever to pry my eyes open, my limbs sated and weak after such an orgasm. When I've finally gained some composure, my lids flutter open, my eyes landing on the cause of such ecstasy.

Ever so silently, I watch in a daze as Noah gently pulls my panties and shorts back up. Once he's made sure I'm properly dressed, he stands back up to his feet, his hard bulge twitching under his sweatpants right at my eye level. My tongue licks the seams of my lips before I crane my neck back to look up at him.

"Go to bed, Skylar," he orders with a groan.

"Are you sure?" I whisper breathlessly, my eyes falling from his face to the way his cock twitches in his pants.

Another groan.

I bat my eyelashes at him, wanting to lavish him with the same pleasure he just gave me. But my words are stuck in my throat when he extends his hands for me to take. I plant my hands in his, and he lifts me up to my feet, our lips just a hair's breadth away from each other's.

"You promised me a kiss," I say on a ragged breath.

"You got one," he retorts with a husky tone that sends shivers down my spine.

"What if I wanted to *kiss* you?" I ask, emphasizing on the word kiss as I press myself on his hard cock.

Noah pulls the strands of my hair, making me tilt my head back.

"You don't want that," he grunts, his eyes bouncing every which way around my face.

"I think I do. Very much."

He gives my hair a biting pull, making me preen with how close I am in breaking his control. My heart jackhammers in my chest when he leans down to my ear, biting the lobe before he whispers, "If you kiss me in any way, shape, or form right now, Sky, you won't leave this room with your cherry intact. I've tasted its sweetness and it's taking everything in me to not steal it from you. So be a good little girl and go to bed. Final warning. I won't give you another one."

I stare into his eyes and see the threat in them.

If I push him, even an inch, he'll snap—my virginity be damned. Since I'm not sure if that's what I want yet, I take a full step back, Noah releasing his grip on my hair, his shoulders instantly relaxing. He then surprises me by threading his fingers with mine and walking me upstairs to our rooms.

When we're both standing under each room's threshold, we hold our gazes for one more minute, neither one happy about putting an end to this magical night.

"Good night, psycho," I finally say with a meek smile.

"Good night, little stalker." He grins with a wink.

And it's with a smile that I close the door on him and the best chapter I could have ever written thus far.

Chapter 20

Noah

Eighteen years old

The next day is killer on my sanity.

I keep reliving Sky's glorious expression on her face when she came all over my fingers and then again on my tongue. How her lush body molded perfectly against mine. The way her full lips pouted when she was denied her pleasure. It took all my strength and then some to pull away from her. To not fuck her right there on my living room couch. I must have beat my cock into submission three times last night and three more in the shower this morning before I was ready to face her over breakfast.

"Good morning, Noah. Did you have a nice night?" Clara asks enthusiastically when I step foot into the kitchen.

"Hmm," I mumble, hoping she is astute enough not to try to bond with me so early on a Saturday morning.

Luckily, Clara's focus is quickly diverted from me to her eldest daughter the instant Daisy waltzes into the kitchen all bright-eyed, wearing one of her the-sun-is-shining smiles.

"You look awfully chipper this morning," Clara greets with a wide smile.

"That's because I am," Daisy announces, ruffling my already mussed hair, and grabs a mug out of the cupboard. "Nothing beats a full night's sleep. Sorry I bailed on you guys yesterday, but I was exhausted. Was the movie any good?" she singsongs as she pours herself some coffee.

"Once you've seen one slasher movie, you've seen them all," I reply, knowing my remark will be enough for Daisy not to ask me about the plot of the movie since I haven't the foggiest.

The moment I walked downstairs last night and saw Sky snuggled into a blanket, all I wanted was to either steal her away and lock her in my room or nestle her to me right there where her big sister could see. When Daisy demanded Sky share her blanket with me, I damn near skipped my way over to her. What happened next wasn't planned, but I sure as shit don't regret it. Making Sky come has become my favorite thing to do.

Unfortunately, Sky might have another opinion on the matter.

Shit.

How should I play this? Nonchalant? Like it was no big deal? Or should I tell her the truth? That she disturbs all of my dreams and I think of little else but her?

Fuck.

How the fuck are we going to go from here? Are we step-siblings that are supposed to hate each other?

Or have we crossed that invisible line on the sand that makes us something more?

I fill my bowl with cereal, my chest tightening as I count down the seconds until Sky shows up, so she can answer all these godforsaken questions running rampant in my head.

But Sky never shows up for breakfast.

And when she doesn't come down for lunch either, my anxiety is replaced with frustration. By the time she shows her face around dinnertime, I'm pissed as all hell. So much so that I refuse to acknowledge her presence in the kitchen when she arrives and says hi to me.

Her forehead wrinkles in confusion, but it quickly vanishes when her mom starts talking to her.

"Hey, stranger. I thought you might be hibernating or something when you didn't come out of your room all day. Let me guess? The muse was strong today and you couldn't leave your writing cave until you got all your words down? Is that it? Will you let me read whatever got you all inspired?" Clara asks with pride shining in her eyes.

"Maybe. We'll see," Sky responds noncommittally, her cheeks blushing. "How was your shift last night, Mom?" she adds to redirect the conversation to a safer topic.

"Oh, good. You know, the usual. I'll just be happy when I get back on the day shift next week. With Curt not being home, I hate leaving you girls all alone at night."

"Mom, we're all adults here," Daisy interjects, rolling her eyes. "You don't have to treat us like we're kids anymore."

"You will always be my babies to me," Clara says, kissing her eldest daughter's cheek, and then pressing another one on Sky's temple.

With the blatant display of motherly affection, I immediately lower my gaze away from the Ames women. I hate it when Clara is this warm and loving to her daughters. It serves only to make me miss my mom more. Miss how I don't have a parent that gives a shit about me like she used to. How Clara evidently does for her girls.

"Well, this baby has a hot date tonight," Daisy croons. "And if it goes as well as I expect it to, I fully intend to prolong it to a breakfast date, if you catch my meaning," she adds, wiggling her eyebrows.

"We all catch your meaning. Subtleness really isn't your strong suit, is it, sis?" Sky retorts with a chuckle.

"Hmm. Can't you postpone it, sweetheart? I really don't like leaving Skylar all alone at home all night," Clara interrupts, completely bypassing her eldest daughter's remark on getting some tonight. The woman sure does like living in denial lalaland.

"First, she's not alone. Noah will be here, too. And second, which part did you miss about we all being adults? Skylar's eighteen, Mom. Not eight," Daisy says, quickly coming to her sister's aid.

I don't miss how Clara looks worriedly to me and then over toward Sky. Instead of saying anything that will only give sway to her concern, I keep my mouth shut and open the fridge to grab the leftover cannelloni from lunch and put it in the microwave. I lean against the counter, my head bowed, pretending to scroll through my phone while I wait for my food. All the while feeling the weight of Clara's scrutinizing gaze on me.

"Okay. You're right, Daisy," she concedes eventually. "Neither of you are kids anymore. No use being such a worrywart." She smiles shyly at us both before looking at her watch. "Oh geez, is that the time? I better get ready if I don't want to miss my bus and be late for my shift."

"I can drive you to the hospital. It's on my way," Daisy offers.

"You're going to the other side of the island? Is that where your date lives?" Sky asks curiously, trying to pin down who her sister is knocking boots with.

If Daisy is going to the rich side of the island, then there is only one person she's hooking up with, and that's Derrick Monroe. He texted me a few days ago saying he's home from college on the mainland for Thanksgiving. I guess Daisy got the same memo and is taking full advantage of his little hiatus back at Thatcher's Bay.

"Thanks, sweetheart. I appreciate it," Clara says regarding Daisy's offer of driving her to work.

Daisy promptly nods and tells us she also has to get ready, leaving Sky's question intentionally unanswered. Not wanting to be left alone with Sky in the kitchen, I excuse myself and take my dinner upstairs to my room, locking myself in.

An hour passes by before I hear a soft knock on my bedroom door. I stare holes at it, wondering if I should open it or just leave Sky hanging like she left me for the better part of the day. It would serve her right. When she knocks again, my resolve breaks, getting up from my bed and swinging the door open for her.

"What?" I grumble, trying hard not to stare at her heart-shaped face or her Cupid's bow lips.

"Are you busy?" she asks nervously, wringing her hands together behind her back.

"Yes. What do you want?" I ask sternly, crossing my arms over my chest.

"Mom and Daisy have left for the night, so I was wondering if you wanted to see a movie with me."

"Not in the mood."

"Oh, okay," she says, her sad gaze falling to the floor for a split second. But all too soon does she remember herself and snap those silver eyes that feel like bullets to my chest right back at me. "Are you angry at me or something? Did I do something to upset you?"

"I've been angry at you since the day you moved in, or haven't you been paying attention?"

"No, that isn't it." She shakes her head, looking suddenly just as angry as I feel. "You're pissed at me because of something else. It's about last night, isn't it? You regret what we did and now you're taking it out on me, aren't you? Well, listen here, buddy. It takes two to tango. You let it happen, too. You touched me because you wanted to. Nobody forced you to," she yells at me, pointing a menacing finger in my face.

"Don't you think I fucking know that?" I shout back, pushing her finger away from me.

"God, I'm so stupid," she mumbles, eyes shut, pressing a closed fist on the center of her forehead before she drops it and looks up at me again. "I really thought yesterday was special. That maybe, just maybe, things would be different between us now. But nothing's changed, has it? We're right back where we started from. Awesome! Message received, Noah. I'll pretend nothing happened either since it's obvious you already have." She turns to leave, but then turns to face me again, true misery starting to water her eyes. "Fuck you, Noah Fontaine. Just...fuck you."

When she turns around to leave me again, I grab her arm and pull her into my room, slamming her back against the wall after I've kicked my door shut.

"What do you want from me, Skylar? You want to be my girlfriend? My sister? What?!" I blurt out hurriedly, on the fringe of losing all control.

"How about a friend? Can't we at least be friends?" she croaks, unshed tears adding a strain to her voice.

"No. I could never be your friend."

"Why not?" she asks, hurt, a stray tear falling down her cheek.

"Because every time I look at you, all I want to do is either yell at you or kiss you," I confess exasperatedly, gently wiping the tear with the pad of my thumb.

"You've already yelled at me today. What's stopping you from kissing me instead?" she whispers, her melodic voice pulling me deeper into her web. She goes to her tippy-toes and presses her temple against mine, making me instantly groan and close my eyes.

"Huh, Noah? Why don't you just kiss me?"

"Because if I do that...if I kiss you...then I'm not going to be able to stop."

"Who says you have to?"

I breathe her in, my breath hitching as her lips draw nearer to mine.

"Little stalker, don't..."

"Stop me then."

But I don't stop her.

I can't.

I never could.

Instead, I lean in and meet her lips with mine, my burdened heart willingly offering itself over to her. I stand still as she curls her arms around my neck, pulling me down so she can kiss me like she wants to. When her tongue breaks the seam of my lips, begging for entry, all my resolve flies out the window. My tongue wrestles with hers, our teeth and lips clashing together as we devour each other.

I pick her up from the floor, her legs entwining around my hips as I walk us to my bed. I lay her down on it, my body covering hers as I continue to get lost in our kiss. Her eager fingers pull at my hair to break our kiss so she can nibble and suck on my neck.

"Sky," I groan as she rubs her hot core on my hard length.

"Hmm," she hums, licking my Adam's apple and then biting down on my bottom lip.

Fuck.

"Sky," I try again, my chaotic mind unable to focus on anything but the way she smells. The way she moans and sighs when my fingers dig into her hips. The way her limber body cocoons itself around mine.

"Baby, please, listen," I beg, my hand already cupping her breast under her sweatshirt, my fingers tugging her perky nipple.

"No. No more words, Noah," she sighs, the heels of her feet digging into my ass so that my cock is pressed firmly on her greedy pussy, giving her the friction she needs. She lets out another one of those long sighs that kills me when the head of my cock rubs at her swollen clit. "I spent all day in my room dreaming about this. About being in your bed with you on top of me. Don't ruin it with words, Noah. Just kiss me."

Fuck.

"Was that what you were doing all day? Thinking about me fucking this greedy little pussy?" I growl, dry humping her cunt with my hard shaft. She nods breathlessly, her nails digging into my shoulders with each thrust. "Did you play with yourself thinking about how I would pop this little cherry of yours?" Another nod, this one accompanied by a loud wail. "Did you come?"

"Every time," she admits on a pained sob. "Please, please, Noah."

"Please what, little stalker? What do you want?" I grunt, before I bite down on the little spot where her shoulder meets her neck.

"Argh!" she cries out. "Please!"

"Please what, baby? I'm going to need you to say it. Be very explicit."

With a knowing smirk tugging at my lips, I pull away from her, going to my haunches, my fingers tightening their grip on her thighs.

Her hooded eyes blink twice at me, her chest heaving for breath, so turned on she can't think straight. Not that I'm any better.

"Tell me what you want and I'll give it to you. Just say it."

I watch her lick her lips, looking so fucking beautiful it takes all my willpower not to just give in before she says the words I long to hear. But I stay strong, running my fingers up and down her legs as I stare her down.

"Say it."

"Fuck me, Noah."

My cock swells painfully as I memorize this exact moment. The moment when my sweet little stalker finally caved and opened her locked gates for me. I pull my t-shirt over my head and throw it across the room. Her half-mast eyes shine as they take in every inch of me.

"Has anyone ever fucked you before?" I ask, knowing the answer already as I pull off her shorts and panties.

She shakes her head, biting that fat lower lip of hers that drives me crazy. I stare at her mound for the briefest of seconds, knowing if I take longer than that, I'll lose my train of thought and just eat her out again. That can wait. First, I want to break her seal and ruin her forever.

I'll be her first, her last, her fucking everything.

I want tonight to haunt her, just as it will haunt me for the rest of my days.

I lean down just enough to pull her hoodie off her, finding nothing but gorgeous glistening skin underneath, two round swollen breasts begging to be fondled with. I run the palm of my hand from her neck, down the valley in between her breasts, to her navel, right down to her dripping cunt and throbbing clit.

"This pretty pussy is mine now, Sky. For as long as I want it, no one else will touch it. Understand?"

She nods again, widening her legs, anxiously waiting for me to stay true to my word.

"Say it," I growl, bending down to lick her belly button. She arches her ass up off my bed, groaning when I push her back down. "Say it."

"It's yours. My pussy is yours. Please."

I can't help the wicked grin that flashes on my face, loving how my nemesis, the girl who has tormented all my thoughts since the day she came into my life, begs to have her virgin pussy filled and fucked. My eyes trail down her naked body, my cock straining in my sweats. When I take longer to say or do anything else, I feel Sky's fingers lightly graze my chin.

"It's okay, Noah. I trust you."

It's the sincerity in her words that kick-starts my heart into drumming wildly in my chest, reminding me that this isn't just a fuck. This is Sky's first time. She's trusting me with her body, heart, and soul. Trusting that I will take care of her, protect her, keep her safe in my arms. I swallow dryly, the adrenaline pulsing through my veins spiking to new heights.

Here's the thing.

I know how to fuck.

I've been doing it since my freshman year. Fucking comes as easy to me as breathing.

And I'm fucking good at it, too.

But as I stare into Sky's eyes, I realize what I'm about to do is as far from fucking as possible.

"Sky," I hear myself stammer, suddenly feeling out of my depth.

"It's okay. I trust you," she repeats with that loving timbre in her voice that wreaks havoc on my heart. She extends her arms toward me, and like a fool, I engulf myself in them, letting her wrap her arms around me.

I let her kiss me, needing her warmth more than I need my next breath. I let her lead me into this new uncharted territory, one kiss at a time. I relinquish all doubt, fall into the kiss, praying she will catch me as I stumble into this foreign abyss. Sky worships my body with her lips, mouth, and tongue, her hands running up and down my back, shoulders, and arms. Each caress she delivers feels like she's branding my skin, imprinting her name on my flesh, and marking me as forever hers.

"Little stalker," I choke out when I can't stand the myriad of emotions taking over me for a second longer.

"I'm ready," she replies hurriedly, desperate for me to possess her.

I push off her just far enough for me to pull my side table drawer open and take out a condom. My teeth rip through the foil packaging, and in quick haste I sheath my cock before nestling myself in between her thighs. I position the head of my cock to her opening, groaning when I see her juices coating it.

"Noah," she calls out to me, placing her palms flat on my chest. "Look at me. Please. Just...look into my eyes, so I can look into yours."

There's this edge in her voice that has me halting my next move.

"We can stop. Tell me to stop and I will."

Inwardly, I curse at what I've just said, but fuck it. I mean every word. If she wants to take this slow, even if at a snail's pace, then that's what we'll do. This right here, is more than enough.

"No," she whispers, her silver eyes deadlocked on mine. "I want this. I want you. Just you."

"You have me," I hear myself say, the words falling through my lips as if they were always hers to hear.

The coy smile that springs free on her face has my heart thumping even faster.

"We'll go slow, okay?"

She nods, biting the corner of her lips as her hands drop from my chest to hold on to my forearms. Ever so slowly, I breach her entrance, groaning when I feel how tight she is around me.

"Noah," she hisses out, her nails cutting into my skin.

My gaze rises from where we are synced together and focuses on her eyes, like she asked me to. Never wavering my gaze from hers, I inch a little more inside her, my legs starting to shake at the feel of her clenching all around me.

Fuck, but she feels amazing around my cock.

Still, I don't press on, waiting for her pussy to stretch and get accommodated with my size.

"Are you okay?" I ask, needing to know where her mind is at.

"Uh-huh," she chokes out, her eyes squinting with pain.

"Baby, if this hurts too much—"

"No." She shakes her head. "Don't stop. Please."

"Always so polite," I tease, needing to do something to get her out of her head a little bit. "If I had a hundred-dollar bill for every time you've said please tonight, I'd have enough for a brand-new muffler."

The little laugh that she lets out has my tense muscles relaxing.

"Don't get used to it," she sasses back with a smile.

"Yeah? What else can't I get used to?" I joke, inching a little more inside her. "Fuckkkkkk!" I grunt when I'm halfway there.

"I can think of a few things," she banters once she's recovered from this last assault.

"Yeah?" I retort, wiping the sweat off my brow. "Like what?"

"I'll think of something," she stutters, her head falling back on the pillow, her breasts rising up to the heavens when I run my thumb over her throbbing clit, sliding my cock a little more until I'm right at her hymen.

With my thumb still flicking her clit, I reach out to her breast and pinch her nipple. On cue, she snaps her head back my way, her lust-filled gaze fixing back on mine.

"While you think on that, just remember that this...this right here...is not one of them."

And in one full stride, I thrust myself deep inside her womb, splitting her open until I'm fully seated to the hilt.

Fuck.

Fuck.

Fuck.

My breaths come out in spurts as I try to regain some control, but by the way her pussy keeps squeezing my cock, latching onto it in a vise grip, I'm not sure that's going to happen anytime soon.

"Sky, are you with me?" I choke out, needing to check in with her.

"Always," she says, her luminous skin looking even more translucent to me.

"I'm going to move now, baby," I warn, needing to prepare her.

She nods anxiously, her hands back at holding my forearms, as if they are the only things that can keep her centered. Slowly, I start to slide in and out of her tight pussy, each thrust driving me insane. While I was doing everything in my power to prepare Sky for this moment, I forgot to get myself ready for it.

This...this...

Fuck.

This is everything.

"Noah," she moans out, telling me that the lingering pain of losing her virginity is now long gone and has been replaced with nothing but pleasure.

Thank fuck for that.

Since I'm no longer the cause of her suffering, I fall on top of her and start to pound into her sweet cunt, my mouth taking hers hostage.

"You taste so fucking good, little stalker. Your mouth is almost as sweet as your pussy."

She moans and quivers beneath me as I keep to my furious tempo, knowing that I'm already close to coming undone with how tightly her walls clench around me. Every little wail and loud moan she lets out only serves to fuel me to drive into her deeper, faster, harder.

"Noah!" she suddenly cries out, her eyes widening. "Oh my God! Noah!"

"Oh, fuck! You coming, baby? You coming on your first time? You coming on my cock? Shit, Sky. Shit! Shit! Shit!" I mumble, vigorously hammering into her so she can ride the wave of her orgasm to its fullest.

Once I've made sure she's seen God in person, I let go and come right afterward. My vision blurs, black spots corrupting my sight. I shake my head, needing to see her face. When it finally clears and I'm welcomed with the most heart-stopping, post-orgasmic smile, something inside my chest cracks, splintering right down the middle. I fall onto my back at her side, still reeling from what just happened. It takes us a minute before we both catch our breaths, the real world outside starting to sneak its way into my bedroom.

"Noah," Sky calls out, turning to her side to face me.

"Yeah?" I reply, turning to lay on my side, too.

"Thank you. Thank you for making love to me," she says with happy tears in her eyes.

Instead of giving her a reply, I press my temple to hers and then offer her a chaste kiss. Then I pull her to me, her head nestling into the crook of my neck as I run my fingers up and down the slope of her back. I swallow the lump in my throat and kiss her temple again the minute she gives in to her slumber and falls asleep.

But I don't sleep.

I can't.

Because she's right.

I did make love to her.

Fuck.

I just made love to the one girl who can never be mine.

Chapter 21

Skylar

Eighteen years old

Sunlight streams in from the window. I open my eyes blearily, pausing when I feel something heavy laying across my waist. It takes a moment for everything to come back. The reality of what happened last night.

I gave my virginity to my stepbrother.

Turning my head, I stare at Noah who's sharing my pillow. His breath is coming out in gentle puffs.

It's amazing how he resembles a sleeping angel; none of the chaos and angst that follows him during the day can be seen.

I feel a little bit like a creeper as I watch him sleep. I think a part of me was sure that he would be gone this morning. Just as he's done any other time we've gotten close.

I'm glad he's here though, because I think his absence would have broken my heart far worse than all the other times he disappeared on me.

A part of me still dreads when he wakes up though. Will he open his eyes and immediately regret everything that happened?

I analyze myself, trying to see if I feel any regret, but there's none to be found. My insides are a little bit achy, but I feel...alive. I think some of the wildness in Noah leaked out and has seeped inside of me.

Noah's eyes slowly blink open, and he stiffens for a moment when our eyes connect. But then I watch as he relaxes, a small smile spreading across his lips.

"You are a little stalker, aren't you?" he rasps in a sexy voice.

I roll my eyes and flush.

"You were watching me sleep, weren't you?" he teases.

I wrinkle my nose at him and I get a little lost in the chaotic blue of his eyes.

His arm that was wrapped around me pulls me closer to him until I'm pressed up against his chest and I can feel his hardening length. "That's okay, Sky, I watched you sleep last night for hours."

His words give me butterflies, not that they're anything special. I'm just feeling so much relief that he's not running, that I think he could say anything at the moment and I would like it.

"How are you feeling?" he suddenly asks in a more serious voice.

I flush deeper, just thinking about everything he did to me, three times, last night.

"A little sore," I admit, and he reaches up his other hand between us and softly runs it across my collarbone, goosebumps emanating from his touch.

"That's too bad. Now that I've gotten a taste, I just want more." He presses against me more and slides a soft kiss across my lips.

Suddenly there's a loud bang coming from down the hall. We both stiffen, and that's enough of a reminder of the fact that other people live in the house to get me jumping out of the bed, pulling on some clothes.

Noah looks completely unworried. He puts a hand under his head and props himself up as he watches me get dressed.

"You don't think Mom and Dad will approve of what we got up to last night?" he teases.

"Don't call them that," I say, wrinkling my nose again. "At least not when you're naked in bed and they're down the hall."

Noah gives me his trademark lazy smile, and like every time I'm with him, I wish I was a photographer and could actually take a good picture. And he wouldn't think I was weird if I spent all my time taking his picture.

I'm sure if I grabbed my phone right now, and started snapping, he'd run from the room.

"We need to get out of here," Noah says when we hear a pot slamming.

"Got any plans today?" he asks, finally sliding out of bed and grabbing his briefs to pull on.

I don't have any plans, other than writing. This was interesting territory to maneuver. Normally, I wouldn't want anyone to hear that I planned on spending the weekend alone in my room, but considering that Noah has been living with me for these last couple of years, he's already quite aware of my hermit habits.

Just as I had that thought, his grin widens. "You were going to spend the day in your room, weren't you?"

"No?" I squeak, although it ends up coming out more as a question than a response.

He steps forward and pulls me against him, his hands sliding up to cradle my face in the way that I love, his thumb softly stroking my cheeks.

"Do you think I can convince you to leave your room today, and instead spend the day with me?"

What Noah doesn't know is that I'm already at the point where I think I'd do anything for him. A dangerous place to be for sure with a boy like Noah, with heartbreak written all over him.

Even if Noah wasn't my stepbrother, I would be scared of the strength of my feelings for him.

But I can't help it.

"What do you have in mind?" I asked roughly.

"It's a surprise," he drawls, moving away and grabbing the pants and shirt he'd discarded last night.

It's amazing that he almost looks as sexy getting dressed as he did getting undressed.

It's also ridiculous how much I miss the heat of his touch. I'd agree to go with him today just so we don't have to worry about prying eyes. I may be sore, but I can't wait to be with him again.

"Meet me out there for breakfast in a few minutes," he tells me as he silently opens my door and peeks out into the hallway. The coast must be clear because he slides out of the room a second later, disappearing from sight. Staring around his room, it's amazing how empty it feels without him in here. I usually like to be alone, but that doesn't extend to Noah. I'm not sure that I could ever get tired of being with him.

"You're a stupid girl," I whisper to myself.

A couple of minutes later though, I leave the room, ignoring the feeling inside of me that I'm heading down a road I'm going to regret. Noah is already in the kitchen, munching away on a piece of toast while my exhausted looking mother tries to ask him some questions. She'll need to sleep for a few hours after having the night shift, but growing up, she would always try to spend at least thirty minutes with us in the morning after a shift before she went to bed.

"Good morning, sweetheart," she says with a soft smile when I enter the kitchen. A small flicker of guilt splashes around in my chest at what we'd done while she was gone, but I push it away.

"How was your shift?" I ask, proud that my voice sounds so light.

I'm really glad that Daisy isn't here right now. Fooling my mother is easy since she's never been one to look too far below the surface. Fooling Daisy though? Not so much. Daisy would've taken one look at me and most likely immediately known what we'd done last night.

"It wasn't too bad. A couple of emergencies came in the door, but nothing too crazy." She lets out a long drained sigh, and takes another sip of the water in her hand before setting it down. "I'm sorry, Sky. I'm exhausted. I'm going to have to hit the hay." She walks towards me and brushes a kiss against my forehead as my eyes meet Noah's over her shoulder. "Any big plans today?" she asks.

"Mmmh, I'm not sure yet. I may hang out with Noah for a little while." My mother rears back at that, trying to hide the surprise on her face.

"That'll be nice," she says. "The two of you don't spend that much time together."

I nod, hoping I look nonchalant. She searches my face for a minute, and fear churns in my veins that maybe she'll see right through me.

But again, she doesn't look that close, and she just brushes another kiss across my forehead before walking upstairs to her bedroom.

Noah slides the plate next to him towards me. There's a perfectly buttered piece of toast there, with cinnamon sugar sprinkled on it. It's my favorite thing to eat in the morning. It shouldn't make the butterflies grow, him making me toast how I like it, but it speaks to the fact that maybe he's been watching me all these years, just as closely as I've been watching him.

Noah grins knowingly, like he can read the thoughts going through my head right then.

"Eat your breakfast, little stalker. And then we'll get going."

I pick up the toast and bite into it, feeling like a lovestruck fool because I swear it tastes better just knowing he made it for me.

After I swallow, I set it down and ask, "Are you going to tell me yet what we're doing today?"

"Nope, it's still a surprise."

We finish breakfast in companionable silence, and I go back to my room to get a quick shower and get dressed for today's outing. Before I leave, I grab some sunscreen and my phone, because those are the only things he's told me to get.

Looking freshly showered himself, Noah has on a beat up hat backwards covering his head when I walk back in the living room. He's lounging in a chair, playing some video game on his phone.

He glances up when I walk in. "Ready to go?" he asks.

I nod, feeling shy for some reason. I find myself wishing that he'd taken my hand. Instead of wallowing in that though, I just follow him outside where his most prized possession is propped in the driveway. I look around for his father's truck, thinking we'll be borrowing it, but the Noah surprises me by walking over to the bike instead. He grabs the helmets seated on top, two helmets where I've only ever seen him with one.

"Are we riding that?" I ask, a slight tremble in my voice.

"I would have thought my intention obvious." He smirks.

I bite my lower lip, looking at the deathtrap he wants me to mount.

"Come on, Sky, live a little," he mocks.

"Remind me again why I gave you my virginity last night?" I gripe as I head towards the bike. "It's obvious you want to kill me today."

He pulls the helmet onto my head and leans forward, close enough that I'm looking to the side of me, sure that someone we know is going to pop out of the woodwork at any moment and catch us.

"No one is dying today," he assures. "And you slept with me because you knew I'm a god in the sack, baby," he teases playfully.

"Modest, too." I scoff, but don't say the contrary.

Not that I have a lot of experience...but, I'm thinking as far as first times go, I'm a very lucky girl.

He hops onto the bike and pats his seat behind him. "Come on, little stalker. Don't get scared on me now."

Taking a deep breath, I slide onto the bike behind him. In my books, the heroines are always fearless and brave, but I'm pretty sure I write them that way because they're the exact opposite of me. Living vicariously through them is all the bravery I can muster.

My dad had a motorcycle while we were growing up. But he never let us ride on it with him. Not that we really ever wanted to. His bike came to symbolize something bad for my sister and me. It was what took him out to the bars whenever he and Mom would get in a fight. It was also what he drove back home in the morning, smelling of cheap perfume and whiskey.

I try to push some of the memories out of my head as I wrap my arms loosely around Noah's waist.

"You have to hold on tighter than that," he yells to me as he starts the bike, and I squeeze him tighter, pressing my body against his and feeling the vibration of the bike between my legs.

Hmmm... Maybe it won't be so hard to replace those bad memories after all.

Chapter 22

Skylar

Eighteen years old

Noah drives us slowly backwards off the driveway, and then we take off, going zero to sixty in what feels like just seconds. I scream as we accelerate and grip on to him tighter, and I can feel Noah's body shaking in laughter at me.

The first couple of minutes, I'm still holding onto him with a death grip, my eyes squeezed close, sure that any minute now we're going to crash.

But after a moment, the fear starts to slip away, and all that's left is giddy exultation. There's a freedom about being on the bike, feeling the pulse of the engine between my legs. I love how the wind whips at my hair, and the world rushes by around us, like we're not really part of it anymore. I can understand now why Noah is so obsessed with his bike, if this is even a small part of how he feels when he's on one. Noah takes off down the main road that goes by the coast, testing the speed limit on the straight shots of land. We ride for about thirty minutes until we pull up to a dock that I've never seen before.

Noah pulls into a parking stall and I hop off as soon as he gets the kickstand up, narrowly missing burning my leg on the hot engine.

Noah slides off with ease. "You'll get better at it," he promises, and my insides jump, thinking of the promise in his words.

That there will be more days like this in my future.

He pulls my helmet off gently, and I swear sparks emanate from wherever he touches me. He pulls off his own then, his hair all over the place. It's grown since the last time I cut it. It's still not shoulder length as it once was, but it's not a crew cut either. It's just long enough that it beckons for fingers to run through its locks, and pull. My insides flip as I stare at this beautiful, golden boy, the sunshine making his hair even blonder than usual. He flashes me a white toothed smile, and I wonder how there could be so much beauty in the world.

For a second, dark thoughts of just how much we don't go together flicker through my head, but I push them away.

At least for today.

For this moment.

He's mine.

I'm sure those dark thoughts will be waiting for me as soon as we're done here.

This time, Noah does take my hand, and I find myself looking around again for someone that we know.

But the dock is deserted. There are ten boats around the dock, but no one is actually around.

Noah leads me to the very end. And my insides tighten with anxiety as I stare at the gentle waves in the water.

There's one boat tied at the very end. You can tell that it's old, but whoever owns it has taken painstakingly good care of it. There's a fresh coat of paint on it and every surface gleams. We come to a stop in front of it, and for the first time this morning, Noah seems...nervous.

"This was my mom's. Well, I guess the dinghy was actually my grandfather's, but he gave it to her as a wedding present, and she always told me growing up it would end up being mine. After she died...it was."

There's a tic in his cheek and he's biting his bottom lip as he does when he's trying to hold in his emotions. It's like watching a storm cloud pass over the sun as despair clouds his features, but he pushes those feelings away a second later.

"She's beautiful," I tell him earnestly, making his face brighten, almost like he'd been expecting a different reaction from me. He holds out his hand and I realize then, belatedly, that he wants to take me out on it.

I glance at the waves licking against the sides of the dinghy and then back at Noah.

"What's wrong?" he asks.

I give him a feeble smile and take his hand, allowing him to help me onto the boat. Then he gets to work on the ropes tying it to the dock, expertly unraveling them and tossing them aside. I'm doing my best to hold my panic attack at bay when he jumps into the dinghy and takes a key out of his pocket. A moment later, the engine rumbles around us.

"Are you sure you have time for this today?" I call out, barely able to be heard with how loud the boat is. It's obvious that the engine hasn't been updated; it's much louder than newer boat engines are.

"Today, I've got all the time in the world." Noah grins, coaxing my insides to be at war with each other.

Under no circumstances do I want to go out on this little boat into the ocean, but I also really want to spend time with Noah.

You just need to suck it up, I tell myself. Maybe today is the day I conquer my fears.

But as we head out, and the dinghy falls and rises as it meets the waves, I'm quite sure that today is in fact not the day I conquer my fears.

On these small boats, it feels like we could flip over at any point.

I grip the seat, my knuckles turning white with how hard I'm holding on. Nausea is building inside of me and I'm starting to hyperventilate. Noah's concentrating on driving the boat, so he doesn't see me falling apart.

I'm in the icy water. Darkness surrounds me everywhere. Every time I hit the surface, I'm dragged back under as if the ocean is desperate to keep me in its grip.

"Skylar!" Noah's voice cuts through the nightmarish memory.

That's when I realize the boat has stopped and we're right by a sandbar.

"Are you okay?" he asks, concerned.

I nod, trying to suck in a deep breath so I don't faint.

"Hey, what's wrong?" he asks gently, squatting next to me and rubbing my skin softly.

"I hate the ocean," I finally spit out.

His eyes widen, almost comically, if I was capable of seeing humor at the moment.

"You hate the ocean?"

"I'm terrified of it."

"But haven't you lived by the water your entire life," Noah asks softly, trying to make sense of what I've said. "You've been on boats before?"

I rub my clammy hands on my knees, trying to get my heart rate under control.

"When I was little, I was out with my dad on his old fishing boat. There was a storm coming, so the waves were extremely rough. I knew, even at that age, it wasn't a good day to go out. But he'd insisted, and I didn't want to let him down. While we were out, a particularly large wave hit us, and I fell overboard... And he took off, not even noticing that I'd fallen out of it."

Noah's face is scrunched in fury when I finish.

"Who saved you?" he murmurs, a tightness in his voice that wasn't there before.

"There was another boat that happened to pass by and saw me fall off, and they came over and saved me just in time." I shiver, lost in that moment again, of the inky blackness threatening to overtake me, and how cold and alone I felt in that moment. I didn't think there was any other place where you could feel as lonely as in the ocean's depths.

"And you've been terrified ever since?"

I nod, wiping away some cold sweat from my upper lip that I'm sure is oh so attractive.

"Why didn't you say anything?" he growls. "Why don't you ever say anything?"

I don't really have an answer, or at least not a good one. I'm so scared of bringing attention to myself, or letting someone down. It's like my cells are ingrained with the need to please rather than to make myself happy. It's a curse I've always had. It's why I'm so angry all the time. Not at the world, but at myself. I let myself down.

I don't even realize that I'm crying until I feel his thumb on my face, slowly brushing my tears away.

"Hey now," he says softly. "None of that." I bite down on my lip and stare down at my hands.

"Sky, you never have to hide from me. Tell me what you love, tell me what you hate, just tell me. I want to know all of it."

I glance up at him, feeling like he actually means every word. The problem is, I'm sure that most people mean things and have good intentions when they say things like this, but it never actually works out the way it should. People break their good intentions all the time.

Or at least, in my experience, they do.

Noah stands up and walks over and starts the boat again.

"No," I squeak out, not ready for another hour or so on the waves. At least right here, by the sandbar, the water is exceptionally calm.

Noah immediately turns off the boat.

"I just need a couple of minutes," I whisper, hating how weak I feel in this moment.

"Want to step onto the land for a minute?" he asks.

I nod eagerly, realizing that the sandbar is in fact big enough for us to go on there. Noah grabs my hand and one of the saddlebags that was attached to his bike, and he helps me onto the cool sand. He motions for me to sit down and then pulls the boat further onto the land so that it won't float away.

"Go ahead, take off your shoes, get comfortable. The tide won't rise enough to cover this place, at least not this time of year."

To my surprise, he pulls out a light blanket and places it on the sand and then takes out a couple of wrapped sandwiches, and a few bags of chips and some apples.

"I'm not much of a chef," he comments, a bit sheepishly as he unwraps one of the chicken salad sandwiches and hands it to me.

My heart is leaping in my chest, and I take a big bite out of the sandwich, moaning in exaggerated pleasure. Evidently, someone making me food is my love language because every time Noah does, I get giddy.

"It's delicious," I assure him, and I'm not lying. I recognize the croissants are from that bakery in town, the one that always make my mouth water when I pass by and I smell them. I don't know where the chicken salad's from, but it's got little dried cherries in it that give me a burst of sweetness with every bite.

It's all delicious.

Here on the sand, the ocean isn't...so bad. Terror still licks at my insides whenever I stare at the waves too hard, but I feel more at peace than I usually do when I'm this near the water.

Don't get me wrong, I've had to endure my fair share of beach and boat trips, but I've rarely felt any moments of peace during them.

I'm wondering if Noah's got a bit of magic in him after all.

The girl stood on the edge of the cliff, staring out at the desolate ocean, wondering if he was out there staring at the land and missing her as much as she was missing him.

"Writing anything good?" His voice cuts through the story I'd drifted into.

I blush and grab a bottle of water, wishing I didn't do that all the time, get lost in my head. But unlike other people, who seem to get annoyed by that particular trait, Noah seems to find it...charming almost.

"Tell me about the story," he says. I roll my eyes, and bite into the sandwich.

"No, I'm serious. Tell me what the story is about."

"I don't share my stories very much," I say quietly.

"Why not? I mean, I've heard of how much your English teacher talks about the stuff you've written."

"Writing feels...sacred to me, I guess," I muse. "I know once the words are out there, that people can say anything about them. I'll read a book and I'll go on Goodreads, and people will have said the most horrible things about something I thought was so great. And I guess... I'm scared of that. Because it feels like I'll be showing a piece of my heart to people, and I'm afraid that they will hate it."

Noah nods, like my comments actually make sense. "But they could also love it too."

I nod and shrug. "But that's the thing, though; negative comments are the ones I feel like I would pay the most attention to. I once read this article by this actress who's basically universally liked. She was talking about how she would watch a ten minute fan video someone posted on TikTok of how wonderful she was, and there'd be thousands of those, and then she'd see a six second clip that was negative, and it would totally destroy her. And of course the question is, why doesn't she just pay attention to the thousands of people that love her? But it just seems to be how it is."

He opens his mouth and I hold up my hand. "Or at least how it is for normal people," I say, raising my eyebrows pointedly.

It's actually one of the things that I love the most about him. He doesn't care. It's like you're either born with self worth or you're not. Other people's opinions are like oil to him; they just roll off and he never thinks of them again. I wonder what it would be like to walk through life that self assured. Because I'm not aware of anything in Noah's background that would have made him that way.

"I know you have that notebook tucked up inside your shirt, Sky. Give me a chance, little stalker. Show me your heart."

He's joking, taking the words that I gave him and giving them back to me, but it feels heavier than that. Does he realize that I have been showing him my heart all this time? I'm wearing it on my sleeve for him right now.

I pull out the tiny notebook that I carry around with me everywhere, just in case the words strike. You never know when inspiration will hit you. Sometimes I'll be walking down the street, and I'll see a glance that someone gives a girl as she passes by, and all of a sudden I'll start imagining his hidden longing, and their story that could be if only she took a second to stop and look at him. Or I'll be in the car listening to a song, and some kind of lyric will spark an entire story. I have notebooks upon notebooks hidden in my room, filled with words that have poured out of my soul from the most tiny encounters.

I hesitate, staring at the cover, but when I look up, he looks so... invested, and I decide to read a few parts.

A lot of this book is filled with sad poems. My experience the last couple of years hasn't lent itself to particularly happy thoughts. But I find one small paragraph that I wrote about him, and I decide to be brave, just this once, and read it to him.

"There was a moment that night when it felt like he looked at me and he actually saw me, that the spark in his eyes was my twin flame. Sometimes at night I imagine that he walked towards me, instead of away. That he'd seen inside my soul, and instead of finding it wanting, he'd found what he'd been looking for his entire life."

"Is that about me?" he asks, his face looking troubled at the thought.

I shrug, "It's just a little something I wrote. I didn't mean anything by it," I add.

Although he may have made love to me last night, everything inside me tells me that Noah is a runner. That even if he did feel something, even if he did recognize me for what I thought I could be to him, it could never last.

He still looks uncomfortable, so I tuck my notebook away, chiding myself for reading something so personal in the first place.

"What do you want in your life, Skylar?" he asks softly. He's staring at the distant horizon. "Do you want to go to school? Do you want to get married and have five kids..."

I snort. "I don't think the two are mutually exclusive," I joke, and he tosses a pebble at me.

"I'm trying to be serious here."

My smile fades and I nod, feeling like I should start asking him questions, because here he is, stripping me bare.

What was I supposed to tell him here? Was I supposed to tell him that for the last couple of years, all I wanted to do was get off this island and move away? Or about my dreams to attend the best English program in the country. Do I tell him that I want to be a New York Times best-selling author, and I want people to know my name? Or do I tell him about another silly dream I had, that I wanted to have a book at the airport. I wanted to walk into one of those places that sells floss and chocolate covered almonds, and see my books tucked in the corner, well-known enough that they would belong there.

Or was I supposed to tell him that falling in love with him was making me wonder if it was even possible for me to leave after all? That none of those dreams come close to winning his heart.

"Go to school, write I guess, if I'm lucky," I finally say casually.

"And you?"

His cheek tics and I know that he's well aware I've given him a simplistic answer, but thankfully, he doesn't press me further.

"It doesn't really matter what I want," he laughs, and it comes out all wrong, bitter like spoiled coffee. "My future's pretty set in stone. Following my dad's footsteps. As soon as I'm done with school at the end of the year, I'll be just another fisherman on his crew. I was born on this island, and I'll die on this island."

Set in stone.

Is anything ever that definite?

I wasn't sure about that so I decide to press him just a little.

"Why do you *have* to do that? It doesn't sound like you want to do that. It doesn't sound like that would be the life you envisioned for yourself."

"Envision?" He chuckles disheartedly. "There is no vision of a different future for me. It's what everyone in my family has done. It's what everyone expects me to do. I'm not like you, Sky. I don't have some crazy talent just waiting to be unleashed on the world. It's a good steady job, and my dad is counting on me to help him. It's all good. I've made my peace with it."

Even as he says the words, it sounds like he's trying to convince himself more than me, and I'm not sure he's being very successful at it.

"What would you like to do, if you could do anything...what would it be?" I ask fervently, reminded about the time I snuck into his computer and saw the hidden folder with all those expensive sail-boats in it.

"I'm not even sure anymore," he finally says after a long pause, sounding almost...ashamed.

"My mom was sick for so long. I poured all my focus on getting her better, and then later, spent whatever time I had watching her die. I guess I've just been existing since then." His shoulders droop. "I think she'd be so disappointed in me if she saw me now. I know she would be."

I flinch at the self-hatred in his voice. Noah always comes across so confident. Yes, I've seen him absolutely devastated, but I've never seen him like this, so laden with self-hatred.

"I think you're wrong about that," I murmur to him.

"Yeah, well, you didn't know my mother, did you?"

I have the urge to flinch away with the way he just lashed out at me, but I know his dark thoughts are the ones that are ruling him right now. The ones provoking him to keep me at arm's length.

"In a way, I feel like I do know her," I say carefully, reaching up and brushing a piece of his golden hair from his tanned face. "I think you're your mother's son. And like her, I think that you're the kind of person who would sacrifice your future to help and make your father happy. I think you're fiercely loyal, and ridiculously sweet on the inside despite your gruff exterior. Just by knowing the kind of son she raised, tells me that I know your mother pretty well after all."

He stares for the longest time dumbfounded at me.

"The way you see me... I'm afraid one day you'll wake up and realize you've got it all wrong."

He says the words so softly they almost fade away in the wind, but nevertheless, they pierce me right in the chest. Because I know that I feel the same way. I'm afraid that this beautiful, broken god of a man will wake up one day and see me for what I am– the mousy bookworm that's better off in the shadows rather than the main stage.

"Not a chance," I whisper, and he leans his forehead against mine, brushing a few soft, slow kisses across my lips. I want to ask him what this is, make him reassure me that he feels what I'm feeling, but I don't.

I just let the moment sit. I let the day pass by, beautiful and tragic at the same time.

Because the best day of your life always has to end.

And I think this one might be mine.

* * *

School feels even stranger than usual with this secret hanging over me. Now when I walk down the hall and see Noah staring at me, it feels laden with so much more than it did before. And when I see one of the girls who is obsessed with him brushing against his arm, I want to run over and shake her, scream to the whole school that he's mine.

But of course I can't do that.

Because if the school couldn't handle one kiss, how would they handle a whole weekend of fucks?

The day passes like that. Looks with hidden meanings and having to watch the school worship him while I have to worship from afar. When another girl comes up to him though, pressing her breasts against his chest to get his attention, something snaps inside of me.

Kyle's just behind me, sending me his usual longing looks ever since I told him we could never be anything but friends. I know it's wrong, but I say hello for the first time since that talk. Kyle immediately lights up, and takes a few steps towards me.

"How you been, Sky?" he asks, trying to go for casual with his one hand tucked in his pocket and his other one gripping the edge of his letterman's jacket.

"Good," I tell him, surprised when I realize that for the first time in a long time, I actually mean that.

I open my mouth to ask him how he's been, when all of a sudden my arm's grabbed in a tight grip.

"Sorry Kyle, I need a few words with Skylar," Noah says through gritted teeth.

A flicker of anger crosses Kyle's face and his jaw tics, but he shakes his head and walks off without another word, well-versed that he is never going to win against Noah.

Noah practically drags me down the hall, garnering a few looks as he does. The bell rings, but he makes no move to let me go to class. When the halls have emptied, he pushes me into the women's bathroom, and clicks the lock.

"What the fuck do you think you're doing?" he growls.

My eyes widen. "What are you talking about?"

He gestures out to the hallway. "With Kyle, what the fuck were you doing?"

"I was just saying hello. He's my friend," I snap defensively, an edge of guilt creeping up my spine because I know that I'd been trying to get a rise from Noah after watching girls paw at him. There's a wild flare in Noah's blue eyes, like I haven't seen before.

He glares at me. "Do you want him?"

"What? No, of course not!"

"So then you were just trying to make me jealous!"

"I —" I'm about to give excuses, but then I just get mad. "What the fuck were you doing letting those girls rub all over you anyway?!" I snap.

A smug look crosses his face. "So *you* were jealous."

I roll my eyes. "And you aren't?"

Anger laces his features, and he's biting his bottom lip again. He's so much bigger than I am, looming over me. He's wild and worked up in the moment, and there's a strange rush in my veins watching him like this. I didn't realize that it would feel like this, to have Noah Fontaine's attention like this...is intoxicating.

"I don't want you talking to him again, and I don't want you seeing him."

I realize then my panties are damp and I'm...desperate for him.

I feel edgy, a strange energy running through me that I don't know what to do with...until I suddenly get an idea. Or should I say... a craving.

"I don't want him, Noah," I murmur, taking a step forward until it's me that's pressing my breasts against his chest. "The only person I'm thinking about, the only person I want...is you."

I brush my lips across his, but he doesn't kiss me back, prefering to just stare at me. I can tell that he wants me; he's rock hard against me... But this feels like a test. A challenge. One I intend to win. I trace my tongue against his lips, and grind against his hard ridge through our layers of clothing. Feeling brave for some reason, I slowly start to lower myself to the ground, dragging my fingertips down his chest as I do until I get to his belt buckle.

Still, he makes no move.

Taking a deep breath, I keep going, tracing his belt buckle before I undo it and then unbutton his jeans, slowly unzipping them.

"I want to make you come," I whisper, licking my bottom lip. "I want to taste you."

To this, he finally moves, his hand grabbing the back of my hair and lacing it through his fingers.

"Is my little stalker as dirty as she sounds right now?" he rasps, his blue eyes hooded.

I gaze at his enormous cock, wondering, not for the first time, how it actually managed to fit in me. I lick at the tip and he groans, his grip in my hair tightening until it's just at the point of pain.

"How bad do you want me?"

"More than anything," I half sob, and he brushes the tip of his cock with his finger and then rubs the pre-cum on my lips. I trace my tongue along them, trying to capture every drop. His eyes are lazy and hot.

"Are you going to let me fuck that perfect mouth?" he asks. And I nod, reaching out and taking his dick like the offering it is. I squeeze it gently, watching as the broad tip leaks with a drop of moisture...and I'm...starving.

I touch my tongue to his slit and take a long lick, lapping up the burst that seeps onto my tongue. I've never gone down on a guy before...obviously, but there's something about this forbidden act that I love. I've heard girls at school talking about this being demeaning, but it's just like Daisy has always said. In this moment...it feels like you own them.

I slide my lips over the head of his cock and begin to suck on him like he's candy. There's no way I can fit him all in my mouth, but I do my best.

"Fuck," he growls as his hands tighten and loosen in my hair, like he wants to take over but he's stopping himself.

I move up and down, sucking up his pre cum. Daisy had once told me that the key to giving a good blowjob was to be enthusiastic, and I definitely nail that condition on all cylinders.

There's a steady stream of praise coming out of Noah's mouth.

"Good girl. Good fucking girl. Sucking my cock so well. Feels so good, baby. Fuck. Yes. Just like that."

He finally gives in to the urge to control my movements and he fucks my face...hard...as his fingers dig into my hair, guiding my movements. Tears are streaming down my face as I choke on his dick.

And I love it.

His breath grows ragged and his movements are uneven as he starts to come. I thirstily drink down everything he gives me, his cum still seeping out of the sides of my mouth. He guides me off his dick and I give the tip one final kiss that has him moaning.

When I glance up at him, he's staring at me like he's awestruck. He wipes his thumb through the extra cum on my face and slides it back in my mouth, feeding it to me. I lick it up eagerly, not even knowing who I am right now.

Noah helps me to my feet and presses his lips against mine in a hard, licking kiss. He's not grossed out at all by the taste of his cum in my mouth, evidently.

"That was fucking amazing," he growls.

"Yes, it was," I respond with a grin.

He shakes his head. "You're full of surprises, little stalker. Because I know that was your first blow job."

I smile shyly and he continues to stare at me.

"No more Kyle," he finally says, and I nod slowly.

"No more groupies," I say back, and he nods too.

We slip out of the bathroom into the luckily empty hallway.

And I've never felt more alive.

Chapter 23

Noah

Eighteen years old

Sky is sprawled naked on the bed, hugging her pillow beneath her head, while I run my fingers up and down the slope of her body. I love how it melts to the mattress, completely sated after I've had my way with her. Sky is never as pliant and soft as she is after I've coaxed a few good orgasms out of her. I could do anything I wanted to her right now, and she would wave the white flag and let me, willingly surrendering to all my wants and demands.

It surprises me that I have no desire to abuse that power. I'm entirely satisfied just softly touching every curve and valley of her body, wondering if there is a part of her that I haven't explored with my fingertips, lips, and tongue. I know there isn't, but just the thought that there is something of hers that I haven't possessed or put my mark on yet is unsettling. The need to brand every little inch of her, making sure it remembers who its rightful owner is, is overwhelming to me.

"Noah?" she calls out, her voice raspy from being sleep-deprived by all the glorious things I did to her and intend to do again before the sun comes up.

"Hmm," I reply, leaning in to kiss the left side of her breast, pulling a soft smile out of her.

"Can I ask you a question?"

"Does it have anything to do with you riding my tongue again? If so, just jump on my face, baby. I'm more than ready to have another go." I smirk, giving a soft tap to her ass.

"While tempting, that's not what I wanted to ask you."

"Pity." I pretend to pout, peppering kisses on her shoulder.

She giggles at my disappointed reply before gently slapping my forearm and turning to her side to face me, giving me an even better view of her body. I run my thumb over my lower lip, feeling suddenly ravenous to sink my teeth in her enticing mound again.

Since I can see that she would rather talk than see God for the fifth time tonight, I pull the bedsheet up to her waist, hoping it's enough of a deterrent to keep me on my best behavior. But when my gaze lands on her perky nipples, taunting me with how sweet they taste on my tongue, I reconsider and tug the sheet all the way up to her chin, making sure it fully covers her chest.

"There. Now you can ask your question."

She rolls her eyes but holds on to the security of her bedsheet just the same. It's only when she grows quiet on me that I realize whatever is on her mind is taking all her willpower to say.

"Hey," I coo, lifting her chin up to meet me. "Just ask. You're safe with me."

"Am I?" she retorts, making my forehead crease. "Sometimes I'm not so sure." I watch her swallow dryly as she inches closer to me. "What are we doing, Noah?"

"What do you mean?" I ask, confused and wondering where this is coming from.

"I mean...what are we? What is this?"

Fuck.

She wants to have the talk.

The words have barely left her lips, and already I feel a chill in the room. Almost as if my libido has been drenched with an ice bucket of reality.

I fall back on the bed, and place my arm over my forehead, staring at her ceiling.

"Noah?" she insists, her tone more alert now. "Did you hear me?"

"Yeah, I heard you."

"And?"

"And I don't know what you want me to say."

From my peripheral, I can see her chew on her lower lip, anxiety getting the best of her. But it wouldn't be Skylar if she didn't shake that shit away as fast as it came and face the issue head-on. She rises from the bed halfway and leans her back against the headboard for support, holding the sheet in place.

"Are we just fucking then? Is that it?"

"Is that what you think we're doing?" I mumble, unable to make eye contact with her.

"I'm not sure. You haven't exactly been very forthcoming with how you feel about all this."

"And you have?" I scoff, my irrational fury making me turn over to my side to face her. "Don't come at me with questions when you don't have any answers for them either. Just because I'm the guy doesn't mean I'm an expert with shit like this."

"Shit like this? Wow. You really know how to woo a girl," she quips with a snarl.

"Fuck," I grumble, rising from the bed, too, and running my fingers through my hair. "What do you want me to say, Sky? This past month has been incredible. Hasn't it? We're having fun. Isn't that enough?"

"Is that what you want? Just to have fun?"

"How the fuck am I supposed to know? Yeah. Maybe. I don't know," I reply, frustrated, pulling the strands of my hair until a few spring loose. "What's the problem with just having a little fun? It's worked so far for us. Why complicate it?"

"Maybe I want to complicate it. Maybe having fun isn't enough for me anymore," she counters sternly.

Jesus Christ.

"We're fucking eighteen, Sky. This is our senior year. If we don't have fun now, then when are we supposed to, huh? When I'm knee-deep in fish guts working on my father's boat? When I have to worry about shit like mortgages and paying bills, knowing that I'll never get off that rat race no matter how hard I try? My future is complicated enough, so excuse me if having fun now when I still can offends you."

I get out of bed and start searching for my discarded clothes on the floor.

"Where are you going?"

"To sleep. Is that also a problem for you?" I arch a menacing brow.

Sky refuses to say anything, and instead falls onto the bed, turning her back to me.

"Good. At least we can agree on something," I mumble, hurriedly putting my sweatpants on.

I pick my t-shirt from the floor and pull it as fast as I can over my head so that I can quickly head toward her door. But just as I grab the doorknob, I stop in my tracks, taking in a deep breath to calm my temper.

Why did she have to go there?

We were good.

We were better than good.

We were perfect.

"Maybe we should just call it? Feels like this, whatever this is, has run its course," I hear myself say.

My heart is beating a mile a minute, just waiting for her to tell me to fuck off, pick a fight, or just beg me to stay. I'd take fucking anything at this point. But when she doesn't say a single word in return, I look over my shoulder to stare at her. She remains so still, it's almost difficult to see if she's breathing or not.

"Sky?" I ask, unable to hide the worry in my voice.

"Just go," she finally whispers, making me cringe at how cold her tone is.

I turn around and lean my temple to her door, ordering my feet to move and do as she says.

"I don't know what you want from me," I finally reply on a ragged whisper.

I hear her softly exhale as I stand there, waiting on pins and needles for her to say something. When she doesn't, I know she's done with me. Unable to stand her silence any longer, I swing her door open and get the hell out of there. Unfortunately for me, I didn't do my due diligence in making sure the coast was clear for me to leave her room. A mistake that is very fucking evident when I find Daisy sneaking down the dark hallway with her stilettos in her hands, gawking at me. Guess I wasn't the only one who was up to no good tonight, not that it matters right now.

I've never had a problem with Daisy.

In fact, right from the get-go, she was probably the only addition to this house that I could stomach. Sure, she looks like a Barbie doll with her golden hair and blue eyes, but her personality was just as reckless and rebellious as my own. She's a rolling stone, unable to be pinned down. I guess we always had that in common. We understood each other. She didn't take any of my shit and I respected her for it.

But by the way she's glowering at me now, our little truce is over and done with. I square my shoulders as she rushes at me like a bull seeing red for the first time.

"The fuck were you doing in my little sister's bedroom?"

"Hate to burst your bubble but Sky hasn't been little in years," I mock nonchalantly, crossing my arms over my chest.

"Cut the shit," she snarls, poking a finger into my chest. "I swear, if you hurt her, I'll cut off your balls and fucking force-feed them to you."

Thing is, I believe her.

Although the two sisters are night and day from each other, Daisy would fucking kill for Skylar. Over the years as I watched them together, I won't deny that I envied the loyalty they had for one another. I never had that. Not after my mom died, at least.

"Don't get your panties in a twist. I didn't do shit to Sky," I lie through my teeth.

Daisy's fixed gaze bounces off me to her closed sister's bedroom door, her mind working double time, trying to come up with a scenario where Sky was safe with me.

"Bullshit." She scoffs, unconvinced when she comes to the conclusion that there is no such world where that would happen.

"Tell you what? Why don't you worry about your own secret booty call and let me deal with mine."

Her face turns all sorts of frightening red as she grabs my chin and sinks her nails into my skin. Any other time, I would have slapped her grip off me, but the pain she's inflicting eases the ache in my chest from how I left things with Sky tonight.

"I'm only going to say this once. Leave Sky alone. She's not like us."

"Us?" I cock a brow.

"Broken. Unable to love anything more than ourselves. She deserves better. Better than you."

At this, I do slap her hand away.

"You have no idea what Sky deserves," I growl in her face, the same one that suddenly changes from being angry to pitying me. I hate that look and she damn well knows it.

"I know that you'll never be man enough for her. Sky is going places. Big places. And you will just be an anchor around her neck, dragging her down. Away from her full potential. So yeah. I do know what Sky deserves and it's not you. Like I said, she deserves better. And I won't let you or anyone else steal her shine, just because they're fucking bored with their lives."

"Are you done?" I seethe through gritted teeth.

"Are you?" she retorts with the same vehemence in her tone.

I nod.

"Good. Keep it that way."

And with that, she passes by me, making sure to clip my shoulder in the process.

I turn around to watch her retreating form, and like the asshole I am, I'm unable to let things go without having the last word.

"Tell me something? Is hiding the fact that you're screwing Derrick Monroe on the down-low his idea or yours?" I smile sinisterly when she halts mid-step, staying rooted to the spot. "Guess I'm not the only one who is so undeserving, huh? Takes a loser to know one, Daisy."

And with that, I walk into my room and slam my door, uncaring if I wake up the parentals or not. The shit that goes on in this house without them knowing is their own goddamn fault for being so fucking clueless anyway.

I fall onto my bed and curse, wondering how this night turned into such a shit show. Not an hour ago I was on cloud nine, having everything I ever wanted right at my fingertips.

Now what do I have?

Nothing.

Daisy will be pissed at me for God knows how long.

And Sky?

Who knows how she'll react.

Will we revert to our old ways of hating each other, or will she just act like I don't even exist?

Fuck!

I grab the pillow from under my head and scream into it, letting out all the agony I suddenly find myself in. Once I've expelled all of it out, I throw the damn thing across the room and focus on trying to get my breathing back in check. Daisy's words continue to drill a hole into my brain, making it hard to concentrate on anything else.

She deserves better.

She deserves better.

Fuck.

Sky does deserve better, and deep down, I didn't need Daisy's reminder to fucking know it. Still, my selfishness rears its ugly head, unable to accept that truth.

Not that it matters anymore.

It's done.

We're done.

And the sooner I can wrap that around my thick skull, the better.

I'm doing you a favor, Sky.

Just take it and run.

Run far away.

Because if you don't, I might just catch you.

And if that happens, I'm not sure I'll have the strength to let you go.

Chapter 24

Skylar

Eighteen years old

"Where's Noah?" my sister bellows, storming into the living room like a woman possessed.

"How would I know?" I retort, mimicking her malicious tone since, unintentionally, Daisy just poured salt into the open wound in my heart by shouting out the name of the boy I've been trying very hard to forget even exists. "I'm not my brother's keeper," I add with a shrug.

"Ah," she interjects, plopping down on the couch beside me before knocking the book I was reading out of my hands, making it fly to the carpet. "But Noah isn't our brother, is he?"

"It's just something people say, Daisy. God, what is up with you? You're acting extra bitchy today," I reprimand, getting up from my seat to pick my book off the floor.

"And you're not?" She frowns. "You've never called me a bitch before."

"And I didn't call you one now either." I roll my eyes. "Again, it's just something people say. And I said you were *acting* like one, not that you were one." I let out a frustrated exhale when I realize my outburst might have hurt her. "But you're right. I'm sorry. I didn't mean to hurt your feelings. I guess I'm in a pretty bitchy mood too." I sigh. "Now, are you going to tell me why you're so upset or are we just going to bite each other's heads off for no apparent reason? Because frankly, I'm really not in the best frame of mind for it."

Daisy picked one hell of a bad day to get on my nerves. I'm already on edge with what happened last night with Noah. I can't deal with her PMSing and taking whatever has her up in arms out on me. Although, I guess I'm pretty guilty of doing the same thing to her just now.

Damn it.

"Why?" she counters, pulling me out of my guilty subconscious.

"What?" I ask absentmindedly.

"Why are you in a shitty mood?"

"You first." I arch a brow.

She stares into my eyes, trying to read something in them. Her gaze is so intense, that I have to turn my face away from her, fearing she'll see something I'm not ready to divulge yet. Daisy shuffles onto the other side of the couch, pulling her knees up to her chin and hugging her legs to her chest while still facing my rigid form.

"Fine. I'll tell you. Our stepbrother is a dick."

"No arguments there," I mumble, but then go silent in thought, wondering why she would say such a thing.

Daisy and Noah are usually on the same wavelength about... well...everything, really, and I've rarely heard them speak ill of each other. My curiosity is naturally piqued, and the urge to know what Noah has done to piss off my carefree sister is more than I can bear. I pretend to flick invisible lint from my knee, keeping my head lowered, waiting for her to spill her heart out and offer up the information without me having to pry it out of her.

"What did he do?" I finally ask when I realize that she needs a bit of prodding to get her going.

I try and play it cool not to let on how desperate I am to know what happened between them. I feel my sister's scrutinizing gaze on me, the weight of it making it hard to sit still.

Shit.

She knows.

She knows!!!

My mind instantly runs rampant with a myriad of excuses to give her, when she surprises me with her next words.

"Let's just say he poked his nose into my business, and I didn't like it."

My exhale of relief is immediate, giving me the fortitude to finally look at my sister head-on.

"I'm sorry."

"What are you sorry about? You didn't do anything wrong. Did you?" she snaps.

I feel my cheeks heat up, but I shake my head in denial nonetheless.

"So you have no idea where the cocky prick is?"

Another shake.

"Hmm," she grumbles, disappointed.

"Why? Why do you want to see him?"

"You know me," she starts to say, taking her phone out of her back pocket. "Like our dear stepbrother, I hate not having the last word in a fight."

I nod, even though I'm dying for her to give me more intel than that. But I can't push Daisy to open up to me. Not where Noah is concerned. I haven't exactly been very forthcoming with my own experiences with our stepbrother. It would be hypocritical of me to demand that Daisy share with me what happened between them when I've been keeping this huge secret from her.

Guilt assaults me yet again of how I've kept her in the dark for so long. I don't really care if no one else knows what has been happening between Noah and me, but keeping it a secret from Daisy feels all sorts of wrong. She's my best friend. She's my only friend. I should be able to confide in her. But actually vocalizing my dirty little secret—that I've been sleeping with Noah in the dead of night—is not an easy feat to do. And now that he's ended it, I'm not sure I'll ever have the courage to come clean. Not to Daisy. Not to anyone. Outing my shame is not exactly something I'm looking forward to doing.

I honestly thought he had feelings for me.

That he felt, whatever this feeling is inside me, with the same intensity that I had.

But no.

He was just having fun.

Those were his words.

His *exact* words.

And it gutted me.

Because while I've been slowly falling deeper and deeper in love with him, he was just passing the time. A wound this deep will take forever and a day to heal. And it would only make things worse if my sister found out, or God forbid, our parents.

"Gotcha!" she yells out, pleased, staring at her phone.

"What? What did you find?" I ask hurriedly, sliding closer to her to catch a glimpse of whatever has grabbed her attention on her phone screen.

"The Monroes are having a Christmas party on their yacht tonight. That's where our brother is." She points at her phone.

"Stepbrother," I correct, staring at the picture that popped up on her social media feed.

Instantly I cringe inwardly when I see Stacy doing a duck face to the camera, while her head is resting on Noah's shoulder. He's not looking at the camera, though. Or at her, for that matter. Instead, he's staring into the horizon, a sea of blue all around them as the sun starts to set. The orange and red hues dipping into the blue abyss behind the couple makes them look that much more ethereal. It's like a stab to the heart, and all too quickly do I look away, not able to take another second of looking at it.

"Come on. Get up," my sister orders, patting my knee, suddenly in good spirits. "We're going to crash that party."

"Hell no," I chuckle halfheartedly. "One Monroe party was enough for me, thank you very much."

"You're coming and that's the end of it," Daisy orders, with steel in her voice, while getting up to her feet.

I swallow dryly, completely unprepared for the disdain in her eyes.

"What did Noah do, Daisy?" I ask, sensing that whatever he did to her is bigger than she's letting on.

"He just messed with the wrong girl. Let's leave it at that."

"But—"

"Enough, Skylar! I don't want to talk about it. Now get your ass off the couch and follow me."

I've never seen her this angry.

Yes, it's true that like a struck match to dynamite, Daisy is easy to set off. But after she's exploded, there has always been a sense of peace afterward. She's never been one to hold on to grudges. That's my field of expertise, not hers.

So what gives?

Not wanting to add gasoline to the already blazing fire, I do as she says and stand up, following her upstairs to her room. Daisy doesn't say a word as she rushes to her closet, pulling out hangers like it's a fire sale. I know the minute she finds what she wants, since her smile stretches a mile wide on her face.

"Perfect," she says, eyeing a little black dress that leaves very little to the imagination.

"You're going to freeze half to death in that thing. It is December, you know?"

"I'm not the one who will be wearing it. You are."

"Like hell I am," I stammer, taking a step back.

"Put it on, Sky. That's an order," she insists, placing the dress on her bed.

I bite my inner cheek, wanting to tell her that she can't boss me around like that, but when she steps closer to me, and gently grabs hold of my hands, all my rage vanishes.

All because my sister's eyes hold a vulnerability in them I've never seen before.

Ever.

Daisy has always been a force of nature.

Impenetrable.

To see her like this has a fist squeezing my heart into a vise grip.

"I need you to come to this party with me. I need you, Sky. Can you do this for me?"

Damn it, Noah.

What the hell did you do?

Suddenly, I'm no longer angry at him on my behalf.

He hurt me.

Hurt me deeply.

But like hell I'll let him hurt my sister.

"Give me the dress," I tell her, gaining a wide smile from her.

"That's my girl!"

I'm not sure what my sister has planned, but whatever it is, I'm on board.

Fuck Noah.

He wants to have fun?

Fine.

Let's see how he likes it when I have a bit of fun too.

* * *

Say what you will about the Monroes, but they sure know how to throw a party. Their yacht is decked out in twinkling lights that challenge the gleam of the stars hanging up in the night sky. I had my reservations about stepping on board, but when Daisy promised that the boat would remain docked all throughout the party, I relaxed.

I've always known that on the other side of the island lived the wealthiest of its inhabitants, but as I walk around the Monroes' yacht, I realize that my notion of wealth doesn't really compare to its reality. I mean, I did get a glimpse of the lavish lifestyle when I went to the

Monroes' party at the beginning of my junior year, but I was probably too nervous and anxious to really take it all in.

I'm sure taking it all in now, though.

This yacht is three times the size of our entire house. With it being three stories high, complete with a helicopter pad and pool, this luxury yacht puts most of the houses inland to shame. A person could probably get lost here and it would take hours before anyone could find them.

I stick close to Daisy as she sashays through the crowd of partygoers, all dressed to the nines with their fancy high-end couture and sparkling jewelry. Suddenly, the idea of crashing such an affluent party has me sick to my stomach. Sensing my unease, Daisy stops one of the various waiters walking about and grabs two champagne flutes for us. The guy doesn't so much as bat an eye when she hands the glass of alcohol to me.

"Here, drink this. It will loosen you up," she orders.

I don't fight her on it or remind my sister that I'm underage and shouldn't be drinking. Instead, I take the flute out of her hand and down it in one go.

"Good girl." She smiles, grabbing another flute for me and handing the empty one back to the waiter. "Now, let's mingle."

I offer her a curt nod and scamper behind her. Daisy flicks her long blonde hair and struts down the deck. With her head held high, and a confidence that can only be described as enviable, she flashes her bright smile to everyone who stops what they are doing just to look at us.

I've always known my sister was beautiful, but tonight there is something different about her. Instead of the short skirts and crop tops she's a fan of wearing, she's done a complete one-eighty, looking like one of the old-time actresses you see in those black-and-white movies. She's the epitome of elegance and grace. In a red dress that probably cost less than fifty dollars, she's outshining all of the women here that paid a pretty penny for theirs.

"Okay. This is a good spot," she says when we reach the main deck where most of the guests are situated.

Guests are dancing gleefully with the classic ballroom tune the pianist is playing on his baby grand piano, all of them enjoying the crystal-clear night. I try not to fidget as I scan the area and come up empty-handed at finding either Noah or Stacy. I'm pretty sure if either one of them sees us standing here, they will make a scene and send us packing. I'm really not looking forward to that shit show happening.

"So what's the plan?" I whisper at my sister, while sipping my champagne, needing the effects of the alcohol to keep me warm.

The dress my sister picked out for me might be gorgeous but it sure isn't warm. I'm freezing my ass off even with the outdoor heating stands placed all around the deck.

"Daisy?" I ask again when she doesn't answer, her eyes discreetly scanning the same perimeter I had a second ago.

"The plan is simple, sis. We're here to show them that we're not to be trifled with. They can't fuck with us Ames girls and get away with it."

"Them?" I arch a brow, confused. "You mean *him*, right? You mean Noah?"

"I mean all of them. Every last person that made us feel less than. That made us feel like we don't belong," she retorts with a sad glimmer in her eyes.

My forehead continues to crease at her puzzling ramblings, but before I'm able to say anything, the bane of my existence finally shows his face. And he's not alone.

Stacy Monroe stares daggers at me as she walks straight in our direction, an uncharacteristically sullen Noah trailing right behind her.

"Oh, hell no!" she shrieks when she reaches us, her face so red it looks like it's about to pop at any second. "Are you kidding me? Did you really think you could crash my party and get away with it?"

"Well, hello to you too, Stacy. Nice boat you have here," my sister retorts, sounding bored. "A little small, don't you think?"

Stacy's nostrils flare in contempt, eyeing my sister up and down like she wants to throw her overboard.

"Daisy," she spits out my sister's name like it's a curse. "You've had your fun. Now it's time you leave. Your kind doesn't belong here."

"My kind?" Daisy retorts with an eerie smile, taking a step toward the youngest Monroe until they are head-to-head with each other. "And just what do you mean by my kind?"

To her credit, Stacy doesn't so much as flinch with the way my sister is glowering at her. With my sister having a good few inches on her, Stacy has to crane her neck back to maintain eye contact with Daisy.

"Trash. That's what I mean by your kind—slutty, filthy trash."

I clench my fist around my champagne flute, ready to pour what's left of the bubbly liquid all over the bitch.

"Really? Is that what you meant by that?" My sister laughs sinisterly. "Careful there, Stacy, because from where I'm standing, you're the one who reeks of filth. Spoiled rotten-to-her-very-core filth."

Stacy's expression turns even more thunderous.

"Leave," she says through gritted teeth. "Leave before I get my daddy's guards to kick you out."

"I'd like to see them try," Daisy deadpans.

I stand there mesmerized at how my sister looks like she is seconds away from murdering Stacy with just her eyes.

"No one is going anywhere," we hear someone say behind us.

We all turn to the disgruntled voice. Derrick Monroe looks like a million bucks in his tuxedo, even if his face does look like he's ready to tear the whole boat apart.

"Derrick—" Stacy starts to pout, but he raises his left hand up to stop her from saying anything else.

"Daisy and her sister are my guests. *My* guests, Stacy. That means you will treat them with the respect and hospitality they deserve."

"But—"

"Enough!" he growls, his angry green eyes piercing his sister to the spot.

Stacy shifts from one foot to the other, uncomfortable with the way her brother is looking down on her.

"Daddy won't like this," she mumbles under her breath, her bottom lip quivering.

"Does it look like I give a fuck?" He cocks a brow.

"Fine. It's your funeral. Just keep them away from me."

"Then I suggest you go home. You've made enough of a spectacle of yourself for one night anyway."

Her eyes widen for a split second and then stare back at my sister with such hatred, a cold shiver runs down my spine. When her loathsome glower reaches me too, I stand up straight, not wanting her to see how she affects me.

She lets out a huff and walks away, leaving Derrick and a mute Noah in front of us.

"I didn't think you'd show," Derrick exclaims, looking at my sister like she's hung the moon just for him.

"You asked, so I came," she replies with a noncommittal shrug.

"Is that all I have to do? Ask to have you coming?" Derrick asks, not hiding how his hungry gaze scrolls down my sister's body from head to toe.

When Noah chuckles under his breath, it pulls my sister's attention off of Derrick and onto him.

"Something funny, Noah?" she questions with the same malicious tone she used on Stacy.

But instead of Noah replying to her with equal venom to his voice, he plants a genuine smile to his face instead.

"Not at all, Daisy. You look lovely tonight. Truly." The flicker of hate in my sister's eyes dims somewhat. When Noah sees that her icy demeanor is starting to thaw, he adds, "I'm sorry for being such a jackass last night. I didn't mean it."

Daisy chews on his apology, not yet satisfied.

"Will it happen again?" she asks, and the way her eyes flicker to me for the briefest of seconds, I have a feeling she's talking about something else than just Noah being a prick to her.

"I don't think so. No." He bows his head and shakes it, shoving his hands into his pants pockets.

"It better not," she warns.

Noah lifts his head up, his eyes finally landing on me.

"Have fun tonight," he says despondently before turning his back to us and walking away.

"Do I want to know what that was about?" Derrick asks curiously, pulling Daisy's chin toward him.

"It's nothing. Just a little fight between siblings. We're all good now."

"Yeah?"

"Yeah." She smiles happily at him. "Now how about you show us around? I'm dying to see what this big-ass boat looks from the inside."

"A tour it is." Derrick chuckles, running his knuckles along my sister's cheek.

This whole night has been a whirlwind, but it's the way Daisy melts into his touch that has me gobsmacked.

Holy shit!

My sister is in love!

When did that happen?

"Are you coming?" Daisy asks, looking back over her shoulder at me, her cheeks flushed.

"I think I'll stay here for a little while longer, then maybe I'll go home. But you two go on ahead. Have fun." I wink with a smile that tells her she's going to have to do some serious explaining to me when she gets home.

Derrick offers the crook of his arm, to which my sister immediately hooks her arm to, and I stand there watching them both walk away, looking like one of those couples you see on the covers of magazines.

I'm still giggling when someone taps me on my shoulder.

"Hi," a guy I've never seen before greets me.

"Hi," I reply on autopilot.

"Couldn't help but come on over here to introduce myself. I'm Gael. One of Derrick's friends from Harvard."

"I'm Skylar."

"Hi, Skylar," he repeats my name like it's velvet on his tongue.

I stand there not really knowing what to say or do, so instead, I just take another sip of my champagne.

"Nice night, isn't it?"

"Hmm." Another sip.

"Shit. I'm so bad at this," he says, laughing at himself while running his fingers through his curly brown hair.

"Bad at what?"

"Small talk." He laughs.

"Me too." I smile, finding his nervousness endearing.

Gael has kind brown eyes, even if he is wearing a tux that's probably worth more than my mom and Curt make in a month.

"How about we skip all the talking and just dance? Promise I dance better than I do chitchat."

"You're doing okay." I grin.

"Yeah? Because it kind of feels like I'm coming off like a dork. Newsflash, I am one."

I let out a giggle because he's being funny as well as sweet.

"That's okay. I'm one too."

His brown eyes twinkle as they look at me.

"Not possible."

"Oh, believe me, it's very possible." I laugh. "But if you're still up for it, I wouldn't mind a dance."

"Yeah, I'm up for it," he exclaims with glee, offering me his hand.

I stare at it for a bit, uncomfortable with holding another boy's hand that isn't Noah's, but then I remember that he's probably done more than just hold hands with Stacy tonight. Without giving it a second thought, I lace my fingers with Gael's and let him lead me to the makeshift dance floor.

We start to sway to the sound of the piano playing a rendition of "Blue Moon," his hands carefully placed on my hips, my hands on his shoulders. He tells me the reason he's spending Christmas break with the Monroes in Thatcher's Bay is because his parents decided that an African safari sounded more fun than spending the holidays with their only son. It saddens me that such a sweet guy could have assholes for parents, but he doesn't seem to be too bothered by it. He asks about my family and my plans for when I graduate high school this year, and I offer the information willingly.

He's easy to talk to.

There's no tension or angst between us whatsoever.

It's just nice.

Innocent almost.

Normal.

My heart squeezes in my chest at how I've never had *easy* or *normal* before. With Noah, everything felt heightened, like at any moment I would burn to ash. The tension between us was always so thick you could cut it with a knife. It had always been like that between us, and when we crossed that bridge where hate and love collide, the electricity between us just intensified.

There's no electricity with Gael.

There isn't even a spark.

Yet in less than the half hour we've spent together, he's made me feel safer in his arms than I ever was with Noah.

"Hey, are you okay? You look sad all of a sudden."

"Do I?" I mumble.

"Yes. Am I that bad a dancer?"

"No, you're fine. I'm sorry. I guess I'm not much fun tonight."

"I wouldn't say that. I'm having a wonderful time." He smiles sweetly.

I open my mouth to tell him that my heart is just not into dancing tonight, when I feel a strong pair of hands grip my waist and pull me away from Gael's grasp.

The hell?!

"Can I help you?" Gael questions a pissed-off-looking Noah.

"Doubt it," Noah seethes at him, turning his attention to me. "It's time we went home."

"I'm not ready to go home," I snap. "I'm staying right here."

"Oh no, you're not." Noah growls at me.

"If Skylar says she's not ready to leave, then she's not." Gael comes to my defense, but when Noah snaps his sole focus back on Gael, I know it was the wrong thing for him to do.

"Don't you ever say her name again. Don't look at her. Don't touch her. Don't even think about her."

The way Noah stares him down, his fists ready to break every bone in Gael's body, is enough for me to know that if I don't want a fight to ensue, I best do what Noah says.

"I'm sorry, Gael. My brother is right. It's getting pretty late. Thank you for the dance, though."

I ignore how Noah cringes when I call him my brother and take it as my own fuck-you to him. Gael's perplexed stare bounces off me and Noah, unsure if he should let me leave with him.

Knowing it will infuriate Noah more, I lean in and peck Gael's cheek.

"Thank you for the dance. I had a great time."

"Can I call you maybe?" he asks, still sounding unsure.

"No."

"Yes." Noah and I say in unison.

Never breaking eye contact from Noah, I ask Gael for his phone and add my digits to it. Once that's done, I thank him again for the dance and leave, Noah right at my heel. Furious that he's acting like a total asshole, I speed up my step, almost tripping on my high heel shoes. Noah's hand immediately grips my arm, preventing me from falling as I walk down the steep ladder to the dock.

"Get off of me!" I shout at him, wiggling my arm.

"There isn't a chance in hell that's going to happen. Move," he growls, his grip on my forearm tightening so I don't lose my balance and fall into the cold water beneath us.

It's only when we are both on solid ground again that he lets me go. I speed away from him, needing to put as much distance as I can from the boy who broke my heart.

"Sky?"

"Sky?"

"Sky!" he shouts out, halting my next step.

"What? What? What?!" I shout back furiously, tuning to face him.

"What do you want from me?! What, Sky? Just fucking tell me!" he yells, raising his arms to the heavens before dropping them to his sides again. I maul my lower lip, shifting my weight from one foot to another. "You're driving me insane, you know that, right?"

"Well, that makes two of us," I snap back.

He scoffs, but there is no heat behind it.

"What do you want, Sky?" he says, defeated. "Just tell me. 'Cause guessing is too fucking hard."

"I want the truth."

"The truth?" he mimics, looking absolutely lost.

"Yes. You once told me that the truth was the only friend I had. Well, that's what I want. The truth."

"And what truth is that?" he questions despondently.

"Why did you pull me away from the party?"

His blue eyes darken at the question.

"You know damn well why."

"No, I don't. Explain it to me," I demand.

"Because I couldn't stand watching every motherfucker there undressing you with their eyes. Is that what you want to hear?"

"It's a start," I quip, my heart jackhammering in my chest when he takes a step closer to me.

"Because the minute you came on board, all I could do was look at you."

Another step.

"Because when that asshole dared to put his hands on you, I wanted to cut them off."

Another step.

"Because anytime you're near, you fucking consume me. I can't think straight. I can't even breathe right."

I swallow dryly as he steps right up to me, cupping my face in his hands.

"Because being in the same space as you, and not actually being with you, feels like cruel torture. And these past twenty-four hours without you have been hell. Hell, Sky. My own personal hell."

"Why? Why does it feel that way? You're only having fun, remember?" I choke out, licking my dry lips. "Fun shouldn't hurt like that."

"No. I guess not. But we both know what does."

"We do?" I breathe out.

"Fuck, Sky. Why did you have to come into my life?" He shakes his head.

Hurt by the remark, I pull away and start to turn away from him. But Noah isn't having it. He grabs my wrist, and turns me around, our chests slamming against each other's.

"Don't...don't turn your back on me," he pleads.

"Why not? Since it's so easy for you to do it."

He lets out a frustrated chuckle.

"You think that shit was easy?"

"It sure looked like that to me."

"Last night was fucking excruciating for me. It fucking killed me to leave your room. Your bed."

"Why?" I whisper.

"Fuck, Sky. Are you really going to make me say it?"

"Yes."

He presses his temple to mine and breathes me in.

"You know why."

"Say it. I want to hear you say it," I demand, the memory of him ordering me to tell him to take my virginity coming to the forefront of my mind.

There is a small smile that tugs at his lips as if he too is being pulled back to that magical night.

"You always did love to bust my balls," he jokes lightheartedly.

I grab hold of his shirt, gripping it in my hands.

"Say it," I whisper, my whole body trembling in anticipation.

"You won't let it go, will you?"

"No. So say it," I reply eagerly.

"I love you, Sky," he whispers with a coy smile. "I'm *in* love with you. And no matter how hard I try, I can't stop. It's a fucking problem."

"A big problem?" I grin, wrapping my arms around his neck.

"The biggest."

"So what are you going to do about it?"

"I guess there is only one thing I can do," he says, running his nose up and down the length of mine.

"And what's that?"

"Love you. I'll love you for as long as you let me."

"And what if I want you to love me forever?" I croak out nervously, tugging at the strands of his hair.

His blue eyes stare into mine, the love he had been so desperately trying to hide all this time right there in his gaze.

"If forever is all I have, then so be it. Forever won't be long enough for me, though. Not nearly enough."

"No?" I rasp, falling deeper and deeper.

"No, Sky. I'll probably love you in this life and the next, and all the ones that will follow. I won't be able to prevent it. Don't you see? It's you, Sky. It's always been you. It will always be you."

Happy tears sting the corners of my eyes as I lunge myself fully at him, his arms wrapping themselves tightly around my waist.

"Promise?" I sob, my heart feeling so full it might float off into the night sky.

"Forever, Sky. You'll have all of my forevers. I promise."

And like a lovesick fool, I believe him.

If only I hadn't.

Chapter 25

Skylar

Eighteen years old

"I need you," he growls, and at this moment I would give him everything. I'm so in love with this boy.

Noah glances around. The noises from the yacht are too close. We could be discovered at any moment.

I wish for a second that we didn't have to hide, but I'll take this relationship however I can get it.

He drags me off the dock, towards the parking lot filled with cars.

"Where are we going?" I ask.

"Just follow me. My bike's parked over there. I need to find somewhere to fuck you."

I roll my eyes. "So romantic," I drawl.

He shoots me a heavy lidded gaze over his shoulder. "Everything's romantic with us, little stalker. Even the fucking."

I nod, anticipation threading through my bloodstream.

It's freezing, and I'm clutching him tightly as the bike starts up underneath us and we speed off in the night. As usual, there's adrenaline coursing through me. I'm turned on as I hold onto him, both because I'm pressed up against his hard body and because of the engine thrumming between my legs.

He takes us down the highway that winds around the coast. I'm wondering for a second if he's going to take us to his boat, because I'm not sure that even he will be able to distract me long enough to have sex on the water.

Before I can say anything though, he pulls off on a small rocky trail with 'No Trespassing' signs all along it. He idles down the bike so it's quieter and takes us down an even smaller winding path in the direction of the ocean. He gets to the edge of a small parking lot and then turns off the bike, walking it in between some trees so it's out of sight.

"We're going to get in trouble, aren't we?"

"Just trust me."

"I do," I immediately say. And I realize that it's the truth. I trust him more than anyone else in my life. It's a scary thing.

He takes my hand and we walk along the side of the parking lot until we get to a small path illuminated by the moon. Taking it down, we make it to a small beach enveloped by cliffs. There's no one else here, and no lights.

"This is old man Winter's private beach. But he doesn't come here this time of year so we'll be totally fine."

Noah suddenly looks at a loss as he stares at the ground.

"Fuck, I didn't bring the blanket I keep in my saddlebag. I really didn't think this through."

I press myself up against him. "Just lay your jacket on the ground. That's good enough for me. I just want you," I whisper.

He groans as he captures my lips in a supple kiss, his hot, wet tongue sliding into my mouth, tasting me.

His tongue takes deep long licks, and it feels like he's fucking my mouth the same way that he does other parts of me.

Finally, he breaks away, his mouth moving to my ear. "You're so fucking beautiful," he murmurs. "I'm so in love with you."

I melt against him and he fists my hair as his mouth goes back to mine, angling my head as we try to get as close to each other as possible. My breasts are smashed against his chest and I mewl and rub against him. His heat seeps into me, keeping me warm despite the cold night. Part of me is still aware we're in public, but this place feels as secluded as an empty house.

It feels like ours.

His smell surrounds me, and I feel close to coming just with all the sensations rushing around. He reaches between us and gently pinches my nipple. I arch into his hand, encouraging him as I gasp in pleasure.

"You're always so responsive," he murmurs.

Noah swallows my whimpers and moans as his hand moves from my breast, to under my dress as he grabs my ass with both hands. He shoves the thin strap of my thong aside, and brushes his fingers gently over my dripping core.

"Come for me, little stalker. Can you do that?"

"Please," I beg, overcome as he slips two fingers inside me and moves them in and out. He licks and sucks my neck and chest, and I'm sure he'll leave a mark that others could see. But I couldn't care less. I hope he does.

It only takes a moment for me to plunge into one of the best orgasms he's given me so far.

"Mine," he growls. "Say it. Say you're mine."

"Yes," I moan. "Yours."

His fingers continue to fuck me through my orgasm, prolonging the pleasure to almost more than I can bear.

He finally withdraws, his fingers slick with my juices, and he immediately slides them into his mouth, making a sexy moaning sound as he cleans them off with his tongue.

"Lay down, baby," he purrs.

I immediately lay back against his jacket that we spread out. He falls to his knees and reaches down and grabs the edge of my dress, sliding it up, past my hips, my breasts, and then finally over my head until I'm lying there in nothing but my bra and underwear.

"You're so fucking perfect," Noah murmurs.

He takes his time staring at my body, his gaze darting all over me like I'm some priceless work of art that shows him something new every time he looks at it. His hand reaches up to my mouth and slowly grabs my bottom lip, his eyes heavy lidded with worship. Noah leans forward and softly licks at my lips, his hands sliding into my hair.

"I need this off," I pant as I grab at his dress shirt.

"Take it off for me," he orders, and I quickly go to work, my hands fumbling over the buttons as I reveal inch by inch of his hard, perfect chest. When it's hanging open, my hands rub all over, marveling at the perfection of his body.

Before I know it, my bra is gone, and he's ripped my thong off, slipping it into the pocket of his dress pants before moving between my knees, spreading my legs.

Before I can say anything, his mouth is covering my slit, sucking and licking as he separates the folds with his tongue while thrusting two fingers into my core at the same time. My fingers thread through his golden locks that look more silver under the light of the moon. I'm riding his face, my head arched back as he creates magic with his tongue. His stubble scratches my inner thighs, and I think I'm obsessed as I glance down and watch his face move between my legs.

He has the enthusiasm part of giving head down perfectly...as well as having the perfect skill.

I'm vaguely aware of the sand sticking to my skin, and the sound of the waves breaking on the shore just beyond us. But it's all drowned out by this perfect moment.

Everything tightens and as he tongues my clit, pleasure tears through me, my harsh sobs getting caught in the wind. My hips are thrusting against his mouth as he licks and sucks and tremors move through my body.

I'm near tears when he finally moves away, his mouth shiny with my juices. "You're the sweetest thing I've ever tasted. Good thing I get to eat your pussy for the rest of my life," he says in a gruff voice.

I know it's ridiculous, the thought that at eighteen you could find your soulmate. But I know with every facet of my heart that we belong together, that he was made to be mine.

Before I can say anything, his lips are pressing against mine, his tongue licking into my mouth so that I can taste myself. I love that he has a piece of me on him. It feels like I've marked him in a way. I feel him fumbling in between us as he unbuttons the top of his pants, and frees his cock.

We're desperate for each other, and he doesn't tease me. He just pushes into my dripping center.

"You're so tight every time," he breathes.

It's definitely a tight fit, and I lose my breath for a moment as my body adjusts to his size.

His hand moves between us and he works my clit, helping my body to relax until the pain is outweighed by the pleasure.

He withdraws slowly to the tip, and pauses, pressing a sharp, sweet kiss on my lips before he pushes back inside. I grab at his neck and shoulders, holding on while he moves in and out of me, setting the perfect rhythm.

Each stroke fucks me deep, and I'm whimpering as he moves. His mouth covers mine, swallowing my cries.

"Come for me, Sky. Choke my cock," he orders, and as if he holds my pussy by a leash, I fall over the edge.

His movements quicken and he kisses me hard, his tongue stroking in and out in almost perfect sync with his dick. He shudders as he follows me over the edge, and I can feel him filling me up, setting off yet another small orgasm.

There's tears in my eyes as his movements slow and I wrap him up with my arms and legs, wanting to keep him a part of me forever.

I want to get all of his forevers.

And in this moment, as he brushes soft kisses all over my cheeks and lips, and tells me that he loves me...

I almost believe that I can.

Chapter 26

Skylar

Eighteen years old

Prom's here, and that means there's only a few more months of school left until graduation. I can't go with Noah obviously, so we're going separately and trying for a few stolen moments during the dance.

I fiddle with the blue dress as Daisy finishes my hair, feeling a bit of deja vu as I stand in front of the mirror, staring at my reflection.

At least tonight promises to be completely different from homecoming...at least I'm hoping it will.

"Just last year I was the one going to prom and now here we are. It's your turn now. I blinked and suddenly we've both grown up," Daisy murmurs...and she sounds so sad that I can't help but turn to look at her.

I want to tell her how thankful I am that she's here on such an important night. Because I am. I couldn't imagine going through this rite of passage without her. A part of me thinks that's one of the reasons why she didn't skip town the minute she graduated last year. That she stayed on this island for me. That she took a waitressing job at The Scarlet Letter Cafe just so she could make sure I survived my senior year. She's never come out and said as much, but what other possible reason could she have?

Anytime I question Daisy about her future, she always responds with a smile, saying that it will be as amazing as I am. She tells me that she's just saving up to get off this island and travel the world but I'm not sure how that will work out since she's always complaining to our mom about how broke she always is. That her money never seems to stretch far enough.

Lately, I've been wondering if the real reason she doesn't leave is because she's waiting on a certain Harvard pre-law student to return to Thatcher's Bay to be her companion in her travels. But if that's the case, if Derrick is the reason why she insists on staying, then why does she always look so sad?

"Daisy?" I start but before I can get a word in, she pulls me into a huge hug, sniffling a bit as she holds me close.

"You're the best person I've ever met," she tells me. "I'm so fucking proud of you."

I start to tear up now too, and I hold her just as tightly as she's holding me.

"I love you, sis. Forever," I tell her, a word that only serves to remind me of Noah and our own promises to each other.

She lets go and holds my arms, staring at me like she's searching for something.

"You're beautiful, sis," she says proudly, and I give her another watery smile before she squeezes me gently and then leaves my room.

Taking a deep breath, I adjust my dress one more time and then head out into the hallway where my mother and Curt are waiting. To my surprise, Noah's there too, leaning against the wall and trying to look like he doesn't give a care, as usual. But as soon as I come into view, he glances up and stares at me, his eyes burning as he slowly takes me in. There's too much emotion there, too many words that anyone could read, and I quickly glance at Mom and Curt to see if they notice. Thankfully they're chuckling over something on the couch and haven't even heard me come in yet.

Giving Noah my own besotted look, I clear my throat, dragging my attention to my mother and Curt who start gushing over me. My mother insists on taking pictures of us, and even the slight brush of Noah's fingertips against my back as we try to look like a sister and brother taking a picture, rather than a couple, sets my skin on fire.

"What time are your friends picking you up?" Curt asks Noah, talking about the limo that his crew had rented for the night.

Noah shrugs, giving his best bored impression. "I passed on the limo. I thought I'd just give Skylar a ride if she needs one."

I freeze, because this is a completely different plan than we'd talked about, but I definitely don't mind. Still, I'm worried that my feelings are written all over my face, with this incredible change in plans. All I want to do is throw myself at him and kiss his perfect lips.

"Do you need to borrow my truck?" Curt asks, and Noah shakes his head. "I borrowed a car for the night," he answers.

Curt frowns for a moment, but then nods his head. After taking a few more photos of us, and telling us to have fun and be safe, we're out the door, stepping into the cool night.

My jaw drops when I see a shiny black sports car, that's so fancy it looks like it came out of a *Batman* movie, parked in the driveway.

"I borrowed one of Derrick's cars," Noah explains sheepishly. "I wanted the night to be special."

"It does feel special. This is more than I hoped, just us getting to go together."

His hand moves at his side, like he's wanting to reach out and grab me. He keeps it down though just in case our parents are still watching from the porch, opening up my door for me, then jogging around the car and slipping inside.

I moan a little as I slip into the cool leather seats. This car smells like money. A lot of money. I'm not exactly sure how to describe that smell. But the interior of this car is it.

Noah starts the car and it turns on almost silently.

"I love this car," Noah murmurs, sounding like he's having an almost orgasmic experience himself.

"Me too," I breathe, admiring the insignia on the dashboard in front of me.

As we pull out of the driveway, he grabs my hand and squeezes it.

"I have a few more surprises for you, if that's okay."

I nod and blush. One thing about getting to know Noah, it's so surprising how thoughtful he is. He's always doing sweet things that I wouldn't have expected before he opened his heart to me. A little part of me wonders if he acted this way at all with Stacy, but I push the thought aside.

We drive down the road, but it only takes me a minute to realize we're not heading in the right direction. "Is this a shortcut I don't know about?" I quip. He squeezes my hand again.

"Just part of the surprise," he says with a sexy wink.

Noah looks like a wet dream tonight. His golden hair is slicked back and he's wearing a black suit and a black undershirt that he manages to make look super expensive, even though I know they're not.

"You're beautiful," I blurt out, my cheeks flushing, because I realize it's the same thought I had at homecoming. I just couldn't say it then.

His eyes soften, and to my surprise, there's a slight blush to his cheeks as well. "You're the most beautiful thing I've ever seen, Sky. I'm the luckiest guy in the world."

A girl wants to hear that, but it's not just the words that are doing it for me, it's how he's saying them. I know he actually means them.

We drive for twenty minutes until he pulls down the same dirt road we'd taken that night we made love on the beach.

I'm always up for sex if that's what he has in mind. I'm up for anything that means I get him alone without the rest of the school and town pawing all over him and trying to get his attention.

He parks in the parking lot and we get out.

"Hmm," Noah says when he sees my stilettos.

"I can take them off," I tell him quickly.

But he shakes his head. "Keep them on. I need some more time to admire how fucking perfect your legs look in them."

Before I can say anything, he's scooped me into his arms and we're setting off down the path like I weigh nothing. I wrap my arms around his neck, and lay my head against his chest, listening to the sound of his heartbeat.

I take a deep inhale, not feeling creepy at all about sniffing him, because I'm pretty sure Noah Fontaine is the best scent in the world.

I forget all about how he smells though when we get down the path to the private beach, and I see a table and chairs set out, and lights strung across the top of them. There are plates of food set on the table, and soft music is playing from a portable speaker. I stare up at him in amazement and find him watching me.

"What is all this?" I breathe.

"I didn't want to share you tonight. I don't care about anyone else. I just care about you. So I thought we could have our own private prom. Is that alright?"

I nod in a daze, at a loss for words for a moment. He sets me down gently on the sand and I slip off my shoes, dangling them from my fingertips as we walk towards the table set up.

I gesture to the fairytale in front of me. "How did you pull this off?"

He smiles smugly. "I did a few favors for old man Winter over the last few years, and then I rented the rest. You don't have to worry tonight about someone coming and busting us."

I smile, thinking about that night that I'll remember forever. I didn't mind the little bit of danger.

He helps me into my chair and lifts the silver lid covering up our dinner with a flourish. There's a delicious looking lasagna, cheese bread, and Caesar salad laid out.

"I have chocolate strawberries for dessert," he says shyly. "But we really can go to the dance if you want." He pulls at his suit jacket anxiously, and I reach out and grab it, pulling him down so I can kiss him softly.

"This is the most incredible thing anyone's ever done for me," I murmur, loving the way his eyes light up.

He settles into the chair next to me and we eat and talk for the next hour. The food is incredible, but the company's even better. Afterwards, we feed each other chocolate strawberries like besotted fools...and then he switches the song and takes my hand and pulls me out of my chair.

"Dance with me?" he murmurs.

The song's haunting, one I haven't heard before, and it almost brings a tear to my eye as he takes me in his arms and begins to sway us back and forth, the twinkling lights and the moon shining down on us.

"I love you," he says, as his hands play with the curls in my hair and his head rests on top of mine.

"I love you too," I whisper, but not for the first time, a thread of uneasiness flickers through me.

Because right now, in this moment, my life feels completely perfect. And I want to hold onto it so badly that I would do anything, give up anything, to keep it.

I only hope that I can.

Chapter 27

Skylar

Eighteen years old

"At this rate, I'll never earn enough to move out," Daisy grumbles as she counts the tips she earned at The Scarlet Letter Café tonight.

"Well, if you're not happy working at the restaurant, you could always go to the community college with me in the fall," I tell her.

"Shit. Dartmouth still hasn't said anything?" she asks me, disgruntled, forgetting all about her shitty job. "You would assume the assholes would at least send you a rejection letter or something. Not keeping you waiting all this time."

"Must have gotten lost in the mail. No worries," I mumble, turning my back to her and opening the refrigerator so she doesn't read my face.

I bite the inside of my cheek when I feel my sister walking toward me until she's standing right behind me, placing her chin on my shoulder and hugging me from behind.

"I'm sorry, squirt. Those idiots don't know what they lost. You can do it without them."

I shrug again and plant a thin smile to my lips.

She pulls away and grabs an apple from the fruit plate on the counter, flipping it from one hand to the next. "Are you sure you can't make it work with the other colleges that accepted you? I mean, that is what school loans are for."

"Not a chance," I reply, steadfast. "No way am I starting my life out with a ginormous amount of debt. I'll just take some creative writing classes on the mainland. It's fine, Daisy. It is what it is. No use crying about it."

My sister's brow furrows, staring at me with wide eyes.

"Wow. You're really taking this well. I'd be a total head case if I were in your shoes."

"Yeah, well, you always did like to be dramatic. I'm a little less neurotic.

"Ouch!" She laughs, placing her hands to where her heart is. "That one hurt."

"I doubt it." I laugh, thankful she's off the college topic.

We're both still giggling when Noah walks through the door, his hair all mussed up and gorgeous. My heart does cartwheels in my chest as he winks at me behind Daisy, making sure she doesn't see the endearment.

"Since I'm not getting any love here, might as well go up to my room and get some shut eye. I'm beat," Daisy utters, strolling past Noah and ruffling his hair.

He chuckles, slapping her hand away as she starts to leave. But then suddenly my sister stops in her tracks and turns toward me, a vulnerable hint to her eyes.

"I know this is going to sound selfish as shit, but I'm kind of glad those morons didn't offer you a grant. I'd miss you like crazy if you had left for Dartmouth. I mean, I wanted you to go, but it would hurt like hell not seeing your face every day."

"I'd miss you too, Daisy," I reply with sadness in my voice.

She gives me a curt nod, not entirely comfortable with showing her underbelly, and leaves the kitchen. When Noah hears the familiar sound of a bedroom door closing, he quickly eats the distance between us, placing his hands on my hips.

"Dartmouth still hasn't said anything, huh?" he asks, concerned.

I lower my gaze from his and shake my head.

Noah places a chaste kiss to my temple, pulling me closer, until my cheek is nestled against his chest.

"I'm sorry, little stalker. I know how important it was for you to get in," he adds, running his hand up and down my back.

I don't say anything, and just let him hug me, his warmth soothing all of my guilt away. I try and put on a brave face when he raises my chin with his knuckles so he can stare into my eyes.

"Daisy wouldn't have been the only one who would have missed you, you know?"

"No?" I swallow dryly.

"No." He smiles sadly. "I would have gone crazy without you."

I curl my arms around his neck, my fingers lightly caressing its nape.

"Oh, yeah? How crazy?"

"Padded cell, straitjacket kind of crazy," he teases, softly tapping the end of his nose with mine.

"Hmm. That sounds serious," I reply, batting my eyelashes at him.

"It would have been," he groans, leaning in to tug my lower lip with his teeth.

Desire instantly pools in my lower belly as Noah uses his tongue to lick his faint bite mark.

"I guess it's a good thing I'm staying then. Wouldn't want them to lock you up and throw away the key."

"No." He chuckles. "We wouldn't want that."

"No, we wouldn't. It would be such a waste," I mumble breathlessly when his hard length presses up against my sensitive core.

"You know what's a waste? Us standing here when I could have you lying naked on my bed this very second."

"Is that so?" I wiggle my brows.

Noah's hands cup my ass, pressing me further against him until I hiss at the small friction he's creating on my clit. Even fully clothed, Noah knows how to hit all my pleasure points, making sure I'm a volcano of need before he's even truly touched me.

Noah's face transforms into something lethal, making me squirm as he bends down to my ear, biting its lobe before he whispers raggedly into it.

"I'm going to count to ten. If you're not naked in my room, thighs spread apart on my bed so I can taste that sweet pussy of yours, by the time I get there, I won't be responsible for my actions."

"What are you going to do? Spank me?"

The glow in his blue eyes when I say it has my pussy flooding like Niagara Falls.

"Don't go giving me more ideas, little stalker," he threatens, making my pulse speed up. "The ones I have are deviant enough. Ten..."

With that warning hanging between us, I'm not sure if I should stay rooted to my spot or run like the wind upstairs to his room.

"Nine."

Anticipation more than fear of the unknown is what gets me to move, running up the stairs, Noah right at my heels. I cover my mouth so that Daisy can't hear me giggling like an excited lunatic as I dash toward Noah's room and start stripping my clothes off. By the time Noah locks the door behind him, he's already at three, eyeing me intently as I unstrap my bra and pull down my panties. I fling myself on top of his bed, raising my knees up high, my legs spread wide before him.

"One," he announces with a growl, his gaze locked on my core. "Such a good little stalker," he praises as his knee dips onto the bed. He crawls his way to me, looking like a predator ready to eat his prey alive.

But where before I would have run from him, now I offer myself as a willing sacrifice.

"Noah," I whisper before his head gets lost in between my thighs.

He raises his head just a smidge, enough for me to see all his beautiful features. "I love you."

The way his hungry expression morphs into utter worship and adoration makes my knees weak. His hands grab my knees, keeping them still as he continues to stare into my eyes.

"All my forevers, Sky. All of them," he whispers lovingly before dropping his mouth to my apex, ensuring that every thought and worry in my head vanishes, until all there is, is him.

Chapter 28

Noah

Eighteen years old

My fingers run through Sky's long brown hair as she lays her head on my lap and takes in the rays of sun shining down on her heart-shaped face. It's one of those warm May afternoons, hinting that summer is fast approaching us. Instead of being excited that graduation is just around the corner, I wish I could freeze time and just stay with her like this. Just me and Sky, sprawled out onto a blanket near the old lighthouse on old man Winter's land, situated on the highest cliff of the island, the sea breeze lightly kissing our cheeks and fanning our hair.

It's been six months to the day that we've been together, and each day feels even more precious to me than the one before. But soon, lazy days like this one will all be over. I'll have to start working on my father's boat, and Sky will be busy with her community college classes, only coming home at night.

That's okay.

At least the nights and weekends will be ours.

Working with my father doesn't seem so bad to me anymore if I can come home to her.

Speaking of home, we should start packing up and getting back. The parentals still don't know about us, but if we keep coming home around the same time after school, then they'll start to connect the dots fast. And I'm not ready for my father to put a damper on our relationship. It's perfect just the way it is.

"We should head back, little stalker. Pretty soon my dad will pick your mom up from the hospital, and we need to be home before they arrive."

"I don't want to," she mumbles sluggishly, wrapping her arms around my waist. "Why don't we stay here forever? We can live in the lighthouse and fish for our supper. We can just disappear and make a life here."

I chuckle at how she snuggles into me, not wanting to end this perfect afternoon.

"As much as I would love nothing more than to shack up with you here, I think we could do a little better than a rickety old, abandoned lighthouse."

Her eyelids slowly open to look up at me.

"Have you...have you thought about things like that? Us living together, I mean?" she asks nervously.

I nod with a smile, swiping the errant stands of her hair off her face.

"And what would that look like? Our home?" she asks expectantly, the silver hue in her eyes twinkling brightly.

"At first, we would probably live in a little apartment in town since we would only have my income to live off of. But after you graduated from college, and got a publishing deal, then we could buy something nicer. Maybe a house right at the beach so your office could face the ocean. It would feel like you were watching over me when I was off at sea."

She closes her eyes, her smile stretching on her beautiful face.

"Tell me more," she whispers, picturing the life we're about to have.

"You'd write your heart out, creating magical worlds in that office, while I earned enough to buy the sailboat I always wanted. Once we could afford it, then we would pick up our things and sail the seven seas. I'm going to show you the world, little stalker. All of it. It will be our own little adventure. Something to help inspire your muse."

She opens her eyes, the sadness coating them instantly making me frown.

"What's wrong, baby? Don't you like our life?"

"No. It's not that." She shakes her head. "I love it. All of it. But you know I'm scared of the water. No, not scared. I'm terrified of it."

"Look at me, Sky," I plead, raising her chin with my hand. "I'll be there to protect you. No harm will ever come to you. Not as long as there is breath in my body. I promise you. I'll keep you safe."

She rises from my lap, only to push me down onto the blanket, her body covering mine. She stares into my eyes, and there is so much love in them, it takes all the air out of my lungs. I cup her cheeks as she continues to lovingly look at me.

"I can't wait for our life to start," she says whimsically.

"Ah, little stalker, it already has."

The beaming smile that crests her face has my heart working double time. Never in a million years did I ever think I could love someone this much. That anyone would ever love me this much. As if sensing that I need to hear the words fall from her lips, she leans down until our mouths are just a hair's breadth away from each other.

"I love you, Noah. I love you so much that sometimes I feel like my heart is going to fly away."

I press my temple to hers and breathe her in.

"I'll never let that happen. Your heart belongs to me now."

"Promise?"

"Always. You have all my forevers, remember?"

She smiles and presses a kiss to my lips. Her sun-kissed lips are warm against mine, and all too soon I am swept away, needing to deepen our kiss. Unfortunately for me, Sky stops it, pulling away before I take her right here and now.

"Nuh-uh. We have to go home, remember? If we start fooling around now, then we'll never make it back in time."

"Fuck it," I growl, pulling her back down to me so I can bite her long neck and then pepper it with kisses. "They'll have to find out sooner or later. Might as well be today. That is after I've had my way with you."

She laughs and then moans when my fingers start to play with her nipple.

"No, not yet. We planned to tell them after graduation, remember?" she says on a whisper, grinding her hot pussy on my already hard shaft.

"Nope. I don't remember a damn thing. Not while that dripping cunt is begging me to fuck it."

"Noah," she sobs, rising just high enough to place her flat palms on my chest as she continues to rub herself against me.

My hands go to her thighs and raise her skirt, helping her keep to the languid tempo.

"Put me in your hand, baby," I growl. "I need to feel you."

She doesn't even hesitate, pulling my zipper down and releasing my monstrous cock from its restraint. But instead of her letting me sink myself inside her like I want, the little vixen shimmies down my body and wraps those full lips around my cock.

"Fuck, baby. Just like that," I praise, threading my fingers through her luscious hair.

Her tongue laps at the angry vein on the outside of my cock, before swallowing me whole again. She relaxes her throat, taking me all the way in, and when I feel the crown of my cock hitting her tonsils, I fucking lose my mind. I pull her up by the hair, making her release my cock. Her stunned expression lasts for a second before my hands grip her waist to seat her right where I want her.

"If I'm coming, it will be inside your greedy pussy, Sky," I grunt, pushing her panties to the side and sinking my cock inside her in one violent thrust.

"Argh!" she wails, her head falling back, her hard nipples taunting me.

I slap her ass hard, waking her up from her momentary stupor.

"Ride me, Sky," I order, my voice dropping an octave.

She snaps her head back, a wicked smile to her lips. And like the good girl she is, she starts to ride my cock to oblivion. Like this, fucking my girl raw, I never last too long. Ever since she's gotten on the pill, condoms have become a thing of the past. There's just something about having no barriers between us that heightens everything. It's as close to heaven as I'll ever get.

Sky continues to drop that perfect pussy on me like she's been doing it all her life, clenching around my cock like she wants to keep it for herself.

Fuck. I'd give it to her with a damn bow on it if I could.

She already has my heart.

My soul.

My forevers.

My body doesn't seem to compare in the mix of things I've already gift wrapped for her.

"Noah!" she cries, already at her precipice.

"I got you, baby. I got you," I grunt, my fingers snaking away from her hip to fondle her clit.

On cue, Sky bursts into flames, screaming my name as she comes beautifully on top of me. Unable to hold on much longer, I thrust into her channel and come inside her while telling her how much I love her. How she is the only person I can't live without. How she is the only thing that gives meaning to my life. After we've both touched nirvana with our fingertips, Sky falls limply on top of me, my arms instantly wrapping themselves around her.

But as this wondrous moment subsides, fear starts to creep up my skin, its ugly nails sinking into my heart, causing panic to chill my bones. The feeling is so overwhelming that Sky immediately picks up on it.

"Noah? What's wrong?"

I stare at her flushed cheeks, how her silver eyes are still hooded from our lovemaking.

"Nothing, baby. Everything is perfect."

Content with my answer, she snuggles back down to me and lets out an exhale.

"It really is, isn't it?" She sighs, nestling her face into the crook of my neck.

I tighten my hold on her, unwilling to let her go.

Because if there is something I've learned in my young life, it's that sometimes love isn't enough to keep the ones you love most in your life.

They end up leaving, whether they want to or not.

* * *

Luckily, when we get home, neither my dad nor Sky's mom have arrived yet. Not to raise any suspicion, Sky runs into the house while I go to the garage, pretending to fiddle with my bike, as if this is where I've been holed up all afternoon. With Daisy working at The Scarlet Letter Café, it's been a lot easier for no one to keep tabs on me and Sky.

Still, we've been careful.

Like Sky, I'm not exactly excited about telling our parents that we're in a relationship. Not that their disapproval will have us ending it, but I know how much Sky hates disappointing her mother. And dating her stepbrother will definitely be a fucking disappointment to Clara.

But then again, it's not like Clara has much morality to say anything about it. She was fucking my dad when he was still married to my mom, after all. Not only that, but she was also my mom's nurse, for Christ's sake. She watched my mom slip away while secretly sneaking off with my father to do God knows what.

Yeah.

Clara and my dad can fuck off if they have anything negative to say about Sky and me being together. We love each other and like hell I'll let two hypocrites like them taint our happiness in any way.

When I hear my father's truck pull into the driveaway, I'm in such a foul mood, reminiscing on the past, that I don't even acknowledge their arrival. Thankfully, my father doesn't pop his head into the garage, preferring to go inside the house to get ready for dinner.

But to my dismay, Clara doesn't follow him in. Instead, she walks into the garage, nervously looking around before she gets the courage to say why she came in here in the first place. Clara never comes into the garage when I'm here. She knows this is my sanctuary. My safe space. And her coming in here uninvited only serves to piss me off more.

When it's obvious she won't say anything before I do, I bite the bullet.

"Can I help you?" I ask, rubbing my hands on an old oil-stained rag.

Like Sky, Clara stalls for a bit until she finds her words.

"Has Sky or Daisy ever talked to you about their dad?"

My brow furrows at the question.

"Only that he's a deadbeat and a waste of a human being."

"Hmm," she mumbles. "He wasn't always like that. We were high school sweethearts. Did they ever tell you that?"

I shake my head.

"We were." She thins her lips as if the memory holds no joy for her. "There was a time when Grant was the most charming man I had ever met. He still is in a way. Daisy takes a lot after him. They both have this way about them. They pull you in with their charisma and *joie de vivre*. When you're young, that type of personality is exciting, thrilling even. You just want to bathe in their light."

"Okay," I grumble, wondering where she is going with this.

"But then life happens, and that same carefree attitude starts to wear you down. Especially when you have to put food on the table and have two infant girls needing you twenty-four seven. Grant didn't take to fatherhood as well as he took to his late nights and parties. One of us had to be the adult, and we both started to resent each other for it."

I let her go off on her tangent, not really understanding why she's telling me all of this.

"It was one thing that drew me to your father. How he, too, had been high school sweethearts with your mom. But unlike Grant was with me, Curt was devoted to Annabelle. There was nothing he wouldn't have done for her."

The hair on the nape of my neck stands on end, hating how she has the nerve to speak about my mother. She lets out a trebling exhale but continues on with her rant.

"I know what you think of me. I know that you hate me just because you think I stole your father away from her. But I can tell you that was never the case. Cancer stole your mother from both of you," she explains, her shoulders slumping. "I watched how your father would come to visit her every chance he got. How it broke him every time he saw her slip further from his fingers. He would come out of that hospital room looking like he had left a part of his heart inside of it. It still hurts him to think of her. There isn't a day that he doesn't suffer from the guilt that he could redo his life, when she wasn't afforded the same luxury."

I fist the rag in my hand, twisting it hard with each word she says.

"Sometimes when your mother was just too frail to have visitors, your father would stand outside her room and just watch her sleep. I would walk over to him and spark up a conversation, just so he wouldn't feel so lost. Our friendship grew from there. And although it was never my intention, I found myself falling in love with him."

My molars instantly grind at her admission.

"Yes, I know how it all sounds. Here I was falling head over heels for a man whose wife was still trying to hold on to the life she had. I live with the shame of it every day. Worse still is that I know there is a part of your father's heart that will never be mine. It will always belong to Annabelle. But maybe it's because I know he loved her so fiercely that I was able to fall in love with him too. Maybe it even made me love him more." She shrugs sheepishly. "I always thought my feelings were one-sided, though. I never acted on them. But then a few months went by after your mother passed and I honestly thought that would be the end of it. That I would never see your father again and he would never know that I had fallen for him. Imagine my surprise when Curt showed up at the hospital, asking me if it would be okay if he could take me out for coffee. Maybe I should have said no and waited for him to mourn your mom longer, but then again, he'd been mourning her since the cancer sneaked its way into your lives years prior to that."

Her crestfallen expression has my head lowering away from her, unable to see the deep-seated turmoil and guilt in her gaze.

"So I accepted his offer for a coffee date, and well, coffee led to lunch dates, then dinner dates, and eventually marriage, as you well know."

"Why are you telling me all of this?" I mumble through gritted teeth.

"Because I need you to understand that sometimes we can't help but to fall in love with the last person we should. That even though the odds were stacked up against us, your father and I did fall in love. Deeply and wholeheartedly in love." The sad smile that tugs at her lips has me paralyzed to the spot as she slowly breaches the gap between us. "And because, Noah, I believe you love my daughter just as much."

When my eyes widen in alarm, she raises her hands in a white flag gesture and takes a step closer to me.

"I'm not here to chastise you for it. Or reprimand you for keeping such a secret from us. In fact, I'm praying that your feelings for Sky are as true as they appear to be."

My jaw tics but I refuse to say anything in return. When she realizes she won't get a confession out of me that easily, she inches even closer to me, a timid smile to her face.

"I can't blame you for falling in love with her. My Skylar is special. So very special. It hurts me sometimes that she doesn't see just how special she is," she laments. "But something tells me that you see it. You see all the potential my baby girl has. Don't you, Noah?"

On reflex, I nod.

How could I not?

Sky is everything to me.

I've never met a girl like her, and I doubt I ever will.

"That's what I thought." She smiles, but it's the sadness in her tone that raises my hackles. My heart drums madly, my hands wringing the cloth in between them as I wait for Clara just to come out and say what she came here to say.

"But we aren't the only ones who know how amazing our girl is. Did you know Sky got accepted to start Dartmouth in the fall? That she got a full ride to attend their creative writing program, one that covers her full tuition and board?"

My heart drops.

When I shake my head, Clara sighs.

"Don't be upset with her. She didn't tell anyone. I wouldn't have found out about it either if the school hadn't reached out to me directly. Apparently, they had been trying to convince her to defer her grant for a year, instead of turning them down completely."

"She told me she didn't get in. That she had to go to the community college in Falmouth because we didn't have the money to send her to a good college," I croak out, trying to assimilate this bombshell.

"It's true," Clara explains calmly. "We could never afford to send her to a fancy university like that. You, above everyone in this house, know our financial circumstances. But, Noah, didn't it ever occur to you that Sky had the grades and potential to go to Dartmouth on her own merit?"

I try to recollect all the classes we had together in the past and remember that Sky never so much as got a grade lower than an A. Fuck! Why did I accept her story about not getting a grant so easily?

Because you wanted to believe it.

Because it was easier to live in your bubble and cast out anything that could take her from you.

My head snaps toward Clara when she places a light hand on my trembling shoulder.

"None of this is your fault, Noah. None of it. My daughter made her decision. One ruled by love. Please don't be cross with her." My forehead creases further in confusion when she pulls her hand away, hope plastered all over her face. "She's made her choice, Noah. But now I think it's time you made yours."

"I don't understand. What do you want me to do?"

Her sad eyes pierce a hole right through my heart.

"Do you love my daughter?" she asks outright.

"More than my own life," I retort without missing a beat.

"Then give her the future she deserves. Give her the opportunity to be the woman she was always meant to be."

My eyes start to sting at the corners, my heart shriveling inside me, finally understanding the underlying meaning of this unexpected heart to heart.

"What if I can't?"

Clara looks me in the eye, her own tears starting to shine through.

"Like I tried to explain earlier, love is never easy, Noah. It's complicated and messy. I'm so sorry, sweetheart, that you even have to make such a decision. It hurts me to know that my baby girl will suffer immensely if you do. That you will suffer, too. But love isn't selfish, Noah. But most importantly, true love will always find a way. Have faith that if it's meant to be between you two, then it will. Unfortunately, that's the only comfort I can give you. I know it's not much of one, but I'll be here with you. I'll be right here with you."

I don't know why I do it, but I fall into her embrace, Clara's body shaking as profusely as mine.

"I can't give her up. I just can't," I cry into her shoulder.

"Shh, sweet boy. Shh." She sobs, running her fingers through my hair. "You have grown up to be this amazing young man. I'm so proud of you, Noah. I know whatever decision you make will be the right one. I truly believe that."

I pull away from her grasp and wipe my tears with my forearm.

"How?" I hiccup. "She'll never go if I ask her to. Sky is stubborn. So fucking stubborn."

Clara's eyes are red with grief, mimicking how I feel inside.

"You'll find a way to convince her. She'll listen to you. She'll listen to her heart."

I lean my head on her shoulder again, playing Clara's words in my mind in a vicious loop.

There's only one way to ensure that Sky will listen to her heart.

And that is if it's broken.

Chapter 29

Skylar

Eighteen years old

The sound of my phone beeping drags me out of the story I'm writing.

Noah: Pick you up in ten?

I smile as I text back a quick *yes* and slide off my bed to freshen up a bit before he gets here.

He's seemed a little off the past few days, so it will be good to have some time together to try and figure out what's wrong.

He doesn't say anything as I walk outside, met with the familiar sound of his bike. I slip behind him, far less careful than I normally am.

We're going to tell everyone this weekend. Soon, I won't have to ever sneak around with him again.

We take off, and I hold him tight, just like I always do. But this time his body is tense, and he doesn't relax for the entire ride.

He takes me to my favorite restaurant on the other side of the island. It's a little hole in the wall that only serves fish and chips. But it's my favorite. He holds my hand as we walk to order, but when we walk to a table, he sits across from me instead of beside me.

And he's not meeting my eyes.

"What's wrong?" I ask outright, making him finally glance up at me. But instead of telling me what's been up with him, all I get is a shrug.

"Just a long day," he answers tiredly.

I nod with a frown.

He'd been helping his dad out today fishing, but it usually doesn't beat him down like this.

"Did something happen with your dad?"

"No," he snaps. "Fuck. Am I not allowed to have a bad day?"

My mouth drops. Noah never talks to me like that.

Before I can say anything, our food arrives, and we spend the next thirty minutes picking at it.

Neither of us says a word.

I'm at a loss for what to say, wondering what could have happened.

"I'm sorry," he finally says, pushing his uneaten food away from him. "I shouldn't have taken my shitty day out on you."

"Yeah, you shouldn't have," I say with a frown, but I let him throw our trays away and take my hand.

"Want to walk?" he asks, and I nod, brushing a kiss across his cheek.

When I move back, his eyes are closed, and his face is pained.

I want to beg him to tell me what's wrong, but I decide to let him tell me when he's ready.

We walk barefoot at the water's edge, letting the waves trickle across our feet.

I shoot him furtive stares, noting how exhausted he looks, and the dark circles under his eyes.

"Noah?" I whisper after we've been walking for a while and not said a word. "Are you okay?"

He startles as if he's forgotten that I was beside him.

"Yeah, I'm good," is all he responds.

I'm at my wits end by the time we get back to the bike and drive home.

I jump off the bike and stomp towards the door, done with his attitude.

"Sky," he calls after me. But I ignore him and trudge inside, immediately heading to my room.

Since it's date night for Curt and my mom, and Daisy's working, we have the house to ourselves. Good thing too since I'm pretty sure everyone would realize that Noah and I are about to have a major lover's quarrel. I slam my bedroom door behind me petulantly, pacing a hole in the floor. The door opens a few minutes later, signaling Noah's followed me, but I don't look up at him. Not until he's standing in front of me with a large box with a very familiar apple logo on it.

"What's that?" I growl, caught off guard by this turn of events.

"I got you a graduation present," he says solemnly.

"I thought we said we weren't—"

"Just open it," he insists.

I grab the box and place it on my bed, sliding off the top cover with trembling hands.

Inside the box is a beautiful sixteen inch laptop, their top of the line one.

"Noah...what is this?" I breathe, my heart stuck in my chest at this gesture.

This computer costs money. A lot of money. Money neither of us have.

"I wanted you to have it for school. To write your stories on it..."

My thoughts turn towards my Dartmouth acceptance letter, and how this is the kind of computer for a school like that...but I push that thought away. I've made my decision. And there's nothing I could ever have in life that would compare to life with Noah Fontaine

"Thank you," I finally say in a tear clogged voice.

I know I should try and convince him to take it back, but what this gift means to me…I can't do that.

"I love you, Noah. Forever," I whisper to him, and he takes the computer out of my hands and sets it on the bed before pulling me into his arms.

"Forever," he murmurs back as he holds me tightly, a shudder wracking through his body.

I don't understand what's going on with him, but I hold him just as fiercely, determined to give him whatever he needs to feel better.

And when we're making love a few minutes later…I wonder why every kiss feels like goodbye.

Chapter 30

Skylar

Eighteen years old

The sound of my phone jolts me out of the restless sleep I'd fallen into.

Noah's recent melancholic mood has been bothering me so much that even in my slumber I'm preoccupied and any little sound will do to wake me up. .

He's been so off lately.

So off it affects the air between us, making it hold an edge of anxious restlessness that our relationship hasn't experienced up to this point. I wish he would just talk to me. Tell me what's on his mind. What is troubling him. Whatever it is we could fix it, together. All he has to do is share the burden with me.

Why can't he see that?

When my phone vibrates again, I reach out for it and grab it off my nightstand, blearily glancing at it.

It's a text from Noah. Or should I say it's a picture from Noah. I click on it, frowning when I see a picture of what looks like him lying on an unfamiliar bed.

A thread of uneasiness joins the apprehension I have already been feeling.

Noah?

I type, watching the three dots on the phone as he types back.

3632 Faulkner Way. There's a party tonight.
Come hang out.

I frown and try to call him, but he sends the call directly to voicemail. I recognize that address. It's Derrick's...and Stacy's.

He hadn't said anything this afternoon about going to a party tonight.

I shake my head and get out of bed, wondering if he's drunk and needs a ride home. I quickly throw some clothes on and then head out into the hallway and down to Daisy's bedroom, knocking on it softly before opening the door.

"Daisy," I whisper. "Can I borrow your car?" She opens one eye and stares at me in a glazed, mostly asleep way.

"Go ahead," she says groggily, waving her hand towards her purse on the floor.

I hesitate for a second, because she didn't even ask me where I'm going, which means she was still basically asleep when she answered, but then I shrug and grab her keys out of her purse anyway.

I just want to get to Noah.

The rest of the house is quiet. Curt and my mom have long since gone to sleep. It's two in the morning, much later than Noah's ever stayed out since we began seeing each other.

I jog towards the car, trying to get ahold of Noah again, but my call once again is ignored.

By the time I get to Stacy's mansion, I'm anxious...and annoyed. If he could have just told me what had him so weird this afternoon instead of getting drunk...I thought we were past this kind of thing.

Taking a breath, I head to the door where I can see through the windows that there is a mass of people inside. It seems the party never stops here.

No one gives me any attention when I walk in. Since I know that Derrick is still in Cambridge, this means this rager is all Stacy's doing. Which also means that the she-devil could appear at any moment to try and kick me out.

I'm determined to find Noah before that happens.

I'm here.

I text him.

He immediately responds.

Upstairs.

I'm trying to think of a good reason why he would be upstairs at Stacy's house party, but my mind still doesn't go where I guess it should go. Because I trust him just that much. So when I walk down to the door he texted me to go, and I knock on it, hearing Stacy's voice call for me to enter still doesn't do what it should.

I'm a stupid fool.

It's only when I open the door and see Noah in bed, lying in a tangle of sheets, that my heart stops. His chest is bare and his hair has that freshly fucked look to it that I've seen so often these last couple of months.

"Noah?" I stammer, right as Stacy walks out of the bathroom in nothing but a pink silk robe.

She shoots me a triumphant look, but I'm still confused as my eyes dart back and forth between them.

He's staring at me like I'm a stranger. Like I'm nothing.

"What did you do?" I whisper, my limbs starting to feel numb. He smiles at me cruelly as Stacy walks towards me and giggles.

"What do you think he just did?" she says as the collar of her robe slips, revealing that she's naked underneath.

This must be what dying feels like. This is how it feels to have your heart shatter into a million pieces.

I can't breathe. I can't think. I should be...doing something. But I'm frozen in this place, wondering how this happened. How our story ended up like this.

A part of me still feels like if he just gave me an explanation, I would forgive him, because that's how pathetically over the top in love I am with him.

And then he shatters me even further.

"It's done," he says monotonously. "We're done."

"Noah, I–everything you've said to me..."

"I said... it's done," he repeats, speaking right over me.

The gaunt thin smile on his face makes him look like a stranger to me. Makes him look like he was never mine to begin with.

"What's done?" I finally breathe out.

"God, you're pathetic," Stacy laughs, bored with our interaction. "What type of stalker are you when you can't even acknowledge what's right in front of your face? Not that I should be surprised. You didn't even know what was happening with your own family and you were living with them twenty-four-seven."

My forehead wrinkles at what she's going on about now.

"Jesus, you're so fucking clueless that you take out all the fun in this." She sighs. "Your family is broke. Like crippling debt broke. Like almost losing your house broke."

"I don't understand," I whisper, my gaze fixed on Noah's instead of her penetrating one.

"God, you're so full of yourself that you didn't even realize what was going on under your own roof. When Noah's mom died she left a mountain of health bills behind. A skyscraper of an amount."

"What does that—"

"Have to do with Noah?" she finishes for me with a sadistic smile. "Everything. Because I made it all go away. Just like that." She snaps her fingers to drive the point home. "I did that for him. Because I could. Because I had the means to do so. What do you have? What could you possibly offer him that I couldn't?"

Love.

The word burns in my throat, but I don't dare utter it. Not here. Not now.

"Wake up, Skylar." She claps her hands in front of me, to pull my attention away from the boy who knowingly is breaking my heart. "This is the real world. Not some fairytale book you're writing. And in the real world, I get the guy. Not you."

I shake my head, not believing what I'm hearing.

"You see, I'm his meal ticket out of this island. I know it and so does he. That's why he always comes back to me. Always. You were just an itch he had to scratch. A minor inconvenience I had to tolerate. But it's over now. The real world is banging at your front door and it's about time you let it in."

The tears are sliding down my face. I don't feel like it's me standing here. I feel like this is someone else's story, a nightmare perhaps. Except I'm not waking up.

"See you later, little stalker. It's been fun," Noah says with another awful thin smile.

I back out of the room, my eyes still locked on his. As Stacy turns her back to me, moving towards the bed to give him a kiss, I turn...

And I run.

I couldn't tell you who was downstairs, or how I got to the car, or even how I got home.

But somehow I end up in Daisy's room, practically shrieking as I throw myself on the floor by her bed.

She shoots up, wiping sleep from her eyes.

"Skylar? What is it?" She reaches out for me, but I flinch away. It feels like if she touches me, I won't be able to handle it. My nerves are splintering. I'm splintering. I've never felt pain like this before.

"I found him. He was in bed with Stacy," I whimper.

"Excuse me. What? Who was in bed with Stacy?" she asks, confused.

"We were together. He told me he loved me. He promised me forever." The word sounds pathetic and fantastical even as they leave my mouth, but I believed him.

Oh, how I believed him.

“Noah? Did Noah do this to you?” My sister growls, slipping away from her bed and going to her knees in front of me on the floor. My painstaking expression is all the answer she needs to hear. "That motherfucker," she spits. "I'm going to kill him!"

But that just sets off a new round of tears. Because I feel like that's what's happened to me.

He's killed me.

"I can’t breathe. Please make it stop hurting," I cry, and she nods, making a soothing sound as she rubs my back, but it does nothing to help me.

"It's okay, sis. It's okay." But then she starts crying too. She's crying with me, and for me. Because when you love someone, their heart-break is yours.

I finally allow her to touch me, and she holds me for the rest of the night on her bedroom floor.

My sobs finally give way to just numbness a few hours later.

“He,” I start, not being able to even say his name, “wasn't the only thing I was keeping from you,” I confess.

“Okay,” Daisy says, her tone holding no judgment.

"I got into Dartmouth. They gave me a full ride," I whisper in a rough, desolate voice.

"What? That's amaze—"

“I wasn’t going to go,” I blurt out. “I was going to stay here. For him,” I admit in a strangled sob.

“And now?” Daisy asks hesitantly.

“I’m going to take it,” I say. “And I’m never going to come back here again."

Tears slide down my sister’s cheeks as she nods slowly.

Tears should be streaking down my own face too, but all I feel is emptiness.

All I feel is numb.

And I make a promise then and there that I'm never going to cry for Noah Fontaine again.

Never again.

I might have died tonight.

But so did he.

Epilogue

Skylar

I fumble with the phone as I type out my father's number.

"Hey, little bird. What's up?" he says, shocking me when he actually answers on the second ring.

"I need to move in with you."

There's a long silence. "Uhh, well–"

"You've never done anything for me, and I never asked you to. But I need you to do this one thing for me now. I can't stay here. I need to leave Thatcher's Bay. Now, Dad. I'll sleep on the couch, the floor if I have to. I don't care. It's not a permanent thing. It's just until I go to Dartmouth in the fall," I spit out. "I'm on the next ferry out of here, Dad. The question is, will you be there to pick me up, or am I sleeping on the streets? Because even if your answer is no, I'm going."

There's another long pause, and I'm sure he'll say no even as I hastily throw my things into a bag.

"I'll be there," he finally says. "I promise."

I don't believe him, because I don't believe in anyone's promises anymore.

But I still leave the house with my bags. And I still get on the first ferry out of this godforsaken island.

And I don't feel a thing when my father's actually waiting at the dock when the boat pulls in.

When I get settled, I'll call my mother and explain why I left without so much as a goodbye. Daisy will make sure she understands.

But no matter what...I'm never going back to Thatcher's Bay again.

* * *

Noah

I think about hurling myself off old man Winter's lighthouse for months after she leaves.

I see it so clearly in my mind. Falling off the cliff and letting the ocean take me under. Letting the waves crush my skull on the rocks—until blue is tinged with dark red.

But I can't muster up the courage to go somewhere she's not.

Not even in death.

The only thing that keeps me going, day by meaningless day, is that she's living her dream.

Even if all my dreams are now dead.

I'm going to love Skylar Ames...forever.

And she's going to hate me just as long.

Get the conclusion to Sky and Noah's story in The Girl I Once Loved, here.

The Girl I Once Loved

Read the conclusion of Sky and Noah's story here.

Sneak Preview

Keep reading for the complete, angsty, second chance romance, the Breathe Me Duet. Available on Amazon and KU at books2read.com/breathemeduet

THE COMPLETE COLLECTION
THE
Breathe
Me
DUET
USA TODAY BESTSELLING AUTHORS
C.R. JANE
IVY FOX

Prologue

Now

Valentina

"Yes. I understand. I'll be there tomorrow at ten. I'll see you then, doctor. Thank you. Goodbye," I reply softly, hoping Dr. Channing doesn't hear the quiver in my voice as I bid him farewell.

I hang up the phone and place it face down on the vanity, my hands shaking so profusely, I almost drop the damn thing on the floor. My whole body can't stop trembling. I hug my stomach and bend over in my chair, just to keep myself from falling off it, slowly breathing in and out, hoping it will settle my erratic heartbeat.

Unfortunately, even if I could steady the irregular pounding in my chest, my stomach has different ideas. The bile of despair and anguish clogs up my throat, leaving me with only seconds to run to the bathroom before throwing up. My knees slam onto the tile, no doubt leaving a bruise, as I purge all these tormenting feelings out of my system. It's a feat of epic proportions how much vile stuff I'm able to hurl out into the porcelain bowl, since my appetite hasn't been what it used to be. Chemo does that to a person. The treatment is meant to save a life, however, it also robs you of every quality it offers.

And in my case apparently, it was a useless endeavor, too.

Dr. Channing's voice said it all. He might not have wanted to come right out and say I was a lost cause over the phone, preferring to see me face to face to deliver the bad news tomorrow morning, but just by his tone alone, I know there is no room for hope anymore.

This is it.

My end.

The day I have dreaded for the past twelve months has finally arrived. After a year of being prodded, poked and analyzed, I have to face the fact that it was all for nothing. My fate has been handed out, and now it's up to me to choose how I will deal with it. Will I crawl up into the fetal position and cry defeat, or will I make the remaining days I still have left count for something?

After I've vomited up all that I'm capable of, I get up from the floor and go over to the sink to rinse my mouth off. I spit out the excess mouthwash and then rinse with water, repeating the process three times before calling it quits. It's no use. I can still taste all my sorrows and regrets on the tip of my tongue. I hold on to the sink's edges, and to my utter misfortune, catch a glimpse of my pale distraught reflection on the bathroom mirror.

Where is the girl who used to fight for what she wanted?

Where is she?

Because right now, I need her terribly.

Unable to keep looking at the mirror's image for another minute, and in desperate need to replace this foul taste in my mouth, I rush out of the bathroom and head into the kitchen. Before I even know what I'm doing, my hand is already pulling the refrigerator door open, retrieving the sealed vodka bottle inside—the very one I had bought so long ago to celebrate when I'd receive a clean bill of health.

Alcohol was just one of the many things I couldn't indulge in, but that was when I still had a dog in this fight. Since I basically just received my death sentence, drinking a few shots is the least of my worries. If I'm going to puke my guts out all night, might as well blame part of it on Absolut.

I grab a shot glass and fill it to the rim, downing it in one go. The bitter liquid burns my insides, but it doesn't dissuade me from having another. My whole chest feels as if it's on fire, but it's a feeling I would rather have ten times over then the sadness looming over my head, seeping its way into my bones.

"You know what you need, Val? Rocky road ice-cream," I say out loud with a halfhearted giggle, trying hard to avoid the fact that I've succumbed to talking to myself in my empty apartment. The vacant rooms are just another painful reminder of how I'll have to face this all on my own. "Yep, that's what you need," I mutter under my breath after drinking another shot, pushing that harrowing thought away from my head.

One pity party at a time, Valentina.

I'm about to reach for the fridge door to grab the pint of chocolate goodness when a certain image stops me in my tracks. My hand goes to the picture hanging on my fridge door, held in place by an Eiffel Tower magnet I bought off Amazon. Without regard to my poor broken heart, I trace over the three faces that once upon a time were as familiar to me as my very own. I put the bottle back on the countertop, so both my hands are free to clutch onto the memory of days where my future was still something I looked forward to. One I still joyously day dreamed about and planned for with them at my side.

Most of the pictures from that time in my life are either in some shoe box stuffed inside my closet or archived in an obscure folder on my laptop, both hidden away from my eyes, so I don't have a constant reminder of everything I lost. It's just too painful to go through the endless amount of evidence of how my life would have turned out if one choice had been made differently.

However, I could never let myself part with this picture. It was our very first after all.

I remember that day like it was yesterday, even though it feels as if it was a lifetime ago. Dad had taken it when Logan, Quaid, Carter, and I had come into each other's lives, unbeknownst to any of us how important we would become to each other. I still remember the beaming smile on my father's face as he watched us sitting on my front porch, wolfing down pizza and telling jokes. We had just met a few hours before, and yet we were so in sync, it was almost as if we had known each other our whole lives.

In the years that followed, Dad used to talk a lot about soulmates. How sometimes in life, we get more than one, and how lucky I was to have found all of mine so soon. It meant we would be able to have more time to grow and nurture our love. To see it blossom into something extraordinary and unique above all others. He didn't warn me that everything had an expiration date though. Even true love sometimes withers away. Just like how a fragile rose, once cut at the stem, loses its beauty and perishes before your very eyes. But Dad had always been a romantic, refusing to acknowledge such pessimist thoughts, and for a little while at least, I did too.

I can't help the tug of a smile that rises from the corner of my lips, as I let myself reminisce on that day, even if my heart is being gripped by a relentless fist of sorrow, telling me to tread carefully.

Logan's blond hair needed a cut that summer. It was constantly falling on top of his stellar blue eyes. Every time I saw him, he was running his fingers through it, making sure nothing got in his way when he looked at me. And Logan was always looking at me.

Quaid still had his braces on, but that didn't deter his bright smile in any way. He was either telling a joke or laughing at one, proudly showcasing his infectious metal grin at every opportunity he could find. With his deep forest green eyes and his shaggy brown hair, it was impossible not to find him endearing, even when he was curled up laughing at our expense.

And then there was Carter—the lone wolf of our little pack. He never said more than an odd word here or there, but that didn't mean he was less observant than the others—quite the contrary. There was never a moment I didn't feel his lingering stare from under his curious lids. He never said much in the beginning, but every time he opened his mouth to speak, I'd become mesmerized. Carter had that effect on people.

Hell, they all did.

Before I knew what hit me, I had fallen for the three friends—unconditionally and irrevocably. At a time where I only had my father to call my own, they crept their way into my heart and became the family I always wanted. We were all so young then, but even at such a tender age, I knew what true happiness was. In retrospect, maybe it was the innocence of youth that made me believe I would always feel that way.

Healthy. Empowered. Safe. Loved.

Deep in my heart, I know they were the reason I had so much hope to begin with. So many dreams I thought I would accomplish with them at my side. Another pained chuckle leaves me as I slide down to the floor, leaning against my fridge for support as I look at each smiling face, taunting me how when I was twelve years old, I had everything and everyone I would ever need or would ever want. I had a family.

Family.

I've heard that word a million times over in the last year. That's who everyone tells me I should rely on during this sensitive time in my life. When you're sick, people react in two ways. Either they offer their condolences, shying away from you as fast and politely as possible, or you get a wealth of curious questions added with an abundance of uninvited advice.

"Why do you always come alone to your doctor's appointments?"

"Don't you have anyone who can hold your hand through your treatment?"

"There must be someone you can lean on during this troublesome time."

"Don't you have any family? Friends?"

"You should seek comfort in the people who love and care for you, Valentina."

"Now is not the time to hold on to family feuds or grudges."

"Don't you have anyone?"

At first, when I was bombarded with such intrusive questions, I made excuses as to why I was always alone. But that was when I still had the energy to lie. After a few months of unsuccessful drug trials, the will to placate their curiosity with civil replies went out the window.

"No, I don't have anyone."

"Yes, I am alone."

"My family is gone."

However, seeing their pitying looks made it so that I stopped telling the truth, too. At least when I lied, I didn't get those. I can deal with people's inquisitive natures. It's their pity that I can't handle. So now I feign ignorance to their probing glances and questions, and change the topic as soon as someone brings family into the conversation.

Family.

Yes, I used to have one. I had a father I adored more than life itself and three best friends who meant the world to me. I lived and breathed for them, until I couldn't do it anymore. My gaze falls back onto the photograph in my hand, where those same three beautiful boys were all smiles and joyful gazes, and me right smacked in the middle of them with my own goofy grin shining brightly at the man behind the camera.

That was my family, and until I take my very last breath, they will remain so—even if only in my heart.

I wonder if they're happy.

If leading the lives they aspired to when we were children gave them the fulfillment I couldn't offer.

Against my better judgment and to my heart's chagrin, over the years, on those lonely nostalgic nights that I desired to feel close to them, Google had been the one friend I could rely on. It gave me small glimpses of all my boys' accomplishments. Now men with established careers, they were able to succeed in all the goals they set out for themselves, while I failed mine so miserably. Pride and sadness breathed simultaneously in one hollowed breath as I got a small peek into their lives. Lives I had been deprived of sharing with them, because of one decision that separated us all.

God, we had so many dreams back then. A bucket list of things we wanted to do in our lifetime. I even wrote mine down and forced my three best friends to do the same, just so we could lie down on the San Antonio grass, look up at the summer sky, and daydream about our lists together. We were so confident we were going to take the world by storm, hand in hand, and that nothing would ever get in the way of our happiness.

It's funny what the memory latches onto. How it chooses to keep some memories so vividly intact, while distorting others so ruthlessly. But those summer days, of whispering our wants and desires to each other, are as much a part of me as is this disease that's killing me.

Those same ambitions seem like nothing but pipe dreams to me now—unattainable and hurtful to recollect.

As expected, the vodka is starting to do its job, pushing my mind to wallow on what could have been if things had turned out differently for all of us. Images of all the places we would have traveled to and visited together, of all the exotic foods and cultures we would experience and delight ourselves in, dance in my head as a cruel joke.

But my wayward thoughts don't stop there. As foolish as the idea is to me now, I can even see myself wearing a white coat in some prestigious hospital, treating the sick and infirm instead of being one myself. And since I've let myself fall into the rabbit hole of regret and failed dreams, another painful image assaults me—one where my belly is bigger than life and four pairs of hands cradle it. Pure love emanating from our entwined hands on the life I would bring into the world.

A drunken tear falls onto the photograph in my hand, and I wipe it off clean before it ruins this small physical memory beyond measure. Just because that life will never happen, doesn't mean I can't hold on to the keepsake that gave me hope it one day could.

Enough, Valentina. Stop wallowing on what could have been and start thinking about what still can be done, I inwardly reprimand. *You want lists? Then let's make new ones.*

I pull myself up from the floor, grabbing the vodka bottle with one hand as I solidly grip on the photograph with the other, making my way to my living room. I sit at the little desk I have in the corner, pushing the medical journals to the floor to make room for what I'm about to do. I grab some stationary paper and write down everything I wanted to do in my life, adding two columns next to it with the titles 'Plausible' and 'Maybe.' I write down each and every thing I at one point in my life dreamed about, while drinking right from the vodka bottle to numb the pain those same written words provoke. I'm not sure how much time passes by, but the buzz I got is a good indicator that I've been sitting in the same spot for hours.

Once finished, I take a good long look at my list. What I had hoped would give me some sort of control and comfort, only deepens the frown on my face. As I start to draw a line over the ones I will never be able to accomplish in time, others stand out as strong candidates for what I can still do.

Visit the Louvre and eat small pastries in a café in Paris.

Dance in the rain in Prague.

Take a nature walk through the Swiss Alps.

Drink wine in the south of Spain and nap under a tree.

Eat gelato while walking through St. Mark's square in Venice.

Skinny-dip on an exotic beach in the Greek islands.

I tap the end of my pen onto the desk as images of fulfilling these dreams accost me. Yes, I want to do all these things, but I don't want to do them alone. When I craved to visit all these places and embark in such an adventure, it was in the company of the men I loved above all.

What would it serve doing any of this without them? It would be pointless and a halfhearted attempt at happiness.

Either drunk on bravery, or too out of my mind with sorrow, I pull three new stationary letters, and on each one, I write the names I haven't uttered in almost ten years.

Logan.

Quaid.

Carter.

In each letter, I write down what my heart still yearns for and end them all with one single question—one that might define the rest of my days.

"Will you let true happiness slip through your fingers a second time, or are you brave enough to take this leap with me?"

I seal each letter into an envelope with a kiss and leave them spread out across my desk. Each one surrounds the photograph of that one childhood memory that changed my life completely. It's oddly poetic that this venerate picture, which celebrates the day all three boys came into my life, is now surrounded by the letters I hope will bring them back into it.

The only difference is that back then, they were able to kick-start my life anew, and time was a concept we had in spades.

That's not the case this time.

Time is no longer an ally of mine, and maybe it never really was. Maybe this had been my fate all along, and I was only given a small reprieve—a small window of happiness.

If they don't hear my call, at least I'll always have those memories to remind me that at one time in my life, I was whole.

I was loved.

And so were they.

Chapter One

Then

Valentina

I wipe my brow with my forearm, the August heat beginning to take its toll on me. Dad said living in Texas would take some getting used to, but I'm not worried. If the warm San Antonio weather is what I have to look forward to all year round, then I'm just fine with that. We arrived a few short hours ago, and already, I can tell how much we are going to like it here. Sure, anything compared to the gray somber streets of Detroit is an improvement, but I like the idea of actually living in a proper two-story house this time—with a back and front yard to boot—and not some shabby apartment in a twelve-floor building, where no one knows their neighbors or even cares to.

This house is a symbol of our new beginning—a place where Dad and I can actually be happy and start fresh.

When packing for our big move, I made sure that nothing in this home would make us think of Mom or her absence. I threw out every little thing that could remind us of her leaving two years ago. Dad said I'd regret not keeping at least a few photographs of her, but if I want a reminder, all I have to do is look in the mirror. I have her dark, jet-black hair, her olive-toned skin and her full, ruby lips. The only thing I inherited from Dad was his golden-hazel eyes, for which I'm thankful. Instead of seeing all the traits I got from my selfish, vain mother, I focus on his and the purity of my eyes.

My dad has the kindest eyes.

Just like the sun beaming above, his eyes are warm and true, and they always burn affectionately brighter anytime they are looking at me. Much like they are now.

"How about you take one of the smaller boxes instead, kiddo?" He chuckles with a wink when he discovers me trying to lift one of the heavier boxes from the U-Haul truck we rented out.

"If I only take the small boxes, then this move is going to take forever, Dad," I exclaim, pointing to the endless amount of larger boxes behind me.

"It'll take whatever it needs to. We have plenty of time." He smiles fondly, picking up the box I was trying to carry, whistling all the way back into the house and leaving me empty handed.

That's my dad for you.

Always Zen, as if he has all the time in the world, and nothing ever gets him riled up. I wish that was something else I could have inherited from him. Unfortunately, I'm more like my mother in that regard, too—always restless and fretful. Or maybe it's because of what happened to me that I always feel like I'm working against the clock. Almost as if I have a certain amount of time to do all that I want to until it runs out. It could also be the reason why I'm so excited to start this new life in a new place. Maybe now I can finally breathe and just enjoy every second, instead of worrying about if the next one will arrive or not.

Most twelve-year-olds would dread being uprooted from their childhood homes. The idea of leaving all their friends behind, having to go to a new school where no one knows your name would be daunting for most girls my age.

Me however?

I see this as an opportunity to actually have all the things I've missed out on.

Aside from the nurses and doctors, who I saw on the day-to-day basis, and the other cancer patients who got their chemo at the same time I went for my dose, I had no real friends to count on. No one to really miss me moving away to Texas. Not even my own mother.

But now that my life is finally my own, I'm going to do everything on my bucket list that I hadn't been able to do when I was sick. And if I'm really lucky, Dad will see how happy and healthy I am, and start living his own life, too. Maybe even start dating. Who knows? The possibilities are endless, and I for one can't wait for us to start living our best life, away from divorce papers and hospital rooms.

Since Dad is adamant in doing all the heavy lifting, I pile three of the smaller boxes, one on top of each other, to bring back inside. He's probably going to frown at my stubbornness, worried that I'll exert myself, but he has to get with the program sooner or later. I'm not made of porcelain. I won't break or have a seizure just because of a little strenuous activity.

That was then.

This is now.

The sooner Dad comes to terms with the fact that all our fears and worries about my health are in the past, the better. And for that to happen, he's going to have to lighten up and give me a little wiggle room to try new things that, up to this point, were unthinkable. For instance, he's going to have to let me do chores around the house, and when I start my new school later this summer, he can't say no when I tell him I want to try my hand at sports. And he's definitely going to have to let me eat junk food like any other preteen.

I can't keep the small giggle of excitement contained at the idea of eating a juicy cheeseburger at the mall, or doing everyday tasks like washing dishes or taking out the trash. It might sound stupid to some, but I welcome the normalcy of it all.

Bring it on!

Normal never sounded so sweet.

With these enthralling mundane images dancing in my head, I jump giddy off the truck with the three boxes in tow, only for the sun's rays to blind me and keep me rooted to the spot. When my light eyes finally get used to the glare, I see two boys across the street, throwing a football from one to the other. I bite my lower lip to suppress the giggle that wants to come out, when the boy with the shaggy brown hair doesn't pay attention to where he's throwing, since he's too busy waving at me, and lands the football right into his distracted blond friend. The brown-haired boy quickly runs over to his friend, now lying flat on the grass, and holds out his hand to pull him up. They are both too far for me to be able to hear what they say to each other, but it must be funny, because they both start laughing, pushing on each other's shoulders as if nothing happened.

Suddenly a loud whistle slices through the air, stunning them into a standstill and embarrassing the hell out of me.

"Dad, what are you doing?" I ask through gritted teeth, my cheeks flushing crimson.

"Watch and learn, kiddo." He winks at me as he waves the two boys over to us.

I can't help but chuckle as I watch them try to make up their mind if they should come over or not. But it must not have been too much of a dilemma, because within seconds, they're both crossing the street and walking up my driveway.

"Hey, are you boys interested in making a few bucks?"

"How few are we talking about, Mister?" The one with the football in his hands asks with a cock to his brow.

"How about ten dollars for each of you? I'd say that's a fair amount for an honest two hours of work for helping me and my daughter unpack this truck."

The other boy, the blond one, looks into the U-Haul and then lets out a long exhale, rubbing the back of his head as he begins counting all the boxes.

"By my count, this looks more like a four-hour job for the two of us, sir. But if you throw in lunch and pay us an extra ten dollars, I can call on a buddy of ours and we'll get this done in the two hours you want."

"You drive a hard bargain, son. Pizza okay with you boys?"

They both nod with bright smiles on their faces, discreetly looking at me every so often.

"Oh, where are my manners?" Dad slams his open palm over his forehead.

I want to roll my eyes at him so bad, but right now, I'm too nervous to do it.

"My name is Eric Rossi, and this lady right here is my daughter, Valentina," he announces proudly, pulling me over to him and placing both his hands over my shoulders, giving me a comforting squeeze.

"Hi, I'm Quaid, and this is my best friend Logan," the brown-haired boy with a full metal grin splitting his face in two introduces.

Even with braces, his smile is infectious, and I can't help my own silly grin from springing forth.

"I'm Val."

"I said that already, kiddo," Dad utters teasingly under his breath.

This time, I do roll my eyes.

"Nice to meet you, Val," Logan adds, stretching his hand out for me to shake, but it's a pointless effort, since I'm still holding onto the three boxes I took out of the truck.

Seeing the error of his ways, he rubs the back of his head again, a shy smile tugging at the corner of his lips, making him look even more endearing.

"So does your friend live far?" I ask, trying to snap out of my awkward state.

"Who? Carter? Nah. He lives right next door to you. We'll go get him," Quaid retorts, pulling at Logan's elbow.

They turn around and stop in the middle of the driveway, talking a mile a minute with each other. Again, I can't hear them, but I really wish I could, since they look like they are about to butt heads. However, whatever they were discussing so heatedly is quickly resolved, and both boys run across our yard next door in a mad dash.

"Welcome to San Antonio, kiddo. I think we just met your welcoming committee." Dad chuckles as he takes the three boxes out of my hands.

"Nope, that doesn't count, since you kind of forced their hand. Offering pizza and cash. You can't bribe kids to be my friends, Dad."

"Ah, Val. Those boys were dying for any excuse to come meet you. I just gave them the golden opportunity they were praying for," he teases, walking past me and back into the house with his load.

I turn to get another box from the truck, when something catches my eye from the second floor window next door. At first, it looks like a shadow lurking behind dark black curtains, but then I catch a glimpse of something shiny. Like a flash of light, it's there, and then suddenly, it isn't.

"Weird," I mumble, and go back to my task, anxious for Quaid and Logan to come back.

Though Dad had a lame way of introducing us, I'm still happy he did.

Sure, when I was thinking about making friends, I presumed I'd start with girls and work my way to boys. But like every other part of my life, nothing is ever as I expect, so why should making friends be any different?

It doesn't matter.

All that matters is that Dad and I will finally be able to live like a normal family and be happy for once.

"Welcome to San Antonio, Val," I whisper my dad's words back to me.

I send a silent prayer to the big guy upstairs to make this home the safe haven Dad and I always dreamed about. Let this home be filled with only love and laughter.

Lord knows we've both shed enough tears to last us a lifetime.

Read the rest of Valentina's story here!

Acknowledgments

This book was pure, delicious angst to write. We felt every word of Noah and Sky's story...and cried right along with them. Life was messy while we were writing this story, most days filled with our own brand of angst. I'd like to think that we channeled all of that into our words, a sort of catharsis for our broken hearts.

You may be a mess right now, but don't worry...true love will prevail in The Girl I Once Loved.

A few thank you's...

To our beta readers, Summer, Emma, Jessica, Sharon, Jackie, Claudia, Dominique, Jennifer T., and Jennifer M., thank you for loving our books. Your help is irreplaceable in creating these stories.

To Jasmine and Rumi, our editors, thanks for making our book baby beautiful and going over every word with such love and care.

To my PA and bff, Caitlin, love you forever.

And to you, the readers who make all our dreams come true. It is a privilege to be able to write our words for you, and we will never take you for granted.

About C.R. Jane

A Texas girl living in Utah now, I'm a wife, mother, lawyer, and now author. My stories have been floating around in my head for years, and it has been a relief to finally get them down on paper. I'm a huge Dallas Cowboys fan and I primarily listen to Taylor Swift and hip hop...don't lie and say you don't too.

My love of reading started probably when I was three and it only made sense that I would start to create my own worlds since I was always getting lost in others'.

I like heroines who have to grow in order to become badasses, happy endings, and swoon-worthy, devoted, (and hot) male characters. If this sounds like you, I'm pretty sure we'll be friends.

I'm so glad to have you here...check out the links below for ways to hang out with me and more of my books you can read!

Visit my **Facebook** page to get updates.

Visit my Website.

Sign up for my newsletter to stay updated on new releases, find out random facts about me, and get access to different points of view from my characters.

Books by C.R. Jane

www.crjanebooks.com

The Sounds of Us Contemporary Series (complete series)

Remember Us This Way

Remember You This Way

Remember Me This Way

Broken Hearts Academy Series: A Bully Romance (complete duet)

Heartbreak Prince

Heartbreak Lover

Ruining Dahlia (Contemporary Mafia Standalone)

Ruining Dahlia

Pretty Madness (Omegaverse Standalone)

Pretty Madness

The Fated Wings Series (Paranormal series)

First Impressions

Forgotten Specters

The Fallen One (a Fated Wings Novella)

Forbidden Queens

Frightful Beginnings (a Fated Wings Short Story)

Faded Realms

Faithless Dreams

Fabled Kingdoms

Forever Hearts

The Darkest Curse Series

Forget Me

Lost Passions

Hades Redemption Series

The Darkest Lover

The Darkest Kingdom

Monster & Me Duet Co-write with Mila Young

Monster's Temptation

Monster's Obsession

Academy of Souls Co-write with Mila Young (complete series)

School of Broken Souls

School of Broken Hearts

School of Broken Dreams

School of Broken Wings

Fallen World Series Co-write with Mila Young (complete series)

Bound

Broken

Betrayed

Belong

Thief of Hearts Co-write with Mila Young (complete series)

Darkest Destiny

Stolen Destiny

Broken Destiny

Sweet Destiny

Kingdom of Wolves Co-write with Mila Young

Wild Moon

Wild Heart

Wild Girl

Wild Love

Wild Soul

Wild Kiss

Stupid Boys Series Co-write with Rebecca Royce

Stupid Boys

Dumb Girl

Crazy Love

Breathe Me Duet Co-write with Ivy Fox (complete)

Breathe Me

Breathe You

Breathe Me Duet

Love & Hate Co-write with Ivy Fox

The Boy I Once Hated

The Girl I Once Loved

Rich Demons of Darkwood Series Co-write with May Dawson

Make Me Lie

Make Me Beg

Make Me Wild

Make Me Burn

Make Me Queen

About Ivy Fox

Ivy Fox is a USA Today bestselling author of angst-filled, contemporary romances, some of them with an unconventional #whychoose twist.

Ivy lives a blessed life, surrounded by her two most important men—her husband and son, but she also doesn't mind living with the fictional characters in her head that can't seem to shut up until she writes their story.

Books and romance are her passion.

A strong believer in happy endings and that love will always prevail in the end, both in life and in fiction.

Join her Facebook Reader Group - Ivy's Sassy Foxes or sign up for exclusive content and my newsletter here - https://www.ivyfoxauthor.com/

Books by Ivy Fox

MF Standalones & Series

The Society

See No Evil

Hear No Evil

Fear No Evil

Speak No Evil

Do No Evil

After Hours

The King

Reverse Harem Standalones & Series

Mafia Wars

Binding Rose

The Winter Queen Duet

The Touched Frost Queen

The Privileged of Pembroke High

Heartless

Soulless

Faithless

Ruthless

Fearless

Restless

Rotten Love Duet

Rotten Girl

Rotten Men

Bad Influence

Her Secret

Archangels MC

Room for Three

Co-Writes with C.R. Jane

Breathe Me Duet

Breathe Me

Breathe You

Hate & Love Duet

The Boy I Once Hated

The Girl I Once Loved

Co-Writes with K.A. Knight

Deadly Love

Deadly Affair

Deadly Match

Deadly Encounter

Printed in Poland
by Amazon Fulfillment
Poland Sp. z o.o., Wrocław

22989682R00222